SCOURGE
— OF —
WOLVES

DAVID GILMAN enjoyed many careers
– including firefighter, soldier and photographer –
before turning to writing full-time. He is an
award-winning author and screenwriter.

www.davidgilman.com
www.facebook.com/davidgilman.author

DAVID
GILMAN

MASTER OF WAR

SCOURGE
OF
WOLVES

HEAD
of ZEUS

First published as an ebook in 2017 by Head of Zeus Ltd
First published in print in the UK in 2018 by Head of Zeus Ltd

9 7 5 3 1 2 4 6 8

A CIP catalogue record for this book is available from
the British Library.

ISBN (HB) 9781784974503
ISBN (XTPB) 9781784974510
ISBN (E) 9781784974497

Typeset by Adrian McLaughlin

Printed and bound in Germany by CPI Books GmbH

Head of Zeus Ltd
First Floor East
5–8 Hardwick Street
London EC1R 4RG

WWW.HEADOFZEUS.COM

For Suzy, as always

And also for my friend James McFarlane,
who was there at the beginning
and helped shape the words

PART ONE
IN THE KING'S NAME
1

PART TWO
THE VALLEY OF SIGHS
127

PART THREE
BROTHERHOOD OF THE SWORD
325

CHARACTER LIST

*Sir Thomas Blackstone
*Henry: Blackstone's son

THOMAS BLACKSTONE'S MEN
*Sir Gilbert Killbere
*Meulon: Norman captain
*John Jacob: captain
*Perinne: wall builder and soldier
*Renfred: German man-at-arms and captain
*Will Longdon: veteran archer and centenar
*Jack Halfpenny: archer and ventenar
*Ralph Tait: man-at-arms
*Quenell: archer and ventenar
*Beyard: Gascon captain
*Haskyn: archer
*Fowler: archer
*Peter Garland: archer
*Othon: man-at-arms

FRENCH NOBLEMEN AND MEN-AT-ARMS
Count Jean de Tancarville: French Royal Chamberlain and
    general of the northern army
Jacques de Bourbon, Count de la Marche, Constable of France
John de Montfort

Marshal Jean de Boucicaut; chief French commissioner
Marshal Arnoul d'Audrehem
Count de Vaudémont: Royal Lieutenant of Champagne
Charles de Blois
Louis de Harcourt: Royal Lieutenant of Normandy
Jean de Grailly, Captal de Buch: Gascon lord
*Alain de la Grave
*Mouton de la Grave: Lord of Sainte-Bernice
*Guillouic: Breton mercenary
*Robert de Rabastens
*Sir Godfrey d'Albinet
*Bernard de Charité
*Countess Catherine de Val

ENGLISH KNIGHTS AND NOBLEMEN
Henry of Grosmont, Duke of Lancaster
Sir John Chandos
Sir William Felton: Seneschal of Poitou
Sir Henry le Scrope: governor of Calais and Guînes

ENGLISH AND WELSH MERCENARIES
*William Cade
James Pipe
Robert Knolles
John Amory
John Cresswell
*Gruffydd ap Madoc

ENGLISH ROYALTY
King Edward III of England
Edward of Woodstock, Prince of Wales

FRENCH ROYALTY

King John II (the Good) of France
The Dauphin Charles: the French King's son and heir
Charles, King of Navarre: claimant to the French throne, King
    John's son-in-law

ITALIAN ROYALTY, KNIGHTS AND CLERICS

Joanna, Countess of Provence, Queen of Naples
Marquis de Montferrat: Piedmontese nobleman
Count Amadeus VI of Savoy
*Niccolò Torellini: Florentine priest
*Fra Pietro Foresti: Knight of the Tau

ITALIAN ASSASSIN

Filippo Bascoli

FRENCH CLERICS, OFFICIALS AND MERCENARIES:

Pope Innocent VI
Jean de la Roquetaillade: Franciscan monk
*Prior Albert: Prior of Saint-André-de-Babineaux
*Brother Pibrac: monk
*Brother Dizier: monk
*Brother Gregory: monk
Simon Bucy: counsellor
Hélie Meschin: Gascon mercenary

* Indicates fictional characters

After twenty-three years of fighting King Edward III has agreed a treaty and released the French monarch from captivity in England, allowing him to return home. France is in chaos, flayed by mercenary bands, a situation which initially suits Edward as it keeps the French King from regaining control. But the vast tracts of territory gained by the English need to be claimed – by force if necessary. French cities' and towns' loyalties cleave them to their own King but reluctantly, one by one, they succumb and agree to be ruled by the English. However, not all towns are so easily convinced. Belligerent lords and self-serving mercenary captains refuse. Thomas Blackstone and the renowned knight and King's negotiator, Sir John Chandos, are tasked with bringing the recalcitrant defaulters under English control.

Outnumbered and still hunted by the French, Thomas Blackstone and his men face betrayal and a final suicidal mission.

PROLOGUE

King Edward III stood at the entrance to the room where Henry of Grosmont, Duke of Lancaster, his lifelong friend and adviser, lay dying. Lancaster raised his hand to stop the King from entering his bedchamber, fearing that the plague, which had once again started its journey of death across Europe, had now reached him.

Edward hesitated. He was blessed by God in victory and peace: should he challenge his own divine good fortune? He strode into the room and pulled an embroidered stool towards his friend's bed. The servants had been dismissed the moment the King mounted the stairs. The words exchanged between these two old warriors would be as private as any confessional. No whispers were to filter down towards waiting servants.

'No, my lord. I beg you. I know not what ails me but it will take me. Step away.'

Edward reached out a hand and clasped his friend's. 'Age will bear us all away when it is good and ready, Henry. It is all in God's hands.'

The dying man wheezed, 'I am glad it takes me before you, sire. I would not bear the grief were it otherwise.'

Edward squeezed his friend's cold fingers. 'So many battles, so many victories and so many of us leaving less than our own shadow on the land,' he said.

'You're wrong.'

'We are never wrong. We are the King,' said Edward, smiling.

'Ah, were it so, eh? No struggle with our own conscience or with those who would try to defeat us by fair means or foul.' Lancaster relented and reached out to grip the King's arm. 'You bless the realm with a burning sunlight that will cast your shadow across this great nation for lifetimes to come.'

Edward's gaze settled with compassion on his ailing friend. How much time was there for any of them? The peace with France was barely delivered; more trials and contests would come their way. But those who had been at Edward's side since he seized the throne as a boy were becoming fewer and fewer in number. The Duke was one of those few.

'What is it we can do for you?'

Lancaster shook his head. 'Nothing for me, Edward. Everything for England.' Even lying on his deathbed the renowned Duke's abiding concern was for the nation he had helped Edward build. 'A month past we saw the portents, the lights in the sky, the eclipse. They say the rain turned to blood in Boulogne. It heralds hard times again, Edward. The pestilence comes more quickly than the dawn. You must look to who can control the territories you have fought so hard for.'

'Our firstborn, Edward, will govern Aquitaine. Lionel will go to Ireland. The Scottish already give us their allegiance.'

'And your sons and those they command will serve you well, but our old fraternity is lost. Brave Northampton is dead; Thomas Holland and Reginald Cobham are ailing and many others are frail, taken one by one as night steals away the day. All gone. And I soon to follow. You have pursued your ambition, Edward. You have achieved greatness for this kingdom and such an inheritance must have its guardian. When the time comes who among the many leads by common consent? A man of loyalty who will speak his mind even at great risk to himself?'

Lancaster gave Edward a querying look. The King knew full well of whom he spoke.

'Blackstone,' said the King quietly.

Lancaster smiled. 'As you said, dear friend. You are never wrong.'

1361

FROM SAINT-AUBIN-LA-FÈRE TO CALAIS

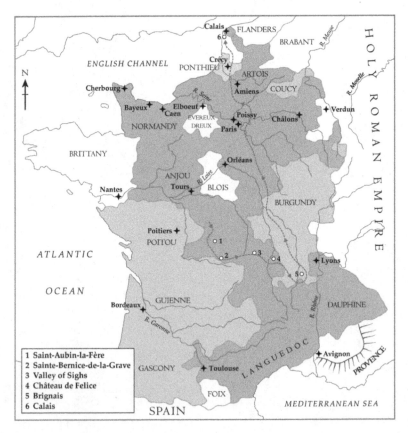

Calais FLANDERS
6
BRABANT
R. Meuse
ENGLISH CHANNEL Crécy
PONTHIEU
ARTOIS
R. Moselle
Cherbourg Amiens COUCY
H O L Y   R O M A N   E M P I R E
N
Bayeux Elboeuf R. Seine
Caen EVEREUX Poissy
DREUX Châlons Verdun
NORMANDY Paris
BRITTANY
Orléans
ANJOU R. Loire
Nantes Tours BLOIS
BURGUNDY
Poitiers
POITOU ○1
ATLANTIC ○2 ○3 ○4
Lyons
5○
OCEAN
Bordeaux GUIENNE R. Garonne R. Rhône DAUPHINE

1 Saint-Aubin-la-Fère
2 Sainte-Bernice-de-la-Grave GASCONY Toulouse L A N G U E D O C Avignon
3 Valley of Sighs PROVENCE
4 Château de Felice
5 Brignais FOIX
6 Calais SPAIN MEDITERRANEAN SEA

BLACKSTONE'S ROUTE --➤--

PART ONE

IN THE KING'S NAME

Limousin France
December 1361

CHAPTER ONE

Thomas Blackstone's men rode to their deaths.

As they eased their horses through the town's narrow streets Sir Gilbert Killbere watched the townspeople who moments before had cheered their arrival. Now, their faces filled with panic, some quickly turned away; others scuttled behind pillars. Killbere knew immediately that he and his men had been lured into a trap by the ill-named Breton lord, Bernard de Charité, who commanded the citadel of Saint-Aubin-la-Fère. Before he could call out a warning crossbowmen appeared on the walls and the first bolts struck home. Horses reared; men fell. An animal-like cry then soared up from the citizens as lust for the Englishmen's death twisted their features anew. Some dared to dash forward onto the bloodied ground and seize the fallen men's weapons. Soldiers appeared from the side streets and shop doorways and roughly pushed the townsmen aside to plunge sword and knife into Blackstone's wounded and dying men.

Killbere heeled his mount as his sword slashed two soldiers reaching up for him. Swinging the blade in swift practised arcs he slew three more as his war horse kicked and turned. Killbere was no stranger to the mêlée of war. He had fought at Blackstone's side since the boy became a man and together they had taken part in every great battle and victory the English had secured in France and Italy. Now he was going to die in a piss-stinking alleyway.

Swordsmen, jabbing low, thrust their blades deep into his horse's flanks and chest. The wild-eyed animal bellowed in pain and Killbere cursed as he crashed down into the mud. Desperately trying to parry the blows that assaulted him, he ripped his shield free from its saddle ties and rammed his sword upwards into the groin of one of his attackers. In his agony the man barged into the others while Killbere, twisting, managed to haul the shield across his body. He felt the heavy impact as a mace slammed into it. A blade jabbed at his side; slithering away, he struck out at the man's ankles and felt the steel cut deeply through unprotected flesh. The man fell, writhing, further obstructing the attackers, his screams joining the cacophony that echoed off the town's walls.

One of the attackers threw himself across Killbere's shield, smothering him with his weight as others grabbed his arms and yanked him upright. They had him now. Sweat and blood stung his eyes. He saw Blackstone's men going down from the overwhelming assault. Jack Halfpenny's archers had had no chance to unsheathe their war bows so the battle-hardened men, the backbone of King Edward's army, fought with archer's knife, sword and raw courage. An English archer's bow was of little use in such a confined place. Crossbowmen were better suited to close-quarter ambush and de Charité had used them well. Killbere saw the young ventenar jig left and right, crying out for the twenty archers he commanded to fall back, but most were already dead or dying so Halfpenny made one last desperate assault on the two men who cornered him. His archer's strength gave him the advantage and he smashed his left fist into one man's face, half turned on his heel and slashed the long archer's knife across the other's throat. Killbere struggled, brought up an elbow and felt bone break in his captor's face. In that split second he saw Halfpenny take a stride towards him. The lad was already wounded in his side but, seeing Killbere being held, was coming to his aide.

'No!' bellowed Killbere. 'Get Thomas!' The warning shout was barely out when those who held him clubbed him to the ground. The last thing Killbere saw before a sickening darkness engulfed him was Jack Halfpenny running for his life. If anyone had a chance to escape it was the lithe archer. That, at least, gave the old fighter a sense of satisfaction.

* * *

By nightfall the lifeless bodies of Thomas Blackstone's men hung from the gibbet in the town's square. Every man displayed evidence of the wounds resulting from the betrayal and ambush by the town's lord. Shadows danced in the torchlight as Saint-Aubin's men and women, relieved from the usual curfew, were permitted to desecrate the dead with knives and staves, making the corpses sway from the assault. Nineteen more of Blackstone's fighters dangled outside of the high town walls as a warning from Bernard de Charité.

Halfpenny had escaped the slaughter amid a hue and cry that echoed around the walls. Clasping a hand over the wound in his side he had forced himself to run hard and fast despite the pain through the labyrinthine alleys until he found a niche in a wall that he could just squeeze into. When darkness fell he had concealed his bow in a narrow crevice between pillar and lintel. It had been his father's war bow and its heartwood that had bent beneath father and son's hand was as precious to Jack Halfpenny as the memory of the man who had taught him to use it. Pushing aside his regret he made his way through the shadows until he reached the high walls. Once the night watch had turned their backs to cheer the brutality being inflicted on the corpses in the square below, he skirted the parapet. Grasping the hemp rope that held the dangling body of one of his men on the outside wall he lowered himself twenty feet down. The corpse sagged as Halfpenny clutched at its clothing. Dried blood soiled the gaping mouth and swollen tongue, half severed by its teeth when the noose tightened. Halfpenny turned his face away from the man he had once commanded, hoping his weight would not tear the man's head from his neck as he slithered down the body, using it to gain extra length before having to release his grip and plunge into the dense briar patch thirty feet below. He prayed that the scattered moonlight did not conceal rocks beneath the thick foliage as he let go of the dead man and fell into the night.

5

* * *

The following day's weak sun failed to burn away the mist that clung to the frost-covered land. Ignoring the morning chill and the skin-splitting roughness of the stone they handled, Perinne and Meulon worked alongside their men to heft stone onto the defensive wall of a ruined building. The rising ground gave the derelict barn a commanding position over the surrounding countryside. They were twelve miles from where the ambush took place in Saint-Aubin-la-Fère and even though the shelter was temporary Blackstone had demanded a low defensive wall be built. He and his men were tasked by the King's negotiator, Sir John Chandos, with securing towns ceded to King Edward in the peace treaty. At each village or town the burghers were called upon to pledge their allegiance to the English King. Some bemoaned what was asked of them, but eventually agreed when they gazed down from their walls at the battle-hardened men who made the demand. Others quickly saw the advantage of being under the protection of a strong warrior king while their own recently released monarch languished in Paris, bankrupt and sorely pressed to keep control over what was left of his kingdom. France was soured by destroyed crops, poisoned wells and the bitterness of defeat. Mercenaries who had fought on both sides of the war ravaged what little food and supplies remained. There were some French lords who resisted handing over their towns to Blackstone and Chandos until money was exchanged, at which point French loyalties were switched with remarkable ease. Those who resisted most fiercely were mercenaries who served the Breton lords. A civil war was raging in Brittany and lands as far south as the Limousin and Poitou were held by each of the warring factions. Saint-Aubin-la-Fère was one such town. Payment had been agreed for the Breton lord to turn over the town and for the burghers to swear allegiance to the English Crown. Sir Gilbert Killbere had taken twenty archers and as many hobelars into the fortified town to deliver the payment and receive their signed agreement.

'Look!' said Perinne, squinting into the morning sun, pointing to a lone figure emerging from the mist and stumbling across the open ground a half-mile away. The men stopped work and watched the man stagger, raise an arm and then fall. Caution made the wall builders hesitate. The woodland that lay three hundred paces to the man's flank might conceal an enemy. Whoever it was that had fallen could be bait for a trap. A war horse jumped the low wall, scattering the men. Its dappled black coat looked as though it had been singed by a fire's embers, part of the reason for its reputation of having been sired in hell.

'It's Jack!' cried Blackstone as he spurred the bastard horse on. Meulon and Perinne grabbed their weapons and ran after him. The fluttering wings of a raptor caught Perinne's eye as it suddenly beat its way skywards from the forest. It made no sound until it found an up-draught that spiralled it above Blackstone's race towards the fallen Halfpenny. Perinne's heart shuddered, not from exertion but from a long-held belief that the screech of a buzzard beckoned death as it called for a man's soul. And now it circled above Blackstone.

As the two men ran forward, Blackstone's centenar Will Longdon rallied the others behind the defensive wall. 'Stand ready!' he ordered. Archers and men-at-arms swiftly prepared themselves for any attack that might surge from the woodland.

Feet crunching on the hard frost, their breath billowing, Meulon and Perinne reached the fallen man at the same time as Blackstone's squire. John Jacob had caught up to them with one of the pack horses. Blackstone's belligerent mount would never allow another to be put onto its back and if Jack Halfpenny lived then he'd need a horse to bring him into the protective wall of the old barn.

'He's alive,' cried Blackstone. He picked up the unconscious man as if he were a child. John Jacob steadied the pack horse as Blackstone draped the wounded man over its withers. Meulon and Perinne had gone twenty paces beyond them, ready to guard against anyone who might have been in pursuit of their fallen comrade. If the buzzard's alarm was a portent of death for Thomas Blackstone then the forest might cloak the enemy.

Blackstone led his horse alongside John Jacob's slow-moving mount, which now carried Halfpenny. Once Perinne and Meulon were satisfied there was no ambush they rejoined the others. Perinne kept glancing skyward but the raptor had disappeared as quickly as it had appeared. As the five men made their way back to safety the squire glanced at Blackstone.

'If Jack has made it back what of Sir Gilbert?'

Blackstone looked around at the gentle undulating landscape. The countryside was plagued with routiers and it was easy to be caught in the open. 'Meulon, you and Perinne run ahead and take ten men back a couple of miles,' he said. 'Scout out the foresters' tracks through the woods. If there's no sign of Sir Gilbert and the others get back here quickly. And tell Will to ready a bed for Jack. He needs his wound attending to.'

The hulking Norman spearman ran off with Perinne at his side. The air from the big man's breath freckled his beard with frost.

Blackstone laid a hand on the unconscious man as the horse swayed. 'They might have run into skinners,' he said. Some of the mercenary bands numbered in their hundreds and a small detachment of men such as that led by Killbere could have been overwhelmed. France was more dangerous now than when the English had fought the French armies. Violence swept across the unprotected towns and villages and the slaughter would continue until King Edward claimed what was rightfully his, and until the French King had reached a settlement with those who committed such carnage without fear of retribution. Or were foolish enough to believe they could cause harm to any of Thomas Blackstone's men with impunity. 'But if those bastards at Saint-Aubin have betrayed us I swear I'll burn it to the ground and kill every last one of them.'

CHAPTER TWO

Jack Halfpenny had quickly regained consciousness when nurtured with Will Longdon's broth and the gash in his side had been treated and bound. Those who served with Blackstone no longer packed their wounds with cow dung and grass because they had learnt better ways to treat their injuries from a woman who had once been thought a witch. She had been a herbalist and accompanied Blackstone when, a year before, he had gone into Milan to kill the man responsible for ordering the death of his wife and child. The so-called Witch of Balon had taught the men well and shown them how to gather plants and herbs, even in winter, and to dress wounds without bleeding the wounded. That she had died under her own hand to save Blackstone made the men honour her memory. Halfpenny had insisted the slash in his side be bound tightly and that he ride with Blackstone despite his hurt. Once Halfpenny had recounted the betrayal anger swept through Blackstone's camp. Men seethed with desire for vengeance. They wanted Saint-Aubin razed to the ground. Blades were sharpened and talk was of the slaughter to come. They waited, alert and impatient, at the camp while Blackstone took his captains to reconnoitre the town's defences.

Blackstone and his captains were lying on the cold ground on the edge of a forest in the shade of its bare branches. They ignored their discomfort as they studied the walls of Saint-Aubin. Their friends' bodies still hung there in a grotesque symbol of defiance against the English King. Halfpenny squatted next to Blackstone and Will Longdon.

Blackstone had questioned him carefully about Killbere's fate but the archer had only been able to tell what he saw. Killbere had been beaten into the dirt. 'We rode in through the east gate. Bernard de Charité stood on the gatehouse wall and welcomed us. Said he accepted the payment for the town and would sign the treaty himself.'

Will Longdon spat. 'Now the whoreson has taken the payment and killed my archers.'

'And the men-at-arms,' said Blackstone quietly, without censure, keeping his attention on the high walls behind which half of his force had been betrayed and slaughtered.

'Aye, I wasn't forgetting them,' admitted Blackstone's centenar, who despite his rank had had only sixty archers under his command, a number now reduced to forty. Those twenty dead men who could loose a dozen and more yard-long bodkin-tipped shafts in rapid succession were precious resources lost to any group of fighting men. The men-at-arms who laboured in hand-to-hand combat stank of sweat and piss as they took the fight to their enemy, but an archer – merciful Christ, Will Longdon crossed himself – an archer was worth his weight in gold and no other man's stench ever smelled sweeter. 'But our bowmen, Thomas, they can't be replaced as easily as a man-at-arms.'

Blackstone looked back at him. Longdon shrugged. The truth was the truth. 'A man like Sir Gilbert was worth ten men-at-arms, Will, let's not forget that,' said Blackstone and then crawled back deeper into the woodland to receive the reports from Perinne and Meulon's scouts.

One of the captains, the German man-at-arms Renfred, shook his head. 'There is no way to scale those walls, Sir Thomas. Fifty feet high at least and over there' – he gestured to where he had just returned from his reconnaissance – 'they have cut the forest back even further. Open ground for at least four hundred yards. If they don't invite us in then I cannot see how we breach the walls. There's a lake that covers the other half of the town. No drawbridge. No postern gate to give access to the water.'

John Jacob studied the battlements and took the twig he was chewing to point out the irregular shape of the town's defences.

'And even if we got under their walls with ladders they would have us in enfilade. Their crossbowmen would cut us down as we assembled the ladders.'

'And we cannot get close enough to mine the walls,' said Meulon.

'This is why Chandos wanted it under the King's control. It's a stronghold worth depriving his enemies of,' said Blackstone. His stonemason's eye studied the walls. They were of recycled stone, a usual means of building up fortifications over the years. Such construction didn't require the skill of a stonemason's cut, but of sufficiently experienced men to lay the stone with mortar. The walls at Saint-Aubin were well built. The expertise of earlier stonemasons who once cut stone for another building nearby, probably a manor house or convent, benefited those who came later. Demolish the old and rebuild the new. Good walls, but once Blackstone was inside them he knew how to bring them down, even though John Chandos and the King wanted the fortress to remain intact.

'Jack?' he said, turning to the bandaged archer who sat propped against a tree, his hand pressing the wound, which still seeped blood. 'What can you remember about the layout? How do we get to de Charité's keep?'

Halfpenny's brow furrowed. He shook his head. 'Like a whore's heart, Sir Thomas. Impossible to reach. A portcullis after the main gate, winding streets. Alleyways and small cloisters running along the street. Some of the merchants plied their wares under them. Stalls and suchlike. I remember them selling bread off one. That smell of baked bread was the last thing I remember before the killing started.'

'Then they've enough grain and fuel for their ovens,' said Will Longdon. 'They'll have months' worth to withstand a siege.'

'No one's going to lay siege,' said Blackstone. 'I want to get inside the whore's heart and cut it out. Jack?'

Halfpenny nodded, knowing the more he could recall the better their chance would be of successfully storming the town. He also knew from experience that his archer's eye always took in more than at first he realized. 'The houses are tightly packed on one side of the street they took us down. That's where they ambushed us,' he said. 'We couldn't turn the horses. We had no chance and Sir Gilbert had men swarming over him. We fought as best we could but when I tried to reach him he commanded me to escape. I hid in a small overhang, that's where I left my bow.' He glanced at Will Longdon. 'I don't want any barrel bow,' he insisted, disdain for the army's replacements, all painted white and packed in barrels, in his voice. 'Mine belonged to my father and I want it back.'

Blackstone placed a hand on his shoulder. 'And you will, but we need to know more.' He turned back into the forest. 'Renfred, take me to the north walls. I want to see for myself.'

The men skirted Saint-Aubin along foresters' tracks. What they saw convinced Blackstone that an assault would be impossible without a greater force prepared to suffer casualties. By the time they reached the edge of the lake it was obvious that the Lord of Saint-Aubin had been blessed with a surrounding landscape that offered him maximum security. As Renfred had said, the open ground was cleared back to the forest by four hundred yards, and from where the men now huddled in the dank gloom of the forest, the frozen lake stretched the same distance to the base of the sheer walls.

Halfpenny pointed towards those imposing walls. 'Where I hid there were steps close by that took me up to the wall head. They hanged the lads from the walkways behind the parapets. I looked over those walls when I escaped but knew I couldn't drop down into the lake. I'd have died under the ice. That's why I went over the south wall.' He turned to look at the bodies that still hung there. 'There's a kitchen window in the north wall, forty feet up. It's a big place and on the other side is a walkway like a narrow bridge across the street below. It connects the kitchen to the main house. It leads through the pantry on this side and the buttery on the other. Once you're through that passage you're into the great hall.'

'How could you know that?' said John Jacob.

'I was lying in an alcove beneath that walkway. I could hear everything that was being said by the servants. I could smell the food and heard what was to be taken where. They were laughing, talking about how de Charité had fooled us. They were leaving their duties to go down into the square. They took ladles, kitchen knives and cleavers. Sir Thomas, I saw what they did to the men they hanged. The lord of the town let the people mutilate and beat them. Two of my wounded men, Haskyn and Fowler, were chased around the square until they were hacked to death. The crowd pissed on their bodies before they died. Those bastards in Saint-Aubin hate the English.'

'And I will give them an even greater reason,' said Blackstone. 'But you didn't see Sir Gilbert's body?'

'No. I saw him struck down, but nothing more.'

'The King wants that town, Sir Thomas,' said Meulon. 'It's important to him. Him and Sir John.'

'Aye, well, the King can't always have what he wants,' added Will Longdon. 'And Sir John Chandos might be a Knight of the Garter and the King's negotiator with these scum but he can kiss my arse if he thinks we've ladders long enough to clamber up any of them walls with their crossbowmen picking us off. And that ice wouldn't take the weight of a fairy's fart let alone men and ladders.'

'Your arse could be offered to them as a target while we assault the south walls. What say you, Sir Thomas?' said Meulon.

'Sir Gilbert kicked Will's backside often enough and I suspect he'd like to do it again. If he still lives. So we had better keep Will's arse in his breeches.' Blackstone and his captains eased back into the trees where the horses were tethered. 'We have to take the town and Sir John is due to join us tomorrow. We need his men.'

A coldness gripped Blackstone's chest which had nothing to do with the chilled air. To picture his men butchered filled him with a bitterness eased only by the desire to avenge them, but to think of Killbere being slain in such a fashion put steel into his heart. His mind's eye saw the French Oriflamme, the great war standard raised in battle against the English. He wished he had seized it when he struck out at the French King at Poitiers. He would raise it now. It signalled no quarter.

13

CHAPTER THREE

What keeps a man alive when he is held prisoner alone without the comfort of comrades or the chance of escape is his own courage and a silent contempt for his captor. When the same man is strapped to a post in the town square, surrounded by the stench of his hanged and mutilated men, it is a determination to somehow find a way to strike back and kill his enemy. They had stripped the injured Killbere down to his breeches and roped him to a post. He had been pelted with human and animal excrement. The chilled air had dried the blood from the blow to his head, encrusting it onto his scalp and beard. No knife or cleaver had been used against him but they had doused him with water and let it freeze on him so that it shrank the ropes that held him even tighter. His muscles had stiffened but he had kept his head raised and stared at his persecutors as they darted forward and struck him with switches. The slender, flexible tree shoots stung as they nicked his flesh.

The children tormenting Killbere scattered when their Breton warlord strode into the square on the third day of his capture to give the veteran knight water.

'You're my ransom, old man,' said de Charité. 'When Chandos comes knocking at my gates I will make even more money from your King. I know you by name and reputation. You're worth more alive than dead.' The Breton nodded to his soldiers, who grabbed Killbere's hair and pulled back his head so that another could ladle water into his mouth. Killbere choked and gasped, but the water would revive him enough to put strength back into his muscles.

'You do not taunt the King of England by betraying him, you

14

stupid bastard. I'll die here at this stake before that happens,' Killbere gasped. 'And you'll be hunted like a sewer rat.'

The Breton was immune to the threat. 'Killbere, you're a fool. Chandos will pay. Your King Edward backs John de Montfort to rule Brittany, my King John arms and supports Charles de Blois. I will stay here at Saint-Aubin and hold the roads north to Paris and west to the Breton March. There are hundreds of routiers riding from the east. Some go south to seize what's left of this country; others ride here to reinforce us. Both Kings seek to bribe the routiers to fight for them and if they cannot be bought then they must be defeated. Chandos needs men who can command. He'll pay to get you back and he will pay for me to convince those who come to support us that their fortune lies elsewhere.'

Crows fluttered overhead, settling onto the decaying corpses of Killbere's men. 'Take down my men and bury them, you vile dog turd,' said Killbere.

One of the soldiers punched Killbere's stomach. The veteran knight's head doubled over the ropes that bound him. He spewed what water he had taken. Sucking air into the pain he forced his head back against the post and sneered. 'Your men must be used to squeezing a whore's tit. They hit like parlour maids.'

The soldier raised his arm to strike Killbere across the face but de Charité gestured him to stop. 'Sir Gilbert, I've seen English arrogance before in the face of an overwhelming enemy. It gives you false courage.'

'We don't need false courage against murdering scum. And we fought your perfume-sniffing King no matter how big his army and won. Look at me, you Breton whoreson. You spill your seed into whores and breed bastards. One chance is all I need and my face will be the last thing you will see before you die. I will take you limb from limb and then spill your guts while you still live. Your head will be sent to Paris with your puny cock shoved into your ear.'

Bernard de Charité took a couple of quick strides, and grabbed Killbere's throat. 'Then perhaps I should take your head now and deliver that to your king!' he hissed, spittle flecking Killbere's face.

'Do it. Send him my head and then by all that is holy you will burn alongside every other wretch in this town. Now take the stench of your dog's arse breath out of my face.'

De Charité slapped Killbere hard. The blow split his lip, blood spilling onto his beard. The Breton turned on his heel. 'No more water for him!'

Killbere raised his head and roared in defiance of pain and death. Children scattered as women darted forward to snatch at them. The sooner their lord put him to death the safer they would all feel. The Englishman was possessed.

Blackstone and his surviving men waited for the mist to clear on the lower slopes of his encampment. The morning sun's valiant efforts to break through the stubborn shroud were once again defeated. The coldest winter for years froze the droplets of mist onto the bare branches; crystals of light glittered. Men wrapped their rotting boots in torn cloth and bound their hands to keep the skin from splitting and their fingers agile. The muffled sound of approaching horses and the creak of leather filtered through the mist. Will Longdon and the archers had already nocked their arrows. If it was an enemy then many would die in their saddles before Blackstone's fighters put them to the sword. Indistinct voices complaining of being lost told Blackstone and the others that at least some of the unseen men were English, but it was no reason to lower their guard because there were notorious bands of English mercenaries across France. Men like James Pipe, Robert Knolles: hardened leaders of tough men released from military service, many of whom were felons granted pardons by King Edward to fight in his army, and now the war was won these killers roamed freely across France. Edward did not encourage the brigands, but it had seemed preferable that they harass the French rather than return home and become outlaws on English roads. However, if they threatened Edward's peace treaty and the towns that now belonged to him they would need to be defeated.

A horse appeared and its rider's shield bore a gash of red, a downward-pointing diamond blazon.

'Sir John!' Blackstone cried out.

The leading horseman, startled by the sudden challenge, pulled up his horse, and like ghosts emerging from a haunted marshland others drew up alongside him. The horseman called out. 'Thomas? Merciful Christ, you could have killed us.' He urged his horse forward to where Blackstone and his men-at-arms stood ready to fight. John Jacob took the horse's reins as the renowned knight and negotiator dismounted. Blackstone eased Wolf Sword into its scabbard as Chandos glanced at the line of bowmen. He extended his gloved hand in greeting. 'Thomas, a man's bowels turn to water when suddenly confronted by English bowmen. I praise God I was not born a Frenchman,' he said, his eyes twinkling with humour. He was ten years older than Blackstone and his grip told of strength forged from a lifetime of swordsmanship.

More of Chandos's men rode forward into the clear air. Meulon, Perinne and John Jacob ushered them to where their mounts could be corralled within the ruins to one side of the camp.

'We saw signs of horsemen yesterday; we didn't know whether they were friendly or not,' said Blackstone as he escorted Chandos into a makeshift shelter: half-broken walls screened with cut branches and covered with bracken. It served to keep some of the rain and chill out and from a distance afforded a degree of camouflage.

Blackstone bent and put flint to his archer's knife, sparking the fire that waited to be lit. 'We went without warmth and food this morning in case whoever it was came upon us was unfriendly. I didn't want our smoke or the smell of food to bring down an enemy on our heads. Better to have an empty stomach than our throats cut.'

The dry kindling took quickly and Blackstone swung a small cast-iron pot over the flames.

The fire offered little warmth but Chandos pulled free his gloves and held his hands near the flames. 'It might have been our tracks you saw, Thomas. I swear we have been going round in circles these past days, but there's a large band of routiers cutting across the Limousin, so perhaps they are closer than I thought. But I have news. You were close to the Harcourt family in Normandy, weren't you?'

'I was. When I was wounded at Crécy I was taken there and nursed back to health. Godfrey de Harcourt served Edward and although his nephew Jean de Harcourt fought on the opposite side, he became my closest friend.'

'And he was slain by the French King because he and the Norman lords were planning treason, and you swore vengeance. Your life was turned upside down because of it.'

'My King and my Prince forgave me.'

'Aye, well, be that as it may, Jean de Harcourt's brother, Louis, has come over to us. He's helping us seize towns and stop the routiers.'

Blackstone kept his surprise to himself. Louis de Harcourt was Lieutenant of Normandy and in the years before had refused every request from his uncle, Godfrey, to fight for the English. 'If that's true then more French noblemen will join him. They'll realize at last that France has lost its power.'

'That and the fact that half of them have been promised lands in England. But I am glad of their help. There are thousands of these damn routiers to stop. I wish to God Edward and the Prince had left the army intact to fight them. But that costs money and the last campaign took much out of the King's purse.' Chandos scratched a crude map of France into the dirt and pointed with the stick. 'They swarm, Thomas, and we face an ongoing contest between them and us.' He drew a zigzag on the bottom of the map. 'These are the Pyrenees. The routiers were due to go and fight in Spain.' He circled two areas. 'But here the Princes of Aragon and Castile have forged a truce in their private war and that has stopped the routiers from crossing over. A French army has been raised by taxes in the south; they're going to try and slow them but we are to block any escape further into the heartland of France. Once the routiers reach the central massif they'll find shelter and the riches of Burgundy will feed them. Now, though, they have no food or supplies and have turned back into Provence to lay waste to the Languedoc. Between them in the south, and war in Brittany here in the north, we might be caught between the two. The Bretons are the immediate problem, Thomas. They are gathering in ever greater numbers and they pay no heed to Edward's demands because they fight on behalf of King John over the disputed territory.'

'And we are supposed to stop them?'

'Aye, before we deal with the other brigands, but we also have to take back the towns that have been ceded in the treaty. Some of these towns, however, are proving stubborn.'

Blackstone stirred the pot. He had been commissioned by the King to retrieve, with Chandos, the towns agreed in the peace treaty, but there was still a frisson of rancour between the two men. During Edward's last campaign they had fought together to seize a town and Chandos had wanted the town's nobleman taken for ransom, but, realizing that the citizens lived in fear of the tyrant, Blackstone had slain him. If a ransom had been paid the harsh ruler would have returned to terrorize the town afresh. Blackstone's actions gave the town its freedom and secured its loyalty to Edward. Nothing had been said about the incident when Chandos and Blackstone were thrown together by King Edward after the signing of the treaty but it had not been forgotten – and now Blackstone needed Chandos's help to seize Saint-Aubin.

'Where's Sir Gilbert?' said Chandos as the scent of herbs reached his nostrils from the pottage being slowly cooked.

'Sir John, I lost half my men and Gilbert might be dead for all I know. Bernard de Charité in Saint-Aubin reneged on the treaty deal. He has the money we paid for the release of the town but he ambushed my men. Twenty archers and twenty men-at-arms.'

Sir John grimaced. He and Blackstone had done their King's bidding for several months and this was the first time a town had turned on them. Most had been relieved the fighting was over and that the routiers would be brought to heel. Chandos or Blackstone would arrive at the gates of a town where the French King's letters were read out commanding his subjects to offer their allegiance to the English Crown. The gates would be opened, the keys handed over and then in the town square a garrison commander appointed. Once the arms of King Edward III were painted above the town gates then Edward's men would ride on to the next town. 'Breton bastard,' said Chandos. 'See what I mean, Thomas? The damned war in Brittany reaches here where we least need it. All right, I can leave you ten archers and the same number of men-at-arms.'

'If Gilbert is alive then I want to get him out.'

'How? Saint-Aubin is a fortified town. Two hundred burghers and at least forty fighting men inside the walls. You'll lose the other half of your men. No, Thomas, Gilbert's fate is his own. We cannot risk more men: we have too much to achieve. I am gathering troops for an assault on the routiers. I have near enough a thousand encamped with de Harcourt and Sir William Felton. He's been made Seneschal of Poitou. They'll hold and wait for my return, and I expect your men to join mine. I'll have a hundred and sixty men after those I leave with you but we need hundreds more. The further south I can go before swinging east the more I'll recruit. The Prince of Wales will soon be given Aquitaine to govern and as always the Gascons have pledged their support.'

Blackstone kept his simmering anger under control but the edge in his voice was enough to alert Chandos. 'Sir John, I have known Sir Gilbert since I was a boy. He took me and my brother to war in '46. I will not leave him to rot – alive or dead.'

'You will obey your King, Thomas, and I am his voice here. If Gilbert is alive de Charité will ask for ransom. We will negotiate. Saint-Aubin needs to be in our hands by whatever means possible.'

'It can be ours if we storm the place and kill the treacherous bastard. I need your help.'

'No!' Chandos turned his back and paced, trying to calm his own temper. 'Thomas, he and your men are casualties of war. There might be a peace treaty in place but we both know the fighting goes on. The civil war in Brittany pits us against those backed by the French and the Bretons who swarm across the land. There are few enough of us doing our King's bidding but we must do it with the resources we have.' He took a breath and gazed at Blackstone, who had not moved from stirring the pot. 'I forbid it,' he said and then, knowing Blackstone's reputation: 'Do not defy me on this.'

Blackstone remained silent. He ladled pottage onto a tin plate and handed it to Chandos. 'No friend of mine dies abandoned, Sir John. Do you want salt?'

CHAPTER FOUR

Within hours the mist had lifted from the valley floor and Sir John
Chandos, belly full but heart clutched with anger, took his leave
of Blackstone's camp. Their parting words barely disguised each
man's antagonism. Blackstone was needed in ten days further
east to stop the advance of the routiers who defied King John and
made claim to the disputed Breton territory in the Limousin. Men
like de Charité who would ignore a treaty and disobey a king. But
these Bretons were gathering in strength and the handful of trusted
men who rode with Blackstone would be useful reinforcements
for Chandos. If Blackstone did not arrive in time then Chandos
would know that he and the rest of his men were dead.

By the time Chandos and his soldiers had gone from sight
Blackstone had gathered his captains. They squatted around the
same fire that had warmed the King's negotiator, but the crude
scratch in the dirt that was France had been scuffed away. In its
place were pieces of stone laid out in an irregular fashion to denote
the walls of Saint-Aubin. The gatehouse, the kitchen, the pantry,
buttery and the walkways were shown with pieces of twig. Spilled
water soaked into the dirt became the lake and handfuls of torn
grass the forest from where Blackstone and his men would launch
their attack.

'Across the ice?' said Will Longdon.

'The night watch are on the other walls. No one will expect
an attack from that side. It's their blind spot.'

'With good reason,' insisted Longdon.

'If we get across the lake how do we scale the walls?' asked
John Jacob.

'We don't,' said Blackstone. 'Grappling hooks will alert them. We need one scaling ladder twenty feet long. We go through the kitchen window.'

'One at a time? That's asking for trouble,' said Meulon. 'The servants will be sleeping there and I don't know if either of us can fit through.'

Will Longdon grinned. 'I can see you stuck like a swollen cork in a bottle, Thomas, but trying to fit Meulon's shoulders in there might be like trying to push through a barrel of lard. If he gets stuck even a prod up his arse with a spear won't shift him.'

'Perhaps we should ram a spear in your skinny arse and shove you up the latrine tower. You'd smell sweeter,' countered Meulon.

Blackstone raised a hand to silence them. 'Whoever goes through that window first kills the servants. You heard what Jack said: they mutilated our friends; they deserve no mercy. Perinne? You can fit through, so can Renfred and John here.'

John Jacob looked at Jack Halfpenny. 'How many servants in there?'

'Six or seven.'

Blackstone's squire nodded. 'Three of us can deal with them.'

'And in the main building? The hall, the chambers? What, another ten or twelve?'

'Aye, but they'll either be in the stables or sleeping in any door-way they can find,' said Will Longdon.

Blackstone nodded. The main force of arms would more likely be billeted away from the main building with quick access to the main gate and square. Once he and his men breached the walls they could be contained and killed. 'Meulon, pick three men-at-arms to go through behind them. Each man with sixty feet of rope to lower from the ramparts for the rest of us. Will, I need you and at least three of your archers on the walls with them before the rest of your men join them. You'll fit through that window. Choose two more.' He pointed to where the walls angled away from what he hoped would be the blind side of the defences. 'Each corner, left and right. If the night watch sees us you have to kill them quickly. Once we are inside the walls, I will go through the great hall with John and Perinne to find de Charité, Meulon will secure the square, archers will take the walls. Their crossbowmen's billets will be by the main gate. Renfred and six men seize the gatehouse and its chapel.'

The men grunted their approval. A gatehouse chapel served two purposes. It gave succour to the ruling lord needing the solace of prayer but also, being at the entrance of a town, was believed to keep ill fortune at bay. A belief soon to be dispelled by Blackstone's men.

'We don't know where Sir Gilbert is,' said Jack Halfpenny. 'If he's still alive then they'll kill him the moment the alarm is raised.'

Blackstone nodded. 'It's a risk but if he's alive I'm hoping they'll use him as hostage. They'll try and buy their lives with his.' He looked from man to man. 'Any questions?'

'There's no moon if these clouds don't blow over,' said Perinne. 'It will be blacker than putting your head up a nun's habit.'

'He's right,' said Longdon. 'It'll be pitch black out there even with the ice on the lake.'

Blackstone thought for a moment. The frozen lake would reflect what light there might be but forty-odd men trying to negotiate across it in the darkness would be slow going. To have them scattered with the risk of going through the ice would put an end to the attack. 'All right,' he said finally, pointing the twig at Longdon. 'Will, have the men cut pieces of the linen we use for bandages. A square of it to be stitched onto the back of every man's collar. I will lead the way, ladder men behind me, and then the others; we follow the white patch of the man in front.'

The men murmured their agreement. The white cloth would show up sufficiently for them not to get separated and be able to follow a straight line to beneath the window.

'Anything else?' said Blackstone.

The attack would be fraught with danger. If the kitchen servants were not silenced quickly then the alarm would be raised before any of Blackstone's men could get inside. It could all go wrong in those first, vital moments. Providing they simply didn't fall through the ice first. The men shook their heads to answer his question.

Blackstone snapped the twig. 'We attack before dawn.'

Blackstone's captains took their men to the crude model that represented Saint-Aubin. The place had once been nothing more than a fortified keep surrounded by peasants' hovels. A hundred years of change had made it a high-walled town with a gatehouse and a population of two hundred. Small by comparison to many but a stronghold that had proved itself valuable to whoever held it. The surrounding area was rich in agriculture and the town was self-sufficient. It had escaped the ravages of King Edward's war. No army would bog itself down with a siege for such a place. And that is why the people of Saint-Aubin thought themselves immune from attack. They were safe behind the walls and they were protected by a knight renowned for his fighting skills.

Each captain outlined Blackstone's plan and the few questions asked were answered; then they prepared themselves for the attack. They had to return twelve miles to the safety of the forest where a long night lay ahead. Muscles would stiffen and there would be no hot food or fires to comfort them. They ate whatever food remained in their cooking pots and prepared to break camp. Men-at-arms cast aside their scabbards and slid their swords into a simple ring on their belt. They tore strips of cloth and tied them to their bridles to deaden the sound of their approach, in case Bernard de Charité had scouts beyond his walls. Will Longdon's archers cut and sewed strips of linen onto the collars of men's jupons. He went among the archers given to them by Chandos. Of the ten men he knew that no more than four had seen any serious fighting. Their chaff and banter told him so. The others were youngsters. Strong lads who had been arrayed and brought under Chandos's command but who looked nervous. When they tried to join in with the veterans' talk of killing fields they were mostly scorned and driven back to silence. One of them diligently stitched a white patch but Longdon saw his fingers were trembling. He knelt next to him and without a word eased the cloth and the needle from his fingers.

'You'll be with me on the walls, lad. Do as I tell you and you'll come through it well enough,' he said quietly.

'I will, Master Longdon,' said the archer.

Longdon deftly stitched one side of the patch. 'Not enough thread. Cut me more. Your name?'

'Peter Garland,' the boy answered.

'All right then, lad. You'll do fine. You have been blessed with serving the bravest man I have ever known. He was once as nervous as you but he learnt his lessons well.'

'Sir Thomas?' said Garland, breaking off more thread.

'Aye. When we went ashore at Normandy back in '46, we took the beach and settled on the cliffs in case the French were ready for us. Thomas was a sixteen-year-old boy who protected his young brother: an ox of a lad, malformed, deaf and mute. But as courageous and as big as bear. Bigger than Thomas even. And Sir Gilbert, well, he's always been a hard man. He was Thomas's sworn lord, not that that meant he was privileged in any way, other than having his protection. We teased Thomas about his father's war bow because it had a draw weight on it that few of us could pull and we got him to loose an arrow at a crow in a tree. Sir Gilbert struck Thomas for wasting an arrow. He was a harsh master, was Killbere. Hard as nails. Hanged men who failed in their duty. But that day, back then, when Thomas could have pointed the finger at us archers who had taunted him into wasting that arrow, he didn't. He took the blow and curses from Sir Gilbert and kept his mouth shut. I reckon whatever angels there are for the likes of us, they had Thomas Blackstone ready to be a leader of men even back then.'

He tied off the stitching and bit through the thread. 'You just do as the other lads do, Peter Garland, and you will see the light of day.' He handed the jupon back to the youngster and patted his shoulder.

'Thank you, Master Longdon.'

Will Longdon got to his feet and stepped away. Perinne glanced his way. Will Longdon smiled. Here he was mothering youngsters. Those who had served with Blackstone over the years cared for those in their charge even though many would also know the lash of Blackstone's tongue. He pushed aside the embarrassment of being overheard by Perinne and looked at the wall builder's men: they had felled a young tree and tapped wedges into its length to split it. They had drilled holes and hammered in hewn rungs. The assault ladder was light enough for two men to carry but it had to bear the weight of a dozen fighting men clambering up it at the same time. Perinne had built many defensive walls and assault ladders over the years; as the men stood back from their labours he lifted the end of the ladder and, using nails for shoeing horses, hammered three into each of the ladder's feet to stop it slipping when it was set against the town's walls.

Perinne caught his friend's arm. 'Will,' he said quietly. 'When Thomas rode out to rescue Jack a buzzard circled. It hovered over him. For a moment I feared for his life in case there was an ambush.'

Longdon frowned. It was unusual to hear the veteran soldier express such heartfelt concern but every man understood how an unexpected sign could be a forewarning. 'Perhaps it called for Jack. He looked half dead when you brought him in.'

Perinne shrugged. 'Perhaps.'

Will Longdon hesitated. How many times had Blackstone been close to death since he had known him? More times than he could remember. They were all mortal and if the forest spirits had beckoned Blackstone's soul then there was nothing any of them could do to stop it. 'It can happen to any of us, Perinne,' he said. 'And you know wherever Thomas is then death is always at his shoulder. I swear there are many others who will die before him.'

Longdon heard his attempt at comforting them both ring hollow. But it was the best he could do. 'Your men have finished the ladder. They're waiting.'

He turned away and let Perinne join his men, who righted their ladder and leaned it against another tree. Perinne pointed to two of his heaviest men and gestured them to test the ladder's strength. When the attack began he, Renfred and John Jacob would race up the ladder with others at their heels. Any fault in its construction meant they would die before breaching the walls. The two men clambered up the twenty feet, followed by another two. Satisfied that the ladder could bear the men's weight Perinne signalled them to take it and return to the camp. He scrubbed a hand across the crow's feet scars on his close-cropped head. A night attack brought its own fears. Thomas Blackstone had taken him and the men into battle many times and not so long past had been trapped behind an enemy's city's walls and had had to fight their way through the streets of Milan. They had been outnumbered and lost good men yet some kind of divine hand had shielded Blackstone.

Will Longdon's storytelling had reminded him of what he knew of Blackstone when Blackstone and other young men like him had stormed the walls of Caen. A dying Welsh archer had bequeathed Blackstone a pendant of the silver goddess Arianrhod. The pagan Celtic charm had not spared Blackstone from personal tragedy but she watched over him, of that Perinne was certain. He wished he had such a charm himself but knew in his heart he would prefer a priest to give him absolution. No man wanted to die unshriven. If they survived the ice then he would go through that window and in the fight that followed stay close to Blackstone. Perhaps some of the goddess's blessing would also shield him.

Perinne spat and buckled on his sword. The time for idle thought was over.

CHAPTER FIVE

Blackstone ran across the ice towards the dark shape of Saint-Aubin-la-Fère's walls. A dull glow emanated from the small window. The cooking fires in the kitchen had been bedded down for the night, the embers deep in the grate's ash ready to be brought to life the next morning. The glimmer, though barely visible, guided the attackers, who had lain throughout the night hours on the frozen ground and then, slowly at first, forced their stiffened limbs to follow the whispered commands of their captains, who in turn rose up after Blackstone. It was pitch black. The clouds had settled low in the sky. No moon, no stars. Only the bobbing white patch on the collar of the man in front.

In the silence of the night all Blackstone heard was the men's rasping breath and the crunch of their weight on the ice. Each footfall sounded like a warning to the night watch on the walls, but he and his men were more than halfway and no alarm had been raised. Men gasped for air as they tried to keep up with Blackstone's long strides and at every step, as they felt the ice give a little more, they became more desperate to reach the black curtain of the wall that lay ahead. And then they were there. In silence, other than their heaving breath, the men went down on one knee, making themselves less of a target should they be seen. No commands were given. Every man knew what role he played. Raising their eyes they saw the blind gaze of their dead comrades hanging from the walls. Contorted in death, their frozen faces told their own story. They had choked to death. No quick release. No snap of the neck. A heel-kicking agony. The ladder went up. Men spat phlegm. Got to their feet. Gripped their swords, slung their shields across their backs. No longer any need to follow the white patch in front. Shuffling forward they spread themselves out at the base of the wall. Waiting for the ropes to drop. Waiting for John Jacob to start the killing.

Blackstone's squire went through the window first, knife in hand. The smell of cooked meat lingered in the air. His mouth watered. A sudden pang of hunger, tinged with envy that there was abundant meat for the Lord of Saint-Aubin even in winter. He settled his feet onto the kitchen floor. There was enough fire glow to show the servants' sleeping bodies. Their backs were pressed against the huge hearth, arms tucked into their chests, curled in on themselves for warmth. As in most kitchens the cooks and servants were men. He took three paces into the room, rolling each step onto the side of his foot to lessen any sound of his footfall. There was no need to check whether Perinne and Renfred were behind him; they moved silently but he could hear their shallow breathing. He stepped past the sleeping bodies and went to the furthest man. Six men would be dead in seconds.

John Jacob's first victim rolled in his sleep. Jacob stopped. Was the man about to wake? The figure coughed and turned to face the hearth. Jacob darted forward, sensed the others do the same behind him, then bent, smothered the man's nose and mouth and cut his blade deep across the man's throat. Warm, sticky blood spurted across his cutting hand. The body bucked. It made no difference. The gurgles of death were each followed by a swift knife to the heart. As the silent killers despatched the servants another three of Blackstone's men quickly passed them. They ducked out of the door, turned left onto the walkway, up six steps to the wall-head defence to drop their ropes to the waiting men below.

Perinne ushered Will Longdon through the kitchen. His bow was unstrung, the cord tucked below his skullcap helmet. His sheaf of arrows was still in the waxed cotton bag that the archers had tugged behind their belts into the small of their backs. Once on the walls the bows would be strung and arrows nocked.

The ropes unfurled down the walls. Blackstone and Meulon

each took a handhold; one of the men-at-arms took the third. They found purchase and clambered up the roughly hewn stone. Sixty feet of heaving effort brought them to the parapet. Sweat soaked their linen shirts beneath their mail despite the freezing air. Callused hands cracked from the hardened, rough hemp. The rope men guarded the walkway but there was no sign of town guards. Blackstone crouched, making his way towards the bridge that would take them across the street below and into the great hall. Men followed him quickly but as he passed Will Longdon, who was guarding the approach, the archer pointed silently below. The curfew demanded the citizens of Saint-Aubin be off the streets in the hours from sunset to sunrise but a night lantern and four flickering torches spilled light into the square. Their glow cast long shadows from the hanged men and revealed in the middle of the square the half-naked figure of Killbere. Head slumped on his chest, his knees bent, the unconscious man was bound to a stake by ropes. Blackstone's heart raced. Was Killbere still alive? That possibility would drive his determination to save his friend. And kill the butcher who had slain so many good men.

Blackstone resisted the urge to run down and release his friend. Movement in the torchlight would alert the guards on the other walls. The darkness and the low temperature were Blackstone's best friend. He hoped that the sentries on watch would be huddled in their cloaks, most of them asleep.

'Protect him, Will. Once the alarm is raised kill anyone who goes near him.' With that simple command he ran across the walkway above the street and plunged into near darkness as he entered the passageway leading to the great hall. Dim cresset lamps gave enough light for him to see the iron-studded door ahead. He grasped the iron ring latch, turned it slowly and pressed his shoulder against the door. There were still no cries of alarm from outside, which meant that Blackstone's men had secured the walls. Blackstone, Perinne and John Jacob moved quickly across the vast expanse of the great hall. The hearth held large logs, which were burning slowly. A long table and benches straddled the room, but no servants slept on the floor or corridor. There was no knowing where de Charité's bedchamber might be but, as in many older fortifications, Blackstone guessed it would be in a wing off the hall where the latrine tower was built.

Blackstone pointed to a handful of torches stacked by the vast stone fireplace. John Jacob and Perinne pushed the oil-soaked torches into the flames. They flared brightly. Flanking Blackstone they reached the end of the great hall, turned down a passage and saw stairs winding their way up. This had to be where de Charité's bedchamber was located. The steps curved right to left and if there were guards at the top then they had the advantage because the wall on Blackstone's right hand prohibited the use of a sword. No challenge was issued, however, and at the top of the stairwell the torchlight revealed the bedchamber's door. Blackstone didn't hesitate as he pushed the door open.

The canopied bed was fit for a nobleman, not a Breton warlord. Fresh reeds on the floor cushioned a woven carpet and a tapestry hung from the walls. There was warmth in the room from a smouldering fire and the smell of stale sweat and sex. The wooden bedframe was decorated with blue and red paint and the feather mattress's bed coverings were of embroidered cloth. Bernard de Charité had plundered far and wide and lived the life of a wealthy merchant.

There was still no movement from the two bodies on the bed. A naked woman lay on her back, arm outstretched, the bedsheets twisted around her torso. Four empty wine bottles lay on the floor and a burnt-down candle's congealed wax dribbled over a wooden table. The remains of a meal made a squalid mess that spilled onto the floor. Next to the woman a man lay face down, mouth open, snoring, with spittle dribbling into his beard. His back muscles rose and fell with his heavy breathing. There was no need for Blackstone and the others to be cautious; the butcher of Saint-Aubin was deeply asleep. The three men relaxed their guard.

'He's a hairy bastard,' said Perinne as he found a bottle that still held some wine. The man's back was smothered in a mat of dark hair, in contrast to his close-cropped head. Perinne offered the bottle to Blackstone, who took a mouthful, passed it back and then went to the window where he could see the first hint of daylight creeping into the darkness.

'Like a bear,' said John Jacob, lifting the drunken man's sword away from the bench that held his clothing. 'And I'll wager he stinks like one. He lives well,' he said, admiring the sword.

'Not for long,' said Blackstone.

CHAPTER SIX

The town awoke slowly as daylight fought its way through the threatening clouds. The chapel bell for matins clanged tonelessly as men and women, hunched and shivering, staggered into the narrow streets to relieve themselves. There were still many weeks until warmer weather would break up the hard ground underfoot and water butts would not need their ice broken. It couldn't come soon enough. Sentries on the night watch who had huddled at their stations throughout the night shrugged off their cloaks. If the guard commander saw them still hunched when he clambered up the steps to the parapet then they would be flogged. A woman squatted in the street, her bladder heavy from the long night's curfew. She yawned and blew snot from her nose. Stiff from the unyielding floor that served as her bed she eased the crick from her neck, her eyes raised towards the high walls. Something dark fell from the sky. Her eyes widened in horror when she saw it was one of the night watch with an arrow through his chest. By the time she had screamed and soiled herself scrambling to her feet others had fallen dead into the narrow street.

Will Longdon had set his men in the perfect position to kill the sentries and as voices raised in panic echoed around the walls Blackstone's men-at-arms had surged into the barracks next to the town's gate. There, de Charité's soldiers were being roused from their sleep and most died desperately reaching for their weapons as Meulon and Renfred's men hacked their way through their ranks. A handful of the Breton warlord's men ducked and weaved their way clear of the slaughter. Naked, grasping weapons, they ran into the square – where Will Longdon and six of his archers had already run down to form a defensive line between the unconscious Killbere and the soldiers' quarters. With practised ease they bent their bodies, pushing their bow staves away from their chests, hauled back the yard-long bodkin-tipped arrows and loosed their deadly shots into the hapless men.

Peter Garland did as commanded and killed with the same relentless efficiency as the others and as the surge of excitement settled he felt the elation of being part of the elite group of men. Jack Halfpenny had retrieved his war bow and stood with his centenar. Ignoring the wound in his side he refused to let the pain from bending the bow stop him from shooting the men who had slain his archers in the ambush.

Within minutes of the town's awakening Blackstone's men had killed most of the sixty men under de Charité's command. The townspeople barricaded their doors but those who had been too slow were forced into the square at sword point while others had their doors broken down and were dragged into the streets. By the time Blackstone had kicked the naked de Charité from his drunken slumber Jack Halfpenny had cut Killbere free. Meulon carried him under one of the arches where others dragged a straw mattress. Renfred and his men seized food and blankets and took them to where Killbere would be tended.

Amid the screams women ran, dragging their children through the streets littered with de Charité's men into the charnel house of the square, where Blackstone's dead men still hung. Their men were forced at spear and sword point to follow. The hapless citizens of Saint-Aubin saw roughly dressed figures shouting at each other in English, and stocky men with war bows taller than themselves pulling bloodied arrows from the soldiers who only hours before had made the townspeople feel safe from any attack. Now that illusion had been wrenched from them by sudden violence inflicted by an invader who seemed to have appeared from nowhere. The terrified people were herded ever closer together by Blackstone's men and watched as a tall, rugged-looking man with a scar on his face dragged the naked Breton warlord into the square.

Blackstone clutched de Charité by the flesh of his cheek, painfully twisting his face. Despite the Breton's obvious strength he could not resist because the Englishman would have torn his face from him. With a hefty shove and a kick the naked man was plunged into the cowering townspeople. Blackstone stood amidst them and looked around at the desecrated bodies of his men hanging from the gibbets. He knew every man's name. He had depended on each of them in battle. Every man had been ready to bleed for the man next to him. His heart thumped hard as if trying to break through the constraints of his leather jerkin. He looked at Meulon, whose glowering expression told him he would cut the throats of every living creature in the town if Blackstone so wished it. Tears stung Blackstone's eyes. He could not express his loss at seeing how his men had died. His voice was no more than a tormented whisper but its tone carried every threat imaginable to those close enough to hear him: 'Get them down, Meulon. And use these bastards to do it.'

Meulon kicked the men nearest to him and then, seeing their captain haul terrified townsmen to their feet, the men-at-arms went into the crowd and did likewise.

Blackstone pointed at the Breton. 'Watch him!' he commanded Perinne and John Jacob. 'He moves, put a sword to his leg.' Blackstone strode on to where Will Longdon attended Killbere. The veteran knight was now wrapped in a blanket and propped up against the wall; Jack Halfpenny had a rag and a bucket and was finishing wiping the detritus from Killbere's chest. Killbere, for his part, was eating a piece of cooked meat and bread and swilling it down with wine. He stared up when Blackstone knelt next to him.

'Don't kill him, Thomas. He's mine. I told that dog turd I would kill him and now I will. I prayed hard for you to come. I knew you would.'

'Did you doubt it?'

'No, but I knew that if Chandos had anything to do with it I'd have been left to rot.' He saw the shadow of the truth cross Blackstone's features. Killbere grunted. 'Aye, I thought as much.

Though I hold no ill will towards him. I'd have done the same if I were him.'

Blackstone placed a hand on his friend's shoulder. He had minor wounds, cuts and rope burns from the coarse restraints, and the matted blood on his scalp had been gently bathed away by Halfpenny. 'Rest first, Gilbert, and then you shall have him.'

Killbere snapped irritably at the attentive Halfpenny. 'Mother of Christ, lad, I'm not a newborn calf to be rubbed down with straw. Away from me before I take a fist to you,' he spluttered, showering those who attended him with bits of food and spittle. He tossed aside the blanket and forced himself to sit up.

Blackstone was unable to suppress a smile. 'It seems being tied to that stake for four days was enough of a rest.'

'And you took your time. I damn near froze to death half naked out there for these inbred peasant scum to hurl shit at me. What were you doing? Whoring? Where've you been?'

The welcome relief of seeing Killbere's antagonistic spirit again soothed Blackstone's grief.

'Aye, you're right. We were drinking and whoring. And then we had to decide whether to come and see if you were still alive and worth saving.'

Killbere grunted. He watched the townspeople being forced to cut down the men he had lost in the ambush. 'We had no chance, Thomas. We fought as hard as we could but they overwhelmed us. Christ, they shot down our lads in one fell swoop.'

Blackstone helped his friend to his feet as Halfpenny stepped forward clutching Killbere's sword belt and clothes. 'Sir Gilbert, we found these in the guard commander's billet. It must have been his reward for launching the ambush.'

'Bring him to me, lad. I'll pay him what he deserves.'

'Will put an arrow through his eye. Him and his men, they're all dead,' said Halfpenny.

Killbere spat. 'Good riddance, then.' He took the clothes without thanks. 'Get yourself away and prod more of those bastards to getting our men off the walls.'

The young archer turned away.

'Jack,' Killbere called after him.

Halfpenny turned.

'You fought well and I thank you for trying to reach me in the fight. I'm pleased you lived. Now get off with you and once our lads are brought down attend to your own wound. There's blood seeping.'

Halfpenny grinned. Killbere's gratitude meant more than he would admit.

'And take that stupid grin off your face before these inbreds think you a village idiot,' Killbere demanded.

Killbere's body shook as he dressed himself but he pulled back from the help offered by Blackstone. 'I'm not a mewling infant, Thomas. I was dressing myself when you were not yet a seed in your father's balls.'

'You can't fight him now, Gilbert. He's strong. And he has twenty years on you. Young men move fast.'

There was still a tremor in Killbere's fingers as he struggled to close his jupon. 'Thomas, leave me be,' he said. He was concentrating on the task at hand but his tone of voice left no doubt it was more of a command than a request. 'And get that bastard dressed and armed.'

CHAPTER SEVEN

Three hours after dawn a frightened priest did as he was bid at the point of Renfred's sword and rang terce. The German man-at-arms let the nervous priest yank the pull rope long enough for the shrill clanging to irritate and then prodded him from the gatehouse chapel to where de Charité and Killbere waited in the square below for absolution before they fought. Killbere had fortified his weakness with brandy and had spurned Blackstone's offer to fight in his place. As Killbere tied his sword's blood knot onto his wrist he turned to Blackstone.

'If he kills me then you can have him. You've a look in your eyes, Thomas. You seek revenge for the men we lost. I will deliver it.'

'These scum hacked them at the end of a rope,' Blackstone said, looking to where his men's savaged bodies lay in a line against the wall. 'They need to pay for that. Men and women. There's no mercy to be had.'

'You don't kill women, Thomas. Never have.'

'These towns need to be taught a lesson. I will burn a swathe across this damned country whether they're held by routiers or French. Their King still has a price on my head. By the time I'm finished he'll have so many heads in sacks he can rule over their corpses.'

'Merciful Christ, Thomas. You'll become a monster if you slay everyone in this town.'

'I will become what they say I have always been.' He gestured to the approaching priest. 'God be with you, Gilbert.'

He stood back as Killbere pulled on his helm and strode forward. There was little doubt that Killbere was the more experienced fighter but de Charité was years younger and the man's strength was obvious from his barrel chest and thick neck muscles. There was a wolfish grin on the Breton's face as he approached the middle of the square. In his mind he had already beaten the weakened veteran knight. De Charité bent down on one knee and took the priest's blessing. A short confession and he was absolved from his sins. He stood back and pulled on his helm, waiting as Killbere faced the priest, who looked uncertain because the Englishman had not bent his knee.

'You're in the way, priest,' said Killbere.

'My lord? You must be shriven.'

'I have confessed a lifetime of sins to many priests before many battles but I have no intention of dying today.'

'Do you fear your sins will not be forgiven by contrition because your conscience bites at your soul?' said the priest uncertainly.

'Get out of the way.'

'But...'

Killbere pushed the stammering priest to one side and advanced. Bernard de Charité hesitated, stunned that Killbere would dare refuse God's blessing.

'Prepare yourself, Breton turd. By tomorrow your head will be spilled from a sack in front of your King.'

De Charité slammed down his visor, raised his sword at the high guard and swung the blade, feet braced at an angle, the power from his shoulders and chest bringing enough strength to bear to cleave a man from shoulder to hip.

As he watched his friend Blackstone involuntarily shifted his weight as if he were fighting instead of Killbere. *Half-step! Turn and thrust! Gilbert! He has you!*

As de Charité's blade swept downward Killbere did not flinch. He made a subtle shift of his body's angle and the Breton's sword tip whispered past his face and chest. It was a movement made by an expert fighter whose instinct as much as his eyes told him where a sword blade would fall. The crowd gasped. De Charité's impetuousness carried him past Killbere, who made no attempt to strike. He waited, shifting the weight on the balls of his feet as a disbelieving de Charité quickly corrected his balance, turned and attacked again.

This time Killbere caught the strike on his own blade, turned it with a two-handed twist and felt the Breton shuffle his weight ready to use the advantage of his strength against him. The crowd stayed silent, afraid to support their lord, but Blackstone's men roared for Killbere. Blackstone glanced at John Jacob; they knew how skilled Killbere was in a fight but he was weak. He would be unable to withstand a sustained attack. Blackstone turned his head towards where he had positioned Will Longdon. The archer held his bow down, an arrow already nocked, his fingers on the cord. If Killbere looked as though he was going to be killed Blackstone could never reach him in time. It would need the speed of an arrow to save Killbere's life. Blackstone shook his head at the centenar's questioning look. Not yet. Wait.

Killbere took a backward step. It seemed ill advised because de Charité braced his left leg, drew back his sword, threw forward his weight and lunged. Killbere couldn't avoid the strike. Blackstone was about to signal Will Longdon when Killbere suddenly swivelled on the balls of his feet, twisted his hips, reversed his sword and struck de Charité's helm with the pommel. The Breton's heels rocked. The blow snapped back his neck and Killbere used his free hand to grab his opponent's sword belt and tip him backwards. De Charité's legs splayed, his sword arm reaching out against the impact of hitting the ground. It happened fast. A roar of disbelief surged from the crowd as Killbere kicked back the man's visor with his heel and then rammed the point of his blade deep into the fallen man's chest. It cut through cloth, mail and flesh. De Charité squirmed but Killbere was leaning all his weight onto the sword's pommel. The Breton's strength nearly threw Killbere off as he bucked and floundered but the veteran knight knew how to kill and his blade could not be dislodged. The Lord of Saint-Aubin screamed, eyes wide in pain and terror, his gaze locked onto the grimacing features of the man who had promised that his face would be the last thing he saw before he died. His eyes dimmed and the gurgling in his throat from the choking blood stopped.

Killbere wrenched free his sword and pulled off his helm, hands shaking from the fight's effort.

'I vowed to take him limb from limb,' he said to Blackstone, who stepped quickly to his friend. 'But I was too damned tired.'

The Breton warlord's head was severed and wrapped in a sack. Blackstone would send the priest north to Paris to deliver the gruesome message that Saint-Aubin was lost and that a favoured ally of the war in Brittany had been slain. De Charité's men's corpses had been unceremoniously thrown into their billet as Blackstone ordered the people of Saint-Aubin to strip wood from their homes and livestock byres. He walked the base of the town's walls letting his stonemason's eye seek out a weakness. He found it in the north wall that abutted the lake. Over the years the dank conditions had weakened the rubble stone used in its construction. The wall had been built in two layers with loose rubble and dirt between them. Blackstone ordered that everything that could burn be stacked along its length. Tar barrels were placed at the base of the wall and casks of oil emptied over the wood. Blackstone was going to burn the place to the ground. The cold persisted but it was fear that made the townspeople shiver as Blackstone looked down on them from the top of the steps leading up to the parapet walkway.

'The Lord of Saint-Aubin-la-Fère was given the chance to fight for his life, but those who had sport with my men will die.'

A fearful moan rose from the upturned faces. They jostled each other like penned sheep but there was no escape.

John Jacob, Perinne and Killbere flanked Blackstone. The squire cast a nervous look at his sworn lord. Blackstone's anger was as unyielding as the frozen lake beyond the walls. He was going to teach the town a lesson and John Jacob feared that he was about to order the slaughter of all the townspeople. Will Longdon's archers were stationed on the ramparts, and the men-at-arms, shields up, stood in a line ready to advance on the unarmed folk.

Three men in the crowd looked nervously at each other and then took faltering steps forward.

'My lord,' said the eldest. 'We serve on the council. And with your permission we will speak on behalf of the people of Saint-Aubin.'

Blackstone gave a curt nod.

'Thank you, Sir Thomas. For years we have lived in fear of routiers,' continued the man. 'They scorched everything for miles around. It was only the protection of Bernard de Charité that allowed us to sleep safely in our beds.'

The second man in the delegation splayed his palms in supplication. 'For years the English King took what he wanted. The war he fought destroyed France. We had nothing. Only our town. It is where we are born and where we belong. It is the only place any of us have known. Our children are our only wealth.'

A murmur of agreement rippled through the crowd. The third elder dared to step closer to Blackstone. 'Sir knight, we had agreed with heavy hearts to deliver our beloved home to King Edward, but Lord de Charité convinced us that it would be a grave mistake, that the English would inflict pain on us in their victory.' He bowed his head, clasping his hands together, voice faltering. 'That we behaved so vilely towards the dead cannot be excused. It shames us. But our lord urged us to wreak our own revenge on them so that we might free ourselves of the burden that has crushed our hearts for so many years. We vented our suppressed fear – and that was wrong. Our true guilt is of being frightened by fighting men such as yourselves.'

The three men fell silent.

Blackstone showed no sign of mercy. 'You will pay. Every one of you,' he said coldly.

A wail of grief rose from the crowd. Women clutched their children to them as menfolk embraced their women. Their death was imminent, exactly as de Charité had predicted.

Killbere turned and spoke quietly to Blackstone. 'Thomas, think a moment on this. Your rage is understandable. The years of war and your own suffering can close a man's heart to mercy. How often have we seen and heard our King vow to inflict terror on a town or a city that has defied him? It was only the tender words of his Queen who softened his anger and made him relent. You loved Christiana when you were still a boy archer. Think of her now. Your wife may be dead, Thomas, but I know she still speaks to your heart.'

Blackstone had still not turned his eyes away from the whimpering crowd.

Killbere gently touched his friend's arm. 'I, more than anyone, wish to strike these people down, but we gain no honour from it. And honour is all we have left in our desolate lives. To kill them in the name of our King serves no purpose other than to inflame hatred against him. You've always had a place of tenderness in your heart. Find it again.'

Blackstone finally turned to face his friend and spoke quietly. 'I am no monster, Gilbert. I would never slay women and children, but an example must be made. You know that. What would you have me do? Walk away?'

Killbere remained silent. Blackstone was right. The English King had won the peace and that which was ceded to him needed to be claimed. And those who betrayed his trust risked everything.

'Do what you did when we seized Balon after our fight at Rheims before the King signed the treaty.'

Blackstone glanced at him. They had captured the town of Balon the previous year and punished those who had tortured a woman thought to be a witch. Blackstone faced the crowd. 'The ground is as hard with frost as my heart is with revenge. You will dig until your hands bleed, men and women both, and you will bury my men and your priest will pray over them. Forty men died. I will take a tithe. You choose,' he said, looking at the town elders. 'Four men to hang. That is the mercy I, Thomas Blackstone, grant you in the name of my King for the betrayal and mutilation.'

The spokesmen nodded their acceptance. Men grimaced at the thought of who might be chosen; women wept; and the children whimpered, not understanding what grieved their parents.

'And when this has been done,' said Blackstone. 'I will destroy Saint-Aubin-la-Fère.'

CHAPTER EIGHT

The pall of smoke hovered above the blazing town, a black shroud heavy in the air. It took a day and into that night for the men, women and children to bury Blackstone's slaughtered men and then as the dawn broke he allowed them to gather what they could carry. Four bodies swung from a gibbet fifty yards from the main gate as the stream of people shuffled their way clear of the blazing buildings and the decapitated body of Bernard de Charité that hung from the ankles alongside the men who had been sacrificed. The townspeople's homes had been destroyed and the corpses of de Charité's men had been laid in the pyre once anything of use had been stripped from them (being garrison soldiers their boots were less worn than those of Blackstone's men). As the inferno took hold the flames soared up through the tower keep and ignited the timber-frame roof like a beacon that would be seen for miles. Blackstone's men loaded supplies stripped from the town after he had allowed every family enough food for a week.

Blackstone and his men sat at the forest edge, their horses shifting weight, snorting breath, and watched the procession of dispossessed with the smoke billowing behind them.

'No one town will take them all in,' said John Jacob.

'They'll split into groups and find sanctuary,' said Blackstone.

'They'll tell the others what we have done,' said Killbere. 'And that will put the fear of Christ into them.' He glanced at Blackstone. 'If any of them survive. They'll fall prey to routiers now, Thomas. They'll be slaughtered out in the open.'

'They've paid the price, Gilbert. We'll shadow and protect them.

That will give them another story to tell. Fear and gratitude work like a horse pulling a cart.'

'You confuse even me at times,' Killbere said with a grin. 'You never intended to harm them, did you? And you let me splutter on a like a damned wet-nurse imploring you to halt any slaughter.'

Blackstone smiled. 'I needed the terror in their hearts, Gilbert.'

'But Chandos and the King will curse you, Thomas. They wanted Saint-Aubin.'

'It's of no strategic importance to anyone now, Gilbert. Its destruction serves a greater purpose. When these people tell their story they will exaggerate every deed and word spoken as surely as any drunkard in a tavern embellishes a tale, and the other towns will surrender without complaint. They'll hand over the keys and swear the loyalty demanded.'

The men continued to watch as the column of people disappeared from view. The intense heat from the flames melted the frost on the branches behind them and as the slow crackle of breaking ice echoed across the lake a louder sound began to be heard. It was the death throes of an ancient town, a place that had withstood siege over the centuries and witnessed the passing of armies. The foundations of the walls were crumbling, the masonry yielding to the searing heat. The men gasped as they witnessed the fifty-foot-high wall collapse from its base and then fold in on itself. Debris from the rough stone infill scattered onto the crumbling ice. The gaping wound that had been the north wall was suddenly cauterized by sheets of fire.

Some of the horses shied and were quickly brought under control but Blackstone's horse's ears pricked forward. It showed no sign of fear at the gush of flame. Blackstone grunted. Perhaps it was true that the bastard horse had been sired in hell. He jabbed his heels and turned it away. The destruction was complete.

The peace was proving as violent as the war.

The priest had been given a broken-down rouncey to carry him and his grisly message to Paris and the French King. The nag's uneven gait threw the pot-bellied cleric from side to side, its bony ribs rubbing his thighs raw. Muttered prayers mingled with every heavenly curse he could muster against the scar-faced Englishman who had sent him on this errand. The blood-soaked sack tied across the horse's loins had dried stiff but a haunting noise had started to wear down the priest's nerves. At first it sounded as though the nag's joints were creaking but when the priest let his mind settle on the sound behind him a stark fear clutched his heart. The noise was coming from the sack. The dead man was speaking to him in a subdued, distorted voice. Heart thudding, the priest hauled the horse to a halt and listened, but the sound had stopped. Heeling the horse forward the grinding began again. The priest squeezed closed his eyes, clasped his hands together and prayed harder than the day he had been given the benefice of Saint-Aubin. Once again he brought the horse to a halt and, like a man scared of something unknown creeping up behind him, eased himself down onto the ground. The moment his sandals touched the muddy track he sank to his knees and prayed again. Moments later the Almighty gave him courage. With eyes still closed he teased the encrusted string and untied the sack. Finally he dared to open his eyes and gaze down. Bernard de Charité's milky eyes stared back at him, his face leering in a broken grin. Mesmerized, the priest gently tilted the sack, and then laughed, releasing the pent-up tension in his chest.

'Ah, my lord. You struck even more fear into me in death than you did in life.' The rocking of the horse had dislodged the severed head's jaw and the grating sound was that of the lower teeth grinding against the upper. 'What's that, my lord? You would beat and curse me again if you could?' He had endured more than one flogging at the Lord of Saint-Aubin's hands. 'I cause you discomfort? It was not I who put you in the sack, and the man who did commands me to take you to those you serve. I do penance at every step of the journey. My arse is as raw as your neck.' The priest's nervousness gave way to distaste for his task and loathing for the dead Bernard de Charité. 'You died too easily,' he whispered vehemently. 'Died without enough pain being inflicted on you for the sins you committed in your whoring life. I pray the legions of Lucifer await you in hell to inflict their punishment.' With a gesture that astonished him in its spontaneity he spat into the upturned face. His action made him recoil and he quickly closed the sack and crossed himself. 'Merciful Christ, forgive me for desecrating the dead,' he said.

'What lunacy is this, priest?' said a voice behind him.

The priest whirled and faced a horde of armed horsemen who stood twenty paces away. He had not heard them approach. His mouth gaped. There were at least thirty men-at-arms; behind them even more followed until they were more dense than the forest that had hidden them.

'The deranged are always with us,' said the tall, barrel-chested man. He eased his horse forward. 'Whether their voice is satanic or heavenly.' He spoke with a strange accent but the words that escaped through the thick mass of grey beard were clear enough to be heard by the hundreds of men behind him. How had they moved so silently? wondered the priest. How had he not heard a jangle of a bridle or the creak of leather and mail? Fear of what he held in his hand had closed the world around him. That and the fact that they had approached downwind. Fighters who knew how to get close to an enemy.

'Which is yours?' said the horseman. 'A voice of God or the mutterings of the devil?'

The priest stuttered, mind racing for an answer as the rider stepped down from the saddle. He stood as tall as the scar-faced Englishman who had destroyed the town but he was older, with an almost white mane of thick shoulder-length hair. The man's callused hands that reached for the sack sported delicate silver and gold rings in contrast to flattened and scarred knuckles. A man who knew how to use his fists, decided the priest; he gave up the sack without protest. The fighting man spoke with a calm assurance, almost conversationally, as if speaking to a child who had been given a gift.

'Now, what have we here?' The man-at-arms pushed back his

cloak and opened the sack. He showed no sign of surprise; nor did he recoil. The blood on the sack had already given its warning. 'Who is this?'

The priest's throat dried as he glanced fearfully from the man on foot to those who still sat unsmiling on horseback. A ravening horde of routiers if he had ever seen one. 'My lord, it is the master of Saint-Aubin-la-Fère, Bernard de Charité.'

'Ah,' said the quietly spoken man. 'Too late, then. I was summoned by him to bring my men and help him resist the English and the pretender to Brittany. A pity. He promised sacksful of gold coin; instead he gazes up at me from one.' He tied the sack closed and handed it back to the priest. 'He had a fierce reputation. Who was strong enough to do this?'

The priest found his courage and his voice again. Now that the barbarian, for that is what every routier was at heart, had declared his loyalty to the dead man he found common purpose. 'A man-at-arms. A knight who fights for England and his violent, grasping King.' He raised his voice and addressed the horsemen as if he were delivering a sermon. 'Who accompanies a man possessed by both the devil and archangel so that he inflicts harsh punishment on one hand and compassion on the other. A double-edged sword that gouges a man's soul and sends him stumbling, confused, into the unknown away from the hearth that has nurtured him, like a spiritually blinded man.'

The man-at-arms sighed and placed a heavy hand on the priest's shoulder to curtail any further incomprehensible rhetoric. 'Who?'

The priest flinched. 'Sir Gilbert Killbere struck my lord down in single combat.'

The routier's chin tilted in recognition. 'Killbere? And the other?'

'Sir Thomas Blackstone.'

Once again the man's eyes indicated recognition. 'And where are they now?'

The priest pointed, arm shaking. 'South. Past what remains of Saint-Aubin. If you are a compatriot of de Charité then you can avenge him. They are less than a hundred strong and you... you...

have...' The priest stumbled as he tried to calculate the press of horsemen.

'Three hundred.' The routier grinned.

'Three...' the priest said, swallowing hard. This was one of the biggest bands of routiers he had seen. 'Then, my lord, ride on and follow the smoke. And in the name of God and the dispossessed people of Saint-Aubin, slay those who inflicted such misery on us and leave their carcasses for the crows.'

CHAPTER NINE

Three days after the destruction of Saint-Aubin-la-Fère, Blackstone and his men waited a mile beyond another town's walls. The citizens of Saint-Aubin knelt at its gates and begged entry; their elders stood before the town's council and declared their misfortune. They behaved exactly as expected. With gestures of ever-increasing passion they wept and bemoaned their fate and pointed to where Blackstone's men waited. Within hours the gates were opened and Blackstone rode into the town to take the oath of allegiance from the chief citizens. They were promised that the town would lose none of its privileges and that the regional lord and his men would serve as seneschal and guardians with the assurance of help from the English King. Blackstone appointed the local lord as garrison commander, ordered that King Edward's arms be painted above the gate and reappointed the town's officials.

'We are little more than debt collectors,' moaned Killbere as they rode towards the next town. 'When you were a boy and a knock on the head away from being the village idiot I was riding across Lord Marldon's domain doing exactly this. Collecting debts from villeins.'

'I was caring for my brother and working in a quarry,' said Blackstone, 'to earn every penny that was demanded.'

'Well,' Killbere sighed, 'they were good days. Days that took us to war. The best war a man could wish for. Better than this. Anything is better than this. Now I collect towns for the King. Where in God's name is Chandos? We need an army to strike at the French. Mark my words, Thomas, the French King is gathering troops. We should ride north towards Paris and put an end to his dreams of glory and stop his men from even leaving the suburbs.'

'North and into the plague?' said Blackstone. 'The pestilence takes its toll in England and Paris. Better to stay out here.' He turned his face to the fine rain that fell and kept his men hunched beneath their cloaks.

Snot dripped from Killbere's nose. 'When a man fights, Thomas, he cares nothing for foul weather, but when he is asked to be an errand boy misery clutches at his heart. Let's go and find some of the Breton bastards who challenge our King and get the blood moving through our veins.'

Blackstone ignored his friend's suggestion and glanced behind him at the column of men. 'Will? The archers Sir John gifted us. They're little more than lads.'

Will Longdon wiped the rain from his face. 'Untested, Thomas. Strong enough, decent pull weights on their bows, but untested. New recruits. They'll be all right. At least he didn't give us Welsh bowmen. God's blood, they can argue for the sake of it and drive a man to pull a knife. I gave half of these new lads to Jack Halfpenny. Jack'll bring them into line.'

'And, John? What about the men-at-arms?' he asked John Jacob.

'Meulon says they're scum, but they seem willing enough. Most are pardoned men. The King needed fighting men so he emptied the prisons and this is where some of them have ended up. I have my lads keeping an eye on them. I've warned 'em that they're following you now and we don't tolerate certain things.'

Blackstone turned to Killbere. 'You've seen them. You walked among them when we camped. Do you think they're ready for a fight?'

Killbere put a finger to each nostril and blew them clear. 'You throw them into a brawl and they'll learn soon enough. I remember you on your first kill. You were puking like a dog. But you learnt quick enough. You had the instinct even back then. You saw how things were. How to attack and where. Most of them will do all right when the time comes. Don't mother the youngsters, Thomas. I know Henry's not here to fuss over.'

'Is that what I did?' he said, his son's image in his mind's eye.

'Aye. Now and then. The lad took risks but he used his noggin. You give these boys a chance and they won't let you down. Not with Jack and Will at their backs. And Meulon will cut the throat of any man who disobeys and rapes.'

Blackstone knew Killbere was nudging him not to be so cautious with untried archers, using Blackstone's son Henry to make his point. The boy had saved their lives a year ago in Milan when Blackstone sought his vengeance against the Visconti, and now the lad was studying in Florence under the guidance of Father Niccolò Torellini. Blackstone's memory prodded him. It was the self-same priest who had held him when he was a badly wounded sixteen-year-old archer on the field at Crécy. Held him and blessed him and given him absolution because his injuries were so bad he was close to death. Sixteen. His own son was not yet that but had shown courage years before he had any right to be tested.

'All right, Gilbert, I'll let Jack and Will command those lads when the time comes. But until it does we do the King's bidding. Chandos has a fight waiting for us so there's time to train them. I won't have my men killed because they're not ready.'

Before Killbere could answer the bastard horse's muscles rippled. Ears forward, its head rose, pulling on the reins. Blackstone raised a hand and halted the column behind him. 'Something's wrong,' he said, trusting the feral stallion's instincts even above his own. They had crested a gently rising hill and made their way into the belly of lower ground. Ahead and to their right flank the edge of a forest followed the gently undulating contours. There was no need for Blackstone's men to question why he had brought them to a halt. The ground suggested a perfect place for an ambush from the curving forest 350 yard-long paces away. The men cast off the chill from their muscles and eased aside their capes. Without being ordered Meulon and John Jacob eased their mounts to either side of Blackstone and Killbere and as they took position Will Longdon and Jack Halfpenny had quietly signalled their archers to dismount and take up position to the front of them. Every fourth man took three horses each and moved them to the rear.

Within minutes Blackstone's men had prepared for an attack. Bird-song had fallen silent, no rooks or crows cawed from the dark thatches of their nests in the tall treetops and yet the whisper of breeze that brushed the men's faces brought no warning of danger. Bridles jangled as the horses patiently stood their ground, but the bastard horse whinnied and bunched its muscles, forcing Blackstone to sit back in the saddle and tighten the reins. Killbere glanced behind them. They would never be able to make the higher ground back there. There had been no sign in the wet grass of anyone ahead of them so if there were enemy on their flank they had kept themselves in the forest for as long as Blackstone's men had been riding in their direction.

'Chandos, do you think?' said Killbere quietly.

'He'd have shown himself as soon as we came over the hill,' said Blackstone. He drew Wolf Sword, its blade scraping loud with intent on its scabbard's metal rim. Moments later every man-at-arms did the same. The forest's treetops erupted in a black swarm of screeching crows. Wings flapping, they cried their alarm as the forest edge wavered and splashes of colour emerged from the dull treeline. The breeze barely lifted the banners and the cut tongues of pennons that followed. Armoured men on war horses were flanked by men-at-arms.

'French,' said Killbere as ever more men emerged from the forest. 'Christ, how many are there?'

'Two hundred at least,' said Blackstone. 'Probably more in reserve. Unless this is just an advance party.'

Killbere glanced at Blackstone's men. 'That's all right then. For a moment I was worried we might be outnumbered.' He grinned at Blackstone. 'God's blood, Thomas, the bastards have us.'

The French had moved across the valley floor and lined up for attack. No challenge had been made, no demand for withdrawal. The French were hunting for routiers and meant to kill.

'Whose banner is that?' said Blackstone.

Killbere squinted as the horsemen turned into formation.

'That's the Marshal of France. D'Audrehem's men. The French

King must think he's the only one who can seize the prize that he's missed all these years.'

'He's not after me, Gilbert, he's clearing out routiers. He doesn't know who we are. He hasn't seen our blazon and he won't have come from Saint-Aubin.' Blackstone studied the line of men that faced them. 'He's an impetuous fool,' he said. 'You remember that he charged our lines at Poitiers and failed.'

'Aye. He wants glory. Let him come then. Will and the lads will cause some pain and then we can get among them.'

The line of French horsemen bristled as they tightened reins and jostled, their front rank knee to knee. 'Stupid bastards never learn,' said John Jacob. 'Our archers will cut them down.'

'But there's enough of them to finish us,' said Blackstone.

Before the French line began their advance the sky darkened on the crest of the rising ground to Blackstone's left flank. Horsemen appeared and drew up their horses. It was obvious that the men were in force. At least two hundred more, realized Blackstone.

Killbere spat. 'Now we might have a problem.'

Blackstone knew he couldn't fight that many. There was no retreat and the horsemen on his flank would have cut off any such attempt. The French had cornered him at last, like a wolf in a trap. He shunned the brief moment of realization that death was imminent. He was grateful his son was in a place of safety and that he would carry on his name. Blackstone heeled the bastard horse. 'Those horsemen on the ridge will hold off, Gilbert. They won't risk getting close to our archers. They'll stay out of it. D'Audrehem's men are enough to finish us.'

Blackstone nudged his horse – fighting the bit – forward and then turned to face his men. Will Longdon had placed his and Halfpenny's archers in a sawtooth formation between the men-at-arms' ranks, arrows pushed into the dirt at their feet. There was little need for Blackstone to raise his voice as he addressed them.

'We're caught,' said Blackstone. 'We can surrender and the French will hang every one of us. And then our heads will be on poles at the gates of Paris.' He unslung his shield from its saddle ties and settled it on his arm. Its blazon of a gauntleted fist grip-ping the cruciform sword beneath its crossguard was decorated with the legend *Défiant à la Mort*. He looked down to where the youngest archers stood under Halfpenny's command. Fear etched their faces; their bodies trembled. They had never faced a cavalry charge of armoured knights before. 'We will attack but if their horsemen get past us then you boys look to Will Longdon and Jack Halfpenny. They will show you courage. Obey their commands and you'll kill many Frenchmen before they kill us.' His eyes swept across the extended line of his men. 'We have danced with death many times.' He hit the flat of Wolf Sword's blade across his shield. 'No surrender!' he called.

His men roared and brought down their blades across their shields. Like a crack of lightning the sound echoed across the open ground. 'NO SURRENDER!' Fear had been rammed down into their chests and smothered with belligerence that gave them the strength to kill and the courage to face their death.

Blackstone kicked his heels and let loose the surging horse as the men – little more than a handful – roared their defiance.

CHAPTER TEN

Blackstone hunched low over his horse's withers, shield raised, sword held low ready to make the first upward cutting blow into the nearest enemy's leg or raised sword arm: mortal wounds that would soon kill. A severed leg or arm flooded blood and seeped bone marrow. In this brutal, unforgiving contest, strength and endurance would be the only thing to keep a man alive; that and the blessing of any angel of war that hovered at his shoulder. The Goddess of the Silver Wheel, Arianrhod, jangled on a leather cord at Blackstone's throat. She was an archer's Celtic charm, a pagan spirit who offered protection. When the time came to forsake him she would ease the fighting man's spirit across the darkening sky. The bowman's guardian angel pressed close to the small gold crucifix that his wife had given him when they were little more than children. A blessing from her to protect the man she already loved.

The front line of French horsemen seemed to waver, uncertain what to do as Blackstone's men hurled themselves forward. Those behind who bore the banners and pennons of the French knights and of the Marshal of France had already turned in retreat. Something was wrong. Blackstone was less than a hundred yards from the front ranks when they too turned their horses. It meant only one thing. The French had drawn in Blackstone and then turned for the forest where they would re-form and outflank him. The killing would be done by those hundreds of horsemen who waited on the hillside. A charge downhill into Blackstone's ranks would force him back straight onto French swords. Hope lay in Will Longdon's archers, ready to loose their arrows on those men on the high ground should they attack Blackstone's flank.

The French seemed to be in turmoil. Many had already galloped into the woodland. Blackstone dared to glance over his shoulder. Thundering horses, bellowing lungs. His own men snarling. Faces contorted in savage determination. A part of Blackstone's memory heard the words of his King from a lifetime ago when they faced the enemy host at Crécy. Blackstone, the boy archer, had trembled with fear as King Edward extolled French courage and ferocity – *furor franciscus*. He had never forgotten those words, nor that Edward assured the English of victory. Now it was Blackstone's men whose ferocity had turned French ranks. And the horsemen on the rising ground had still not spurred their horses.

Blackstone's horse barged a French man-at-arms' mount as he struggled to heel it away from the English charge. The horseman swung wildly, but Blackstone had struck him on his blind side. The man had no means of delivering a blow. Wolf Sword's blade almost severed the man's left leg behind the knee. The razor-sharp edge cut through flesh, bone and tendon and then went on to slash into the horse's flank. Screams of pain rent the air as Blackstone's men bludgeoned their way into their enemy.

As Blackstone's momentum carried him through the French front ranks, the bastard horse swinging its huge head like a pole hammer, he realized that those Frenchmen who had first retreated into the forest were now slowing those behind them making their own desperate bid to escape. The forest had clawed at the French as surely as ranks of spearmen on the battlefield. There were barely forty men left to fight. A dozen French horsemen scattered; riderless horses from those already slain ran after them. Chaos was Blackstone's friend as the remaining men-at-arms were killed. Killbere's flail brought down a young horseman. He quickly got to his knees and threw open his arms in surrender but Perinne was at Killbere's shoulder and had already swung down with a killing blow. Crazed horses, nostrils flaring from effort and the stench of blood, barged and pushed into each other. John Jacob heeled his horse between Blackstone and a Frenchman who had managed to bring his mount under control. As the man raised himself in the saddle to strike down on Blackstone's helm, Jacob lunged, his sword point ramming into the man's exposed thigh and the soft flesh of his buttock. The man's head threw back, then spasmed as he vomited. He slumped, defenceless, his horse once again out of control as it surged away. The man held on for thirty yards and then fell into the grass. He writhed, wounded leg pulled tightly into his chest, his screams rising above others who were in their death throes.

One of Blackstone's men had gone after the wounded horseman and quickly dismounted. Blackstone didn't recognize him or know his name: it was one of the men gifted by Chandos. The man-at-arms put his foot against the wounded man's throat and stabbed down into the defenceless man's other leg. He struck again into the man's shoulder, ensuring the downed man would know even more pain before he died. Once again he plunged his blade, not yet delivering the killing blow.

Blackstone spurred his horse forward and as the gloating killer was about to hack again into the downed man struck him across his helmet with the flat of Wolf Sword's blade. The blow threw the man down and by the time he staggered to his feet Blackstone had dismounted and was standing over him. The man spat blood and cursed and, without thinking, lunged at Blackstone who struck him down again, using the sword's pommel.

'No man who serves with me tortures another to death,' snarled Blackstone.

John Jacob and Killbere reined in as Meulon joined them to stand over Chandos's man. The fight was over, the dead scattered on the ground, their horses running. Blackstone looked at Meulon and nodded towards the badly wounded Frenchman. Meulon bent and quickly cut his throat, ending his agony and his life.

'Get to your feet,' Killbere ordered the humiliated man. 'On your feet, scum, and beg Sir Thomas's forgiveness.'

The glowering men were as formidable as any enemy and the man had the good sense to crawl to his knees and lower his head.

'I beg it, freely, Sir Thomas,' he said.

'He's one of those put under my command,' said Meulon. 'William Cade, pardoned murderer. Him and the nine men-at-arms that came with him. They ride together.'

Killbere spat. Meulon gestured with his knife. Better to rid themselves of unreliable men. Blackstone shook his head. He looked past them to where the horsemen had finally begun to approach slowly down the hill. 'We need every man. Back to Will and the others before those men spur their horses on.' He looked down at Cade. 'On your feet. You inflict torture on a man ever again and I will kill you myself.'

He turned his back and mounted. The hundreds of approaching horsemen, who were now less than a half-mile away, had still not surged towards them. Perhaps, Blackstone reasoned, there was no need. They outnumbered Blackstone's few by so many that the killing could be a leisurely affair. All he could hope for was that his archers would bring down enough of them to give him and the others a chance to quit themselves well. He glanced down the line. Men crossed themselves. All had been shriven by the pot-bellied cleric at Saint-Aubin. All except Blackstone and Killbere. If it was his fate to die this day then it caused him little concern. It meant he would rejoin his wife and daughter and that thought caused a warm glow in his chest that dispelled any fear.

He looked to where Will Longdon and Jack Halfpenny stood with their archers. 'Will, Jack,' he called. 'Those tree stumps are your markers. The first is at eighty paces, the next a hundred and thirty-three and where that small ditch runs is the two-hundred mark. Give them time to get close. Kill them at a hundred and eighty and those that fall will hamper the men behind them.'

The advancing horsemen came on at the walk in a wedge formation, their leader astride a sturdy cob, ideal for travelling over rough terrain. These weren't cavalrymen on war horses, they were men who roamed far and wide and had strong, uncomplaining mounts. Their leader was too big for his horse. His feet dangled, his massive frame seemingly broader than the animal beneath him. His chest was as large as a barrel and the long grey hair and beard

61

obscured much of his face. The open bascinet showed two glaring eyes. Blackstone kept his gaze locked on the man. He seemed fearless as he drew up his men on the limit of an arrow's range. There were still English and Welsh bowmen who could arch their backs and whip their bodies forward to gain those extra yards, yet the man stayed unmoving. Was he, Blackstone wondered, tempting his archers to risk using their arrows to little effect? The two groups of fighting men waited in silence. The three hundred bore no pennons or banners; nor were they clad in armour but dressed in leather and mail with a cloak for warmth and a shield without blazon.

'Routiers,' said Killbere quietly. 'French are using them as well as trying to stop them.'

'What are they waiting for?' asked Perinne.

'Wanting us to break and run,' said John Jacob.

'Or piss us off so that we charge,' said Meulon.

The routiers' leader raised a hand and called across the divide. 'I will approach,' he called. 'Keep those bastard archers' fingers off their bow cords.'

'He's heard of you,' said Killbere, turning to look down the line at Will Longdon.

'Aye, and he had better not be my father because then he's a dead man anyway,' he answered.

A ripple of amusement rose from the men. Death might be moments away but contempt of any kind cheered them.

'Come forward!' Blackstone called.

The rider heeled the shaggy-coated horse. The closer he got the more Blackstone sensed he knew the man. He carried a spear rather than a pike. A simple killing weapon also favoured by Meulon: a pole eight feet long with a sharpened twelve-inch blade at its tip. Good for close-quarter fighting in the hands of an expert like Meulon.

'I know this man,' said Blackstone quietly.

Killbere glanced at him. 'I hope to Christ he's not *your* father as well, Thomas, otherwise there's going to be a death in the family today.'

'I'm looking for Thomas Blackstone, a boy archer rewarded as a knight and a farting old bastard by the name of Gilbert Killbere who should be lying dead beneath a horse on the battlefield of Crécy fifteen years back.'

'By all that's holy. It's him,' said Killbere and raised himself in the saddle. 'You ugly, broken-toothed whoreson! It's you who should be rotting in the mud at Crécy!' he guffawed. 'It's Gruffydd ap Madoc!' he said to Blackstone, whose memory opened the door to the time he was an archer with his first command and had been protected by the giant Welshman when aggressive spearmen questioned Blackstone's right to wear a Welsh archers' goddess at his neck.

Gruffydd ap Madoc pulled up his horse at fifty paces. 'Well? Do you intend to fight and die or invite me to eat?'

'You ride with the French?' Killbere shouted, knowing the routiers could be in the King of France's pay and that there was still enough time to charge their lines. It would take only minutes for the hundreds to kill Blackstone's few men.

Blackstone gathered the reins and urged the bastard horse forward before the Welshman had time to answer. 'No, Gilbert. The French took fright when they saw them. They thought they were with us.'

Killbere spurred his horse to join Blackstone as the scar-faced knight reached the mercenary leader.

'God's tears, Gruffydd, the last time I saw you, you and Gilbert went down beneath a horse. You with a spear in your hand and him trying to kill its rider.'

Gruffydd ap Madoc beamed and cuffed Blackstone on the shoulder. Blackstone remembered him doing exactly the same thing all those years before and, like then, damn near failed to hide the grimace of pain.

'And you were hacked near to death from what I saw. And your men still look as rough as a thistle-eating hog's arse. Nothing has changed!' said the Welshman.

Killbere drew up alongside him and extended his hand. 'I thought you dead all these years.'

'And I you. I should have guessed you were too belligerent to kill that day.'

'I was dragged from beneath that horse, but you?'

'The good Lord alone knows how I got away. I was hurt but I crawled through the mud and woke up two days later among the dead on the battlefield with a scavenging peasant trying to steal my knife, so I rammed it down his throat. Good days, Killbere. Days when we knew who we fought and why. Since then I have sold my sword. North-east. Up near the German border.'

Blackstone studied the bear of a man. Fifteen years was a long time in a fighting man's life. What drove them to fight for their King was behind them once they had been released from their service. The brusque man before him had championed Blackstone back then against antagonistic Welsh spearmen. But now? The hundreds of men behind him were battle-hardened, there was no doubt about that, and they looked ready to hurl themselves forward at the slightest gesture from their leader.

'How is it that you appear on our flank,' said Blackstone, 'as if you have been following our trail? Why have you travelled so far from the German border?'

The Welshman laughed, exposing his broken teeth through the thickness of his beard. 'To kill you.'

CHAPTER ELEVEN

King John II pulled his ermine-lined cloak around his neck as he walked across the vast raised courtyard of the royal manor at Vincennes. He and the immediate members of his council had moved the four miles south-east of Paris to what had once been his ancestors' hunting lodge in the Vincennes forest, but which over two hundred years had become a fortified château and retreat for French royalty. It also offered John and his family safety from the claustrophobic streets of Paris, now suffering from the pestilence, where a hundred people a day were dying. Legend and superstition said that the name of St Roch should be invoked to cure the plague, but if this failed it meant that the supplicant had grown too wicked and that God intended their end. A few miles along the Seine at Argenteuil only fifty survived from the population of eighteen hundred. To John's mind the curse of the English and the foulness of the pestilence went hand in hand. And St Roch was deaf to those who prayed.

'Sire,' said his son, the Dauphin, 'we do not wish to impose more discomfort on your grieving heart that we know mourns for France, but Blackstone's continuing presence stabs at us like a dagger point wielded by the English King. It is Edward's doing that Blackstone secures the towns ceded in the treaty. Does he intend to inflict this torment on us for ever? Blackstone has destroyed Saint-Aubin-la-Fère. That was not in the agreement. Nor was the death of Bernard de Charité. His head was sent to Paris.'

The King turned away from the gaggle of counsellors. He had spent four years in captivity after being captured at Poitiers by the Prince of Wales and escaping death by mere yards at the hands of Thomas Blackstone. The King's courage in battle was readily acknowledged, but the whispers, even of those close to him, were that had he even half as much political wisdom as bravery on the battlefield the nation would have survived. John had alienated Norman nobles and they in turn had plotted against him and joined forces with his son-in-law Charles of Navarre. Such conspiracies, John had decided when being forced to surrender at Poitiers, had been as if the stars had aligned themselves against him. Not even a divine king could alter the fate cast by the heavens. And then after captivity he had returned to a scarred land, torn apart by routiers and civil war. The north of France was plagued by bands of English, German, Breton and Navarrese mercenaries. Charles of Navarre still harboured ambitions to seize John's crown and it seemed the English King was unconcerned because such disruption kept the French monarchy at bay and less able to control events. And there was a private war being waged by Count de Vaudémont, the Royal Lieutenant in Champagne, against the German princes the Duke of Lorraine and the Count of Bar: a bitter struggle beyond France's eastern frontier fought by routier armies. At every turn King John faced lament from his subjects. More than 120 castles were still held by his old enemies in Normandy alone, castles that English and Gascons refused to leave in accordance with the treaty. Peasant farms and great estates alike were stripped bare by foraging mercenaries. Churches had been pillaged, stripped of everything so that services could not be undertaken –the wind gusting through windows bereft of glass blew out the candles. What manner of men stole glass from a church? Of what use could it be to them?

Days had passed into weeks and then months while he tried to bring unity and wellbeing to his country, and in the end a part of him had begun to yearn for the years spent in England, despite the guilt that crept alongside such thoughts like a witch's daemon. How could he not hanker after that time? He had been living in luxury, more a guest than a prisoner of the English King, not suffering like the French people. Along with other noblemen held after the battle and whose ransoms were still being raised, he had enjoyed great comfort, even gifts. Living in the Savoy Palace he had attended balls and tournaments and enjoyed the gaiety of the victorious English court. When King Edward's mother, Queen Isabelle, had attended her last tournament on St George's Day at Windsor Castle he had joined the English royal family and suppressed the humiliation of watching English knights beat those who came from across Europe.

He felt acid gnaw at his stomach. Such extravagance was being paid for by his countrymen, who had been stripped of everything. And while John was lavishly entertained, enjoying days of falconry and unfettered travel between the noble houses of England, his nation had been left in the hands of his son, the Dauphin, who defied his own father and rejected the treaty. The Dauphin and the Estates General had poked a stick in the English lion's eye and brought Edward and his ravening army back to France. Were it not for the hand of God and the mighty storm that had slain so many of Edward's men then the English King would never have signed a treaty of peace. And now? Desolation was everywhere. Memories of defeat and the sight of Thomas Blackstone fighting the Prince of Wales on that St George's Day tournament had been pressed between the pages of time, like a child's collection of flowers and butterflies crushed between the leaves of a book. And even now he was not being allowed to forget the scar-faced Englishman. Even now.

'We do not wish to hear about Thomas Blackstone,' said the King to his son. 'He should not inflict any more distress upon our family or our nation and we will not discuss him again.'

John raised his face and closed his eyes, breathing in the cool country air. It smelled clean and sweet and he had no desire to contaminate it with any talk of Thomas Blackstone. Birds were not yet nesting but they sought their old places of safety in antici- pation of the fullness of spring that would eventually rebirth the countryside. Nature's hand easing away the ugliness of the ravished landscape was something to be cherished. John the Good turned to his son again. 'When we were released we gave Edward the kiss of peace and vowed to honour the treaty. Blackstone is not the only Englishman carrying out his King's command.'

King John glanced towards the older man who stood a few paces behind the Dauphin. Simon Bucy, longtime friend, senior adviser and the man who had led the French Parlement and who had endured the years in Paris trying to help the Prince Regent rule France in John's absence. Bucy's face was a mask of inscrutability. Ever the diplomat, the favoured counsellor would never show any sign that might indicate even a hint of disloyalty to the young Prince. It had been Bucy's duty to support the Dauphin through those years of John's captivity, to stay close and advise in the King's name. John turned away. It would be unfair to press Bucy in front of his son. He would wait. They already spoke long into the night about how best to salvage France and make her the greatest country in Christendom once again. Long conversations without the Dauphin's presence. Without the habitual coughing and sniffing. That a son's ailments could be so intrusive and irritating! Charles had always been a sickly child and now even as a grown man his physical looks and demeanour suggested little more than an illness-ravaged, indecisive twenty-three-year-old youth. He had lost his hair and fingernails, all, if rumours were to be believed, due to being poisoned by Charles of Navarre. John suppressed a sigh. If only he could have been blessed like Edward with warrior sons and no in-laws trying to stab him in the back.

The King watched a pair of linnets dart in and out of a bush as they began the task of ensuring that their old nest was still in place. They were an example of industrious endeavour. Exactly what was needed for the French to rebuild their country. Their songbird trills were a delight. He would let them nest and rear their young and then he would have nets set and snare them. They would make a delicious pie.

'We tire,' he said and walked away with a dozen lackeys close at his heels.

As Simon Bucy followed the King, the Dauphin placed a hand on his arm. 'A moment,' he said.

Bucy held back.

'Does our father not see the threat that Blackstone might still be to us?' said the Dauphin quietly.

Bucy hesitated, nervous that his absence from the King's side would be noticed. 'Highness, our sovereign lord has the greatest task placed before any monarch. His country is in ruins and he is near bankrupt with a ransom still to pay the English King. Thomas Blackstone plays no part in his future.' Bucy could see that the Prince, who at times could be more petulant than his father, would need a better explanation. He lowered his voice. 'My Prince, in the past your father and I tried to have Blackstone killed, but we failed. We set the Savage Priest on him and Blackstone slew him in combat. Blackstone must surely be guarded by Satan's imps. And when you graciously kept me at your side while our King was held prisoner, you and I contrived to send him to the assassin in Milan who had murdered his wife and child. And that too failed. Blackstone is a force of nature that I doubt any man can destroy.' Bucy did as he had always done when offering advice to either King or Regent. He would pause as if considering the great weight that his interrogator had placed upon him and that brief hesitation always convinced those listening that his answer had been given with the utmost care and consideration. 'Should we not abandon any further attempt to rid ourselves of him? Perhaps we should be grateful that when the Jacquerie scorched the land it was Blackstone who helped rescue your family. It was he who gave you what short time was left with your children before they were so cruelly taken.' Bucy lowered his eyes briefly, a mark of respect and shared sadness. Barely two years after Blackstone had rescued the Dauphin's family at Meaux, Charles's three-year-old daughter Jeanne and her baby sister Bonne, his only children, died within two weeks of each other. The Dauphin had taken the bereavement badly.

'Our children are gone from us, Simon. Perhaps it was God's punishment for not putting Blackstone to the sword when we had him in Paris. Our sin must have been to have let such a scourge on our land live.'

'No, highness. Forgive me but that is not true. You were in his debt. And you paid that debt by telling him where the assassin was. There would have been no honour in killing him when he came to Paris under truce.' Bucy concealed his agitation at being held back from being with the King. Such a delay might raise questions and the last thing he wanted was to have to explain to his sovereign lord that his son still harboured an unquenchable desire to kill the rogue Englishman. There were greater and more pressing concerns to attend to.

'You do not understand, Simon. You do not see the future. Our father will not live for ever and when we are king we will face the threat that Blackstone and men like him bring. We may not be a warrior or master horseman like our father, we may not even have the strength to wield a sword, but we have sufficient intelligence to foresee that Edward will promote Blackstone here. The day will come when we will take back France. We will avenge Crécy and Poitiers. It may not be this year or the next. But do not doubt us, we will take the realm back from the English and when that day comes we do not wish to have Thomas Blackstone defy us as he has defied his own King. Our way ahead will be easier without him.'

The comment gave Bucy pause for thought. There was no denying the Dauphin had strength of personality despite his physical frailty. Had it not been for his stubbornness in denying King Edward the full terms of the original treaty more of France would have fallen into the hands of the English. Even when Edward had invaded with the greatest army he had ever assembled, the Dauphin had stayed behind the walls of Paris and let the English King fail to seize the great cities, denying him supplies by burning the crops and food stores before Edward could reach them. In many respects the ailing Charles had outfought the great warrior King without even leaving the royal palace. And the boy had been astute enough to keep his father's counsellors close to hand, himself included. Perhaps Charles had the vision to see what might befall France if Thomas Blackstone were given more power and authority, and, most importantly, more troops.

'Then how could we succeed when we have failed so many times before?'

'You would not remember because you were engaged in attempting to save your estates from the Jacquerie.' It was a gentle rebuke, but pointed none the less. 'But when they swarmed across our land the guards found a poacher in these very grounds. He had dared to clamber over the walls to kill our game. He was apprehended. We had him show us how he laid his traps and then how he enticed the prey into them. It was skilful and took patience. He tempted those he wished to kill into moving from a place of safety into his snares. He understood his prey and used that knowledge against it.' The Dauphin's smile reminded Bucy of a grimacing corpse whose tinder-dry skin stretched across its skull. 'We have already set a course of action,' said the Dauphin. 'And we will share it with you when the time is right. Simon, think to your own future and decide who best to serve in order to save France.'

In a dismissive gesture the Dauphin turned his face away to gaze across the manicured gardens.

Simon Bucy bowed and, gathering his cloak around him, walked briskly towards the royal quarters. He served the King loyally and always had done. And would continue to do so. But – there was always a but in the corridors of power – would John have the vision and strength that was required to strip the land of marauding fighters like Thomas Blackstone?

CHAPTER TWELVE

Wolf Sword was suddenly at the Welshman's throat. Blackstone had moved so quickly that even Killbere was taken by surprise. Gruffydd ap Madoc guffawed and slapped his thigh. 'I would kiss the Pope's arse if he created a miracle so that the world could see the look on Killbere's face.' Gruffydd made no move to defend himself but his eyes locked on to Blackstone. There was suddenly no humour in his voice. 'Thomas Blackstone, lean forward and press your sword point into my throat and every man with you will die. Lower your sword and let me explain.'

'It had better be a good explanation, my friend, because if it is not your head will be in the mud before my death,' Blackstone said and lowered the blade.

Gruffydd ap Madoc sighed. 'Christ, you were a mad archer back then, throwing yourself into the fight, and it would appear everything I have heard about you over the years is true. You're a fearless bastard and I wager you place your life in Arianrhod's hands, but I didn't know that you had attacked Saint-Aubin. Bernard de Charité sent word weeks ago for us to fight in the war in Brittany against John de Montfort's troops. It was time for us to leave what was left of the Germans and make some money in the Limousin. Had we got here earlier I would have been forced to make a decision whether to take de Charité's gold and fight you or turn my back. What do you think I would have done, Thomas?'

Killbere grunted and poked a finger in Gruffydd's chest. 'You and I faced French cavalry at Crécy, and we both saved the other's life. Men who endure that do not turn on each other like rabid dogs.'

'He has hundreds of men, Gilbert, and perhaps they didn't share your danger. They ride for profit,' said Blackstone, looking at the Welshman.

Gruffydd nodded. 'You're right. These men are drawn to me because I put food in their bellies and gold in their purses, but what Killbere said is true. And I would have killed any of these men behind me who would have challenged me. They know that. And what good would it do for me to kill Thomas Blackstone? I would be showered with wealth by the French King and his son but I would be cursed by every Englishman and God knows you English cause enough trouble without me adding to it. There's fighting and money to be made elsewhere.'

'You could have helped against these French,' said Killbere.

'I did. I stood my ground and let them see our strength. They were only a couple of hundred Frenchmen going south to join their army.'

'Perhaps you were waiting to see whether they turned and ran or overwhelmed us,' said Blackstone. 'Then you could have claimed that you had blocked any chance we might have had of escape.'

'You're beginning to sound like a damned politician, Thomas. Merciful Christ, I held back because the French knew we were not with them. They saw us and thought we supported you. Now, are we going to sit out here all day or can we join forces and ride on? The French go south to fight routiers.'

'And we are on the King's business,' said Killbere. 'There's no pillaging to be had. You and your men will stay poor if you ride with us.'

Gruffydd's eyebrows raised as he looked questioningly at Blackstone. 'Some payment for our help? Three hundred men at your back is no bad thing.'

'You ride with us to join Sir John Chandos and if he agrees you can have the money from Saint-Aubin.'

'How much?' said Gruffydd ap Madoc.

'One and a half thousand gold francs,' said Blackstone.

The Welshman grunted with pleasure. 'You have it here?'

'Of course,' said Blackstone. 'The sack is strapped to my pommel.' He glanced down. 'Ah. Pity. It must have slipped free during the fight,' he said drily.

Gruffydd blinked twice and then threw back his head and laughed. He gathered his reins and turned the horse. 'You taunt your enemies and tease your friends, Thomas.'

'Did you think I would carry that much money?' said Blackstone. 'What fool would? The money is on a writ pledged by the King. Chandos will pay you.'

The stocky horse wheeled under Gruffydd's hand. 'So be it! Ha! You are a man worth following, Thomas. My men will bring up the rear behind your own and we will obey your commands.' He guffawed again and spurred his horse back towards his men.

'Gruffydd!' Blackstone called.

The Welshman turned.

'Your men at the rear but you ride with Sir Gilbert and me.'

Ap Madoc grinned, knowing full well that if Blackstone sensed betrayal then he would be the first to die. 'So be it!' He nodded in agreement and urged the horse away.

'God's blood, Thomas, these Celts are touched. He's as possessed now as he was back then. Better he's with us than not,' said Killbere. He studied Blackstone for a moment. 'We fought hard, him and me, smothered in gore and with a rage to kill. We took the fight to the French and we bled for our King. There was honour in it.' He watched the burly Welshman reach his men. 'But we cannot trust him now. Mark my words on that. He's dangerous.'

'Tell the captains to keep our men away from his. You're right, Gruffydd ap Madoc will be a good ally until he decides not to be. Once he gets the smell of plunder he will turn on us no matter what he says.'

'Aye, especially if he finds out what we carry in our saddlebags, and that you told him a thousand less than we have. I was fearful the coins would jangle when that bastard horse of yours shifted its weight.'

* * *

They rode south-east for six days, skirting the towns that already owed Edward fealty. There were still a half-dozen more that were required to paint the English King's arms above their gates, but they could wait. By day and night the uneasy fellowship of ap Madoc's mixed band of routiers rubbed like a wet boot on a man's heel.

'Keep your stench downwind,' Will Longdon taunted the riders, whose ranks were mostly Welsh men-at-arms bolstered by mongrel packs of English, German and French routiers. After the Welsh it was the English who made up most of their numbers. Some had deserted the English army years before to find a more profitable occupation; others had been discharged like so many after the last great invasion. It made no difference which King they had served, the reality was they were only good for war and thousands of such men roamed the countryside in various bands, led by captains, all men of fighting experience. All driven by lust, greed and necessity.

'Sleep with your hand on your cock and you'll wake to find your throat cut one morning,' they jeered back at Longdon.

'Sleep with your knife and you'll wake without your cock,' others cried.

'If it can be found,' shouted another.

Gruffydd ap Madoc grinned and said something in a language that Will Longdon could not understand. The men who rode closest to the big Welshman roared with laughter.

'A hundred paces and a couple of dozen sheaves of arrows and I'd teach them to cry for their mothers in English,' said Longdon to Jack Halfpenny who rode at his side.

'If Sir Thomas trusts them to fight with us then we had best not antagonize them, Master Longdon,' said Peter Garland from a horse length behind them.

'Do dogs' bollocks swing?' said Longdon. 'You have to show scum like that contempt. It's expected. Us to them, them to us. How else are men to show they are men? Taunt and insult. It's necessary.'

'For what?' said the young archer.

'For friendship,' said Will Longdon, shaking his head as Jack Halfpenny grinned at the lad's innocence. 'And trust,' he added. 'How else am I to go among them and find out their true intent?'

Will Longdon had gone out with a half-dozen men that day and brought down a deer. That night he took a haunch to some of ap Madoc's men, guided by campfire and raucous voices. The routiers had looted wine and brandy from German lords' cellars and had clearly been imbibing freely. Blackstone's men, in contrast, had settled into their own defensive routine and smothered their cooking fires and extinguished candle stubs as darkness fell. The distance between the two camps was as broad as each group's discipline. They were a day's ride from where Sir John Chandos expected a routier army to be, and that was close enough for Blackstone to insist on caution. Let ap Madoc's men behave as they wanted but Blackstone and those who had long fought at his side knew the value of letting darkness and silence cloak them. If any sneak attack were to come in the night it would be against the routiers, illuminated by their scattered firelight across the open field.

Will Longdon was welcomed to a campfire by men dulled with drink and he played up his own part accordingly. The meat was packed into the embers, covered with stones and more wood stacked on top. It would take hours to cook but the soldiers would wake to a succulent breakfast. Will's generous gift was rewarded with a small cask of brandy. Ap Madoc's men bragged of how they had raided the French–German border for a year. They had fought and killed without restraint and they had been well rewarded by the French Count de Vaudémont.

'We burned the ignorant peasants out, slaughtered everything that moved,' one of the men grunted, eyes glazing as he looked into the flames.

'Aye. Cats, dogs, women and children. We swept through them like wildfire—'

'And their militia,' interrupted another.

'And them,' agreed the man. 'Impaled them on sharpened poles...'

One of the men stabbed his knife point into a piece of dried fish. 'And they squirmed!' he laughed. Others joined in. Will Longdon grimaced. It was enough to be thought of as a smile of approval of the men's cruel actions.

'The Germans ran like chickens from a coop with a fox after them,' said another, taking a bottle from his lips. 'We stripped their churches like their women!' More laughter. More slaps on the back. Men belched and farted.

'Gruffydd ap Madoc took no prisoners unless they were worth ransom. We have *moutons*, *livres*, francs, florins. Money is money.'

'Aye, and enough plate from noblemen and churches to furnish our own castle!'

'If you have money,' said the man next to him, leaning blurry-eyed into him, 'we would take it. You have money, bowman? Eh? Your captain stripped a merchant's wealth lately?'

'No, we suffer with a pauper's stipend from the King,' Will Longdon answered, adding, 'No looting, no rape.' He spat in pretence. 'We live a poor life compared to you lads.'

'You!' a man across the campfire said, pointing at him. 'Even you are worth something. Dead, that is. Better dead for us. You would have been lying face down in the mud if we'd got to you before your captain burned out de Charité's town. We were set to make money from killing you and those fighting against the Bretons. Count yourself lucky, archer.'

Will Longdon could barely make out the man's face in the dim light but he could see from the hunched shoulders and extended arm pointing accusingly at him that it wouldn't take much for the man's belligerence to tip into violence.

He bit back the challenge that surged in his chest. One stride across the fire and his archer's knife would be buried in the man's throat. He'd kick embers and then cut and slash his way clear. Drunken men were slow off the mark and he saw in his mind's eye the order of the killing. Instead he grunted as if burdened by drink. 'First you'd have to find us. We know how to hide!' He grinned. 'Three hundred of you and a handful of us! What chance would we have? Eh? We know when to run. And I wager we can run faster than any of you. Chickens and foxes, eh?' He squawked like a chicken.

The men laughed. Longdon staggered to his feet and slapped the man's shoulder next to him. 'I need to piss.'

The man snatched at his arm and he suddenly seemed less drunk than a moment earlier. 'Archer! You're on the wrong side. You understand what I'm saying?' His grip was fierce but it made little impression on Will Longdon, whose arms were cords of muscle and sinew.

The men fell silent and turned their faces towards him. 'You think you fooled us, archer?' said the man who had threatened him.

Longdon's muscles tensed. His arm was still held. His knife hand.

'You bring a haunch of meat. Why would you do that?'

Will Longdon stared them down. And bluffed. 'You know why.'

The men glanced at each other.

'Bring your men over and join us,' one of them said.

'How much?' said Longdon. 'You want us, you have to pay.'

They grinned and Longdon's arm was released.

'That's what we thought. All right, we'll talk again.'

Will Longdon gave a convincing stagger as he stepped away and the men jeered good-naturedly. Despite the darkness he quickly found his bearings and remembered where he had entered the men's camp. A few hundred paces would bring him back to his own men. As he stepped past one of the last campfires he saw a half-dozen shadows flit between the scattered firelight as they made their way towards Blackstone's encampment. But the man leading the others changed direction and stopped next to one of ap Madoc's men who was feeding his fire; the flames surged, showing Longdon the man's face clearly.

William Cade.

CHAPTER THIRTEEN

Will Longdon reported his information to Blackstone and Killbere before the day's ride began and Gruffydd ap Madoc joined them at the front of the column.

'They bribe men to join them?' said Killbere. 'What's unusual about that? There are thousands of footloose men in France looking to make a living. Plunder and the promise of it is what we all seek. Every man needs to eat.'

Longdon winced. 'It's more than that, Sir Gilbert. It's a feeling, is all. Something not right. They aim to do us harm, I reckon. They're whoresons, every one of them. They slaughtered women and children and impaled the men who fought against them. They are as bad as the Hungarians in Italy who burned their prisoners alive.'

'Yet they have not caused us harm,' Killbere said. 'And we have ap Madoc's word that they won't.' He snorted and spat. 'But Thomas knows my thoughts on that.'

Blackstone tightened the saddle cinch on the bastard horse. It snapped its head back, trying to bite him with its yellow teeth, but he had already looped the opposite rein over his arm to restrict its predictable response. 'You're certain you saw William Cade in their camp?'

'It was him,' said Longdon.

'Aye, well, the likes of him would sell his arse to a mendicant monk if he thought it got him closer to the Pope and the gold in his coffers. We'll watch him,' said Killbere. 'He might be deciding which side offers the most profit.'

'They need archers and even though there are few of us we'd

give them the advantage in a fight. They came to kill us, Thomas, but now they say they'll stand with us,' said Will Longdon.

'And they will because they'll be paid. But then they'll go their own way because we will have Chandos's men at our side and they won't risk an equal fight. When Meulon returns tell him to keep an eye on William Cade.'

The bastard horse protested as Blackstone pulled himself into the saddle but once Blackstone's weight settled it calmed, ducked its head, yanking the reins as if to let him know its strength, and then it snorted, head raised and ears pricked. Meulon and Renfred appeared a thousand paces away on the edge of a forest. They had reconnoitred ahead the previous day and slept in the barren wasteland overnight. Meulon stood in the stirrups and raised his spear; then he waited with Renfred beside the trees. A chill wind gusted, crackling the pennons. Windswept trees lurched, bent from the constant exposure to the eastern gales that coursed over the bleak landscape. Their bare branches, not yet softened in leaf, clawed out for the riders. As the wind shifted and caught the fluted branches an eerie moan rose up. Half-world creatures lived in such places. These forests harboured wolves and boar and hid friend and foe alike. Better for a man to ride out in the open. Better to die under a blade in battle than dragged from his horse by an unseen assailant whether of this world or the next. Superstition. It could cripple men's minds or make them strong.

'Thomas?' said Killbere. 'You think Meulon has found Sir John's force? My bones ache with this constant riding.'

'You'll soon have your fight, Gilbert. That'll warm you.' He grinned. 'Once we're through that forest.'

Killbere and Will Longdon crossed themselves when they looked to where the German captain and Meulon waited, the big man signalling with his spear again, this time lowering and pointing towards the gloomy forest.

Killbere grunted as Gruffydd ap Madoc rode towards them to join the head of the column. 'Madoc's more superstitious than any of us put together. He might not follow us through there.'

'Then he won't get his money,' said Blackstone and spurred on the bastard horse. He would be the first to enter the bleak and ancient woodland. Once he was far enough ahead of the cantering horses not to be seen he quickly brought Arianrhod to his lips and kissed the silver wheeled goddess.

'Hold up!' the Welshman called as Blackstone nudged the bastard horse onto a woodcutter's track.

He turned and looked at ap Madoc, who had brought his horde of men to a halt. 'We cut through the forest we save a day,' said Blackstone. 'There's a track. And we'll come up behind Sir John's force.'

'You don't know that,' said the long-haired Welshman. 'You put three hundred men down a narrow track and they can be ambushed.'

'By goblins and faeries?' taunted Killbere. He glanced at the dense forest. 'They're the only ones who could hide out of sight. No army can lie in wait, Gruffydd. Do the spirits of the dead frighten you?'

'The dead?' ap Madoc snorted. 'The dead?'

'Aye, didn't you know this is called La Forêt des Morts?' He suppressed a smile as the man who had once fought so fearlessly at his side nervously licked his lips.

'I'm not fearful, if that's what you think,' he blustered. 'But some of my men come from such dark and forbidding places. They've seen ancient forests swallow a man whole.'

'Then they shouldn't live in Wales!' said Killbere. 'Dark, miserable, pissed wet through, godforsaken place. It's enough to make a man yearn for war to get away from it. Did you never wonder why so many Welshmen serve in Edward's army?'

'I know this forest,' said Blackstone, cutting off a belligerent war of words before they could gain purchase. 'My men and I used to raid here when I lived in Normandy.' It was true, he had, but like many others he also knew that a place earned its name for good reason and the Forest of the Dead was no exception. When plague had swept across France years before the forest dwellers had died their agonizing deaths and their bones were found everywhere by hunters and raiders. The woodsmen and their families had tried to run from the pestilence but it had overtaken them before they reached the clearing that Blackstone remembered being further on. 'I've been through it before, Gruffydd. It keeps out the routiers. Only those who know the truth of the place will venture in. No ambush, only the wailing of the dead.' But even as he said the words a chill ran down his spine. 'We hold our nerve,' he said and heeled the bastard horse onto the forest track.

The last time he had travelled through the dense forest, he'd seen bones of the dead scattered either side of the track. The way was overgrown now but the semblance of a path was still visible because wild animals had adopted it as a hunting trail. What had not been there the last time were the human bones dangling from branches above the track. Leg bones, arms and hands, a rib cage and skulls swinging in the wind that whistled through the forest, their grinning teeth seemingly moaning in a creaking howl. Bleached and beaten by the weather, rattling like hollow dice in a tavern game played with the devil, these were warning signs not to enter the Forest of the Dead, placed by those who had taken the woodland as their own. It was too late to turn back. Blackstone led the men at a steady pace through the trees relying on his memory as to where the woodcutters' village had been so that he might find their hovels and then the track that led out of the forest. By midday the trees opened into a broad overgrown clearing and his mind's eye showed him where the huts had once stood. Since then the forest's tendrils had sneaked across the open space and suffocated what remained of the hamlet. The villagers' bones had long been taken by animals but he still felt the presence of the dead as the wind blew through the gnarled and twisted trees. His imagination suddenly taunted him. Had he been lured into a place of death so that he too would die there? He spat and expelled the fear with it. They needed to ride south-east and although the sun had disappeared behind the thickening clouds he looked to where the moss grew on the trees' bark. Moss needed moisture to thrive and would never face the sun.

'Stay here,' he told Killbere, who was waiting at the head of the column, and eased the bastard horse forward. His eyes sought out the dark cloak of moss on the tree trunks, then he turned his back and faced south, urging his horse across the opening, angling its direction towards the lower quadrant. It was as close as he could get to facing south-east. As he turned in the saddle to call the men a movement caught his eye. It was fleeting but the drab brown shape blurred against the far treeline. Alarm suddenly squeezed his chest. It was no animal that had moved but the figure of a man who had darted back into the trees. And it was faceless.

He kicked his heels and the bastard horse needed no further prompting. It lunged into the overgrown clearing, its weight and strength tearing aside any clinging plant. As Blackstone surged forward Killbere led the men after him and, seeing Blackstone with Wolf Sword in his fist, armed himself. Whatever Blackstone had seen had caused him to gallop forward and this might be an ambush. Blackstone had a forty-yard lead when he suddenly veered out of sight into the trees. Killbere swore under his breath. What in God's name were they riding into? There was no room for a column of three hundred men to swarm across the clearing. Only the first forty or so of Blackstone's men managed to forge their way forward, as Gruffydd ap Madoc's horsemen blocked each other's progress. The Welshman rode at Killbere's side, no sign of fear, eyes focused on the dense forest.

'Go left!' Killbere commanded so that the men could strike in two columns. Ap Madoc made no complaint and swung his horse as Blackstone's men split and followed both of them. Their horses struggled through the undergrowth, hooves rising and falling, chests forcing aside bracken. Despite the chill their flanks were soon lathered white with sweat from their exertions. As they reached within thirty yards of the far side of the clearing Blackstone reappeared and raised his sword arm to halt their surge.

'Hold back the men!' he called. Momentarily confused, Killbere and ap Madoc yanked their reins and slowed their horses. 'Gilbert and Gruffydd with me.' He turned his back and heard Killbere order Perinne and Meulon to hold the men. Horses snorted and fought their bits, dismayed that their sudden race for the forest had been curtailed by their riders.

The two veteran fighters rode to where the clearing merged into the forest once more, searching out Blackstone. They saw him on a cleared track and then he disappeared from view again. Killbere glanced at the Welshman. Both men were mystified but they stayed alert, glancing around at the dense foliage.

Ap Madoc grunted. 'The old gods have kept me safe for many years, Gilbert, but I'll wager that your Thomas Blackstone might one day taunt them enough to abandon me. He rides into the unknown in a place of death and then calmly calls us forward.'

'If Thomas is unharmed and he's called us then there's no danger,' said Killbere.

They followed Blackstone around a bend in the track and came into a settlement of fifteen or more huts crudely built of wattle, mud and thatch. The cut branches and hurdles that penned their pigs and chickens between each hut helped their semi-concealment. A horseman passing by would not see them unless they rode into the hamlet. Rabbits hung from poles and a deer carcass, recently gutted, was stretched onto a gutting frame. There was no smoke coming from the roof smoke holes but now that they were close and the wind was in their faces they sensed the dank smell of wet fire. These wood dwellers had doused their fires when the intruders rode into their forest. Blackstone sat astride the bastard horse and looked at the dozen faceless men dressed in ragged clothing. Their heads were covered in coifs but their faces were bandaged with a gauze-like material that obscured their features. What was left of their hands, also bandaged, gripped staves and axes.

'Mother of Christ,' Killbere whispered. 'Lepers.'

CHAPTER FOURTEEN

Blackstone faced Killbere and ap Madoc. 'They tell me they've been living here for three years. There are fifty or more of them. Men and women. A few children. They scavenge, trap and hunt.'

The two men stayed back.

'Come closer,' said Blackstone. 'You'll not be infected.' He looked at the bandaged men who stood defiantly in a half-circle in front of their huts. 'They need no leper's clapper out here. They're free men. As free as they can be.' Blackstone dismounted to show Killbere and ap Madoc not to be afraid. 'When Christiana and I escaped from the Savage Priest in Paris we hid in the leper colony north of the city walls. They offered us food and kindness. We accepted both.'

The man who seemed to be their leader said something, his voice muffled behind the cloth across his face. Blackstone was near enough to hear him. 'Then we will give you what we have in return,' Blackstone answered. He looked back to where Killbere and Gruffydd still sat uneasily. A third figure had ridden forward from the clearing. William Cade looked at the diseased men and women.

'Burn them out,' he said. 'Kill them and put their bodies in the fires. They infect the air we breathe. Best to be rid of them.'

Killbere turned on him. 'Keep your whoreson mouth shut. You have no business here and you do not tell Sir Thomas Blackstone what to do. Get yourself back to the others.'

Cade was unperturbed by Killbere's anger. He shrugged and then spat. 'If you don't have the stomach for it, Sir Gilbert, the Welshman will do it. He and his men have slain women and children in their droves.'

'Be quiet,' said ap Madoc. 'What I have done is my business.'

'You think Sir John will want any of us to ride with him once he learns we've breathed the same air as lepers?' sneered Cade, drawing his sword. 'Stand aside. I'll do it myself.'

Gruffydd ap Madoc suddenly swung an arm as thick as a man's thigh and caught Cade across the chest. The blow tumbled him from his horse but he rolled and quickly got to his feet. His fighting skills were in his blood as the leper's affliction was in theirs. Blackstone took three of his long strides and gripped Cade's sword arm as he prepared to lunge at the Welshman. Cade's muscles were taut from years of fighting but Blackstone's grip stopped his strike as surely as if his arm had been severed.

'That's the second time I've had cause to stop you. The next time I'll kill you,' said Blackstone quietly. He released his grip and shouldered the tough killer aside. 'Ride back to the men and send Renfred to me with the sacks of flour on the pack horses.'

Once again William Cade bowed his head from the admonishment. 'I beg forgiveness, Sir Thomas. I thought only of you and the men. The air here is foul and we always slay lepers.'

'It seems to me you would slay any living thing given the chance,' said Blackstone. 'Get yourself back.'

Cade sheathed his sword and climbed into the saddle. By the time his back was turned Blackstone looked at the two men who still waited at a safe distance. 'When we get to Sir John I want rid of him,' said Blackstone.

'You should have let Meulon cut his throat when we had just cause,' said Killbere.

Gruffydd ap Madoc knew nothing of the incident when Cade had tortured the Frenchman. 'He came to me last night to sell his sword,' he said.

Killbere glanced at Blackstone. The Welshman's confession was in his favour. 'We know he skulked in the night to see you,' said Killbere. 'Not hard to imagine why.'

'We deal with him later,' said Blackstone. 'Right now I've got us lost in this damned forest.'

'And the flour's for them by way of barter? To get us out of here?' said Killbere.

'Aye. We'll get more when we reach Sir John. They'll lead us out.'

'I'll get back to the men,' said Killbere.

'And I to mine,' said ap Madoc.

They turned their horses.

'Your friends are frightened of us,' said the leper.

'Yes.'

'They should be. Who knows how we become afflicted. But you are not afraid.'

'You heard what I said about my escape from Paris.'

The leper turned and instructed the others. 'Stay alert. Some of those men wish us harm.'

'You'll not be harmed if I say you won't,' said Blackstone.

'I accept your word,' said the leper. 'But we are vulnerable now. No one has ever ventured into this forest since we settled here. The bones of the dead and the legend kept all but you away. And now your men know about us others might return.'

'I give you my apologies. What will you do?'

'Move deeper. We do not blame you, Thomas Blackstone.'

Blackstone's chin lifted in surprise at the man addressing him by his name.

'Your man called you Sir Thomas. There are many men known as such but I know who you are. Come,' said the leper, and led the way towards one of the huts.

They stood aside and appeared to offer no threat. Blackstone knew it would have been an act of folly for them to cause him harm, but his senses were alert as he stepped into the windowless hut. A dull glow from a tallow lamp lit the room softly as the leper went to an iron-edged wooden chest and lifted the lid. His disfigured, bandaged hand held up a surcoat. The armorial design of a chevron against green background was barely visible beneath the ingrained dark stains on the worn cloth. Blood had soaked and dried, permanently discolouring the linen.

'I wore my lord's blazon,' said the leper. 'Henri de Crosin.

We fought you at Poitiers. I was twenty paces from you when you tried to kill our King. I recognized your shield the moment you entered the forest.'

Blackstone's sense of being watched had been borne out.

'I was stricken with leprosy a year later,' said the man. 'Spared in battle and condemned to a living death.'

'Which takes a greater courage,' said Blackstone.

The man grunted. 'Perhaps,' he said. 'But I was outcast.' He replaced the treasured cloth from a time when he was as sturdy and strong as the man who stood before him and stepped closer to Blackstone so that he could see his eyes were infected: skin bubbled the flesh around them and the thin gauze showed similar disfigurement below the covering. 'And then, like you, I was banished. You by your Prince, me by my fate. Banished from my wife, my lord, my town and my children. And now here you are, giving us your protection.'

Renfred's voice called from outside. 'Sir Thomas?'

'And your flour,' said the leper.

Blackstone sensed that the man smiled.

The leper stepped out of the hut. Blackstone followed. Renfred had dropped two sacks of flour onto the ground and kept his distance from the gathered men.

'Ride back. I'll follow,' said Blackstone.

The German captain hesitated, looking nervously at the gathered men.

'Go. There's no danger. Have Sir Gilbert form the men into column again. We're leaving.'

Renfred tugged the reins and spurred his horse.

'I will lead you out,' said the leper. 'There are animal tracks we use when we go to the towns to beg. There's a convent that gives us alms and food that help us trade among ourselves. When I leave you at the forest's edge, turn south for eight leagues, then east for another six. You will find the men you seek there.'

'You've seen them?'

'Chandos? Yes. We saw his banner. We know our enemies

from the past, Sir Thomas, but perhaps it is they who will rid us of the brigands.'

'Your name?' said Blackstone.

'Robert de Rabastens.'

'You have my thanks, Robert.'

Rabastens nodded and then placed a bandaged stump on Blackstone's arm. Blackstone never wavered but looked into the man's eyes. 'Before you meet your enemy you will pass close to the village of Sainte-Bernice-de-la-Grave,' said the leper. 'For many years before Poitiers, ten or more, I served at my King's command. I fought pagans in the Holy Roman Empire, routiers in Lorraine, the English in France: any enemy that challenged my King. My wife and children saw nothing of me. I never watched my children grow. I had made a vow before God that if I survived fighting the English that day at Poitiers that I would return home. I was wounded and spent weeks recovering and by the time I reached the outskirts of Sainte-Bernice I knew it was more than battle wounds that ailed me. So I did not go back, but let it be thought I had died. My wife remarried the lord of the manor, Mouton de la Grave, who took in my sons and they in turn took his name. Two died of the plague but the third, Alain, is near enough a grown man. Lord de la Grave is a good knight and he may stand in your way. He is loyal to King John and even with the King's command I do not think he will relinquish his town or his loyalty easily. I ask a favour...'

Blackstone placed his hand on what remained of the man's. 'No harm will befall your son from me or my men,' he said.

A tear glistened in the once proud man's eyes. He nodded his thanks.

'I shall tell him that his father still holds him close in his heart.'

Rabastens shook his head. 'I am dead. Let it remain so.'

CHAPTER FIFTEEN

As the men filed their way out of the forest Blackstone did not look back. The leper who once fought as a man-at-arms at the French King's side had melted back into the shadows. Courage on the battlefield Blackstone understood, for it was underpinned by rage and fear; but the fortitude to survive the loss of that life as a soldier and then abandonment by family and community was something he could not comprehend. His own grief at the loss of his family was tempered with loving memory, which gave him the strength to fight on; he doubted he had the kind of resolve needed to endure a living death like the leper.

They rode sixteen miles south without incident. Killbere and Gruffydd ap Madoc traded stories of the years since Blackstone last saw them fighting shoulder to shoulder on the field at Crécy.

'It was the nun that did it for me,' said Killbere. 'Damned if she didn't steal my heart. I remember it as if it were yesterday.'

'As do we all,' said Blackstone.

'I have not mentioned this story for at least two years,' said Killbere.

'Not so. We hear this story every time Gilbert stops to take a piss.'

'Having your cock in your hand brings back memories,' said Killbere defensively.

'You didn't marry the nun?' said the Welshman.

'She was promised to others,' chirped in Blackstone. 'The whole damned monastery.'

Killbere scowled. 'It is true she was a woman who had an appetite but you can only do so much praying in your life. The loins ache for physical comfort.'

Gruffydd grinned. 'By the sound of it, it wasn't an ache but an itch.'

'I see I am in coarse company. Where is your respect for a man's confession of love?' complained Killbere.

'Let's be clear, Gilbert. Your heart was ruled by your balls,' said Blackstone. 'But what confuses me was whether this was the first nun or the other?'

'There were two?' said ap Madoc.

'Oh, at least,' said Blackstone. 'But I know only of two.'

'You mock a man unfairly,' said Killbere in a wounded tone. 'She was an angel searching to bring heathens like me to the Mother Church.'

Gruffydd laughed. 'Lead me to her! I'll abandon the old gods.'

'Gilbert reverted to his heathen ways and beat the monks, and... I've forgotten, what did you do to the nun?' said Blackstone.

Killbere ignored the question. 'And then, years later, I was riding in the forest and found Thomas here surrounded by men ready to kill him. That was just before Poitiers. What he fails to mention is that I saved his life that day.'

'And he has told the same story ever since,' said Blackstone.

As the wind settled Blackstone saw, several miles ahead, the murky haze of smoke that smothered the clouds. He spurred the men across the rolling ground and then urged the horses on as it rose before them. As they crested the hill they saw that where a village had once huddled a mile ahead bitter-tasting smoke now swirled through the destroyed houses. Bodies lay scattered: villagers desperate to escape the terror that had swept down on them. Smouldering corpses lay scattered along a track through a small coppice whose trees had been seared by wind-whipped flames. Wherever these people had been running to they had been too slow or the violence that had come upon them had been too swift. Blackstone and his men trotted forward, swords drawn, but there was no sign of the attackers. The hamlet was bereft of livestock and spilled corn told a story of grain stores being looted. A cow lay dead, its udder empty. Milked and slain to deny others. Rats scurried over the fallen bodies; some burrowing into carcasses via open wounds. As the men skirted the burning village Blackstone saw trampled ground. Horsemen must have used the shallow river that meandered along the far side of the buildings to approach, probably at first light, masking their noise with the sound of water, and churned up the bank when climbing ashore. The hoof prints showed there must have been a large group of horsemen. A hundred or more. At least.

Blackstone called to Gruffydd ap Madoc. 'Split your men and encircle the village. Then sweep through in force. If the raiders are ahead of us we will be on their heels. This killing is only hours old.'

For a moment it looked as though the Welshman would argue but the ferocity of the recent attack stopped any objection he might harbour at being commanded by Blackstone. As ap Madoc wheeled his mount and shouted his orders, Blackstone led his men along the track. They would be the first to strike against any enemy that remained at the slaughtered village. The mud of the track was churned up: whoever had attacked this place had swept through the hovels, struck down the villagers and surged onward down this path.

A half-mile down the track the woodland opened out into another clearing. A low-walled fortified house stood two hundred paces away. The gates were open and a dozen bodies slumped over the parapet here and there. The attackers had overwhelmed a local lord or seneschal, the man responsible for protecting the villagers. Blackstone's men quickly fanned out as Will Longdon dismounted his archers and formed a defensive line across the clearing. If there were still raiders behind the walls they would be brought down moments after any attempt to escape. Blackstone and his men looked at the scene of destruction. The lord's house sat within the centre of the walls, surrounded by a courtyard. A small family chapel had lost its roof, its bare timbers smouldering. No sound came from behind the walls. Blackstone eased the bastard horse at the walk, his men following. Whoever the house belonged to its owner had secured it as best as he could. It was the kind of stronghold common across France. A local lord and his family with a small retinue of footsoldiers, probably no more than twenty or so men. Crossbow- and pikemen usually, the kind of small force that would be called upon by the King in time of war. There were thousands of such local fiefs, and once brought under the fleur-de-lys gave a French king a great army. The kind of army that the English King had defeated on the field of battle.

The trees had been cleared far enough from the walls to give the lord of the manor's men a good killing ground but it appeared that this attack had been so sudden that the alarm had been barely raised before the swarm of men overpowered the defences. Meulon and John Jacob had gone forward and reconnoitred the far side of the walls. Meulon reined in.

'The ground is churned from the gates, around the walls and then beyond the far clearing,' said the Norman.

'Whoever was here was in force, Sir Thomas, but it looks as though they've gone,' said John Jacob, handing Blackstone a torn piece of cloth. It bore bloodstains. 'There are a few bodies at the foot of the walls brought down by crossbows. This was on one of them.'

Blackstone turned the cloth over and looked at the design of a barbed arrowhead.

'Bretons,' said Blackstone.

'Some of the men fighting for Charles de Blois,' said John Jacob.

Blackstone called Perinne forward. 'Take five men. Follow the tracks. Be back before nightfall.'

Perinne turned his horse and called the nearest men to him.

'All right,' said Blackstone, 'let's see if anyone survived the attack.'

He led the men through the gates. It was too small a fortified house to warrant a portcullis or defensive ditch and there was no sign of the gates being smashed open. Peasant smocks lay abandoned just inside the gate.

'Like as not they talked their way in,' said Killbere. 'They kill and chase villagers, take their clothing, beg for entry and once the gates are opened quickly kill the sentries. And then it's a quick gallop from the trees and the routiers are in.'

Blackstone glanced at him.

'You can be sure they're part of the horde that John Chandos is hunting,' said Killbere in answer to the unspoken question. 'Sure of it.'

Blackstone nodded. It made sense that the closer they got to Chandos the more evidence there would be of the Breton routier army that was gathering. Inside the walls there were signs of the fight all around them. Bodies lay where they had fallen: another twenty or so of the knight's men, crossbows flung from their hands, some with swords still in the scabbard – so quick had been the surge through the gates that those in the yard, perhaps still running for the walls, had had no chance to draw them. Three servants were propped against the main house entrance, their blood splattered across the iron-studded door. Kitchen knives and a hand scythe had been their only weapons, useless against battleaxe, mace or sword, but their death at the entrance was testimony to their courage as they had tried to stop the killers from entering their lord's house. One was disembowelled; another had a severed arm; their companion's throat had been cut.

Wisps of smoke swirled as the breeze caught embers in the deep thatch that covered the buildings to one side of the yard. Soldiers' quarters most likely, thought Blackstone. Four attackers lay dead at the feet of two men who had fallen half in, half out of the entrance.

'Small company of men,' said John Jacob.

Meulon eased his horse towards them. 'No sign of anyone alive out here. A few attackers dead near the grain store along with servants. Five women inside. Raped. Throats cut. I covered them with sacking.' He hesitated. 'And what's probably their children. They spared no one. Their blood-lust was up.' He spat. 'Bastards should be spitted and roasted, Sir Thomas. If these are the skinners we're after they need no mercy shown them when it comes to it.'

'Once they got over the wall in numbers these people stood no chance,' said Killbere. He glanced at Blackstone. The sight was eerily reminiscent of when they had fought the Jacquerie while searching for Blackstone's family a few years before. They had come across a similar scene of a local lord's household butchered and raped. Blackstone had remained stony-faced.

'All right. Secure the walls. Bring in Will and the others. Renfred, ride to ap Madoc, tell him what we've seen and ask him to hold the ground around the village. Have him post men on the hills and then ask him to join us. Meulon, have the men guard the gates. Whoever did this won't be coming back but it pays to be vigilant. We'll look inside and then move on. There's no point in staying in this butcher's yard.'

He tethered the belligerent horse away from the others and, with Killbere and John Jacob, stepped up to the house's main door, past the dead servants and into the gloom of the stone walls. The damp air drew their breath into a mist. John Jacob walked ahead, sword ready. He shouldered open a door that led into the great hall. Embers still crackled in a fireplace; the stonework was smudged with smoke and the smell of it lingered in the room. John Jacob bent and pressed a torch of bound faggots into the glow, blew on it and, once it flared, held it aloft. The glow reached into the farthest corner. Tapestries had been ripped from the walls, benches overturned. Wine and scraps of food had spilled across the dining table. The killers had obviously stayed long enough to raid the kitchen. A body slumped by a wall panel in a spreading pool of blood, still wet, that settled across the floorboards beneath the scuffed reed covering: another servant, his head caved in, blood plastering his matted hair across his face. A meat cleaver had fallen from his hand but there was no blood on its cutting edge. It had been a futile attempt at self-defence. A hunting dog was close by, its skull crushed.

'Killed the man's dogs. There'll be others outside, I'll wager,' said John Jacob.

'Put the light over here, John,' said Killbere, pointing to a dark corner of the room. A narrow passage almost concealed a door.

'Bedchamber,' said Blackstone. 'Have a look, Gilbert.'

Killbere cautiously opened the door with John Jacob at his side and the flaming torch pushed forward. Blackstone heard the veteran curse. 'God's tears, Thomas, these are vile men who have gone before us. Killing will be too good for them.'

Blackstone joined them at the entrance to the bedchamber. A woman of about forty years had been tied spreadeagle across the bed, and her clothes ripped from her. She was no servant: the quality of her gown told them that. It was obvious she was the knight's wife. Her head was twisted to one side, her mouth slightly open, eyes glazed in death. That she had been raped was beyond question and then they had mutilated her. Killbere gestured towards what was concealed behind the door. A man, beard and hair grey, blood streaked, was bound to a chair. John Jacob put an arm across his nose and mouth to filter the stench in the room.

'Tied him up and made him watch them do that to his wife,' said Killbere, 'and then, after they gelded him, they gutted him.'

A clothes chest had been plundered, those pieces not wanted discarded.

'Searching for jewellery and gold,' said Killbere as he moved to the far side of the bed and saw that some of the timbers had been levered up. 'A man usually hides his treasures close to where he sleeps.' He spat the stench from his throat. 'Enough of this, Thomas. Let's be gone.'

The three men left the room but as they strode back across the hall a shadow lurched from an alcove, a glint of steel slashing down. Blackstone turned on his heel, Wolf Sword raised, but he slipped in the still wet blood from the slain servant. John Jacob threw the burning torch at the attacker who instinctively shielded himself from the flying sparks. In the instant of the attack the men saw that the assailant had a lame arm and a blood-encrusted scalp. He was obviously weakened. This was the last, desperate lunge of a brave man.

Blackstone was already on his feet as the man fell and before Killbere instinctively delivered a killing blow Wolf Sword blocked Killbere's strike.

'Wait!' Blackstone commanded.

The man squirmed onto his back, favouring his injured arm across his chest as Blackstone stood on his other wrist, forcing him to release his sword.

'Murdering scum,' spat the assassin. 'Be done with it and burn in hell.'

John Jacob kicked the sword away. Blackstone and the others looked down on their attacker. It was doubtful he had yet seen his seventeenth year. The lightness of the whiskers on his face were those of a boy. His leather jerkin was darkened with a patch of blood over his left shoulder. His age was not unusual; there were many like him in the army.

'We are not the ones who did this,' said Blackstone.

The boy's face creased in uncertainty. How long had he been unconscious? Blackstone wondered. The lad must have come to thinking the killers were still in the house.

'Get to your feet, lad, and keep your hand away from that knife on your belt,' said Killbere.

The boy's strength seemed to have deserted him. He half raised himself but then slumped. Blackstone's gesture stopped John Jacob from reaching down to help him. 'Let him do it on his own,' he said, wanting to test the boy's determination. 'Come on, boy, you can't lie down like a beaten dog. On your feet.'

Blackstone's taunt gave the boy strength and he got first to one knee and then to his feet, lifting his injured arm to stop its weight causing him more pain.

'Who are you?' said the injured boy. 'Where're my mother and father?'

Killbere and Blackstone exchanged glances.

'A lord and his wife?' said Killbere.

The look in the boy's eyes was enough of an acknowledgement.

'They're dead,' said Blackstone bluntly.

The boy grimaced. He looked at Blackstone. 'Where?'

'Best you don't see them,' said John Jacob.

The boy looked towards the bedroom door and took a stride forward but Killbere blocked his way. 'Listen to us, lad. Leave them be.'

He had the good sense to step back from the veteran knight, who looked as formidable as the taller scar-faced man who stood at his side. 'You're English,' he said uncertainly. 'Routiers.'

'We're not mercenaries. We serve the English King. We travel east to fight the skinners,' said Killbere.

The young man hesitated. 'The English are our enemy, but I'll ride with you because I must avenge what has happened here. Will you take me?'

'No,' said Blackstone.

'What?'

'You're injured and your blood boils. I know what it's like. You lose reason. When you kill you need to unleash the blood-lust, but also to let your mind rule your actions. Bring those two together and it's formidable. You don't have the experience to fight like that.'

'Treat my wound and let me join you, otherwise I'll go alone.'

'Horses are gone,' said John Jacob. 'There's no food left and your wound will poison you. You won't get far on foot. You'll be wolf bait in two days.'

The boy lowered his head, the turmoil of his anger forcing him to beg. 'Please,' he whispered. 'Help me avenge my family and all those loyal to us who were killed here.'

'Where is this place?' said Killbere.

'Sainte-Bernice-de-la-Grave,' the boy answered.

Blackstone hid his surprise. 'You're the son of Mouton de la Grave? Lord of this manor?'

'I am,' said the boy.

Blackstone nodded to himself. Fate, it seemed, had brought him to the leper son's door.

'All right, you can ride with us. Your father had more courage than most fighting men; his son deserves a chance to follow in his footsteps.'

The boy struggled for a moment with the realization that he had suddenly been accepted. 'I'm grateful to you. My name is Alain de la Grave.'

'I know,' said Blackstone.

CHAPTER SIXTEEN

Blackstone and the others stepped outside. Gruffydd ap Madoc sat on horseback flanked by fifty or so of his men. Meulon, Renfred, Will Longdon, Jack Halfpenny and all their men were on their knees, hands behind their heads, weapons laid on the ground in front of them. Alongside the Welshman was William Cade. Two of his men stood over Peter Garland and Will Longdon who knelt, hands bound in front of them with ropes around their necks.

Gruffydd ap Madoc raised a hand when Blackstone and Killbere stepped through the doorway, John Jacob behind them, helping the wounded boy. 'No further, Thomas.'

Blackstone stopped and placed a restraining hand on Killbere.

'Whoreson bastard,' said Killbere.

'Ah, Gilbert,' sighed ap Madoc, 'now you guessed this might happen, don't tell me you didn't.'

'You kill us now, Gruffydd, and Chandos will hear of it sooner or later. And then the King,' said Blackstone.

The big Welshman shrugged. 'I know, I know. Thomas, I have a fondness for you and Killbere is a good companion to have at your side when the French throw their weight at you, but this is business. A transaction has taken place and I have mouths to feed and men's greed to quench.' He patted the saddlebags that were slung across his horse's withers. 'You lied to me, Thomas. Now what kind of friendship can be based on distrust, I ask you?'

Blackstone looked at the sneering William Cade, who leaned across his pommel. 'So that's what you were doing in ap Madoc's camp last night. Telling him about the gold from Saint-Aubin.'

'It seemed only fair that I be paid for my efforts. Chandos is more frugal with the King's gold than a nun selling her cunny.'

'You could have taken the money sooner,' said Blackstone to the Welshman.

'No, that would have caused bloodshed between us. This place presented itself. You inside the walls, me outside with my men.'

'Take the money,' said Blackstone. 'And take the ropes off my men.'

'Ah, now, Thomas. You show me no respect. Am I a fool to be taunted? If I do that the moment I turned my back a flight of arrows would find their mark. And then you will have the gate closed knowing I cannot lay siege to you. I take these men as hostage and leave them at the far end of the village. That will give me enough time to be long gone and out of range of your archers. You can see that makes sense, can't you?'

'Harm them and you and the murdering bastard next to you will be my blood enemy. I swear it, Gruffydd, I swear it in front of every man here.'

William Cade tugged on the rope around Will Longdon's neck. 'You threaten us when we have the lives of your men in our hands?' He laughed.

Blackstone quickly strode forward a half-dozen paces through his kneeling men. Horsemen's swords cleared scabbards and those Welshmen who carried spears lowered them in anticipation of Blackstone attacking ap Madoc. But Blackstone had moved so that he could face both antagonists and that they would see the reality of his threat in his eyes. He stood as close as he dare without Will Longdon and Peter Garland being yanked down and dragged away. He looked directly at William Cade.

'If you know anything of those I have killed then you will know that I do not make idle threats. I say again, harm them and you will know more pain than you thought possible before I kill you.'

Gruffydd ap Madoc scowled. 'I intend no hurt to befall them, Thomas. I seek only a safe retreat from your anger and your archers.'

Blackstone pointed at Cade and the threat was unmistakable.

His voice hardened. 'It is him I warn, Gruffydd, but if my men suffer injury you will both be held accountable, no matter who inflicts it on them. Blood and death will follow you.'

William Cade tossed the rope holding Will Longdon to one of the men. 'If they're too slow to keep up and fall and scrape their knees, what then? You'll bring more than curses down on our heads? No matter what threats you make, Blackstone, you bleed like any other man and I will not turn away when the day comes. I've killed tougher men than you.'

Blackstone didn't answer. He had made his promise and saw that it had struck the pardoned murderer as firmly as the blow he had given him before.

The Welsh veteran was losing patience. 'William Cade and his men will have their share of the gold francs so there is no cause for him to bear malice towards these two archers or to test your desire for retribution. You wait long enough for us to clear the village and then you can do what you want. Give chase and we will turn and fight, and you are not stupid enough to pit yourself against hundreds of men.' He wheeled his horse. 'I bear you no ill will. Neither you nor Gilbert. I take what is needed and that is all. Sir John Chandos can keep the writs bearing the King's seal and all that they promise. Gold coin is gold coin and when men die every day there is no damned time to wait for a fucking writ! Stand your ground, Thomas, and then come for your men.' Gruffydd ap Madoc spurred his horse and cantered from the yard. His horsemen turned to follow and Will Longdon and Peter Garland fell in at the rear of the horsemen. They would be obliged to run as the horses trotted.

Will Longdon glanced back. 'It's a mile or so, Thomas. No more. Even I can run that.'

And with that the men cleared the courtyard. No sooner were they through the gates than Blackstone's men quickly armed themselves.

'We give chase, Sir Thomas?' asked Meulon, buckling his sword.

'We can keep them in sight long enough.'

'No. I don't want to give Cade any excuse to kill Will and the boy.'

'He's a twisted creature, Meulon, he'll take pleasure in plunging a knife into them,' said Killbere. 'Give them space.'

'How long do we wait?' asked Jack Halfpenny.

'Long enough to bind this man's wound,' he said, beckoning John Jacob to bring Alain de la Grave forward. 'Jack, gather your bowmen and hold these walls in case they change their minds and return. Meulon, you and Renfred ready the men. Gilbert, pick ten men and hold this place until I am back. We might need it.'

'Thomas, leave Halfpenny and the archers here. Bowmen are no good to you in the trees but the rest of us are.'

Killbere was right. The thought of trying to keep any of the men-at-arms out of an ambush was the wrong choice. Blackstone laid a hand on his friend's shoulder. 'We'll take all the men but I'll lead. I want you on my flank. Split the men. You take Renfred; I'll have John and Meulon with me.'

Alain de la Grave had been propped against the wall, his leather tunic eased off him and the blood-soaked linen shirt cut away from the clinging wound by one of Jack Halfpenny's archers.

'I will come with you,' the Frenchman said.

'No. There will be time enough for that.' He looked to Halfpenny. 'Search the kitchen and cellars. See if the raiders left any honey. Wash that wound, smear it into the cut and then stitch it. Bind him tight with clean linen when that's done.'

'Aye, Sir Thomas.'

'You'll need brandy for when they use needle and thread on you,' he told the boy.

'I will be all right,' de la Grave said bravely.

'As you like,' said Blackstone and turned to the waiting men. 'We go slowly. Sir Gilbert will ride around the village and use the stream to come up behind any of those bastards who might be waiting. The Welshman will not use all those men; there are too many of them. But sixty or so could be waiting. The rest of us will ride straight into the village. If we have no choice we ride back here behind the walls.'

He brought the horse to the head of the men and rode through the gates. Like a sword blade from the coals hammered on a blacksmith's anvil the old rage beat in his chest.

CHAPTER SEVENTEEN

Gruffydd ap Madoc led the band of mercenaries away from an enraged Thomas Blackstone. The world they lived in brought fighting men together but it also demanded that each look to his own wellbeing, and there were times when old bonds of comradeship had, by necessity, to be loosened. And two and a half thousand gold francs meant there was a lot of slack. He kept the horses at a slow trot so that the two men at the rear with ropes around their necks did not stumble. Even without inflicting further humiliation or pain on these men he knew Blackstone would seek him out. He glanced back and saw the huge body of horsemen behind him. One thing was certain, with this many men it would be impossible to hide their tracks, and if Thomas Blackstone followed then he would have no problem finding them. He resisted the urge to heel his mount into a canter. Once the men were released at the village then he would give the horses their heads. No matter what trail he left behind the greater the distance between him and Thomas Blackstone and Killbere the better. He knew Blackstone would not be foolish enough to attack so many with so few, but he also knew that the Englishman would one day find a way to confront his theft and betrayal.

Will Longdon felt the rope's knot beneath his chin as he ran to keep up with the mercenary, twenty paces ahead, who had been tasked by Cade with holding the length of rope. Peter Garland ran alongside, and he too kept his chin high to avoid the chafing hemp. Both men's lungs burned. Will Longdon spat phlegm from the back of his throat. Sweat stung his eyes and the shirt stuck to his back beneath his jupon.

'Peter, almost there, boy.'

The young archer glanced his way and nodded with gritted teeth. It was obvious to Longdon the boy's fear might get the better of him. And what he also knew in his heart was that William Cade would hang them, no matter what assurances Gruffydd ap Madoc had given Blackstone. He needed the boy to be thinking clearly because if they were to escape the noose they had to do it before they reached the village and the Welshman brought the horses to a halt.

'Peter, listen. You hear me?'

Once again the boy looked his way and nodded.

'We have to take our chance before we reach the village. We can't trust them. You understand?'

The boy's brow furrowed with uncertainty and then he understood what the veteran archer was telling him. He nodded. 'How?'

'The last bend in the road before we reach the village. The forest is on the left of the track and is dense enough for us to hide in until Thomas and Sir Gilbert come looking for us, as they surely will. Cade was humiliated and the turd will take his revenge, I'm sure of it. You hold tight onto the rope.' Both men were grasping the length of rope in front of their faces to ease the chafing. Longdon gestured with his clenched fists. 'When I tell you, you pull hard, dig in your heels, let your back take the weight, like drawing your bow. You understand? Curve your back and yank the rope. If we don't pull the riders from the saddle we might rip the rope from their hands. Then we run. Into the undergrowth. And we keep running until we find the filthiest shit hole to crawl into. Somewhere they won't poke their noses looking for us. They won't search for long. Not with Thomas and the others on their way. With luck the Welshman doesn't want a fight even if he does outnumber us. Understand, boy? Use your strength and then run. I've a knife in my boot so I can cut the rope but we need to get distance between us and them. Got it? We run and hide.'

Peter Garland looked frightened.

'Aye, me too, lad,' said Will Longdon. He smiled, and drew

another deep breath from the exertion. 'But it's the fear that gives us legs.'

He looked ahead. William Cade had eased his horse free of the jostling riders and as the two men who held the ropes approached him he made a small gesture with his hand, a movement that indicated something ahead that was higher than the riders' heads. Will Longdon squinted through the sweat. His archer's keen eyesight picked out a chestnut tree with an overhanging bough. It was barely twelve feet above the track. A rope thrown and tied off on a horse's pommel would haul him and Garland fast enough to break their necks.

'Mother of Christ, help us,' he whispered to himself as his gut instinct was confirmed. 'Peter. We do this now. Hear me? There's no more time!'

The young archer's eyes widened but he nodded. Longdon held his gaze a moment longer and then, as the horses ahead slowed under Cade's command, he gathered the strength in his arms and back and heaved on the rope. Out of the corner of his eye he saw Garland do the same. There was immediate slack. The riders were taken by surprise at the archers' strength and the ropes fell free from their grasp. The two archers ran for the cover of the trees, trailing the telltale lengths of rope. Cries of alarm went up but the horses, plunging in distress, impeded each other and were unable to turn quickly enough for their riders to see where the two men had gone.

No sooner had Longdon plunged into the forest than he was sawing the rope around his neck with the short-bladed skinning knife hidden in his boot. Garland tried to keep pace but the tangled bramble kept catching his legs. Will Longdon jumped across a hurdle of fallen branches towards him. They had made barely thirty yards and as Longdon cut Garland's bonds he could see horsemen urging their mounts into the trees. The moment Garland's hands were free he took the knife and freed Will Longdon's bindings. And then desperately tried to cut the length of rope from his own neck.

'Hurry!' hissed Longdon. But the rope was thicker and was

taking longer to cut than the veteran archer's. One of the horsemen saw them and although he cried out to his comrades Longdon realized that the others could not see them because a tall swathe of bramble obscured their position. The horseman was urging his horse to twist left and right through the trees in their direction. Longdon snatched the knife and took a fistful of Garland's rope and with more strength than the boy possessed cut the rope, yanking the blade across the hemp. The rope separated but the force of his efforts loosened the knife from his grip and it tumbled into the undergrowth. 'Leave it!' said Longdon.

They turned and, ignoring the tearing thorns, pushed deeper. Lungs raw with exertion they ran for their lives but the crashing sound of the horsemen was getting closer. Will Longdon could hear running water but there was no sign of the river that skirted the village. If they could reach it and it was fast flowing they might have a chance to be swept beyond the horses. He dared a glance over his shoulder. Garland was keeping up but one of the horsemen was now less than twenty paces behind them and had found a gap in the trees to force his horse through. Cade's man gripped his sword, ready to cut them down. Further back two other horsemen urged their horses towards him. Will Longdon's instincts took over. The memory of charging horsemen at Crécy and Poitiers flared in his memory and once again he summoned the heart-stopping courage it took for men to stand their ground and kill their enemy.

'Run, boy! Run!' he yelled as he turned to face the horseman. He snatched a fallen bough, its branches flayed like a witch's claw, and thrust it at the horse. It reared; the rider yanked the reins but the huge beast had lost its footing and fell sideward. Longdon hurled himself at the cursing man, who was already half up as the archer's weight struck him. Longdon hit him hard in the face with his fist and the man reeled but he was strong enough to absorb the blow and threw himself onto Longdon. In that moment the archer knew that while he was sturdy, the other man was heavier and stronger. He was ten years younger and knew he had the advantage. Neither man cursed, each holding their breath from the exertion as they grappled. Cade's man suddenly had a knife in his hand. Longdon snatched at his face, clawing at the man's eyes. He brought a knee up into his groin and Cade's man grunted, but even that did not lessen his grip. Will Longdon pulled the man's weight down onto him, smothering the knife hand as it got caught in the undergrowth. Longdon pushed his thumb into the man's mouth and clutched the flesh of his face, tearing the lips and cheek open. The man bellowed, but the agony gave him added strength. The two men rolled, each fighting for the knife. Will Longdon headbutted his opponent. Blood splattered the man's face as his nose cracked. And then as the horseman gradually gained the upper hand Longdon reared up, throwing his weight against him. But the man's grip held firm on Longdon's jupon and the archer knew that if he fell onto him the knife would find his belly.

Suddenly the ground gave way and both men fell, still clutching each other, through the undergrowth and down the stone-strewn embankment. Within seconds they hit the river. Will Longdon's attacker had tumbled beneath him and Longdon fought to keep his body on top as they plunged into the shallow water. The man seemed weaker and the archer realized he must have caught his head on a rock; although he still flailed Longdon suddenly had the upper hand. He forced his knee into the man's back, grabbed his collar with one hand and his hair with the other and twisted his head, forcing it beneath the water. The man squirmed, legs kicking, his desperation to survive the fight forcing strength back into his body. Will Longdon found that deep-seated place within himself and drew on its killing energy, forcing the power from his shoulders into his arms and fists. And then the man went still. The archer kept his weight on the man's back until he was sure he was dead.

Exhausted but still alert for the other horsemen, he slumped back into the waist-deep water and steadied his breathing. Voices carried from the forest above. He stumbled to the embankment and pressed himself into the dirt wall. He dared to glance downstream but there was no sign of Peter Garland. He should have made good his escape now Longdon had bought him time. The voices sounded closer. Longdon smeared mud and dirt from the riverbank onto his face and jupon, then grabbed handfuls of grass and weed, pushing it here and there into his belt and neck opening. Anyone riding close by would not recognize a man half submerged, camouflaged with mud and leaf.

There was nothing more Longdon could do other than wait and hope that Cade and ap Madoc's men would ride on. The light fluttered before his eyes. He pushed aside the overhanging undergrowth but still the grey light flickered through the trees. He blinked. He felt the chill of the water on his thighs and waist. It tugged at him. The water was deeper than he thought and he shivered from its chill. Sweat from the fight slithered down his spine. He suddenly felt weak and his head began to pound. He touched the wet hair on the back of his head and his hand came away covered in blood. Like the man he had killed he must have cracked his skull on the downward plunge and his urge to survive had smothered the pain from the injury. He cursed beneath his breath. It felt as though he was falling asleep. He had lost all sense of time. How long had he been hiding? He snatched back his head as his chin drooped onto his chest. Horsemen were approaching. If he couldn't stay awake they would find him and then he would hang. Just like the current pulling at him, unconsciousness was carrying him away. He slipped lower, chest-deep, tried to find his footing but couldn't. He cursed disbelievingly. He thought he had won the fight.

Like a lover's gentle enticement the river eased him away.

CHAPTER EIGHTEEN

When Gruffydd ap Madoc saw the archer's hanged body he hauled William Cade from the saddle and threw him to the ground. Cade's men drew their swords but ap Madoc's Welshmen quickly boxed them in.

'You dog turd! I gave my word!' His great bulk loomed over the English mercenary, sword point hovering over Cade's throat.

Cade scuttled backwards away from the blade but the Welshman planted his boot onto Cade's chest. 'I owed Blackstone,' Cade spat. 'He humiliated me in front of my men.'

'Humiliated?' said ap Madoc, rolling the word on his tongue to savour its meaning. 'Made you look like the sewer rat you are. Stopped you torturing a man is what I heard.'

'It was me who told you about the gold!' Cade said hastily.

'And I paid you your share. There won't be enough gold to keep me alive anywhere in this peasant-shit country now you have unleashed Thomas Blackstone. I will be hunted. Even if I go to the French they will use me to bargain with the English. I'm a routier! I have no ally. We fight for each other. No one will save me from the rope or Blackstone's sword. Every damned Englishman will be happy to hunt me like a cur dog so they can please him.' The sword pressed closer to Cade's throat.

'Wait, wait! I can be of use to you.'

The Welshman murmured in his own language. '*Mor ddiwerth â rhech gafr.*' Ap Madoc's horsemen sniggered and voiced their agreement. He spat, the globule landing on Cade's chest. He pressed the sword under the man's chin and a trickle of blood ran down his neck. 'As useless as a sheep's fart.'

111

It would take only the slightest pressure for the blade to pierce Cade's throat. 'I beg you. Listen to me. I rode with Sir John Chandos. I know where all the towns are that are to be ceded to Edward. I know where all his troops will be. I can lead you away from them all. You need never see an Englishman again.'

'Except you.'

The sword hovered. There was some value in what the treacherous bastard said. Once word got out that a man serving with ap Madoc had caused the Welshman's pledge to Blackstone to be broken then, in the time it takes to break wind, Cade would be forgotten. It would be thought the mercenary leader himself had strung up the English bowman. Even routiers needed some kind of honesty. Those who paid for their services expected they would keep their contract. He glanced up at the men who rode with him and who benefited from their raiding together. They were veterans of the wars and even those who came late, the 'Tard-Venus', who drifted in looking for plunder, were ruthless but dependable. Dependable as long as there was money. And none wanted to face the wrath of any army or organized body of men because of a treacherous act. There were others who would hang, draw and quarter every one of them because of their past actions.

'I have enough shit on my boots,' said the Welshman raising his sword.

Blackstone and his men approached the village. They rode slowly and deliberately, looking for any sign of ambush. It seemed unlikely, Blackstone reasoned; the Welshman could have slaughtered them in the courtyard. There would be no need to risk injury to his own men in the open. No, this was a simple case of theft and, for the thief, buying time. They brought their horses to a halt on the muddy track when they saw the body hanging from the low overhang. Gruffydd ap Madoc and his men were long gone. And with them any thought Blackstone had of him being a brazen cutpurse. He was a murderer.

The rope creaked as the wind moved the bough. The body swayed.

'Cut him down,' said Blackstone, keeping his eyes on the dead man's face, grieving for the loss of a comrade, regretting the needless death of a fighting man. The thought that his trust of Gruffydd ap Madoc had brought it about flayed him. But, he answered himself, it was an Englishman's betrayal. Cade had told the Welshman about the gold. Greed and treachery had led to this.

Two men went forward to retrieve the body as a third lowered the rope tied around the tree trunk. The men cut the rope and laid the dead archer gently in the grass at the side of the track.

'I would not have thought it of the Welshman,' said John Jacob. 'He fought at Sir Gilbert's side all those years ago.'

'A man changes, John,' said Blackstone. 'Perhaps he did it as a warning for me not to follow him.'

'And will we?'

'In time. First we must bury the dead and attend to the King's business.' He eased the bastard horse closer to the dead archer. The men stepped away as he gazed down. 'Put him across a horse and bring him back,' said Blackstone.

He looked up at the cut rope. As frayed as the past.

Killbere led his men along the riverbed around the flank of the village. They could see through the overhanging trees that there were no horsemen in sight but they were downwind and the stench of the rotting corpses wafted sickeningly over them. There would soon be more creatures of the forest feasting on the dead if there weren't already. Killbere glanced left and right as his horse picked his way through the river stones beneath its hooves. A body lay face down, his leather jerkin billowing from the air trapped beneath it, which had allowed the dead man to float and be caught against the riverbank. Killbere brought the men to a halt. It was a good place for an ambush and using a dead man as bait was not uncommon. With practised ease some of the men urged their horses up the lower left-hand bank to shield those in the water in case a sudden charge came out of the village. The others stayed alert, scanning the high bank opposite; it was smothered with undergrowth, the trees diminishing the light. Killbere gestured and Renfred eased his horse forward and quickly dismounted, turning the dead man over.

'It's one of Cade's men. He's been in a fight. Half his face gone. Ripped and beaten.'

'Let him rot,' said Killbere, keeping a wary eye on the surroundings. The nearside bank showed no sign of horse's hooves. 'If he's down here he must have come from up there,' he said, pointing to the high bank. He rode forward, peering into the gloom of the river that darkened the closer it flowed nearer the village. The overhanging branches interlocked creating a roof, keeping the damp chill trapped. That and the stench. Some of the villagers had tried to run for the safety of the river when the village had first been attacked but the killers had blocked any retreat. There were bodies lying on the low muddy bank, half in, half out of the water. Hair swirled in the slow but insistent current. A woman's arm flopped into the water, her hand waving gently in macabre farewell.

Further ahead in the gloom a body was caught on a fallen tree branch. The man's arm had caught the branch and the submerged trunk had stopped him floating further downriver. Killbere stiffened and then spurred his horse. He dismounted and waded quickly to the man who wore a jupon like the rest of them. Killbere wrapped his arms around Will Longdon. Dead or alive? He couldn't tell.

'Will, you're safe now, man. You're safe. We've got you.'

Renfred was at his side and eased the unconscious body out of the water and onto the bank. Killbere clambered after him. Renfred laid a hand beneath Longdon's jupon.

'His heart beats, Sir Gilbert. But he's lost blood and the cold water has taken its toll.'

'Fetch my blanket from my bedroll and bring my brandy flask,' said Killbere, kneeling and gently tapping his palm against Longdon's face. He tugged away the ferns and grass from his collar and belt. Renfred draped Killbere's blanket over the injured

114

archer as Killbere lifted his head and dribbled brandy between his lips. 'Come on, lad. You've been hurt worse than this before now. Come on,' he urged gently.

After a few moments Will Longdon spluttered. Killbere grinned at the others. 'I've known this whore-mongering archer since Morlaix, and in those twenty years I've never seen Will Longdon refuse brandy.' He slapped Longdon's face harder. Longdon flinched and opened his eyes.

'Mother of Christ. Sir Gilbert!' he gasped, looking dazed, eyes darting back and forth at the faces grinning down at him.

'You're still a malingering whoreson, Will Longdon,' said Killbere. 'And now we find you skulking in a river dressed like a damned woodland fairy,' he said, clutching the torn ferns and grass in his fist.

Longdon groaned. 'Aye, well, I couldn't go back without bathing or you'd have complained I stank after the exertions I endured.'

Killbere nodded. 'We saw Cade's man back a ways. It looked as though you had a fight on your hands. God's tears, Will, you're getting old and slow.'

Will Longdon grinned. 'That's the truth, Sir Gilbert. A drop more brandy might warm what blood I have left in me.'

Killbere eased the flask to his lips. 'I'll take payment from your purse when I find it.'

Longdon sighed. 'I would expect nothing less, Sir Gilbert. Where's Peter Garland?'

CHAPTER NINETEEN

Blackstone withdrew the men behind the gates of Sainte-Bernice. They tipped the bodies of de la Grave's defenders over the walls and posted guards. Night beckoned so it made no sense to ride on to meet Sir John Chandos; besides, the boy archer needed to be buried and Will Longdon's wound stitched. Once that was done the captains set about organizing their men. Perinne had returned from his patrol and reported that the tracks left by the attackers had been lost at the edge of a dense forest. Food was cooked and sentry duties allocated. Alain de la Grave was asleep next to the fire that now blazed in the great hall. The blood had been sluiced from the floor and the bodies of the dead servants taken outside and placed downwind. Killbere pulled off his boots, still wet from wading in the river, and settled his feet in front of the fire. Candlelight glimmered as the men laid down their blankets. Except for their turns at sentry duty they would all sleep inside the great hall.

'I swear I have heard more sense coming out of a pig's arse,' Killbere said, extending the brandy flask to Blackstone, who shared the fireside. 'Bretons slaughter their way through territory because they are not part of the treaty. We have routiers hunting routiers, the French army chasing them up, Englishmen chasing them down. King John paying brigands to abandon the towns they hold so that Edward can nail his name above the gates. French towns ceding to Edward, some refusing, others being bribed. We pay gold coin on behalf of the Crown and make an alliance with three hundred mercenaries led by a treacherous Welshman and are betrayed by an Englishman stealing the King's money who served Sir John

Chandos, Knight of the Garter, friend of the King and a fine judge of men.'

'It's called peace,' said Blackstone, handing back the flask.

'Thomas, I want a simple life. Show me my enemy and let me kill him. Raise the flags, beat the drums and let the trumpets blow across the battlefield.'

'Perhaps that will come again if Edward doesn't get the territory he won.'

'That *we* won. We serve our sovereign lord, Thomas, but it is our blood that nourishes this godforsaken land.'

'That's the price we paid, Gilbert.'

'And gladly. But are we to spend our days wandering the land like tax collectors? The time will come when everything due *is* paid. What of us then? What about taking the cross and going on crusade?'

Blackstone's eyes widened. Killbere shrugged.

'To seek out a decent fight, Thomas. We defended the Pope against the Visconti. Why not do more?'

'We fought for Florence against the Visconti. Don't confuse the two things, Gilbert.'

Killbere rubbed his feet, warming to the idea. 'But, Thomas, think of it. You have several hundred men still under contract to Florence. Master Elfred still commands them; they're still being paid. The bankers in Florence would back you. Then Edward would smile graciously in our direction and give us more men and, who knows, perhaps more money. We could ride to warmer climes and fight the Moor. It's an idea worth considering.'

Blackstone got to his feet and laid a hand on his friend's shoulder. 'First let's do our duty, then we retrieve the King's gold. In the meantime I shall check the perimeter and you keep an eye on the boy there,' he said, meaning de la Grave.

Killbere's tone softened. 'We lost a good lad, today, Thomas. This Frenchman is no archer. It's a poor exchange.'

'But he has courage,' his friend answered and stepped towards the darkness.

* * *

There was enough light from the moon behind the clouds to see the dark shape of the walls and the forest beyond the clearing. Blackstone went up onto the walkway. He could see shapes moving beyond the walls and the snuffling told him wolf and boar had come from the forest to feast on the dead. The corpses in the village and those slain here at the manor house would feed the scavengers for weeks to come. The crows had already pecked the soft flesh. Eyes jabbed from sockets and tongues plucked out. The carnage was nothing compared to a battlefield but the gentle beauty of this lush countryside deserved life. He stood still and let his vision grow more accustomed to the near-darkness. Sentries patrolled their posts, their cloaks pulled tight. Night spirits flittered through the forest seeking out the souls of the dead. He could sense them, felt their cool touch on his cheek. It was no breeze that caressed him or drizzle that settled on his beard. It was the tears of those damned to half-life between earth and heaven. He kissed the silver goddess.

'Sir Thomas?' said an approaching shadow.

'Will. You should be with the others. Get some sleep.'

'I've done the rounds,' said Will Longdon. 'Didn't much feel like sleeping yet.'

'Your head?'

'Thudding like a drum. All stitched. Meulon did it. Christ, his hands are like bloody hams. I swear I've more cord in the back of my head than on my bow. And he's stitched me so tight I've a permanent grin on my face.' He sensed Blackstone smile in the darkness.

'He's changed since we lost Gaillard back in Milan,' said Blackstone.

'Aye. He's more ready to kill, if that's possible. Give him half a chance and he would go after the Welshman alone. Maybe we should let him.'

'In good time,' said Blackstone.

They fell silent as they walked the walls.

'I should have saved young Garland,' Longdon said after a while. 'I tried, Thomas. I got us away from Cade's men, cut his rope, but then I had a fight on my hands. Didn't think they'd catch him.'

'There's no telling what happened. We lose a man and we go over it a hundred times. But no amount of flogging ourselves brings them back. We go on. Carry them with us.'

The two men passed a sentry. It was one of Meulon's men-at-arms. Blackstone greeted him. There was nothing to report from his post other than the scurrying shadows from the forest and the unsettling sound of night creatures crunching bones.

'Go and rouse a half-dozen men. Bring torches and drop them over the walls where the bodies are. Let's give the dead some peace for the night.' The man hesitated. 'Go, Will and I will stay at your post until you're back.'

The man went down the steps into the yard and set off towards the hall.

'Talking of hams, Meulon went through the cellars and found some food and drink for the lads,' said Longdon. 'The murdering scum who did the killing here had missed it. I've left a smoked ham and wine with Sir Gilbert. He's sharing it out now with the men.'

'Good. Make sure they keep some for the sentries when they come off.'

'Already done.'

The two men gazed across the shadowed land, both silent now. Their journey together had been a long one. As long as Sir Gilbert Killbere had been with them. Since the beginning. Half a dozen torches flickered from the great hall as the men ran across the yard towards the ramparts. Blackstone turned to Will Longdon. The approaching flames cast light across his face. Will Longdon felt something tighten in his chest, a tension that was not from the beating he had taken.

'Will,' said Blackstone quietly. 'When we reach Sir John you choose the archers that he offers. Find me hard men, the best there are. I want gristle and muscle behind those bows. I want men who will use every arrow in their bag and then follow us with sword and archer's knife in their fists. I am going to rip the heart out of every mercenary company I find. I will give no quarter to these murdering scum. And when we have done that I will find Gruffydd ap Madoc and William Cade and kill them.'

This was no simple threat or desire for revenge, Will Longdon realized. It was as devout a promise as a man who submitted his soul to God and became a priest. It was a pact being made with heaven or hell and the veteran archer was uncertain which it might be.

'Sir Gilbert wants a crusade. I will give him one,' said Blackstone.

CHAPTER TWENTY

The peacocks at the royal manor at Vincennes screeched. King John the Good smiled with delight as they entertained him with a flourish of colour. The dismal weather was as depressing as the blanket of grief that settled over his kingdom. How had the greatest nation in Christendom been trammelled by the barbaric English? How, indeed, he wondered, could he and his fellow hostages, many of whom were still held in London, have been so well and kindly treated by Edward, but returned to such desolation? It was not dissimilar from the torture that he had inflicted on his enemies. One foot in a cold bucket of water, the other in scalding. Soon it was only the cold water that was required to break the victim. This chill of despair he felt now was like the plunge into the cold water.

'Highness,' said Bucy. 'You sent for me.'

'We are melancholy, Simon. We were thinking a moment ago of how cosseted we were by our cousin Edward in England, how here there is nothing but discomfort and waste. The English stroke us with a velvet glove on the one hand and scourge us with the other.'

Simon Bucy stood nonplussed. Matters of state needed to be attended to. An army of several thousand had been raised in the south and Bretons were gathering in force in the south-east to challenge the English-backed John de Montfort. The Breton mercenaries worked in King Jean's favour. Brittany was not part of Edward's treaty and the fiefdom was to all purposes controlled by Charles of Blois, supported by the French King.

'Sire, I am grieved to hear that, but the Bretons will pose a threat to the English and Brittany will at least still be held for us. Meanwhile, the English are securing the towns laid down in the treaty while routiers destroy others. Sir John Chandos will be soon be here with his commissioners and he will require the final handover to the English Crown of those towns that remain.'

King John nodded, but Bucy could see that his attention was elsewhere. He was gazing across the vast walled courtyard. Over the years Vincennes had been fortified and if one was not behind the safety of the walls of Paris the royal manor was perhaps the next best place to be. The building work had continued over the years and it was the King's desire that the royal family and the retinue of advisers and servants could all be accommodated.

'The fountain does not seem to flow with the same power,' said the King.

'Sire?' said Bucy, looking towards the centre of the courtyard where a fountain spurted.

'Do you not see?' said the King impatiently.

Bucy's age and long experience serving the King and the Dauphin had schooled him in the art of showing no reaction to their capriciousness. The fountain was fed from the nearby suburb of Montreuil and a lake had been built at Saint-Mandé to feed it. It was just one of many extravagances the King had demanded. No different perhaps than the keep that was still being constructed whose four connected towers would stand a hundred feet and more above the château. A place a threatened king might retreat into at a time of war. Or a place to be incarcerated when madness finally struck. The truth, Bucy knew, was that the huge edifice was being built to accommodate the Dauphin's art collection. Perhaps the madness was already upon them.

'Highness, the weather is freezing and perhaps one of the clay pipes has cracked. I will have workmen investigate it.'

'Good. We take some pleasure from it and there is little of that to be had these days.'

'My lord, you sent for me. Was it to attend to the fountain?'

'Are you becoming senile? There are other issues to hand. We must consider our army's standing in the south and I intend to journey there.'

Bucy waited, his thoughts chasing possibilities. The King would surely not dare take to the field against the routiers. Did he still crave glory? Had not the English tarnished such endeavours? 'I see, your grace. A journey,' he said flatly.

'If our army has secured the south then we have it in mind to travel to Avignon. To the Pope.'

Pope Innocent VI was a Frenchman and looked kindly on John but to Bucy's mind there was no cause for the King to travel across what was still a war-torn France to see the Pope, no matter how successful the French army might be.

'Avignon? Twenty thousand died of the pestilence. They say it has passed, but there is still a risk,' Bucy said.

'It has passed,' said the King. 'Now we must see the Pope.'

'The Pope,' Bucy said, keeping his voice free of censure. 'For a blessing, sire?'

'Of a kind.'

Bucy waited. Since the King had returned from being held prisoner in England he had seemed incapable of finding the means to begin rebuilding France. Was it because the English King's demands were still being met, that his ransom had not yet been paid in full? Was that what stripped the volatile King of France of his energy?

'We have been at prayer and reading the prophecies of the Franciscan,' said the King.

Bucy's thoughts stumbled in the face of the King's fecklessness. For years John had schemed and planned and brought both high emotion and cool logic to his single-minded desire to rid France of the English, but now he was talking of fountains and a Franciscan monk. There were no Franciscans in Paris. None at Vincennes.

'De la Roquetaillade,' said the King, annoyance creeping into his voice at Bucy's dull look of incomprehension.

Merciful Christ, Bucy almost whispered. Back in '56 a trouble-some monk had been cast into prison in Avignon, just before the great battle at Poitiers. He had railed against the corruption of priests and predicted that France would be brought down by tyranny and brigands. Was the King interpreting this to mean that Edward was a tyrant? Bucy wondered. But there was no denying that after the battle routiers had swept across the countryside. And still did, as prevalent and deadly as the pestilence itself. The Franciscan's mind might have been afflicted by starvation and privation but he had also proclaimed that the lowly would rise up against the great. That had certainly come true. The Jacquerie uprising had slain thousands. And then Bucy thought he understood.

'The Anti-Christ,' he said. 'He predicted the pestilence and the Anti-Christ. Do you believe, sire, he meant Thomas Blackstone? We had news that there had been a skirmish between him and d'Audrehem's men, who were forced to retreat, though we are uncertain whether their attack was deliberate or he was mistaken as a routier. He serves Edward but—'

'Blackstone? A common killer? He is beyond our concern or our interest,' the King interrupted. 'And a court fool could predict pestilence. Are we to relegate you that role, Simon? Do you have no comprehension? De la Roquetaillade predicted – after the chaos and poverty, once our chastisement had been endured, and against all known custom – that the King of France would rise to power again and be elected as the Holy Roman Emperor. To rule as the holiest monarch since the beginning of time. Such an emperor would cast out the Saracens and Tatars from Europe and would convert the Muslims, Jews and all other heathens. Simon, heresy would be conquered.'

Anxiety gripped Bucy. Was the King of France losing his mind? Prophecy was one thing but to conjure reality from it another. Events swept across a nation and it was easy to attribute superstition to such times. 'Highness, I do not understand why you would need to visit the Pope. If our merciful Lord Jesus Christ meant to bestow such a blessing on... you,' he faltered, the incredible thought slowing his speech, 'then surely the Pope would... know. Would he not? A king rules by divine providence but a pope is God's representative in this world.'

'Even a king cannot force the hand of God, Simon,' said John.

'One must exercise patience. For some time now we have been a widower. And such grief is not unlike experiencing the death of France.'

'Sire, France lives. She is wounded but she can be healed by your hand.'

'Wounds heal slowly, Simon. We thought that we should bring together France and Provence. Do you see? Slowly but surely we will ready ourselves for the future.'

Like watching a stonemason turn a rock in his hand to fit it correctly into a drystone wall Bucy saw a piece of the puzzle fit. The Pope and Avignon were in the territory of Provence, which was ruled by Countess Joanna, Queen of Naples. And Naples was a fief of the papacy. If King John wished to marry the Countess then he would need the blessing of the Pope. And that seemed unlikely. The Pope would see Provence being absorbed into French territory as a threat. The King would also, Bucy admitted to himself, need the hand of God to protect him. Joanna had already been twice widowed and (rumour had it) by her own hand.

'A marriage and also to take up the cross and fight the Saracens. Money and honour,' said Bucy as if thinking aloud. 'But, highness, how does that help France if you are not here to rule?'

King John the Good looked at his trusted counsellor. 'When France rises from her sick bed and breathes freely again I will lead her to glory.'

Bucy felt the grip of fear clutch at his bowels. The King was going to abandon France to her fate. He bowed. 'I will begin to look into the journey, highness.'

He turned quickly on his heel, fist clutching his cloak to his chest, desperately trying to keep his pounding heart from escaping. Only the Dauphin had the cunning and the foresight to save France. And if he had such plans then Bucy would heed the advice given to him earlier. The Dauphin would one day take back what the English had seized and Simon Bucy would side with him. And if the Dauphin had a plan to stop Thomas Blackstone then he would embrace that as well. The way ahead was clear. Now there was hope.

PART TWO

THE VALLEY OF SIGHS

January 1362

CHAPTER TWENTY-ONE

Blackstone and the men left Sainte-Bernice and followed the churned earth left by the brigands who had slaughtered the villagers and the lord of the manor along with his wife and every living thing within its walls, except for Alain de la Grave. Blackstone had the boy's parents buried despite the hard ground, and covered the shallow grave with rocks to keep the predators from digging up their remains. The creatures that came out of the forest had enough to feed on.

The torn earth led Blackstone and his men across the steepening ground for two days until the tracks were swallowed by woodland. In the distance mountains peeped above the miles of dense trees. It would have been madness for so few men to follow the killers. With another day's ride eastwards they smelled the smoke of camp-fires before they crested a rise and saw the host gathered by Sir John Chandos. There were a few banners snapping in the bitter wind, and the smoke was lifted and carried away quickly. Here and there tents were pitched for those lucky enough to have them. Makeshift rails had been made to tether horses and Blackstone saw that Chandos had secured the rising ground to his advantage. Sentries huddled in groups rather than single men at various posts. If a surprise attack were made by the Bretons these groups would quickly form up, a fact quickly demonstrated as Blackstone and Killbere rode across the skyline and a company of men levelled their pikes and locked their shields. A cry went up. 'Riders!'

Blackstone kicked the bastard horse side-on so that the shield slung from his saddle was seen by the sentries. One of the men lowered his shield. 'It's Sir Thomas!' The others followed his example. Their faces, deep-etched with tiredness and campfire smoke, creased into grins. The man who had recognized Blackstone stepped forward. He was sturdy, thickset and full-bearded. He looked to be a veteran. His clothing, mail and weapons – the knife and battleaxe tucked easily to hand in his broad belt, snug against his torso – proclaimed a man comfortable in the field of conflict. His was a hard-worked body, used to long days without food and, Blackstone thought, steadfast and efficient in a fight.

'My lord, we heard you were coming. A man of your rank and reputation is welcome.'

'I'm as common as any man here,' said Blackstone.

'Aye, my lord,' said the man, 'that may be, but these sons of whores are what you would scrape off the bottom of your boot. They stink, rank with sweat and dry hog shit from sleeping rough. Were it not for our King's payment most would be off looting. You might be common, Sir Thomas' – the man grinned – 'and I dare say your stench is no better than ours, but believe me, my lord, you might as well be the Archangel Michael compared to this lot.'

He turned to the ragtag bunch of fighting men behind him. They jeered with good humour. Blackstone was reminded of the vast army that he and the others had once been a part of and how the men, insolent and ribald, gave no man their respect until he had earned it. Blackstone grinned at them.

'I would be glad to have them at my side, rather than under my boot,' said Blackstone.

'And now that you're here we might just stay,' shouted one of the men. 'We've a seneschal leading us and he's a whip for a tongue. Hard on his men, Sir Thomas.'

The criticism of the man designated to lead them into battle raised a murmuring of agreement.

'What of Sir John?' asked Killbere.

'He's here. We'll take you and your men to him, but he's handing over command. That's all I know.'

'Sir Gilbert,' one of the men called. 'I was with Cobham at Blanchetaque. I saw you there.'

'You got your arse wet wading across, then,' said Killbere.

'And my blade – with French blood.'

'The King said the fish would all speak French after that,' shouted another. 'That's how much blood we spilled.'

The man who stood before Blackstone raised a hand. 'All right, gobshites. Look to your duties. We don't want Sir Thomas thinking that talk is all you're good for.' He looked up at Blackstone and Killbere. 'They're good men, every one gathered here across these fields, and they'll fight hard for someone they trust,' he said. His meaning was clear.

'And do they fight for you?' asked Blackstone.

'If they do not then they get a boot up their arse. Most were at Poitiers with my Lord Warwick. We know you held the hedgerow that day, Sir Thomas. You and Sir Gilbert.'

'It was a day to remember,' said Killbere.

'And never forgotten,' said the soldier.

'Take me to Sir John,' said Blackstone and nudged his horse forward.

As they walked the horses through the scattered men, those who recognized the shield and its motto, Defiant unto Death, stood with respect. And as those men stood then the murmur whispered across to others who glanced towards the new arrivals. And they too got to their feet. There were those who had not fought at Crécy, and some not even at Poitiers, but they had all heard of the man who had fought in every great battle and they wanted to see whether Thomas Blackstone's appearance lived up to his legend.

'No bowmen,' said Will Longdon, scanning the scattered troops. 'Not a bloody archer in sight, Thomas.'

'Then that means you'll have to work harder,' said Meulon.

'And about time,' added Perinne.

'The only time I saw Will work up a sweat was in that brothel a month back,' chirped Renfred. 'Sir Thomas? A horseman.' The German pointed to a man-at-arms weaving his horse through the troops on the ground.

Blackstone recognized the man's blazon of five scallops set

against a black cross, and when he reined in he saw it was Beyard, Lord de Grailly's captain, the man who had escorted him across France when he had returned from exile in Italy. De Grailly, the Captal de Buch, was one of the greatest Gascon knights and held the hereditary title of Master of Gascony. If the Captal was here then there could be no doubt of who would lead the fight.

'Beyard,' said Blackstone. 'Good to see you again.'

'And you, Sir Thomas,' said the Gascon. 'I would come closer and offer you my hand in friendship and welcome, but I remember your horse is of ill temperament.'

'Well remembered,' said Blackstone. 'The Captal is here?'

Beyard shook his head. 'More's the pity. He's now counsellor to Charles of Navarre. They're tucked up in the Pyrenees. Navarre had a hereditary claim on Burgundy but he's been forced to think again. It's politics, Sir Thomas. A plague on us all. Sir John is this way.'

The soldier stepped back. 'Good fortune, Sir Thomas. Captain Beyard can take you on to Sir John.'

'Your name?' said Blackstone.

'I am Ralph Tait.'

'Then, Master Tait, I will see you again.'

Sir John Chandos stood before a modest tent and a glowing brazier. He was as grimy as any of the men, and like them he looked weary. Drizzling rain had started again and the damp smudged the furrowed lines on his forehead. A face ploughed by the responsibility of being the King's negotiator in France.

Blackstone nudged the bastard horse towards one of the wooden stakes with an iron eyelet hammered into the ground. Killbere did the same but kept his horse out of kicking distance of Blackstone's mount. They dismounted and tethered the horses.

'Beyard, I will call the captains before dark and give them my orders. Have yours ready,' said Chandos.

The Gascon acknowledged the great knight's command and spurred his horse. The moment he was out of earshot the King's vice chancellor in France changed his tone. 'You took your time. You're damned late. Another day and we would have been gone from here.'

'We'd have followed the stench of your latrine pits,' said Killbere.

'Gilbert, I swear it's you I blame for making Thomas Blackstone so damned independent in thought and action.'

'I taught him everything, John. Especially how to not give a pig's arse for authority other than the King's.'

'And the Prince,' said Blackstone. 'When he lets me give a pig's arse. When he doesn't exile me or strip away the towns I fought for. When he's had a good night's sleep after a bellyful of good Gascon wine. Then, he and I get along. Until the next time we fall out.'

'Honour is a tenuous thing, John,' said Killbere. 'We offer it to men who often don't appreciate it.'

Chandos handed them two beakers of wine. 'We're soldiers. No one said it was going to be exactly as we want it. Which is why' – he looked at Blackstone – 'we need discipline.' He poured more wine into his own beaker. 'He disobeyed me, Gilbert, to go off and find you. I told him you weren't worth the effort. That you would already be dead. That there were more important battles to fight.'

Killbere nodded. 'Quite right. Which brings us back to that pig's arse. John, we fight for each other. Nothing will change that.'

Chandos addressed Blackstone: 'So you killed the bastard who captured Gilbert?'

'I did that myself,' said Killbere. 'And then we burned the town.'

'It was to be held,' Chandos berated them.

'No, it was a punishment for betrayal,' said Blackstone, helping himself to more wine, and then topping up Killbere. 'And Sainte-Bernice is abandoned as well. Routiers slaughtered everyone. Men, women and children. And the lord of the manor.'

'Holy Mother of God. The King is inheriting a wasteland. He needs every town he can get.'

'Not those two,' said Killbere.

'We lost one of our own as well,' said Blackstone. 'We came across French troops, d'Audrehem's men. They either mistook us for routiers or the King of France still has a warrant out for my death.'

'They saw your blazon?' said Chandos.

'I believe so.'

Chandos gave the news some thought. He shook his head. 'No, Thomas. King John knows you ride with me and that you serve Edward. See it as an error.'

'Aye, an error that would have made us crow food,' said Killbere. 'They knew who they challenged.'

'Then most likely it was a knight or some such who bears a personal grudge against you. God knows there are enough Frenchmen who would like to see you dead. But they backed off, did they? So, you see, they saw you were Edward's man.'

'No, it wasn't that simple. We fought enough of them to make them run, but that was because they thought us reinforced by a few hundred routiers led by a Welshman, Gruffydd ap Madoc. We both know him from the old days, but he had been bought off by the bastard at Saint-Aubin to ride against the likes of us. I planned to bring him here to fight with us and promised him payment.'

'Then where is he? Three hundred could sway the battle.'

'We were betrayed by the man you gifted us. William Cade. He told ap Madoc about the gold we carried from Saint-Aubin. They took two hostages so we couldn't pursue them. They hanged one of our archers. Cade took his men with the others. I intend to find him, get back the gold and kill Cade and the Welshman.'

Chandos grunted and poked the charcoal. 'There's scum everywhere. Cade was a freebooter. He raided around Paris. He fought for whoever paid the most. Even the French. It's what men do. How else are any of us to live if we don't sell our sword?'

'And you got rid of him by putting him in my company?' said Blackstone.

'Don't complain. He was worth having in a fight.'

'He's a man who takes pleasure in inflicting pain,' said Blackstone. 'He would torture a wounded man to death. He was more than scum and you put him among us.'

'It was his choice. He and his men came to me when I left Paris after the first negotiations. I didn't gift him, Thomas, he asked to join you once I offered you men.'

Killbere glanced at Blackstone, and then said, without concern in his voice, 'Aye, well, he couldn't have known we were taking towns in the Limousin.'

'He seemed to know,' said Chandos. 'He asked if I were joining forces with you. I thought nothing of it. Should I have done?'

'No. He probably thought there was some glory to be had by riding with Thomas,' said Killbere, brushing aside any doubts Chandos might have had.

Chandos grunted and nodded vaguely towards the troops. 'There's enough food for you and your men, for a couple of days at least.'

'We have enough to look after ourselves,' said Blackstone.

'As you like. Have your men camp behind us on top of the slope, Thomas.'

'Where are your bowmen?'

'Up there. Fifty of them, no more, but they are well sited for any attack that might come. They'll buy us minutes' grace if need be.'

'Is there a centenar?'

'No. A ventenar commands them.'

'Your fifty and mine. I have a centenar who knows how best to use bowmen.'

Sir John looked towards Will Longdon and quickly identified the veteran who rode ahead of the archers, his war bow in its waxed linen bag across his back. 'Tell my ventenar you are to command them. His name is Quenell.'

Blackstone turned to the men behind him. 'Will, you heard Sir John. Work with his archers. Meulon, Renfred, Perinne.' He nodded at his captains, who turned away their horses without needing to be told what to do, well versed over the years as they had become. 'Alain, go with the men,' he told the young Frenchman.

'And him?' said Chandos.

'Sainte-Bernice. It wasn't just the village and manor house

pillaged, they also slaughtered his parents. He can ride with us. He's old enough to fight and he has bad blood for the killers. He's the Lord of Sainte-Bernice now and he signed it over to us, for what it's worth.' Blackstone took a deep draught of his wine. Killbere warmed his backside against the brazier. 'Who do you have?' asked Blackstone.

'William Felton, who is Seneschal of Poitou, and Louis de Harcourt. They're the main commanders.'

'How many men?'

'Between us we have a thousand.'

'Against?'

Chandos shrugged. 'De Harcourt and Felton are out there now patrolling with their men. But my estimate is that there are two thousand Bretons and they won't be dislodged easily.'

Killbere swallowed the last of his wine. 'On the King's last campaign Felton got himself captured at Rheims but he escaped. It was said he broke his parole. He's a miserable bastard. Hard-nosed Northumbrian. But the King likes him well enough.'

'A man back there said he's in command,' said Blackstone.

'I'm due to return to Vincennes and continue negotiations for the handover of the remaining towns.'

'Then we stay with Felton?' said Killbere.

Chandos pulled out a folded document. The wax seal had been broken. He poured both men more wine. 'King's orders. I'm to do the talking, Thomas, and you the fighting.' He gestured with the folded document. 'He's in command but you know this country-side so you're to advise him.'

CHAPTER TWENTY-TWO

Blackstone and Killbere walked their horses towards Blackstone's men encamped on the high ground.

'Thomas, you know that Felton will piss his breeches with frustration. He'll be obliged to listen to the advice of a man who's socially inferior. Handle him with care.'

'I will,' said Blackstone, 'but he's got a reputation of having the heart of a lion and being unafraid of death.'

'Aye, and that'll make his pride ready to burst like an overripe grape if you challenge him.'

'I'm hoping Louis de Harcourt will side with me.'

'A blood enemy of Edward now fighting for him? He might not. His brother became your tutor and friend after Crécy but Louis never came across to join our ranks. No matter that he now takes payment from Edward, he might think you turned his brother back then.'

'I didn't. The family was already split.'

'God's tears, I hate family quarrels.'

'Be thankful you don't have one.'

Killbere grunted and said, 'William Cade seemed intent on joining us, Thomas. Is there more to it you think?'

'Perhaps. If he was near Paris who knows who paid him.'

'But why kill one of our lads?'

'To make me come for him.'

'Aye, that makes some sense. But it won't be to draw you away from fighting the Bretons. It's more than that.'

'Then when we find him we will find out.'

'And while we're talking about distrust,' Killbere said, 'keep an eye on Chandos. His shit isn't covered in gold. He takes handouts, y'know.'

'He's the King's vice chancellor in France. He's Edward's negotiator. Why would he do that? He has power and prestige enough.'

Killbere spat. 'When I dragged your arse ashore all those years ago you were as dumb as blood pudding. Haven't you learnt anything? Do you not listen to gossip and rumour and then apply your mathematical skills as a stonemason and divide up the percentage of what are lies and what's truth? Edward gave Chandos old Godfrey de Harcourt's castle at Saint-Sauveur-le-Vicomte. That's the stronghold that holds the Cotentin, you remember that, don't you? Whoever commands that has the key to invade Normandy. Charles of Navarre has fiefs in Normandy and guess who pays Chandos to look the other way when Navarre's men raid and harass the French?'

'If that's what Chandos is doing then it's because the King wants it.'

'Oh, I'm not saying the King isn't playing a double game. He promises the French there will be no Englishmen raiding while his chief negotiator turns a blind eye. When have I ever loved the French? I hope they rot and one day we rule this godforsaken place we fought so hard for. What I am saying is do not trust so easily.'

'Gilbert, Sir John's reputation is renowned. Look at the responsibility he's been given. He landed with sixty archers and fewer than forty men-at-arms and but within days he added a further forty hobelars. Between him and Louis de Harcourt they've now raised a thousand men. We couldn't do that.'

'Because we don't have the King's warrant or money. All I am saying, Thomas, is that when these damned glory hunters get a command ripped out of their hands they can cause trouble. If they ignore your advice, you're the one in the pig shit.'

'Gilbert, when I was a young archer you taught me that without honour we are nothing. We will follow Sir John because he is the King's loyal servant and we serve the King.'

Killbere sighed and rubbed a hand across his whiskers. 'Aye, I taught you well, right enough. Still, no harm in keeping eyes and ears open.'

As they reached the top of the slope John Jacob came forward and took the bastard horse's reins. It immediately lurched and tried to bite him, the big yellow teeth snapping, but Blackstone's squire had long since learnt how to handle the belligerent beast and quickly brought it under control. 'There's trouble with Sir John's archers,' he said, nodding to where Jack Halfpenny and Will Longdon stood facing a bunch of Chandos's bowmen, who looked angry. Blackstone and Killbere strode quickly towards the men.

'Jack, what's going on?' said Killbere.

'Sir Gilbert, these men accuse us of betraying Peter Garland,' said Jack Halfpenny, one hand resting on Will Longdon's arm. Will looked as though he would strike at the man opposite him at any moment.

One of the belligerent archers stepped forward and faced Killbere, who was a couple of steps ahead of Blackstone. 'Sir knight, we gave young Garland into your care and this man' – he pointed at Will Longdon – 'tells us that the lad and him were taken but that he escaped. No centenar runs from his men, and we'll not be led by a coward.'

Will Longdon's archer's knife was in hand before anyone realized – except Meulon, who had anticipated violence and was standing close by. He snatched Longdon's arm and blocked the archer's lunge. Longdon stepped into a wall of muscle and bone.

'Easy, Will,' said Meulon. 'The man provokes a fight,' he added, glancing at the accuser who had his own knife in hand, 'without knowing the man he challenges.'

'Enough!' said Killbere and cuffed Longdon's accuser, who stumbled backwards but had the good sense not to retaliate. 'If you want to know about that boy, you speak to any one of our captains and they will tell you the same story as Will Longdon here. He was hanged by the man who rode with you, William Cade, and it is he who set his men on our archers and it was they who damned near killed this man here. He fought to save Peter Garland. Know this and live with the knowledge. And then you serve under his command. Understood?'

The men muttered their understanding and agreement.

'Your name?' demanded Killbere of the archer.

'I am Richard Quenell, ventenar to twenty of these men.'

'Then you shall remain so,' said Blackstone. 'You and Jack Halfpenny both,' he said, pointing to his own man. 'And serve under Will Longdon.'

'I will, Sir Thomas. I thank you,' said Quenell, dipping his head in respect for Blackstone and in gratitude for retaining his rank.

Killbere's pockmarked face scowled as he and Blackstone turned away. 'Mother of Christ, Thomas. We must choose our own men and not be put upon. I would not be surprised if when the time comes these archers put an arrow in our backs.'

'You're the one who struck him. Not me.' Blackstone grinned. 'I'll make sure I'm nowhere near you when the fight comes, just in case his aim is off.'

Sir William Felton was getting on in years, thought Blackstone as he attended the gathering of captains. Probably, he guessed, in his fiftieth year, though it made no difference: Killbere was about the same age and as aggressive in a fight now as he had been years ago. Blackstone studied Sir William. He came up to Blackstone's chest and the two lions of his blazon ranged against a red background on his surcoat seemed to stretch as he drew a deep breath. He scratched grubby fingernails across his weather-beaten face where pig-bristle whiskers sprouted.

'Two days, no more,' said Felton as he pointed with a stick at the crude model of the landscape that stood between Sir John's force and the Breton horde. 'At least two thousand. They're disciplined. Well fed. And well led. I couldn't make out whose banner led them but I recognized some who had been at Poitiers. These whoresons will give us the fight of our lives.'

He looked at the men gathered around him. Louis de Harcourt stood next to Chandos. In contrast to the squat, muscular Felton, de Harcourt was almost as tall as Blackstone, his gaunt, sunken features etched around a hawk-beaked nose. He looked to be the most noble of everyone present and when he spoke it was with a quiet authority, his Norman accent reminding Blackstone of de Harcourt's uncle, Godfrey, who had abandoned the family to fight for England. It was Louis's brother Jean who had befriended Blackstone. Seeing de Harcourt lifted the trapdoor to a thousand memories in Blackstone's mind.

'They come in two columns, half a league apart,' said de Harcourt. 'They are organized. Scouts are a league ahead, mounted crossbowmen on each flank – not many, I saw two, perhaps three hundred. Like us the men-at-arms wear no heavy armour. And I saw nothing of their plunder. Sir William?' he said, deferring to the English knight.

'Aye, they have it. A hundred men or so guard it at the rear. Pack horses mostly and a few carts. Supplies and plunder.' He looked to Chandos. 'I recommend we ride hard and get further north of them.' He pointed to the bits of rock and sticks that represented their proposed route and battleground. 'There, beyond the mountains on the reverse slope and we'll secure the heights.'

The men murmured their approval.

'That's your decision, William. I depart for Vincennes in the morning. I'll take fifty men as escort and leave the archers with you.'

Felton turned to the gathered captains. 'Order of march. I take the right flank, de Harcourt the left and...' He glanced at Blackstone. '... you'll take the vanguard.'

Killbere grinned with anticipation but Blackstone simply nodded. Felton seemed to be waiting for an answer. 'You make no comment, Sir Thomas?'

'I was wondering why you would race to meet them. We exhaust ourselves and our horses. The land here is already hard going. We have come a long way east and the freezing air spills down from the mountains. We don't know the ground there but a few

141

miles from here there's a monastery. It sits high in the land. Its vineyards will be in ruins but there's a river that feeds a lake and there's marshy ground that could be to our advantage. The Bretons are looking for a fight and they come straight for us. We hold the vineyard and divide our force and we have them in a pincer. They would have no choice but to attack uphill and try and fight through the terraces. If they wheel away the lake and marshland are on one flank, and the rest of us on the other. They would be forced into a bottleneck. They would have no escape.'

There was a stunned silence for a few moments. Felton's face coloured. Blackstone had embarrassed him in front of the captains. He glanced around and saw on the men's faces that they thought Blackstone's proposal to be better than his plan.

'I know the monastery,' said Louis de Harcourt, breaking the awkward moment. 'It sits above a place known as the Vallée des Soupirs. Blackstone is correct. The vines will have rotted but the stakes will be there and the terraces are steep.'

Felton ground his teeth but he held back the curse that festered on his tongue. Such *radaillons* had proved successful in battle before. The contours of those ancient terraces had helped funnel the French onto English swords at Crécy. Is that what Blackstone remembered? One great victory. One day's slaughter? If that was all Blackstone could offer by way of a military strategy then his reputation as a successful war leader was undeserved.

'It is a plan that has no guarantee of success,' said Felton. 'My route puts us directly in their path. It will be done with once and for all. It serves our King's wishes to destroy these Bretons. It will take Charles de Blois another two years at least to gather such a fighting force again.'

'I will guarantee they will turn onto the road and have no choice but to face us,' said Blackstone.

'Guarantee?' Felton scoffed. 'There is no guarantee in war.'

'Only that a wrong decision will lead to defeat. I know this place and I know how to force their hand. Half a day's ride instead of two and onto ground that will give us victory.' He glanced at

Louis de Harcourt. '"The nature of the ground is often of more consequence than courage."'

De Harcourt guffawed. 'Vegetius! The precious book my brother loved. He taught you well!' He laughed again, and nodded, 'Yes,' remembering his own studies and quoted further from the ancient book of war: '"And if your forces are few in comparison to your enemy then cover your flanks with a city, the sea or... a river."'

The men looked at Sir William Felton. He had been defeated. He glowered at Blackstone. 'Your name will be tarnished for ever if we are defeated.'

'And yours will be praised when we win,' said Blackstone.

CHAPTER TWENTY-THREE

Winter sun crept across the landscape just as a fawn might ease itself into the open from the depths of the forest, cautious and unwilling to challenge the chill air that persisted beyond the trees. There was insufficient cover for men to hide in ambush close to the forest's edge so Will Longdon was obliged to settle his archers forty paces back into the trees. It would mean a muscle-cramping night. No fires would be lit for their smoke would linger in the high branches, which would be spotted several miles away. But there would be no complaint, or at least none spoken aloud. The men's curses would be reserved for the men-at-arms who slept beneath their blankets sheltered from the wind by the craggy ground behind them. No doubt the damned knights would have fires. The wind favoured them, blowing the smoke away downwind from any approaching enemy. Bastard hobelars, bastard knights, bastard noblemen, every bastard man-at-arms who waited to kill those that the archers would force onto their blades.

Will Longdon had left Jack Halfpenny with his twenty archers on the slopes with Killbere where they would face the initial assault when the Bretons charged uphill. Halfpenny's men were in the safest position. Down here in the forest Longdon was not content to let the archers sit in what little comfort was offered by the leaf mould blanketing the forest floor. A thousand years had softened the ground and, despite the damp, it was a bed that offered some comfort. 'Off your arses,' Longdon told them. 'We put ourselves at risk being here. There are enough horsemen to turn and ride through us once we shoot into them.'

Longdon and Quenell set their men to sharpening stakes thirty paces back from the forest edge. The archers would be able to step forward of them and hold their ground but if a charge came their way then they could sprint behind the sharpened stakes, which would be hidden from view until it was too late for the riders to see them. The slender boughs dug in at an angle would pierce a horse's chest and the archers would set on the fallen riders with knife and sword. They could not dig pits to entrap the horses forward of the treeline as that would have given the ambush site away. The archers were few in number, but they could loose several hundred arrows in the first minute. The shock of sudden and near silent death from the sky would throw the mounted troops into disarray. Some would charge forward towards the high ground where the English and Gascon men waited; others would surely turn and charge the archers. The risk was how many Bretons would be courageous enough to attack. Will Longdon nursed the fear in his stomach. His archers would have a chance if only a hundred or so charged into the trees. Thirty or more would go down on the stakes, the rest would hurtle after them and that's when the lightly armed bowmen needed help. It would be a lung-rasping run to the other end of the forest into the clearing and then they would need to steady their breathing and turn to face the Bretons. Will Longdon prayed that Perinne's men had placed the extra sheaves of arrows there for them. And that Perinne had not spotted any more buzzards circling. The raptors had faced a hard winter and scoured the land for food, but today they would abandon their hunt and be calling up men's souls. Longdon glanced up at the rising ground. There was no sign of movement except from crows in the sky. Nothing seemed untoward. Nothing suspicious that would alert the Breton mercenaries. With luck the killing would be efficient and his own losses few. He blew snot from his nostrils and wiped the sweat from his face as he sharpened another stake.

The narrow valley would lead the Bretons towards those who waited on the higher slopes where a small lake fed into a river.

The ever-resourceful Benedictine monks – now absent, having abandoned the monastery during the winter when the routiers came through – had created the catchment area from the mountain run-off that fed down onto the lower hills. It served as a reservoir that gave them fish to eat and its cleanliness was assured because it was the river below the monastery that carried away offal from the animals butchered in their kitchens and ordure from their latrines. In order to control the water level they had built a sluice that released the excessive winter snow melt.

The reservoir was the length every peasant used to measure his field – 220 yards – but unlike the ploughman's acre the dam was as broad as it was long. The monks had used the natural saddle of the land to trap the water by building a stone wall between the rock face that jutted forward on either side to secure the sluice gate. The irrigation channels for their crops and vines were controlled by small wooden gates barely as wide as a man's spread hand. If the monks did not control the winter flow of water then the dam would overspill, the irrigation ditches would founder and the retaining wall crumble beneath the water's pressure. At the base of the sluice gate a small opening allowed a steady stream of water to pass. This fed down into the river and served to keep the water level fairly constant.

'You're certain you can do this?' said Louis de Harcourt as he stood with Blackstone and Killbere on the high ground, looking down across the lake and the flowing river. Will Longdon's archers were a long way below in the forest. If the Bretons were trapped between the trees and a sudden fast-flowing river then their choice would be to try and turn into the forest and face an unknown number of archers or to surge upwards and assault the men-at-arms who held the high ground. Blackstone knew it was a gamble which the enemy might choose. If all went as planned the Bretons would be split: some on one side of the river; others beyond it. Whatever happened, his plan would disrupt the larger force. But Felton was correct – there were no guarantees.

'It can be done. I have already been down there. Once we open that sluice gate the Bretons will be trapped. The river will flood and the marshland beyond the turn in the road will be swamped after they bring their horses across the ford. It's shallow enough now but not when the water reaches it. We will trap many of them this side. Those in the rear will be slow to turn with the supply wagons and pack horses. We take those after the fight.'

Blackstone's eyes were on the fighting ground. He was taking a risk and if he got it wrong then his men would die and Sir William Felton would make certain all the blame for the failure of destroying the Breton horde fell squarely on his shoulders. De Harcourt studied the younger man. He couldn't remember whether he had ever seen him at Castle de Harcourt many years ago during those days when the family was split between serving France and England. A time when his brother Jean de Harcourt had taught Blackstone the skills of the sword after his bow arm had been broken. He shook his head, knowing he had not. Blackstone glanced at him.

'You doubt me?'

'No, I was thinking of something else.'

Blackstone nodded, accepting the explanation, his concentration back on the small lake and the sluice gate. Timing was everything.

'You cannot turn the sluice gate wheel. The handle is missing,' said de Harcourt.

'I go in the water and haul on the chain.'

'That's too much for one man, even a man as strong as you. It cannot be done.'

Blackstone grinned and gestured towards Meulon, who was organizing the hobelars into their battle positions. 'Meulon will be in the water with me. Two of us can do it.'

Louis de Harcourt knew that Meulon had been a sworn man to his brother but when the French King had executed him for treason then Meulon had sworn allegiance to Blackstone.

'Our families are still linked, even by the men who fight. All right,' said de Harcourt, accepting that there was no more to be discussed. 'I will be on Killbere's left. I pray you do not freeze to death in there and that when you open the sluice that the water does not take you with it.'

'You and Sir William stay hidden until Gilbert calls for you, my lord. That way the Bretons will see only him and his few men. They'll think the heights are lightly defended. Then, when you break cover, stand fast with Sir Gilbert. Meulon and I will join you once we are out of the water. Gilbert has men ready to hold us with ropes we will tie about us.' Blackstone grinned. 'What could go wrong?'

CHAPTER TWENTY-FOUR

Renfred sat astride his horse two miles from where Blackstone and the men waited. The wind whispered up the valley and swept around forest and ancient vines. It was, Renfred realized, a sigh rather than a ghostly moan. And the valley had rightly earned its name. He kept his cloak tight around him, grimacing at the thought of another winter in France and hoping that Blackstone would take them south, perhaps even back to Italy. For summer at least. Winter everywhere was the bane of a fighting man's life and Blackstone fought throughout the year. Renfred's eyes glistened from the snap of wind but he was thankful that the rainclouds seemed to falter in their journey towards him and settled across the distant mountains. The forests shimmered in the wind but so too did the horizon at the end of the valley road. He wiped his eyes, turned his head slightly to one side to settle his vision and then looked again. Had it been the height of summer he might have considered the wavering body of men that appeared to be an illusion created by heat haze. The enemy were in sight. The two columns of Breton routiers had come together across a broad front and rode steadily towards him. If Sir William and Louis de Harcourt had been correct in guessing their number then of the two thousand at least several hundred breasted the valley. And given the breadth of the valley that meant that they would ride ahead in three waves one behind the other. Renfred grinned. As the valley narrowed and the river flooded they would be forced to merge ever tighter. Knee to knee on horseback. Cursing and berating horse and man. Forced to do Thomas Blackstone's bidding.

He turned his horse and spurred it away.

* * *

John Jacob stood at Killbere's side. 'There,' he said, pointing to where Renfred signalled.

'I see him,' said Killbere. 'They've entered the valley,' he called and looked across to where Jack Halfpenny's men crouched on the other side of the lake. The hurdles that Blackstone and Killbere had ordered built nestled against the old vine supports on the top three terraces. Anyone looking up onto the rising ground would see nothing more than overgrown and abandoned vines but as many men as possible crouched behind the hurdles. The others waited on the reverse slope where the horses were tethered, out of sight.

'Thomas, make ready,' he said to Blackstone and Meulon. Stripped down to shirt and hose, Blackstone and Meulon eased into the dam, gasping with the pain of the icy water.

'Mother of Christ,' wheezed Meulon.

For a moment Blackstone could not speak. Chest-deep the ice-melt strangled him. Despite each man's layered muscle both felt the water's vice-like grip and the pain it caused in their joints. A sudden fear gripped Blackstone, as frightening as the prospect of not being able to accomplish their task. Even if they succeeded would they be able to fight afterwards?

'My balls have taken refuge somewhere behind my lungs,' Meulon said, forcing a laugh as they struck out for the sluice gate.

'At least you still have yours,' gasped Blackstone. 'I think mine have shrivelled and dropped off.'

Heaving for breath, they reached the wooden gate and the chain, as thick as a man's wrist, that cranked it open. The windlass was long gone but as Blackstone gripped the slimy metal and heaved on it he felt a satisfying give in the tension. Meulon moved to his side and readied himself to put his hands above Blackstone's on the chain.

'Not yet,' said Blackstone. He peered over the low stone wall and tried to stop himself shivering long enough to gauge where the enemy had reached. Another half-mile and the Breton front ranks would be close enough. Once they saw the water pour down the slope into the river there would be no time for those first two rows of men to wheel their horses and retreat. Those who rode in the third rank might have time to start but they would be caught by the flooding river and be bogged down in the marshland. Blackstone's body tensed; his mind fought the urge to yield to the uncontrollable shivering that would strip them of their strength. The rope tied beneath their armpits was already chafing. 'We count to fifty and then open the gate,' said Blackstone.

Behind his thick black beard, Meulon's teeth chattered. 'You do the counting. My brain has been seized by a river god.'

Blackstone nodded. 'One... two... three...'

Will Longdon crouched in the shadows with his archers as the massed horsemen rode by. Earlier he had instructed the bowmen to place stone markers every fifty paces into the path the horsemen would take and now they rode near enough the 150-yard mark. Back from the treeline the low branches hid them from the high-riding horsemen but the archers would soon move quickly to the fringe of the forest and then the element of surprise would be short-lived. He glanced along the line of bowmen. Quenell turned his head and looked, waiting for Longdon's command. Every man clutched a fistful of arrows in one hand, his war bow in the other. More arrows were tucked into their belts. Their killing time would be brief, so they had abandoned their linen arrow bags. They could hear the men's voices as they rode by. They were relaxed, some shouting and laughing – there was no sense of danger. The wind shifted slightly. A couple of the horses caught the men's scent in the forest and tugged at their reins, but the riders quickly brought them under control. Will Longdon licked his lips. His mouth was drying. He wished he was with hundreds more archers. Wished they stood in sawtooth formation between the men-at-arms as bugles and drums heralded death to the French army. He pushed the memory of the great battles from his mind. The damned Bretons seemed to move at a snail's pace. How many more, for Christ's sake? He edged a few paces closer to the edge of the forest, extending his arm to keep the others back. He crouched again. Now he could see the broad column of men spread across the valley. Some were swinging wide of the others, finding ground to ease their horses across. A hundred yards. Getting too close. He turned. All eyes were on him. He nodded to Quenell and swept his arm forward. As one the archers moved forward quickly. Longdon was five paces ahead of them and the first to step into the open. He jabbed his fistful of arrows into the ground. Some of the riders saw him, and then shouted a warning as the line of bowmen appeared. By the time the cry of alarm went up they heard a man's voice call out a command.

'Nock! Draw!' There was a brief creaking of heartwood yew being drawn back.

Seeing the archers suddenly on their flank had caused turmoil among the nearest horsemen. Riders yanked reins and spurred horses, turning them into those who rode alongside them. In the few seconds it took for Will Longdon's cry to be heard the horsemen's own yells of panic redoubled.

'Loose!' The sudden whoosh of yard-long arrows caused the riders to look up into the sky. A natural reaction to see where death might strike. And by the time those who kept their eyes skyward had blinked the dark shower fell onto them. Before the arrows had struck into the seething mass the next was already arcing high, and then another. The archers kept a steady rhythm. *Nock!* Draw back. *Loose!* Pluck an arrow. *Nock!* Draw back. *Loose!* Pluck another arrow. *Nock! Loose!* There had been no need for Will Longdon to command his men to mark their targets before shooting. Shooting into the packed men was already bringing down man and horse and no one had yet dared to turn their horse and charge into the ambush. Some of the riders surged forward, taking others with them. A jammed knot of men turned this way and that and anyone trapped in that mêlée died. Men bellowed in pain as arrows tore through their legs and into their saddles. Others slumped forward with a yard-long shaft sticking out of their shoulders, bodkin points ripping through heart and lungs. As each man and horse fell the chaos deepened. Horses reared and whinnied from the pain of being struck by arrows while the men lucky enough to evade the storm fell under the hooves of the panicked animals. Blood slicked riders' saddles and horses' flanks. And still the rhythmic whisper of death fell. As Bretons caught in the killing zone began to reorganize a flood of water seemed to appear as if from nowhere. It swirled and gurgled across the smooth boulders, raising the water level, spilling beyond the low riverbank. Horses panicked when the water began to stream through their legs. The rapidly flowing water added to the confusion. By the time Will Longdon's men had loosed as many arrows as they could, some of the horses' hooves had sunk deep into the muddy bog. Those riders who had survived the initial onslaught now spurred their horses from behind the dead and dying and surged, sword in hand, towards the vulnerable bowmen.

'Now!' shouted Will Longdon. 'Come on, lads! Run!'

The lightly armed archers needed no further encouragement. As Longdon and his men turned and raced for the safety of the forest, dodging patches of bramble and thick undergrowth, horsemen raked their spurs, bellowing cries of revenge and death. Behind them another sound rose up: the agonizing screams of horses running into the sharpened stakes.

Longdon cursed. His lungs burned and his legs ached. The younger men he commanded were already gaining ground. Grasping his remaining arrows in one hand and his bow in the other he veered left, aiming for another narrow forester's track, hoping the trees would slow down the horses in pursuit. Quenell was a dozen paces ahead of him. Longdon wanted to urge his men to run faster for the far side of the forest but his lungs needed the air to keep him going. He'd had no time to ease the cord from the horned nock at the tip of his bow and now it was proving unwieldy as he ran through ferns and under low branches. But then his second wind came and he felt the surge of power in his legs. He almost laughed aloud at the joy of it. He glanced back. The chasing horsemen were close. It made no difference. Once they reached the safety of the open ground on the far side of the trees they could turn and, with the fresh supply of arrows brought by Perinne, bring those riders down.

All would be well and the killing would be swift.

And then his bow cord snagged a gnarled branch and he fell.

As his head struck the ground and the rock-hard tree root, he felt the thundering vibration of the approaching horses.

CHAPTER TWENTY-FIVE

Moments before the archers struck at the approaching enemy Blackstone and Meulon trod water, hanging onto the sluice-gate chain.

'Twenty-nine, thirty, thirty-one...' He peered across the low wall. Will Longdon's men were already killing Bretons. 'They're close enough. Heave!'

They brought their weight and strength to bear and the chain creaked against the wheel. Immediately they felt a greater tug on their feet from the gate's narrow gap.

'God's blood. It's flowing fast,' said Meulon, grimacing as they flexed their arm and back muscles and the sudden rising of the gate sucked them closer to the hole.

'Hold on!' Meulon cried. The gate was open, the chain notched as Blackstone was sucked under. Meulon reached down and grabbed his arm and hauled him above the surface but they had underestimated the force of the trapped water in the lake.

'Ropes!' Blackstone yelled.

The two men on the bank each took the strain of their rope but they quickly lost ground. One of them cried for help. Killbere was as close as any man and grabbed the end of one rope while John Jacob and two others quickly jumped to his aid. Three men on each rope managed to hold Blackstone and Meulon from being sucked through the sluice gate.

'Heave!' Killbere shouted. 'Thomas! We cannot hold you. Pull yourself towards us. Hurry man, the Bretons will be upon us.'

Released from the restraints of the sluice gate the tongue of water roared free. Blackstone and Meulon were still out of their depth but now the pressure of the water pressed them against the stone wall. Blackstone gripped the coarse rope and tried to pull himself against the overpowering weight of fast-flowing water. Meulon was being sucked beneath the surface. He bobbed up, muscles stretched from holding on to the rope. He looked at Blackstone and shook his head. Then Blackstone went under, a great fist seizing him and tugging him down. He opened his eyes and saw the churning white water thunder through the sluice gate's maw. They were going to drown. He hauled himself up hand over hand, shook the water from his eyes, saw that the men on the shore were being pulled ever closer to the edge. No one was strong enough to hold them.

'We go,' he spluttered to Meulon. 'Or we drown. We'll go under and they won't pull us up.'

Meulon immediately understood. He nodded. The freezing water and the strength needed to stay above the surface was taking its toll.

'Let go!' Blackstone shouted.

The men on the bank looked dumbfounded, and kept their grip despite their feet sliding ever closer to the edge, but then Killbere understood. 'Release the ropes!'

The command was not to be contested and John Jacob and the others let go. Blackstone and Meulon disappeared beneath the surface. Killbere and the others leaned quickly forward and saw the two men spewed from the dam and tumbled down with the gush of water. Bretons were already two-thirds of the way up, forced into a tight group as they spurred their horses up to the terraces, yanking reins left and right as they found a way through the old vines and onto the terraces. They had seen Killbere and the others and believing they were so few raised their swords, drew tight their shields and charged.

'To your front!' bellowed Killbere. His men-at-arms dropped their hurdles and lunged with sharpened blades on ten-foot-long ash poles. Horses veered; riders fell; Killbere's men stood ready to kill the fallen. Horses tumbled downhill, hooves kicking, legs breaking, crushing men trying to scramble upwards. Those behind faced an assault course to find a way through, but their sheer weight of numbers soon began to show. Horses bunched, men rode harder and faster towards what seemed like just a handful of men. Killbere had tried to keep sight of Blackstone and Meulon but now stood his ground with John Jacob as the Bretons began to push into them.

'Now, Jack!' Killbere bellowed, his voice rising over the clamouring yells and screams.

Across the other side of the dam more hurdles dropped and Jack Halfpenny's archers loosed their arrows into the attacking men's flanks. They died, unable to turn their horses away from the ambush and the contours of the ground and the dam's spewing stream of water.

Killbere and John Jacob strode forward, shields high, swords slashing. Others stood at their side, men versed in inflicting violence efficiently, hacking men's limbs in the knowledge that that would be sufficient injury to take them out of the fight and to kill them. Blood gushed from severed arms and legs; shock and pain did the rest. Without thought of the men under their feet Killbere and those with him moved steadily on. Ash lances speared more horses, causing confusion amid the riders swarming uphill, yet the Bretons persisted, every man fighting for himself, throwing himself onto the English ranks in a desperate attempt to live. But then Beyard the Gascon edged his men forward, forcing the Bretons to swerve back onto the steep ground that made the horses lose their balance, stumble and fall.

The Bretons now realized that their attack was being weakened by forcing horses into the fray and that they should abandon their mounts. They joined the unhorsed mercenaries on the lower terraces, re-formed into a fighting block of men, like a memory of the great battles that had gone before. One among them led them forward once more.

'Hold!' Killbere called out, making those of his men who had gone ahead to finish off the wounded, retreat back to where he held the line. Now unencumbered by their horses, the Bretons swarmed towards the English and Gascon lines. Killbere saw that the sheer weight of the attack might crush them. He turned to the man carrying Blackstone's banner. 'We need Sir William. Raise it!'

The flag bearer lifted the long sapling that had been cut to carry the banner and raised it high.

Alain de la Grave stood further down the line. Killbere glanced at the boy hunched behind his shield, eyes barely visible above the rim. There was no sign of enemy blood on him or the shield.

'John! Pull him back,' said Killbere. 'God's tears. One strike on the shield and he'll have his nose smashed and then his throat cut. He was told to stay with the rearguard.'

John Jacob hesitated.

'I know,' said Killbere, 'you're not his wet-nurse but Thomas promised to keep him alive. Go!' he shouted as the Bretons got within thirty paces. 'Send him for Sir William! We need those men now.'

Blackstone's squire turned and ran behind the line of men. Sweat stung his eyes, the hauberk chafed and the days of cold and wet had blistered his feet. Cursing to himself that fighting was hard enough without protecting a boy who clearly had few skills on the killing field, he reached Alain just as the routiers' front rank clashed. He saw the boy falter; another stride and he was with him, using his shoulder to push him aside, sending him sprawling and taking his place in the line, ramming his sword low and up into the soft underbelly of a Breton.

'Close!' he yelled as he stepped back. The men either side immediately moved, shields tight, and closed the gap he had left. He kicked the fallen boy. 'Up!'

The young Frenchman glared angrily as he scrambled to his feet, retrieved his fallen sword, and was about to argue when the ferocity of the assault nearly broke through the line. Anger was quickly replaced by fear. The killing was only feet away and he saw the sickening reality of blade on bone and flesh.

'Get back to the horses. You're needed there! Move your arse!'

The boy flinched as the men behind John Jacob gave way; one went down with a sword thrust to his throat, and the Breton shouldered aside the next. John Jacob spun, caught the attacker with an unexpected low slash that almost severed his leg below the knee. The man's mouth gaped silently, eyes wide in terror, and then air filled his lungs and he screamed. He was already tumbling forward as the shield wall closed behind him. He sprawled, and Alain desperately shuffled backwards as John Jacob plunged his sword into the man's neck. He looked at the stricken boy. 'Go,' he urged him again. 'And tell Sir William and de Harcourt we need them now.'

Alain ran back to where the horses and the rearguard waited. The Bretons were going to break through. Felton and de Harcourt were leaving their flanking attack too late. John Jacob ran back to where Killbere stood his ground. The dead at his feet were testament to his prowess and they impeded those who had to step over them to attack him. He was hard pressed. Once John Jacob was at his side the two men pushed back their attackers again. There were so many Bretons and so few who held the ground in front of them. The mercenaries could not fail to scale the heights and win the day. And then they would teach those who defied them what it meant to die a slow and agonizing death.

'Where the fuck is Sir William?' Killbere complained bitterly. 'Sir William!' he bellowed above the din of the fighting. 'SIR WILLIAM! God's blood.'

At last Louis de Harcourt and Sir William's men swept from Killbere's left flank in a pincer, just as Blackstone had ordered, and it was the over-confident Bretons who died like netted fish as Killbere and the fighting men closed on them. They died in their hundreds. Arrows cut them down; men-at-arms hacked them to death. Their own horses trampled and crushed them. Blood-splattered, Killbere and John Jacob fought their way down onto the next contour where the terrace widened and the torn earth from the desperately scrambling horses' hooves slowed the advancing men even more. Horse carcasses became obstacles for sweating, grunting men to clamber over and around. Survivors began to run downhill. Killbere wiped the sweat from his eyes. The stream of water still poured down into the river.

It ran with blood.

Blackstone and Meulon had barrelled downriver, the surging water sweeping them over back-scraping river boulders. Blackstone raised his head, squinting against the stinging spray, watching Meulon four lengths beyond him as the big Norman used his arms like paddles to guide his body through the rapids. As both men fought the torrent the Bretons were trying to attack the heights. The tableau of chaos and shouts of the men came and went as Blackstone was repeatedly ducked beneath the water. None of the riders seemed to notice the two bodies being swept rapidly downstream.

Blackstone saw that where the river curved ahead some of the Bretons were already trying to turn their horses away in retreat. He glimpsed other horses too: some writhing from their wounds; others, riderless and panicked, galloping this way and that, trying to find a way out of the place of death. Men were scattered across the ground, lying beneath a field of arrows. Will Longdon and his archers had inflicted many casualties on those first riders to enter the valley, he thought, and then his back caught another river boulder. The impact made him gasp; he half rolled, threw out his arm and cupped his hand to drag his body away from the white water that tore itself across low jagged rocks. He straightened his legs and, like a fast-moving skiff, just missed the deadly, bone-crushing rocks. His eyes blinked away the whipping spray and he saw that Meulon's rope was almost within grasp as it snaked behind him. The two men would soon reach the bend in the river where marshland had slowed the Breton advance, and now their retreat. Blackstone snatched at the twisting rope, missed, and lunged again, throwing his chest free of the water, almost blinded by the slap of water as he half ducked his head beneath the surface.

His fingers touched the coarse rope. Closing his fist he felt the satisfying bite of Meulon's weight as the rope went taut. Forcing his turned shoulder back into the water he grasped the rope with both hands and was pulled through the water like a sledge through snow. Meulon's body slowed as Blackstone's acted like an anchor, giving the big man a chance to aim for the riverbank before their aching and bruised bodies, pummelled by the freezing water, were plunged helplessly into the mêlée of men in the marshland.

Meulon squirmed, twisting this way and that, trying to use the current to push the weight of his body into the riverbank. They were almost on the fringe of the forest and Blackstone saw him stretch up his arms to catch an overhanging branch. It must have been rotten because it snapped under his weight. Blackstone felt the rope cutting into his hands, but he used Meulon's weight to steer himself closer to the riverbank on the far side away from the Bretons. Then, as the river struck a bend, a gully to one side took some of the force of the water and Meulon managed to wrench his body into its muddy gap. The rope immediately slackened. Meulon stumbled, but found his feet in the waist-deep gully; he turned and hauled on the rope, pulling Blackstone towards him. Moments later he snatched at Blackstone, just before his leader was swept past the safety of the riverbank, and the two men fell into the shallow creek. At least here they were concealed from the turmoil that still raged across the river on the valley floor.

Blackstone vomited river water but Meulon ignored that as he grabbed him by the rope that was still tied beneath his shoulders. The man's strength didn't seem to be diminished as he threw Blackstone down into the mud beneath the rotting vegetation on the bank. Horsemen were crashing through the forest, heading towards those beyond the river. Blackstone and his Norman captain could not see the riders but the noise of the trampling horses told them they were close. As the sound faded they yanked free the ropes and carefully slithered up the bank and into the trees. Their backs were bruised and grazed from the boulders but the mud had a strangely soothing effect on their wounds and once they had brought their shivering under control they clambered further into the undergrowth.

As they crawled they heard muffled shouts and screams from the distance. The fight continued beyond the forest. Meulon pushed aside a clump of ferns and bramble and they came face to face with the contorted body of a Breton mercenary with an arrow in his chest. Dirt and blood clogged his mouth; leaf mould half covered his face. Beyond him a horse lay dead with a broken stake in its chest. The clamour of the fighting became more distinct.

Blackstone snatched the fallen Breton's sword and Meulon grabbed his mace. 'It's Will and Perinne,' said Blackstone.

CHAPTER TWENTY-SIX

When Will Longdon fell the horseman had turned his mount to trample him beneath iron-shod hooves. Killing Englishmen was in his blood, but to kill an English archer gave a visceral satisfaction and slaked an appetite to slaughter these silent killers. Richard Quenell had turned at the sound of the horseman bearing down on them. He saw Will Longdon fall. A thought flashed through his mind. Longdon had caused his humiliation; if he were dead then the way ahead might be open for him to take Longdon's place as centenar. As quickly as the thought had arrived he pushed it from his mind. Longdon's sworn lord, Thomas Blackstone, could have taken his rank from him, but had not. And even though the veteran knight Killbere had struck him, it had been a light punishment. Quenell had challenged the centenar, a man of senior rank, and he had been put in his place. A lesson had been learnt and he had been accepted into a band of men who wore their loyalty as proudly as their blazon. He nocked an arrow and loosed at the looming figure.

It was a difficult shot. His aim instinctive. The rider's mouth gaped from shock and pain, his head thrown back as the bodkin-tipped arrow punched into his chest and blood choked his throat. As he fell from the saddle the horse veered and ran into a concealed stake. As it screamed in agony Quenell ran forward to the fallen archer. Longdon was stunned but he was trying to get to his feet. Quenell reached down and grabbed the older man, dragging him up. He put his face close to the archer.

'They're still coming!' he said. Other horsemen were in the forest. 'Can you run?'

Will Longdon looked confused from the blow to his head. Quenell gripped his jupon and shook him. 'Run!'

It took only two deep breaths for Will Longdon's senses to return. He grabbed his war bow and without a word turned and sprinted for the far edge of the forest.

Ignoring bramble cuts and whiplash branches they ran for their lives, cutting through the trees onto the narrow forester's track. Behind them came the increasing sound of more riders punishing their horses through the undergrowth, swerving this way and that to avoid trees as they sought out the archers who had ambushed them. Longdon's lungs heaved but he realized that he still gripped the half-dozen arrow shafts in his fist. If they had to turn and fight they could still kill some of those who pursued them.

'The others are through,' gasped Quenell.

Ahead of them the trees thinned and daylight flooded the meadow on the other side. Longdon blinked away the tears of exertion and saw the ragged line of archers had turned 150 paces or more from the treeline to face the approaching enemy.

'Now we kill more of the bastards,' said Will Longdon and put on a spurt.

Barefoot, sluiced with sweat and caked in mud, Blackstone and Meulon followed the clamour of battle and ran into the clearing. Will Longdon's men were formed up in a ragged line where Perinne and Renfred's one hundred mounted men-at-arms had been waiting; the archers seemed to have paused their killing as Blackstone's captains were now riding hard into the surviving Bretons who had been foolish enough to give chase through the forest and emerged to find themselves in yet another ambush. Twenty or thirty Bretons had wheeled and fought but they were being overwhelmed. Many were already lying dead on the ground either from the archers' skill or the men-at-arms' charge. Horses ran loose; handfuls of unhorsed mercenaries scattered, running for the trees. If they ran clear of the hobelars then Longdon's archers brought them down. Some corpses had three arrows in their back.

Blackstone and Meulon came face to face with four of the mercenaries who thought they had escaped the killing. Disbelief creased their features as the two wild men appeared. Barefoot, hair and beards caked with mud, grass and twigs, shirts ripped, hose blackened, they didn't look human, but like huge pagan forest dwellers that had finally emerged into daylight. However, whatever doubts the Bretons had were quickly dispelled. These two men were armed and were charging at them.

Meulon's great strides gained ground on Blackstone and he sidestepped a sword strike. The turn of his body meant he was already swinging the flanged mace from a low position in a fast arc that caught the first Breton under the chin as he stumbled forward. His head snapped back. So did his neck. He was dead before he fell. Blackstone parried the second mercenary's sword thrust. The blade he had taken from the dead Breton did not have the fine balance of his own Wolf Sword, and the pitted blade had a poor edge to it. He sidestepped, allowing the man's lunge to carry his weight forward. Letting the blade pass him he grabbed the man's forearm, blocking him with his body strength, and smashed his forehead into the man's nose. The Breton's legs gave way and as Blackstone stepped over him he thrust his blade into the back of the man's neck.

Blackstone and Meulon stopped, level with each other but ten paces apart, as the two surviving Bretons attacked. The scar-faced knight and his long-serving captain stood their ground. Years of experience served as their shield. One of the Bretons saw Blackstone take a step forward. His bare feet looked to have slipped in the wet grass. He went down onto one knee. Caught unawares. Head lowered. The Breton attacked, obeying his instinct and half raising his sword ready for a sweeping cut. Blackstone lifted his head, looked into the man's eyes, saw the startled awareness that he had been duped. Screaming defiance, it was the last breath he took as Blackstone tilted his blade and let the man's momentum drive it up below his breast bone. The blade severed lungs, heart and spine and its bloodied tip protruded from his back. The inferior blade snapped. The man's weight fell onto Blackstone, who went down beneath him. Rolling clear he saw that Meulon had the second man on the ground, a knee in his chest, his free hand pinning the man's sword arm. The mace was raised; the man screamed for mercy. And then fell silent.

Blackstone and his friend stood and watched as Perinne and Renfred's hobelars killed the remaining Bretons. Those few who escaped had already galloped into the trees. The meadow's crop of goose-feathered shafts was being harvested by the archers as they went among the dead and retrieved what arrows they could use again. Will Longdon raised an arm to Blackstone. By the time he and the throat-cutter reached him it was plain to see that every man had been blooded.

'Thomas,' said Will Longdon, weariness creasing his face, 'I lost four of my lads.'

Blackstone nodded, and placed a hand on his friend's shoulder. No words were needed. He stepped past him to where Perinne was bringing the mounted men back together, steadying them after the killing in case of a counter-attack, although that was unlikely. The Bretons were in retreat down the valley and all the survivors would be in full flight.

'You look as though you've been rolling in boar shit,' said Will Longdon to Meulon.

'And you stink of it,' the Norman answered.

'Aye, well, that's because some of us have been fighting and men soil themselves when they die.'

'You archers don't get close enough to fight.'

'Then it must be your own arse you're smelling,' said Longdon.

Meulon laid an arm across Longdon's shoulder and grinned. 'You moan like an unpaid whore.'

'And your armpit reeks of a feral dog.'

'Come on, I'll help you collect your arrows.'

'Aye, well, don't go dragging your great paw along the arrow shaft when you do. It takes skill to bind them goose feathers. Something a throat-cutter wouldn't understand.'

They bickered their way across the killing field until enough bloodstained arrows had been gathered and then waited for the next attack. Side by side.

CHAPTER TWENTY-SEVEN

Blackstone waited in the field with the men but the Bretons did not return. The day grew short and as the light behind the clouds begin to diminish he led them back through the forest towards the heights. The valley was strewn with corpses: a thousand men or more must have died in the confines of the ambush and the assault higher up. The riverbank had been torn away in places and dead Bretons, either wounded by Longdon's archers or killed in the assault and fallen into the torrent, now lay twisted and caught on fallen trees and rocky outcrops at the river's margin. The force of water from the dam had flooded grassland and forest edge. The current was gentler now that the sluice gate had been closed. When Blackstone and Meulon saw the devastation they realized they had been fortunate not to have been swept to their deaths or pummelled even further along the boulder-strewn riverbed. If the river hadn't crushed them then the horde of Bretons waiting to attack would have had them at their mercy.

Blackstone led his men back towards their lines. The higher they climbed the more dead they stepped over. Men heaved their attackers' corpses downhill, clearing the assault line. Killbere strode along one length of the terraces, John Jacob on the other. Beyard and his Gascons were doing their fair share of looting the bodies before tossing them aside. Jack Halfpenny and his archers had left their vantage place to pick their way among the dead retrieving what arrows they could, and they too looted. Felton and de Harcourt's banners fluttered further to the rear.

'Looks as though Jack and his men brought down more than their fair share,' said Will Longdon.

'As did you, Will,' said Blackstone. He raised an arm towards Killbere, who acknowledged his approach.

'And Sir William will be claiming all of this as his own doing,' said Meulon as he plucked a silver-handled knife from a mercenary's belt. 'Small reward for what we did today,' he said, tucking it into his boot.

'Best to let a vain man have his glory, my friend. It was a small price to pay to get what we wanted.'

By the time they had scrambled up the terraces Killbere stood waiting.

'I thought you had gone with the fishes,' he said, grinning.

'It looks as though you had a fight on your hands,' said Blackstone.

'Nothing like the old days. We lost twenty or thirty men. Mostly Sir William's. They were untrained and ran down the damned hill like girls at a county fair. Thank Christ there were enough of them to smother these bastards. By the time they'd tripped over their swords and de Harcourt's men closed the ranks we got them organized.'

Blackstone's amused look of doubt made the veteran knight shrug and relent.

'Aye, all right,' he admitted, 'they fought well enough. But they were a breath away from being late. John here saved young Alain's neck and sent him back to fetch the lazy bastards. Not as disciplined as us but they played their part. It was a good enough day. Better had you and Meulon been at our side instead of being so damned foolish. God's blood, man, what were you thinking? A few more men and we could have pulled you out of the dam.'

'There was no time. We'd have drowned.'

Killbere glanced at Will Longdon, Perinne and the others who had fought in the ambush. 'You lads stop them down there?'

'Will did more of the killing than us,' said Perinne, nodding towards Longdon, 'but we killed those who thought they had the better of us.'

'Get the horses to the rear and then help secure the line in case those whoresons try a counter-attack.' He turned to Blackstone. 'We hurt them, Thomas, but there might be enough of them left to try their luck again.'

'No, Gilbert. They're spent. We've given the King the upper hand in his private war with the Bretons.'

Killbere grinned and spat. 'Better still, we have pissed off the French.' He looked back towards the hilltop. 'Pig-face is up there, pleased as a virgin bride.'

'I'd best go and congratulate him.'

'And then let's be about our own business, Thomas. This has whetted my appetite for a decent fight. Let's track down William Cade and the Welsh mountain goat he rides with.'

CHAPTER TWENTY-EIGHT

Sir William Felton and Louis de Harcourt stood further up the hill, just below its crest, beyond which the horses were tethered. They were bloodied, but their squires were busy cleaning their weapons and scrubbing their surcoats. The two men were stripped to their undershirts, plunging their hands into a bucket and sluicing blood from their faces. Felton looked up as Blackstone approached.

'You didn't drown then?'

'I came close enough,' said Blackstone, helping himself to the knight's wine flask. He swallowed a couple of mouthfuls and watched the two men being fussed over by their squires as they were handed bolts of cloth to dry themselves.

'Did you get any fighting done?' said Felton.

'Enough,' Blackstone answered and took another mouthful of wine.

'You're free and easy with another man's drink,' said Felton.

'And you were almost too late in committing your men. What were you waiting for? A winged angel with an invitation from the King? Killbere had to send a lad to summon you. Could you not hear the fury of it all?'

'Damn you, Blackstone. You weren't here to see the carnage that could have happened had I not thrown my men into the fray at the correct time.'

'I told you that Sir Gilbert was in command and if you had listened to him you would not have lost so many men.'

'Men serve to fight and die.' He snatched the flask from Blackstone's hand and strode to where a fresh shirt was being unpacked for him by his squire.

'You waste men's lives needlessly. Every man has his place in a battle. Throw a man's life away and you weaken everyone who fights. You have Sir Gilbert to thank for holding the line at your leisure.'

Louis de Harcourt stepped quickly between the two men because Sir William had turned and taken an aggressive couple of strides towards Blackstone. De Harcourt knew that Felton's rank should not be challenged by Blackstone, but he also knew Blackstone's reputation when it came to defiance. Thankfully his action stopped Sir William from doing anything rash. There would be only one outcome and Thomas Blackstone, had he struck the Seneschal of Poitou, or done worse, would have once again felt the wrath of his King. Despite being King Edward's enemy for so many years, and by association Blackstone's, Louis de Harcourt had now thrown in his lot with the English and felt protective towards the man who had sacrificed so much for the de Harcourt family.

'It is difficult to time when best to strike, Sir Thomas. Too soon and we would have lost the element of surprise. And then even more men would have died,' said de Harcourt.

The two men, seeing de Harcourt's gesture of reconciliation, understood in that moment that conflict between them should be avoided. Sir William grunted dismissively and sat on a fallen tree trunk as his squire helped him off with his sweat-laden shirt and into fresh linen.

'You can go your own way now, Blackstone. I have my duties to return to and de Harcourt rides with me,' said Felton dismissively.

'My men need payment. We serve the King. Sir John knows this,' said Blackstone.

'Then take your claim to him. Chandos made no mention of it to me. Besides, I have my own and Louis's men to feed, clothe and pay. Take your gang of cut-throat vagabonds and seize what you can elsewhere.'

'My men take precedence,' Blackstone insisted. 'I gave you this victory. If we had listened to you we would likely be lying dead beneath Breton hooves. You fought in other great victories standing at the Prince's side, but they were victories not of your making.'

Sir William Felton's temper broke. 'You gutter rat,' he snarled. 'You were given honour by the Prince's hand. That he knighted a common archer is not for me to condemn but when you are in the territory that I control then you take your orders from me. There is no money. There is no food. You will not benefit from our supplies or our protection. Ride on, Blackstone, and rob others but you will not thieve from me.'

Louis de Harcourt raised his hand to try and stop Felton's aggression. 'William, if he is due payment on the word of the King then he should be paid.'

'Not by me and if anyone questions my reasoning then I will tell them that the great legend Thomas Blackstone deserted the battlefield at the time of the attack.'

Louis de Harcourt was barely quick enough to step aside as Blackstone suddenly had Wolf Sword at Felton's throat. His squire reached for a knife.

'Unsheathe that blade and your master dies,' Blackstone told him.

Blood drained from Felton's face. His mouth opened and closed but no words came out. Wolf Sword was unwavering, as steady as Blackstone's voice. 'You accuse me of desertion and cowardice?'

'Thomas, in God's name. No such charge would ever be laid against you. Not while I am alive. I swear,' said de Harcourt. He saw that his words had no impact on Blackstone. 'I swear it on Jean's soul, Thomas. He loved you like a brother.'

'And I him,' said Blackstone but his sword didn't move. 'But if bad fortune befell you, Louis, this favourite of the King would slander me and my men. I would rather kill him now and let his death be a shield of truth for us all.'

Felton felt the razor-sharp edge against his throat. It would take only the slightest pressure for his throat to be cut. He was in the wrong and it was not worth dying for an ill-considered insult. 'I beg your pardon,' he said. 'I beg it freely and swear I would not cause ill will between you and the Prince or the King by such slander.' He swallowed hard even though his throat had dried. 'I spoke in bad temper and in haste.'

'I bear witness, Thomas,' said Louis de Harcourt. 'Accept his apology.'

For a moment no one who saw the exchange between the Seneschal and the scar-faced knight knew whether Blackstone would let the insult die. Felton's eyes closed when he felt a trickle of blood dribble down his neck onto his clean shirt. And then the pressure was released. He drew breath. De Harcourt sighed with relief. Blackstone lowered Wolf Sword and looked around at the men who had witnessed the argument and the near death of Sir William Felton. The silence was broken only by Wolf Sword being pushed into its scabbard.

De Harcourt and Sir William watched Blackstone turn away. He heard Louis de Harcourt speak quietly to the Seneschal: 'You should attend mass and thank Christ, William. I know how close you came to death.'

Blackstone trudged down the hill to where Killbere and the men waited. Will Longdon and Jack Halfpenny had gathered their archers and were cleaning and repairing what arrows could be used again.

'We could do with more,' said Will Longdon. 'Especially with Quenell and his men joining us.'

'They asked for that? They're Sir John's men and Quenell blamed us for Garland's death. I'll not have any bad blood, Will.'

'There is none. We've made our peace. He asked me if they could serve you.'

'And you agreed.'

'I told him I had some influence with you and if he shared his booty then I would consider it.' Will Longdon grinned. 'Thomas, a man has to have something for his efforts.'

'And have I already accepted him?'

'Oh aye. We have an agreement.'

'Did I make a good decision?'

'I would say so.'

'Then it's just as well I considered the matter carefully.'

'And you'll find others wishing to ride with us,' Longdon said, nodding to where Killbere and the men-at-arms were gathered.

The hobelar, Tait, who had first challenged Blackstone when he entered Chandos's camp, stood with Beyard. Some of the men were trading with each other, exchanging knives and silver-inlaid belts stripped from the dead. Others had found well-honed swords and decorative scabbards, spoils of war that the Bretons had seized from others and which they no longer had any use for. Killbere tugged off one of his boots and ran a hand inside it. He looked up as Blackstone approached.

'Damned nail kept digging into my foot. It was a distraction I didn't need during the fight. But Jack Halfpenny found this pair that fit me better than they do him.' Killbere changed his footwear, got to his feet and stamped the ground. 'If I didn't know better I'd say they were made for me.'

'And I'll wager the Breton who killed the man who first wore them said the same,' Blackstone said, taking his jupon from John Jacob.

'And how is the old boar on the hill?' said Killbere.

Blackstone refastened his sword belt and pulled his fingers through his hair. 'Chastised,' said Blackstone with a grin.

'Sir Thomas?' said Tait. 'Me and my men serve Sir John Chandos. There's twenty of us and now we wish to serve you.'

Blackstone looked at the rugged man and his equally vicious-looking hobelars. Some carried slight wounds; all showed signs of bloodletting in the close-quarter fight. 'You said Sir William had a whiplash tongue. Then you should know that my punishments leave a harsher mark. I hang men who rape and those who fail in their duty and cause harm to any other of my men.'

Tait nodded. 'Sir Thomas, your men have told us all we need to know. If you will have us, we will ride with you and be honoured to swear allegiance.'

'All right, your captain will be Renfred. You hold no ill will towards Germans?'

'Providing he holds none to us.'

Blackstone looked towards Renfred. The German studied the men for a moment. 'I take no argument on my commands. You obey and we will have no ill will.'

'Then we have agreement,' said Tait.

Killbere grinned. 'Well, Thomas, we build our strength back again. Beyard brings his thirty Gascons to our ranks.'

Blackstone turned to the Gascon. 'Beyard, what of your Lord de Grailly?'

'He's with the King of Navarre in the Pyrenees. He has no need of us for now. But we Gascons are sworn to Edward and the Prince of Wales, so if we fight with you, we serve them.'

'And with Tait's men that makes fifty more men at our side, Thomas,' said Killbere.

'You and your men are welcome, Beyard,' Blackstone told him. 'When we camp tonight you and Tait will bring your men to me and my captains and give me their names.'

Killbere turned his back on the men and whispered, 'And how do we pay them?'

'Felton refuses us, Gilbert. So we find Gruffydd ap Madoc and William Cade and we take back the gold that is now rightfully ours.'

'All of it? Even the King's share?'

'All of it.'

CHAPTER TWENTY-NINE

They buried their dead and rode south.

'The French army are somewhere ahead of us, Thomas,' said Killbere. 'A skirmish with a couple of hundred of d'Audrehem's men is one thing but an army of thousands might test us too far.' He grinned.

'The problem isn't only d'Audrehem's men it's the army from the north trying to catch the routiers between them. If they're using their fight against the routiers to entrap us then we keep out of their way. We secure the towns we're supposed to and then find Cade and the Welshman.'

'Debt collectors again,' Killbere moaned.

'We do the King's bidding but we find those murdering bastards, take our revenge for Peter Garland and get back the gold. But this countryside gets harsher, Gilbert, and the Auvergne is home to brigands coming up the Rhône Valley. The more men we have with us the better.' He turned in the saddle and called the Gascon captain forward. 'Beyard.'

The Captal de Buch's man spurred his horse alongside.

'Chandos will wait in the north. Like us he takes the towns for Edward but the further south we go the closer we get to those Gascons who ride with routiers. They are going to be crushed by the French,' said Blackstone. 'They have an army of thousands and your Gascon brothers will die at their hands. Would they come over to us to save themselves?'

'Without plunder? I doubt it, Sir Thomas. How else are they to be paid? They would take their chances with the French.'

'Chandos told me there was a large force of routiers down in the Rhône Valley,' said Killbere.

'And that means they might threaten Avignon and the Pope,' Blackstone added.

Beyard scratched his beard, his face wrinkled with uncertainty. 'Gascons already loyal to King Edward ride with the routiers to fill their purses and seize whatever can be had, so that when the Prince arrives, they are not beggars at his door.'

'He's right,' said Killbere. 'They've nothing to gain by coming over to us. Not now, at least. They've free rein to loot and kill but if they took your offer then they are manacled by your command.'

Blackstone knew they were right but also knew it was unlikely that his small force would be strong enough to secure all the towns decreed by the treaty. He needed help but, as Beyard and Killbere had made clear, there was only one good reason, other than loyalty, why fighting men followed one leader or another: plunder. 'I've seen Avignon threatened before and the Pope usually pays off the routiers. Once the Prince of Wales becomes the Prince of Aquitaine then the Gascons will fall under his rule, and they would not defy either him or the Captal de Buch. I can see why they wouldn't abandon the chance to extort money while they can.'

'The routiers have not scoured Gascony because of the Captal's loyalty to Edward. But the territory's borders will become greater when we and Chandos clear towns held by the French,' said Killbere. 'We must give the Gascons the power to determine their own fate.'

'Then we offer now what might be denied them later,' said Blackstone. 'The Gascons can have their pick. The treaty says the towns keep their existing privileges. I appoint a seneschal in each district and make Gascons captains of any walled town. Then they would have a foothold. All they would need to do then is bend the knee to Edward and swear their allegiance. Choosing their own territory now is better payment than gold or plunder.'

Beyard nodded at Blackstone's proposal. 'I'll wager they'll threaten the Pope, take his money and then turn to you.'

'Thomas, if they come over to you Chandos might think it's a show of strength,' said Killbere. 'That you intend to seize territory for yourself.'

'Then he'd be a fool. Gilbert, we don't know whether the French are hunting us or their attack was just misfortune, but if we stumble across a French army and they strike then it's simple enough for them to say they thought us to be skinners. Our heads will be on poles. Let us at least gather men at our back. No harm can come from it.'

'Sir Thomas, I'll take ten of my men and leave the others with you. It might take me some time to contact those I need to convince. When I send word how will I reach you?' said Beyard. 'I don't know whether I can draw the Gascons away from the other routiers. There are French and Bretons who fight at their side, and the Hungarians would want to be in the front rank if there's killing to be done. I'll choose only Gascons and only those I can trust.'

'How much time, Beyard? A couple of weeks or more, do you think?' said Killbere.

'I know my way down there. If we don't ride into trouble I will be at Avignon in fifteen days,' said the Gascon captain. 'And then however long it takes to recruit the men.'

'And we will be riding several days south,' Blackstone said. 'There's a monastery at Saint-André-de-Babineaux. You know it?'

Beyard thought for a moment. 'South from here, you say? There's a Franciscan priory I know in that valley and Saint-André is beyond it, I think. It's hard riding, Sir Thomas. Valleys and mountains and not many routes in – the River Allier is, what, west or east of it? Is that the monastery you mean?'

Blackstone nodded. 'Between the Allier and the Loire. Routiers have taken one of the walled towns nearby. Look for us at the abbey. If we ride on we will leave word. Take what supplies you need and choose your men well. Take your best. You'll need them.'

'Aye, Sir Thomas.' The Gascon captain turned his horse and cantered back to his men.

'Gilbert, are we likely to come across any of your favoured nuns at Saint-André?' Blackstone teased.

'God's tears, Thomas, if it were likely do you think I would let the likes of Will Longdon near such a place? Anyway… no, there's none that I can remember.' Killbere looked askance at a grinning Blackstone. 'And if by chance there are I will make sure your bed stays cold.' He nodded towards the horsemen riding towards them. 'Perinne and the scouts.'

Perinne and four of his men drew up. 'Sir Thomas, we've found routiers.'

'Cade and the Welshman?' said Blackstone.

The stocky fighter shook his head. 'No. Might be Bretons. Perhaps some of those who escaped the fight. But they wear the arrowhead blazon that we found at Sainte-Bernice. Same people who slaughtered the boy's parents.'

'How many?' asked Killbere.

Perinne shrugged. 'No more than we need for a decent fight. About the same as us. They're camped on broken ground. Boulders, trees, a fast-flowing stream. They've lookouts. It would be hard to get close without being seen.' He looked from Blackstone to Killbere. 'We could avoid them. Go around their flank.'

Killbere spat. Perinne grinned. The answer was obvious.

Darkness blanketed the uneven ground. The routiers' campfires cast their glow across huddled men. Their voices carried across to where Blackstone and his captains lay watching from three hundred paces away. Beyard had not yet departed with his men and he settled on the wet ground with the others.

'Will Longdon and his archers could kill half of them in their blankets,' he said.

Blackstone studied the dozen or more campfires, watching as occasionally a figure rose and cast a shadow. 'Hard to say how many there are,' he said. 'But the size of those fires means there must be a half-dozen men or more seeking their warmth. If we shoot into them many of them will scatter into the night.'

'Let's go in at dawn,' said Renfred. 'Men are stiff and cold, their bladders full and their eyes half-closed.'

'Perhaps,' said Blackstone. 'Where are their horses?'

Perinne lifted his chin, indicating the darkened bulk of boulders beyond the firelight. 'Treeline comes over those rocks. Hard ground to cover at night. I don't think we could get close enough to scatter the skinners without alerting them. We are downwind for now so they won't pick up our scent but look at the way those flames are dancing this way and that.'

'Breeze is veering,' said Blackstone.

'And no telling when it shifts behind us and those mounts get restless once their nostrils smell our stink,' said Killbere.

'Sir Gilbert,' said Meulon, 'these men are riding hard. They've covered a great distance since Sainte-Bernice. If they are good at what they do then they will be in the saddle as dawn breaks. We should kill them now.'

Killbere grunted. 'He's right, Thomas. We've their firelight to guide us.'

'I don't see any sentries posted,' said John Jacob, 'but I'll wager they'll be somewhere. I'd put them on the rising ground near those rocky outcrops. I could get close enough. The stream there and the breeze in the treetops would mask our approach.'

There was a murmuring of agreement among the men.

Blackstone glanced at the night sky. Cloud obscured the moon. 'We wait until they are curled in their blankets and the fires have gone down. Fewer shadows but enough light to guide us. Perinne, you and Renfred take a few men apiece and circle around those rocks. If their sentries are there then they might be armed with crossbows.'

Killbere sighed. 'And the last thing I want when I'm creeping around like a priest leaving a whore's bed is to have a bolt in my arse.'

Blackstone sensed the men grinning in the blackness.

'Sir Thomas,' said John Jacob. 'What about the boy? Alain de la Grave won't be easy to keep back with the horses once he learns his parents' killers are down there.'

Killbere huffed. 'Christ, Thomas,' he whispered, 'we can't take him. He'll trip over his spurs or piss himself. He's no killer.'

'They raped and mutilated his mother, Gilbert, and the man he thought of as his father was gelded and gutted. He needs to rid himself of that. He comes down with me. It's time he learnt to kill.'

CHAPTER THIRTY

Perinne and Renfred had bound their boots with torn cloth to deaden any sound of leather scraping against rock. They left their swords with the rearguard and each man was armed only with a knife. They went forward before Blackstone and the others slipped into the darkness. Ever wary of the wind shifting and betraying their scent to the horses they felt their way around the rock formation, guided by the snores of one sentry and the muffled cough of another. Renfred clambered through a break in the rocks and crawled, hand outstretched in the darkness, his fingers finding the way forward until he felt the boulder slope downward. Straining his eyes in the near blackness he made out what looked to be the dark shape of a boulder but one that hunched and moved: the shadow became a man that coughed and spat free the phlegm. Cloth and steel scraped the rock face yards away, followed by the sound of a body falling as Perinne killed the other sentry. Alerted, the wheezing sentry moved away from what little comfort he had found against the boulders. Renfred slipped over the edge and reached out, yanking back the sentry's head. The man's knees buckled and before they touched the ground a knife had been driven beneath his chin. His gurgled last gasp for life was choked with blood and the sudden flailing of his arms ended as quickly as it had begun.

Blackstone kept Alain de la Grave at his shoulder. The boy trembled with anticipation and fear but his eagerness to keep up with Blackstone's fast pace, and not stumble, gave him something to concentrate on. Spurs removed, scabbards discarded, axe, knife, mace or sword in hand, Blackstone's men had fanned out and swept into the camp. Blackstone moved quickly to the nearest fire, held a restraining arm back against the boy, and plunged Wolf Sword into the sleeping man's neck. He gestured for Alain to ram his blade into the already dead man's chest. Blackstone needed the boy to know how hard it was to penetrate muscle and bone. Alain hesitated, but then felt his blade sink into the corpse, and as the body rolled saw the blazon that he had last seen during the attack on his family at Sainte-Bernice. He jabbed the sword in again. Blackstone looked at him and nodded. Now the boy knew how to kill.

Guillouic, the bastard son of a cobbler from Croissic in south-eastern Brittany, had spent the better part of his twenty-odd years living by his wits, his blade and his ability to inflict terror. He had served with the French army off and on but preferred the freebooting life of a routier where more profit was to be had and unrestricted pleasure indulged in without the discipline of arrogant French lords. The Breton civil war suited him. Three years ago he had joined Breton brigands. A drunken fight with their leader over pay and the savagery of his victory startled even those among them who had wallowed in blood. The humble cobbler's son was a force to be reckoned with and the fury of his killing meant the leadership passed to him without challenge.

He and his men had raided south, their actions uncontested. Paid by Charles de Blois, who was backed by the French King, the plunder they seized was a bonus, like the torture and rape that was their reward when the few defenders of the walled towns fell. The Breton civil war promised to last for years and the Bretons' wave of terror had subdued towns and villages into the Limousin where de Blois held territory. And Guillouic knew that all that he and his men needed to do was to avoid the English who rode throughout France accepting allegiance from French towns and villages. He had the good sense to keep his force small. Never more than sixty or so men, enough to seize towns and scavenge off the land. Days before he and his men had seen the columns of thousands of men make their way northward. They were destined for a great battle but he and his men had kept their distance and avoided being drawn into fighting alongside so many. Better to stay quick on the hoof and to choose their own fights.

He grunted as he rolled tighter into his blanket, the warmth of the fire against his back. By the time summer came around he and his men would have enough plunder and money to see them through the following winter. Sleep proffered him twisted images scattered here and there through his dreams. They made no sense and did not immediately drag him to wakefulness. But somehow a small spark of animal intelligence warned him that the grunting sounds that been snuffling pigs rooting in a forest in the dream was something more. Sudden panic forced him instantly awake. Heart pounding, he saw figures looming out of the darkness. Where were the sentries? he thought instantly, then forgot as he saw the raiders sink their blades into his sleeping men. Their grunts of pain were barely audible. His cry of alarm stuck in his throat. If he alerted his men the intruders would be quickly drawn to him. He rolled clear and lunged into the night but his shoulder caught the legs of one of the attackers. Guillouic's body was well muscled, corded with sinew, lithe and fast. But the man he rammed barely moved from the impact. He might as well have run into a boulder. His neck snapped back and he saw a bearded face, eyes glaring down at him. A bloodied knife blade slashed down and he turned away just in time; the cut missed his throat and sliced into his shoulder. The wound seared his flesh. And then a huge fist caught the side of his head. It rocked him backwards. A fragment of light exploded in his mind and like a felled beast he slammed into the ground. This had to be a dream from which he would soon awake. The fires must have died down for he was cold. The darkness engulfed him.

Bodies lay where they had slept, blood-soaked blankets cocooning the dead. Seven routiers had survived into the grey dawn. All were wounded and sat, heads slumped, glancing here and there at their attackers, knowing that no matter how hard they begged the Englishmen who had slipped into their camp would not offer mercy. Most of the fires barely smouldered but Jack Halfpenny and Ralph Tait had gathered dry kindling and some of the fires burst back into life. Englishmen, the dawn chill hunching their shoulders, squatted and warmed themselves and then balanced cooking pots over the flames. They stepped over and around the men they had killed, their interest focused on food after their long night. The dead were going nowhere and those bodies that hampered the Englishmen from getting near the fires were thrown clear.

Guillouic sat with the survivors, his bloodstained shirt sleeve torn back and used to bind his wound. The sour taste of exhaustion and fear coated his mouth. He begged for water.

'Ask again and I'll piss on your head,' said Killbere as he walked past the defeated men.

Ralph Tait's men had been given responsibility for watching the prisoners.

'Tait, make sure these bastards aren't given anything before we hang them,' Killbere said. He looked back to the bloodied man – 'You'll die unshriven, you scum. Hell awaits you and there you'll know what thirst is' – and walked off. As he approached Blackstone he saw Meulon hand him what looked to be a scabbard belt.

'Gilbert, Meulon found this on one of the men.' Blackstone handed Killbere the belt. It was a strap finished in deep blue velvet with an ornate gilded buckle. Enamelled rosette mounts shaped by a craftsman's hand adorned its length.

'A French knight's belt. These skinners must have ambushed a scouting party. It's too small for your girth, Meulon, but it might fit me.'

'Sir Gilbert,' said Meulon, 'I will trade it for a barrel of wine and a warm woman in the next town but this was not taken by these men. It was seized when we fought d'Audrehem's French troops. I saw William Cade loot it.'

'Then these men have done business with him and ap Madoc,' said Blackstone. 'Who had the belt?'

186

Meulon gestured towards Guillouic. 'I was about to cut his throat but I saw the belt and clubbed him. The information he has might be worth more than the belt's value.'

Guillouic stared as the belligerent pock-faced veteran strode back towards him. The big man with him bore a scar down his face. He was the younger of the two but despite that the Breton could see that the tall Englishman was in command.

'On your feet,' Killbere commanded and gave Guillouic a kick.

The wounded man staggered to his feet. The loss of blood had weakened him and he swayed.

'You,' said Blackstone, pointing to a less injured man next to him. 'Hold him up.'

The routier wrapped an arm around Guillouic, taking the man's weight.

'The man who gave you this belt. You know him?' asked Blackstone.

Guillouic shook his head. 'An Englishman. Traded it for brandy we had taken from a monastery,' he said weakly.

'How many men with him?'

Guillioc shrugged. 'No more than twenty.'

'No Welshman? Three hundred riders?' said Killbere.

'That many and he needn't have traded, he'd have taken.'

Blackstone turned to Killbere. 'They've split from ap Madoc. He's riding alone again.' He addressed Guillouic. 'Which direction did he go?'

'I don't know. South, perhaps. He told us nothing.'

'How long ago?' Killbere said.

'Who knows? Sir knight. I beg you for water,' he said, avoiding Killbere's eyes.

Killbere was about to say something but Blackstone spoke first. 'You shall have water.' He called to Tait: 'Have a bucket brought from the stream for these men.'

The veteran knight scowled. 'You know what these scum did, Thomas.'

'I know but they can slake their thirst before they die. There's sufficient agony awaiting them,' said Blackstone and turned away.

The man who held Guillouic let him fall. 'Lord,' he begged, 'before I die give me brandy and in exchange I will give you information about the Englishman.'

'Tell it first,' said Blackstone, 'and you can be numbed by drink before I put a rope around your neck.'

The routier pointed to the slumped mercenary. 'This man's name is Guillouic. He leads us. I heard him speak with the Englishman who said that he had a woman whose name was Felice. And that if we wished to join him, she paid well.'

'Where is she?' asked Blackstone.

'That I don't know, lord.'

Blackstone glanced down at Guillouic. 'You?'

The Breton mercenary gave a wheezing laugh. 'Let me live and I'll take you.'

'He's lying,' said Killbere. 'He bargains, is all.'

Blackstone studied the wounded man. 'Let him drink and then hang him.'

'Then you will never find him.' Guillouic spat.

'I know the woman: Felice Allard. She is the wife of a famed French knight. You have nothing to give me.'

He watched the man's face fall as he lost his final gamble for life.

Blackstone and Killbere walked back to the men. The scent of herb-laden pottage wafted on the morning breeze, blanketing the stench of death.

'You know this woman?' said Killbere.

'I've never heard of her.'

'What? But... then perhaps he does have information.'

'No, you were right, Gilbert, he was buying time. I made up her husband's name and he didn't challenge me. But we have her name and we will find her.'

* * *

Blackstone's men went about the business of striking camp. The routiers' horses had been examined and any beasts in better condition than those serving his men were exchanged. The others were cut loose to roam the countryside. Alain de la Grave dogged Blackstone's footsteps.

'I wish to kill him,' said the young Frenchman when he learnt that it was the wounded Guillouic who had led the routiers that murdered his family so brutally.

'No, the man will hang,' said Blackstone.

Alain's face crumpled with hate. 'I beg you, Sir Thomas, let me injure him as he injured my mother and father.'

'I said, no,' Blackstone repeated. 'Your hatred has been vented on those you killed in the night.'

'They slept. I want to see his eyes when I strike him. I want to hear him scream.'

'No, he will hang.'

Tears of frustration formed in the young man's eyes. His head shook from side to side. 'It is not enough,' he said in a whisper. He turned away to join the men saddling their mounts and securing the plunder that had been stripped from the dead routiers.

Killbere gave Blackstone a quizzical look and turned away.

'What confuses you, Gilbert?'

Killbere raised a dismissive hand. 'Nothing.'

'Spit it out.'

'You have a short memory, Thomas. When the assassin killed your wife and child you brought him down with an arrow and then trampled him to death beneath the hooves of your horse. You stood by and heard him scream for mercy, you heard every bone crack and you watched him die. What is so different between that and what the boy wants?'

'He's a boy. He has a chance to learn the skill of war. If I let him kill Guillouic in cold blood it will poison him for ever. You were there when I told him that if his blood-lust cools and his mind guides his hand, then he has a chance to become a fighter. This isn't the way.'

Killbere spat. 'For God's sake, Thomas. Who among us has not stepped into hell? He's French and you deny him revenge. He'll turn against you.'

'My order stands,' said Blackstone and walked to where the surviving routiers were being led to the hanging tree. The man granted brandy in exchange for information staggered but leered, happy in his befuddled state that the reality of his death was being tempered. Guillouic was aided by one of his men. The nooses were set and the ropes quickly hauled. The kicking, choking men swung wildly for a few moments. Blackstone's men stopped breaking camp and watched them die, then, when the bodies' shudders ceased, went back to readying their departure.

Blackstone looked across to where Alain de la Grave stared at the corpses swaying gently in the breeze. Blackstone thought of his own son's courage, which was untainted by a thirst for revenge. Henry Blackstone bore the goodness of his mother and the defiance of his father in his heart. It was that thought and the memory of meeting a brave man struck down with leprosy, abandoned by his family, who wished nothing more than for his son to live, that made Blackstone want to give this boy a chance at life without the bitter desire to kill in cold blood. It was a poor inheritance. Blackstone was no stranger to it.

CHAPTER THIRTY-ONE

The woman lay naked across a sable bed covering. The fire in the bedchamber's grate burned brightly, its glow shading the contours of her body. Her long dark hair feathered her breasts. She lay with her arm outstretched, sweat from lovemaking glistening on her aroused nipples as her breathing settled. She stretched her legs from the pleasure as William Cade, breathless from his exertion, rolled off her and then eased onto his side, pulling his fingers through his sweat-soaked hair.

He grinned. 'Each time I return your lust exhausts me.'

Unperturbed she slid from the bed and trod lightly across animal-skin rugs that cushioned the fresh reed floor covering. She poured water from a jug into a bowl, wiped down her body and rid herself of his seed. 'Then perhaps you should find yourself an old crone,' she said without turning to face him, knowing her rebuke would sting. She could almost feel him flinch.

'You're a bitch on heat, nothing more,' he said, enjoying the malice of his words. He reached for the bottle of wine on the stool next to the bed, which was fit for a queen. The embroidered canopy kept the flies and spiders away and the feather mattress was thick and firm enough to support the weight of two rutting bodies without sagging. The bolster had a quilted cover as a headrest so soft it near suffocated a sleeping man. Linen sheets cooled the body after exertion but comforted the skin during the night. It was the most luxurious bedchamber he had ever slept in, fit for any fighting man who had gold in his purse and a willing whore beneath him. And if rumour were to be believed this ornately decorated bed had once graced a royal palace and a royal mistress. How it came to be here was a story yet to be told. Unless, of course, Cade thought, the bitch had been the mistress.

'Did you fuck the King?' he asked, eyes closed, concentrating on the bottle tilting to his lips. He drank deeply. There was no answer. He felt her next to him and then the tip of a knife kept his chin tilted and the wine spilled down his chest onto the sheets. Wide-eyed he stared at her. At any other time her nipples pressing against him would be arousing but now whatever heat had been in his groin had cooled. 'Christ, woman, what are you doing?' he spluttered. Her free hand grasped his hair and pulled his head back further as the blade levelled across his windpipe. He was uncertain whether the wetness he felt was blood or wine, but he dared not move.

'I use you, don't ever forget that. You are my pleasure, not the other way around. The moment you no longer satisfy my need is when you will find yourself in the courtyard below with the other routier scum.' She put her lips closer to his ear. And whispered: 'I take pleasure in killing. Always remember that. And do not ever forget your place here.'

The blade tightened against his taut throat. He could see the fire glow in her eyes. 'Yes,' he whispered. 'I understand.' A slight tug on his hair prompted the good manners that had been abandoned by his impertinence. 'Countess,' he added.

Freed from her threat he gathered his clothes and then – telling himself that she was a mad bitch of a widow but at least she paid him well for the prisoners he delivered to her every once in a while – he dressed in the poorly lit passageway. She was a source of income that he could not afford to abandon, nor was he prepared to lose the opportunity of sharing her bed. She might be high born, but to him she was little more than a common whore – albeit, he had to admit, a dangerous one. The thrill of their sexual coupling outweighed any fear that she might carry out her threat.

William Cade had recruited more men to ride with him. They

were a disparate group of brigands, men who rode in small groups that he had convinced to join him and his band. The extra men numbered no more than fourteen: three Englishmen, seven French, a German, a Hungarian and two Spanish who had travelled north to find more prosperous territory. They had been fighting for the Spanish Princes in a quest for plunder, and had been sorely disappointed when the warring parties had agreed a truce. There would soon be a surge of mercenaries from Aragon and Castile that would add to the roving bands that scoured the southern provinces of France. William Cade had given his new recruits a dozen gold pieces. All of them had gladly thrown in their lot with the Englishman.

And died an agonizing death.

He clattered down the staircase into the courtyard where his men were eating their breakfast. His men slept alongside their horses in the stables, watched from a distance by the Countess's men, all of them French soldiers who greatly outnumbered the routiers. He plunged his head into a horse trough and glanced at his followers. None dared offer any comment on his good fortune in being taken to the woman's bed.

It was two weeks since he had returned with his hapless victims and now four of the routiers he had enticed to join him swung from a gibbet. An Englishman had died first, grateful for the rope after torture had been inflicted on him. Wooden cages held the others. The Spanish had sworn and threatened when seized, their sword skills mortally wounding four of the Countess's men. They were hamstrung by their guards as the Hungarian made a run for it. The garrison troops had strict orders only to maim, not to kill, and two crossbow bolts in his legs brought him down and rendered him helpless. The bloodied bolts still protruded from his legs, denying him any chance of comfort in the cage. The German had proved the most difficult to capture. He had wheeled his horse the moment they entered through the town gates – some deep-embedded instinct had alerted him that a trap was about to be sprung. It took several pikemen to kill his horse but even then he

193

fought with such ferocity that he killed four of those who attacked him. By the time he was brought down the Countess had decided that such courage deserved a long agonizing death.

It was the French prisoners who had begged the loudest for mercy. Battle-hardened men who had fought for the King, they protested they had served loyally.

'And now you slaughter at will,' the Countess had said. 'And there is a price to pay for the road you have chosen to travel.'

Two of them had been dragged out of the cage and taken through the gates to a nearby river. Hands bound, they were secured with ropes and tossed into the current. As they dipped below the surface, twisting their faces away from the surging water, Cade's men hauled the ropes and played them like fish until finally they drowned.

The torture of the captured men went on for days, each morning bringing more pain and suffering. The German was hanged, drawn and quartered. His screams silenced the crowds who gathered to watch him die. Snarling dogs darted forward to snatch at his entrails and turned on each other as they fought over the offal. The blood was sluiced and then the next man to die was dragged out, screaming for mercy. But the Countess had no mercy. Her acts were as callous as those committed by any routier.

William Cade's men were a means to an end for the Countess. Mercenaries had slaughtered her family two years before and she had sworn eternal revenge on routiers. Inflicting cruel death on those captured gave her a twisted pleasure. She paid Cade and his men to entice other routiers to their deaths. Cade received an extra bounty but he knew there was always the threat that he would one day be seized and put to death by her. He was a turncoat. The English mercenary had sold his sword to the French Crown two years before, and had been sent by the Dauphin to help gather taxes. Countess Catherine had offered him the opportunity to earn more money and his master the Dauphin had liked the idea of routiers being entrapped – and an Englishman was the perfect tool. As a reward the Dauphin had forgiven the Countess the tax she owed. Let her spin her web, Charles had decided, and whomever she ensnared meant one less mercenary flaying the land.

Cade spat and gestured his men to join him. There was still one caged prisoner waiting to die and before the Countess came to watch his agonized death there was time enough for Cade to have some sport with him.

CHAPTER THIRTY-TWO

Sir John Chandos stood before King John and the Dauphin Charles. The King sat on an ornate gilded chair; his son was similarly seated but a half-pace behind his father. Bucy and a handful of senior counsellors fanned out behind them. The chill in the great hall at the royal manor at Vincennes was eased by a roaring log fire. Chandos was no longer dressed as a fighting man but presented himself as the diplomat he was, wearing his cloak bearing the blazon of a Knight of the Garter. The English King's representative was known for his negotiating skills, empowered to make the demands on the French necessary for Edward's territories to be secured under the peace treaty but without causing offence. Despite earning the respect of all who had dealings with him, Chandos, in the eyes of the French Crown, represented the hubris of victory over them. He had fought at every major victory – Crécy and Poitiers – and King Edward had given him the stronghold at Saint-Sauveur, once belonging to the Norman traitor Godfrey de Harcourt. Chandos not only had the right to demand the speedy delivery of the ceded towns, but he also held the key strategic castle that would allow another English invasion through the Cotentin peninsula.

'We have heard that you have gained the loyalty of our subjects in Poitou due to your even-handed treatment of them,' said the King. 'That we should bear their loss is painful enough but to hear that you appear to have treated them more kindly than our own Seneschal had done causes us further grief.'

'Sire, it was not I who gained their affection, it was your concern for them. All I did, highness, was to guarantee them the privileges that you had already bestowed upon them.'

King John gave a rueful smile. The loss was no more bearable but Chandos's words were diplomatic and offered a modicum of healing balm to a monarch stripped of wealth and swathes of his country.

'And now you continue to pluck the fruits of France and lay bare our orchard,' said the King. 'Our cousin Edward is determined to see us beggars at his door.'

Simon Bucy winced. It would serve no purpose to antagonize Sir John. He was the King of England's voice in France. There were already difficulties with some of the French towns refusing to swear loyalty. The strategic port of La Rochelle was due to be handed over to Edward but the citizens had made additional demands to protect their privileges. They seemed less concerned with the territorial gains of Edward and more with their own wellbeing. King John had been obliged to send Marshal Arnoul d'Audrehem to placate them before he took the army south to deal with the routiers. It was, thought Bucy, as if the French were fighting a fire on different fronts.

'Sire,' Chandos continued, 'Edward wishes only for the peaceful transition of the towns and territory ceded to him. I am charged with securing—'

'And what else are you charged with, Sir John?' the King interrupted, unable to restrain his characteristic rage at anyone opposing his will and inflicting theirs on him. 'We have heard that Englishmen have defeated a Breton army. Your men, Sir John? William Felton and the last of the de Harcourt traitors, Louis?'

Sir John Chandos did not avert his gaze. 'Sire, the Bretons were routiers. The very scum we both wish to defeat.'

The open sore that was Brittany seeped poison. Bucy knew that Chandos's reply was a veiled challenge. The French King was fighting a proxy war against the English for Brittany and for him to openly admit to Edward's representative that he was funding routiers would inflame the ongoing tribulations that beset France. Chandos had trapped him.

Bucy quickly stepped forward in an effort to deflect the King from making matters worse, but the Dauphin leaned forward, a raised hand cutting off Bucy's reply to Chandos. 'Sir John, the defeat of the Breton routiers came as a surprise to us all. We had heard there were too few English and Gascons to challenge their journey north. That Felton and Louis de Harcourt were successful was no mean feat. I wonder if you employed routier captains to help you achieve this success. Men like... Thomas Blackstone.'

'Your highness, Sir Thomas is no mercenary captain. He is tasked by Edward to aid me and others in securing the towns. That is his role.'

'Was he there, Sir John? Did he fight?' insisted the Dauphin.

'He was there and, yes, he fought.' Chandos was obliged to answer truthfully. The animosity between the House of Valois and Thomas Blackstone would always cause friction in the ongoing negotiations.

The Dauphin leaned back, satisfied that he had been able to put Sir John on the defensive but more importantly that he had found out where Blackstone was.

Bucy felt caught between the King and his son. It was important to change the subject away from another defeat and the Dauphin's obsession with Blackstone.

'The transfer of the towns according to the treaty is of prime importance,' he said.

'And, with respect, it has been going too slowly,' said Chandos.

'Sir John, there have been delays, of that we are aware. His highness has done all he can to give his blessing and assurances to our people but Marshal Boucicaut has been confined to his sick bed. There are inevitable delays.'

The French commissioner for the transfer of the towns, Boucicaut, had lain sick for weeks and Chandos had said little. The time had been well spent raising troops to defeat the Bretons but now that there had been some success he would apply pressure. 'I am aware of his illness but now we must press forward. He must accompany me or we shall request a new commissioner.'

'Must?' fumed the King.

'Sire,' said Chandos, 'it is your highness's honour that I fear for. Boucicaut's illness might be seen as delaying tactics. It is possible that it is his loyalty to you that makes him drag out his debilitation.'

Bucy barely kept the exasperation from his voice. Chandos had diplomatically deflected the King's anger. 'We are grateful for your concern, Sir John. We will do everything we can to assist you.'

The King suddenly stood. The Dauphin got to his feet. The angry scowl on the King's face seemed to herald an insult to Sir John, but he turned on his heel and left the room, followed by his advisers. Only Bucy and the Dauphin remained.

'Our father has returned to a ruined, land, Sir John. Like a man entering his home to find that thieves have stripped everything of value. It is a difficult time,' said the Dauphin.

Chandos bowed. 'I understand, your grace.'

'We will adjourn,' said Bucy, 'and await the King's pleasure.'

Sir John bowed again, and made his exit.

The Dauphin waited until the heavy doors closed behind the English envoy. He turned to Bucy. 'You see, Simon? Blackstone is still used against us. You cannot dismiss his continuing interference in our lives.'

'He plays a small part,' said Bucy.

'Do you not hear what the people are calling him? Wolf of the North. He strikes fear wherever he goes. How does a man gain such a reputation other than by inflicting humiliation and terror on our citizens? The plague savages France but we are flayed by a scourge of wolves. Ravening beasts led by the likes of Thomas Blackstone.'

Bucy's allegiance still hovered between the King and his son. If Blackstone was snared and killed as the Dauphin had previously intimated, that might give succour to the King. Was trying to seize Blackstone a path worth pursuing when France was being ravaged by brigands and seized by the English King? His every instinct told him that it was not worth considering. All their previous attempts to kill Blackstone had ended in failure. The men who followed Blackstone were few, and his violence was directed against the

Bretons and mercenaries who stood in Chandos's path. But there was always the *chance* that the Dauphin could deliver a victory against Blackstone. It would diminish King Edward and raise the spirits of the French and their monarch. As he pondered, Bucy realized that, without him being fully aware of it, he had actually made the decision to align himself closer to the Dauphin. But his deep-seated loyalty to King John died hard.

'I look forward to hearing how you plan his capture and death,' said Bucy.

The Dauphin sniffed, blew his nose into a handkerchief and then discarded it. A servant stepped forward and retrieved it; another of the Dauphin's staff offered a fresh one. 'When a wolf approaches a trap,' said the Dauphin, dabbing his nostrils, 'he is wary. He will often avoid poisoned bait because his unerring instinct tells him to do so. Offer a ravening beast choices, ultimately it makes no difference which one he decides to take. The trick, Simon, is to be the one offering them.'

Bucy was none the wiser. He was still not being told what the plan was. Bucy wondered whether the Dauphin's idea to seize Blackstone was so beyond the realm of likely success that he did not wish to divulge it.

'When will you tell me, your grace?' Bucy said.

The Dauphin's watery gaze studied him. 'Our thoughts are not for our father's ears, Simon.'

There was the test of loyalty again. The tug that would yank him clearly into the Dauphin's confidence and make certain that Bucy gave him his full support. He could back out now, excuse himself, tell the Dauphin that it should be discussed once Sir John Chandos had left Vincennes. To buy time to consider the best action to take as he went between father and son. But then, he suspected, he would never know. Would never be embraced. And Bucy had once before experienced that visceral taste of lust on his tongue when it seemed Blackstone would be slain. The emotion repelled and excited him simultaneously.

'He will never hear those thoughts from me, your grace.'

The Dauphin's parchment skin stretched into what passed for a smile as he bared his yellowed teeth. Spittle gathered at the corners of his mouth. It was the face of a cunning rodent about to feed. 'Very well. The Visconti have still not produced in full the money owed for our sister's betrothal. That money is needed to finish paying the ransom for our father into the grasping hands of the English King. There was a vendetta between Bernabò Visconti and Thomas Blackstone. It is thought to be settled. Perhaps it is. Time has passed. There has been no threat. No attempt. But we know the Italians, Simon: they brood; their feuds fester. So who is to say that the Viper of Milan has not sent agents into Florence to seek out Blackstone's son?'

Bucy managed to stop his mouth from opening and closing like a beached fish. Had the Dauphin commissioned the assassination of the boy?

'Sire? To what purpose would you have Blackstone's son killed?'

'If I cannot snare and kill Blackstone here in France then we must at least rid ourselves of him. If his boy dies at the hand of an assassin Blackstone will believe it to be the Visconti who have reached beyond their walls and had the boy slain. He will go to Florence. He will then wage war against the Visconti. He will be gone.' The Dauphin smiled at Bucy again. 'Simon, we have laid traps and one of them will snare him. And if he slips the noose of one then he will find himself in another.'

CHAPTER THIRTY-THREE

The vendetta between Bernabò Visconti and Thomas Blackstone had been settled on the killing ground outside the walls of Milan little more than a year before, when Blackstone slew Bernabò's bastard son. The swordsman had arranged the assassination of Blackstone's wife and daughter and justice had been delivered by Wolf Sword's honed steel. The bad blood between the Lord of Milan and the scar-faced Englishman had been settled. Blackstone's act of revenge had allowed his son Henry to take up his studies in Florence under the watchful eye of Niccolò Torellini. The Florentine banking family, the Bardi, supported King Edward's conquest of France and fate had drawn the banking family's priest, Torellini, ever closer to the English King. The Italian acted as a go-between for the English Crown and his master, and he delivered information from his spies who moved in the shadows of the courts of Paris and Milan.

Father Niccolò Torellini knew that the will of the Almighty had placed him in a position of guardianship over Thomas Blackstone, and now his son Henry. What other reason could there have been for Torellini to be the one summoned by the English King to give Thomas Blackstone the last sacrament when he fell near mortally wounded at Crécy? The years had passed and fate had entwined their lives. And so it was that when the vendetta had ended Henry, now in his fifteenth year, had been sent to Florence to continue his studies. He was safe in Florence and the privilege of study was his greatest joy. Henry Blackstone's intelligence indicated that as soon as he completed his secondary schooling and entered university he would continue his studies in Latin so that he might be considered for training in one of the professions, perhaps a notary or lawyer. Father Torellini had been as much a guardian as well as mentor and there was mutual respect between the priest and Henry's father. The boy wished never to bring shame on his father's name and even though his classmates' jibes about his heritage were sometimes barbed, like any teenager's hot-headed, thoughtless words, Henry Blackstone let them wash over him. What were words when he had faced violent death? He avoided trouble and never spoke of the terror and savagery in his past, nor of the time he had been obliged to kill to save his mother and young sister. Those experiences had matured him and resilience was embedded beneath his modest demeanour. What Henry Blackstone did not realize was that Torellini's influence ensured that there were those who shadowed him as an added precaution against his father's enemies. A precaution that proved necessary.

Three weeks ago, after his regular class, Henry Blackstone had left his secondary school and visited his tutor. Commune schools were notorious for rowdy students. When the incident that nearly cost him his life occurred it was thought to be a simple act of aggression on the part of youths from another district. Florence was divided into four quarters and as he was hurrying back from his lessons for a game of football with fellow classmates, Henry ran through a piazza in the Santa Croce quarter, then ducked along a narrow street, a well-trodden path home. District pride was flaunted by each quarter displaying its own banner and if violence broke out between one neighbourhood and another the banners would flutter and street gangs would draw blood. It took little to cause offence and even an unintended insult that damaged another's pride could spark a fight. Such *umori*, erupting into running street fights, were not uncommon. And Henry Blackstone's school had recently beaten another commune school from Santa Croce in a wrestling match, with Henry playing a part in his team's success.

He had been cornered by four youths, older, taller and stronger than him. They taunted him for being an Englishman, then threatened him for crossing their district, something he had done on numerous occasions without incident as he went back and forth to his tutor. He had tried to talk his way out of a situation that he knew could quickly turn dangerous but the youths' leader struck out. Henry took the first blows and tasted blood; then he half turned and used the aggressor's weight to help wrestle him to the ground. With a surge of strength he delivered a blow to the youth's throat. Choking for breath, the youth writhed as Henry rolled clear. His defence had momentarily surprised the other three but their disbelief ended quickly when one of them unsheathed a dagger. Henry snatched at the knife in the fallen youth's belt and crouched, blade held low, ready to strike. Everything he did was instinctive; fear honed into grim determination, no less than when he had been forced to kill years before. Then he had been in the company of men who knew the real meaning of violence. He had shared danger with English bowmen and seen his father lead men into battle. This attack was little more than a feeble reflection of what he had experienced.

He made no sound. He issued no challenge. His eyes locked onto the most determined of the three who danced forward, jabbing and slashing. The other two held back. The attack was ineffective and it was obvious the youth lacked the skill needed. He had only bluster backed by strength. Henry dodged again, head tucked in, feet dancing left and right, looking for an opening. Enraged at his lack of success his attacker threw himself forward with what he thought would be a killing strike. Henry Blackstone saw it coming and allowed the blade to stab forwards, then sidestepped and rammed his own knife into the youth's groin. The boy's screams echoed through the colonnades as blood pumped in squirts with every heartbeat. He sat in his own pool of blood, hands clasped to his groin. Henry stood ready for the other two to attack but when they saw the result of their friend's attempt they turned and fled along with their leader. Henry looked down at the youth, who was slipping into unconsciousness, his body tilting as if falling into sleep. The boy tried to say something but his life was already slipping away.

Henry knew the alarm had been raised and that the state police, the Eight of the Guard as they were known, would soon arrive. He threw down the knife, wiped the blood from his hands, then gathered his fallen books and sat on the colonnade's steps. His hands trembled; shock from the sudden violence arrived before the police. He breathed slowly and deeply and calmed himself. In the few minutes it took to regain his composure he watched his attacker die.

Le Stinche, the municipal prison, had stood for sixty years and the place reeked. Putrid vomit and excrement assailed Henry's nostrils as he and his police escort approached downwind along the Via del Luvio. Men, women and children were separated inside the prison walls and he was grateful that he was placed in a single cell. There was barely enough light to see the scuffed straw on the floor that served as a bed or the wooden pail for his ablutions. Cries of agony punctuated with screams of excruciating pain echoed around the damp walls. He shuddered. Torture was a daily occurrence in Le Stinche and no matter how hard he tried to block out the terrified sounds he could not. He found a prayer to recite until the monotony of his whispered words made him fall asleep.

He awoke in darkness, so black that he could not see his hand in front of his face. It had to be night. He rolled into the straw and curled in on himself. Whatever the outcome of his arrest he suspected he would need his strength – it was a lesson learnt from his father – so he let himself sleep once more.

A key turned in the lock and the heavy door opened. He blinked awake without any idea of how long he had slept. A dark-cloaked figure pressed past the jailer. It was the same man who escorted him to Florence, one of the hospitaller order, the Knights of the Tau, who were sworn to offer protection to those travelling between places of worship on pilgrimage. If Fra Pietro Foresti was here, Henry knew, then it had been Niccolò Torellini who had sent him.

'Come,' said the cloaked figure and without waiting for any reply turned away from the door.

Once they reached the street Henry blinked in the sunlight. The Tau knight strode ahead along the northern side of the prison walls onto the Via del Palagio, past vegetable sellers on the other side of the street who were crying out, enticing shoppers to buy their wares.

'My school's not down here,' said Henry.

'Did I give you permission to speak?'

'No, but this is the wrong way.'

Fra Foresti ignored him.

'May I speak, Fra Pietro?'

'You're an educated boy. Had you employed that education and spoken to those who attacked you, your circumstances might not be as they are.'

Henry Blackstone kept pace with the striding hospitaller.

'Well?' said Fra Foresti. 'Rats chewed your tongue in Le Stinche?'

'You had not given me permission to speak,' said Henry.

Fra Foresti slapped him across the back of his head. It stung. Henry winced. Fra Foresti had not broken stride. 'You're insolent.'

'I meant no offence,' said Henry. Although the boy had appeared disrespectful, the opposite was the truth. Another of the young Tau knight's order had died trying to save Henry's mother and sister just over three years before. 'They were intent on wounding me, perhaps more. Words would have been of no use, Fra Pietro.'

'A civilized man only kills when every avenue has been explored.'

'There was no avenue,' said Henry. 'They blocked it with their knives.' He cast a glance at the Tau knight. He felt certain he saw the corner of his mouth twitch in what might have been the beginning of a smile.

As they walked past a merchant's house Fra Foresti suddenly grabbed Henry's collar and pushed him into the doorway. He glanced up and down the street, nodded to someone unseen in the crowd behind them and then pushed open the heavy, ornately carved door. A servant ran from the cool interior of the house. From what Henry could see the servant had been expecting them and with a gesture urged them to follow him. They strode across marble tiled floors beneath a vaulted portico, then stepped into a colonnade bordering a fragrant garden with the comforting sound of a gurgling fountain. Henry saw that there was a gallery on each of the two floors of the house and silk curtains swayed in the breeze; there was little doubt that the dwelling belonged to a wealthy Florentine merchant. They followed the servant up the wide steps to the first-floor gallery. A door was opened and they stepped inside. A man in his sixties, his clothing denoting his status and wealth, bowed in greeting and respect to the Tau knight. Then he turned on his heel and left the gallery through another door. The room extended across the windows and the Tau knight stepped around the room's dividing wall and looked back at him. Henry stepped forward and saw Father Niccolò Torellini sitting in a chair in front of the open window, the delicate silk blinds moving gently from the breeze.

'Father Torellini,' said Henry, bowing.

'Henry, we thought you had been involved in a street brawl but it appears there was more to the attack than we thought.' He gestured to a table that held food and drink. 'Eat.'

Fra Foresti stepped to the window as Henry reached hungrily for the tray of cut meats and flagon of wine. He forced himself to refrain from stuffing his mouth like a starving man. As desperate as he was to eat and drink he knew he was being observed by the influential bankers' priest.

'Since you came to Florence under my protection I have had you watched and followed. The incident that took place yesterday seemed at first observance to be nothing more than rival youths fighting among themselves. You moved so quickly through the crowds the man I had following you lost sight of you. No matter, you are unhurt and another's blood has stained the pavement. We traced the other three boys. They were persuaded to confess.'

Henry washed down the meat with a mouthful of wine. Being persuaded to confess meant only one thing. He imagined the screams he had heard in prison belonging to those boys.

'The boy you killed was Filippo Bascoli. He came from a poor family, like the other three, and had been paid by a stranger to attack you. They intended to kill you.'

'Who paid him?' said Henry. His stomach had knotted and the food stuck halfway in his gut. If someone had been bribed as an assassin then others would follow.

Torellini nodded as if he had read his thoughts. 'They failed this time. None of the boys knows who approached their dead friend. He gave them a small payment to go along with him. We are faced with a dilemma, Henry. If a rich man's son whom you might have injured in sport, or insulted, sought to cleanse his wounded pride by paying these young men, then we do not know whether the death of the antagonist will stop him from doing so again. If it is an extension of the vendetta from the Visconti against the Blackstone family, then assuredly they will try again.'

'I could continue my studies in another city. Would they find out?'

'You are right, that might serve the purpose and secure your safety. I have sent for your clothes.'

'And my books?'

'And your books,' Torellini said smiling. 'But we will not take the risk of relocating you. The *fratelli* of Tau are sworn to protect pilgrims and as it happens a small party are due to travel to Canterbury. Four of the Knights of the Tau safeguard their journey along the Via Francigena. I too will travel. We go to our ally the Marquis de Montferrat in Lombardy, a friend to your father, and his guides will take us across the pass in the Alps. Then we will ride to the Pope at Avignon. The Bardi have a house there where you and I and Fra Foresti will stay.'

'I remember that house, Father Torellini. You once took my mother and us children there when the Savage Priest hunted us.'

'Quite so, Master Henry. Well remembered. It seems that the name of Blackstone will always draw those seeking death to your family. For now we are guests of a friend. We are safe and I have men watching the street. I have arranged for you to bathe and sleep here and then we leave at first light. Our party will separate until we are beyond the city walls. Each group will leave by different gates in case there are people still looking for you. We will use the Porta della Giustizia.' Torellini saw the significance of the east gate cross Henry's features. It was where criminals were hanged. 'Yes, Henry, you will see those who attacked you hanging from the gibbet. They attempted murder and had they been allowed to live they would have spoken of your survival. That news will be known soon enough, no doubt, but we must delay it reaching the ears of those who commissioned the crime. The harshest sentence was passed on them. They were hanged this morning.'

Henry felt a twinge of regret for the three boys. They had been bribed to accompany the killer and now they had paid the price. Boys from poor families dying for a few pitiful coins in their purse.

'Will I stay at Avignon and continue my studies?'

'No, Henry. I doubt that even there you are safe. There is only one place where you will be. Once we arrive I will find out where your father is and deliver you to his side.'

CHAPTER THIRTY-FOUR

Blackstone knew that finding the woman called Felice was a near impossibility. They would question villagers and itinerant travellers as they rode further south and perhaps that fickle bitch Fate would bless him with the information he needed. William Cade and Gruffydd ap Madoc had obviously separated and the hordes of mercenaries that were known to be gathering in the south would soon be confronting the French army. After Guillouic's men had been killed Beyard had left to ride south to try and recruit other Gascons to join Blackstone. Distances proved hard to predict accurately and Blackstone's intended week's ride to the monastery at Saint-André-de-Babineaux took twelve days once they had rested after killing Guillouic and his men. Their route crossed broken ground, coarse grassland and boulders that made the going hard, and rivers that flowed in strength, which meant the men took longer to find a ford. They had to be careful in the mountains and forests to find a route that did not place them on narrow tracks where an ambush could be sprung. The vast Auvergne wilderness could not be policed easily by the French and was a favoured retreat for routiers when conditions became difficult in the lowland areas. Once gathered in strength they would use the mountainous terrain to sweep down into the Loire valley and beyond. But the routiers were not completely invulnerable. Food and supplies were short in this harsh landscape, which meant they could be isolated and hunted down by local lords and their militia.

Alain de la Grave had remained sullen during the slow trek south and bore the brunt of John Jacob's temper when he failed to attend to his duties in an efficient manner each night the men camped. John Jacob said he wished Henry was still with them as his page rather than the self-centred French boy. Blackstone had said little to Alain but he could see that resentment still burned in the boy. Killbere's advice to kick his arse was ignored. Young men needed time to wrestle with their grief. Anger was Alain's response to it, Blackstone told him.

By the time Blackstone and his men sighted the monastery at Saint-André-de-Babineaux it seemed the boy had accepted his lot. As Blackstone's men approached the widening valley they rode through scattered hamlets, with small timber-framed houses hugging close together and tumbling downhill boulder-like: a handful on the approach; a dozen more further on within the valley, on left and right. Most of these small hovels had fallen thatch roofs. Some were burnt out; others had collapsed through neglect. There was no sign of life. The wicker pens that had once held livestock were broken down or rotten. Forlorn doors swung half open on snapped leather hinges.

'Skinners have been here, Sir Thomas,' said Meulon. 'A while back, but they left nothing.'

'Except the monastery,' said Will Longdon, pointing towards the honey-coloured stone buildings in the distance that had been built into the lower craggy slopes. Some of the cloistered buildings bore grey slate roofs, others warm terracotta tiles. A four-storey tower rose up beyond its small church. Other buildings sat in a regulated square design around the central courtyard. The monastery had a fine view across the valley floor and was bathed in the southern light and warmth for much of the day.

John Jacob rang the bell at the entrance. Moments later a leather-faced monk opened the viewing hatch. John Jacob declared that Sir Thomas Blackstone, King Edward of England's envoy, requested hospitality for himself and another knight and their men. He passed through the document bearing the orders given to Blackstone by Sir John Chandos. The King's seal would give the prior sufficient assurance that the men at his walls offered no threat. The hatch closed and the men waited as the sound of sandals scuffing the stone floor retreated. It seemed that no sooner had they gone than they hurriedly returned.

'Told to get his arse back to the gate and let a King's envoy be given shelter,' grunted Killbere. 'I need a hot bath and meat on my plate. Benedictines are a sour lot but if they have a misericord then at least they'll break the rules and eat meat.' He suddenly looked concerned. 'There'll be meat, d'you think? I didn't catch any stench of livestock.'

'Gruel most likely,' teased Blackstone as the gate was opened and the monk gestured them towards the stables and dormitory. 'Gruel and sore knees. We'll be expected to pray for our supper.'

'Then I shall pray they let us kill a pig or have a ham already prepared in their smoke house,' said Killbere as they dismounted in front of the stables. John Jacob took Blackstone's horse's reins and quickly led him into a far stall away from the others.

'Captains, see to the horses – we'll pay for feed. Then bed down in the dormitory. Tait,' Blackstone called, 'in case you and your men haven't been guests at a monastery before, we do not drink ourselves into a stupor, we do not fight and we attend prayers at vespers and matins. We are under the prior's roof and we behave accordingly.'

'Aye, Sir Thomas. Understood,' said the hobelar.

The porter monk stood back, waiting for Blackstone to join him. 'I'll pay my respects,' said Blackstone. 'Coming?'

Killbere's face crumpled. He glanced around at the monks in their black habits who tended their vegetable gardens. 'I am never comfortable surrounded by scurrying crows pecking away in the dirt. I'll stay with the men.'

'As you wish,' said Blackstone and followed the gatekeeper monk.

'Thomas,' Killbere hissed, putting fingers between his lips indicating food. 'Don't forget to ask about the meat.'

Blackstone followed the porter past a wood yard and vegetable plots where a dozen monks bent at their labours. Some were lay brothers, not tonsured, and used mostly for labour to alleviate the burden on the monks whose time would be better spent in study and prayer. Most likely local men who had sought sanctuary from the threat of brigands and who wanted little more than a dry bed and a meal each day. They dared to raise their cowl-covered heads, giving the tall fighting man a sideways glance before quickly returning to their tasks. Opposite the stone-laid path that Blackstone trod was an arched entrance leading to the church and cloisters and beyond that the quickening breeze told his nose that there was livestock. He went through the arch and saw goats, sheep and cows penned in the distance and protected by walled enclosures. A number of two-storey buildings extended beyond one side of the church, and opposite these were the granary, bakery and workshops. He guessed that there would be near enough forty monks and a prior living there. They were self-sufficient with vegetables, livestock, milk and cheese, and honey if they had hives out on the edge of the trees that ran alongside the soft meadow valley beyond the walls.

The weathered porter moved quickly into the cloisters. The dull light was still bright enough to expose the column's capitals; carved grimacing faces stared blindly at Blackstone as he went deeper into the shadows. Blackstone's stonemason's eye admired the skill of the craftsmen who had cut and laid the walls hundreds of years before. The old monk stepped aside, ushering Blackstone into a bare room with a boarded corner that served as a bed, and gestured silently for him to wait. The monks indulged in speech only after midday prayers and the bell for sext had already started its steady clanging. Blackstone looked through the small window. The monks had abandoned their tools and were washing their hands in a water trough before hurrying to prayer. Other monks in ancient times had planned these buildings carefully, he thought. A tributary that tumbled down from the forested hills must feed their well. It was a mystery to him why such a place had not been pillaged for the wealth of its food if not for any silver in its chapel. There would be reliquaries and plate and most likely relics of saints that could be plundered.

Blackstone ran a hand across the bare-planked bed nook. The walls were boxed with the same wood. At least that would offer some warmth from the chill of the stone walls. He had shared a room similar to these in another monastery a lifetime ago with his wife and children. They had been pursued by a vile enemy then but had escaped. Almost. Blackstone had been obliged to abandon Christiana and she had been raped. It had been John Jacob who had rescued her and saved Blackstone's son Henry. The room suddenly pressed in on him. He stepped outside, ever wary of a situation that seemed normal in violent times. Could these monks be something else? Disguised routiers? Did they draw outsiders in and kill them in their sleep? He cursed himself for having such thoughts. Better to concentrate on where he and his men might make a stand if this place were attacked. That series of small stone houses that were, he guessed, given over to retreat or meditation? Each had a walled garden so anyone attempting to strike hard and fast would have sufficient obstacles in their path. If his own men were caught in the open during the coming days this monastery could serve as a stronghold. All these inner walls would make it a good defensive position.

Time passed and his thoughts settled. There was no denying that the solitude of the monastery and its natural surroundings created a calmness within him. Such feelings could lull a man into carelessness when in enemy-held territory. He grunted to himself: *You will not seduce me.* He kissed the silver-wheeled goddess at his throat and then tucked her away. Better to let the small crucifix he wore next to her be visible in such a place.

The porter reappeared, beckoned and waited for Blackstone to join him. 'The prior will see you, Sir Thomas,' said the monk, now that he was allowed to break his silence.

The prior stood before a window that showed an elevated view of the valley below. He was younger than Blackstone expected, a man most likely to have seen forty years of life, but not the venerable sage that so many monasteries had at their head. He extended the folded document that identified Blackstone.

'I am Prior Albert. You are welcome here, Sir Thomas. I have arranged for our armourer to give your men quarters in our dormitorium.'

'Thank you, Father. We will pay for the care and feed of our horses.'

'I am grateful. We are self-sufficient but contributions are welcome, as are you and your men. Routiers have been slowly cleared from these valleys by levies of the Seneschal but the threat is always there and I hope you are here to attend to those who remain. Levies are not experienced fighting men.' His eyes noted Blackstone's stature. 'Unlike you and your men. You are here to sweep away those who still blight this region?'

Blackstone tucked the document into his jupon. 'I have orders to reclaim towns in the name of my King,' he answered. 'I have sent one of my captains south to recruit more men. I have given this monastery as the place they should return to.'

A frown creased the prior's brow. 'I doubt we have sufficient food to cater for the men you have now; if they increase in numbers then we will certainly not have enough supplies.'

'A meal a day for my men for two days will be ample, Father. I have bowmen with me who can hunt and bring in fresh meat, which we'll willingly share—'

The prior raised a hand. 'We follow the Rule, Sir Thomas. We do not eat the flesh of four-legged beasts. Fowl, yes, but nothing more. You are aware of this, surely?'

'Indeed, but I see you have a misericord. Does that not mean you allow your monks to eat meat or cooked offal on the non-fasting days? The refectory remains your sanctuary for the strictness of the Rule.'

Prior Albert smiled. 'Your eyes are as sharp as your knowledge of our discipline. And you are familiar with some of our weaknesses.' He shrugged. 'Yes, we allow meat on certain days but not partaken in the refectory. If you wish to hunt then we will accept your offering.'

So, Blackstone thought, there it was. The monks bent the Rule

215

of their founder, that was common enough. What else might influence them to be less strict about their behaviour other than their desire to taste meat? Could they be bought by routiers? Is that what kept them unmolested? 'I have asked myself why you have been spared any assault from the routiers.' Blackstone's tone challenged the prior.

The prior nodded. 'It is a fair question.' He raised a hand to gesture towards the distant view. 'You saw the ruined houses when you rode here?'

'We did. Which is why I asked. If they raided and burned the villages then they would have stormed these walls and seized anything of value. You and your monks would be dead.'

'It was not routiers, my son, it was the pestilence. It swept through these valleys a year ago. No more than two days' journey on foot was a Franciscan priory. Not one of the thirty friars survived.'

Blackstone sensed the Benedictine monk was not too distressed by the death of those from another order.

'Most of the stones from their buildings were put to good use,' said Father Albert. 'Here,' he added in what appeared to be an apologetic tone. 'To strengthen our walls. Just in case of attack.'

'But you were not harmed by the plague. You and the brothers,' said Blackstone. 'So you stayed here... in safety. Did you not help those who needed it?'

'Those who left the safety of these walls to help the infected died the same agonizing death. I ordered the houses boarded up, and where the pestilence was most virulent I had the houses burnt.'

'With those infected inside?'

The prior showed no sign of regret. 'Sir Thomas, when the boils burst the stench is beyond description. We burned every corpse. Two hundred people died in this valley, including eight of my fellow brothers.' He gazed out across the ruined hovels. 'We left the ruins in place and marked their doors with the sign of the plague and no routier dared venture near us.'

'We saw no red crosses on any door when we rode in.'

'They are there, my son. Faded, perhaps, but there. And the

news of the plague that killed every living soul in this place spread as quickly as the pestilence itself. We have been left in peace ever since. And, as I told you, we are blessed that there are those in these valleys who kill routiers for the vermin they are. I suggest you rest here for a few days; time passes slowly here and we find it gives men a chance to pray and reflect. See the week out. We have sufficient food. You would be most welcome and I would be pleased to share a meal with you and to hear how the peace treaty goes. I beg you, do not deny me the pleasure of your company.'

'Your gracious invitation is most welcome, Father Albert,' said Blackstone. Good manners always helped an invitation to be extended and gaining the trust of the prior might yield more information.

'Excellent,' said the Prior. 'And once you and your men are rested and have enjoyed the succour of mass then you can acquaint yourself with those who share your intent to rid us of those devil's sons.'

'And where would I find them?'

'Two, perhaps three days' ride from here you will find Countess Catherine de Val.'

'And her husband?'

'Dead. Killed by routiers.'

'And she has soldiers to protect her?'

'Yes. At the Château de Felice.'

CHAPTER THIRTY-FIVE

'It's not a woman's name, Gilbert, it's a château. And she has armed men behind the walls,' Blackstone said.

'William Cade?' asked Killbere as he and Blackstone hunched over a plate of food, along with their men, in the guesthouse. A flickering candle on the rough table between them dripped wax onto the scrubbed tabletop.

'I don't know,' said Blackstone, toying with the melting wax. 'I questioned the prior and found the route. We leave at first light.'

'We're going to assault a castle?' said Killbere, wiping his plate with a piece of torn bread and then cleaning his eating knife on his sleeve.

'I don't know what we'll do until we get there, but if good fortune has smiled on us then Cade might also fall into our hands. And if we find him we find ap Madoc and the gold and then we avenge Peter Garland.'

Killbere glanced around the refectory. 'They're meagre with their servings here.' He winced, and his belly growled. 'If I could find one of the lay monks he might be persuaded to grace my plate with more food. Would they be offended if I asked for more? Anyway, it makes no sense William Cade going to a place that has kept brigands at bay.'

Blackstone pushed his plate forward. 'Finish this.'

Killbere happily obliged. 'I know you, Thomas. When your hunger deserts you it means impatience rules your belly not your head.'

'We need to rest the horses but I'm tempted to leave now.'

Killbere eased a piece of food from a tooth. 'As I feared. A day's rest hurts no one. Neither man nor beast. Did you ask about whether they would permit us to eat meat? This pottage is little better than Will Longdon's fare and my knife barely cut the cheese. Why not stay a few days, let him and Jack go and hunt? Put strength back into us. Some of the men still carry wounds; they may be slight but they can irritate a man in a fight, and if you've a mind to go scaling walls and street fighting, then we'll need every man here. And if Cade is there then we need to find out more.'

Killbere watched his friends who seemed distracted. 'Thomas, you're already planning an attack. I can see it.'

'Not yet, Gilbert. Not until we see what we're facing. Did you see any plague crosses on the doors of those ruined hovels when we rode in?'

'Most of them didn't have doors, just wicker shutters. But on the others? I didn't notice. Why?'

'Prior Albert said the plague killed everyone around here and that it kept the skinners away.'

'Understandable, Thomas. If we had known then perhaps we would not have come this way.'

'Yes. Perhaps.' Blackstone appeared distracted. 'Something's not right. We'll stay two or three days, get some fresh meat and rest.'

Killbere knew his friend well enough to realize there was more to Blackstone's change of mind other than resting men and horses. 'And?'

'We watch and we listen. I'll go out with Will, and I'll take John and Meulon with me. Stay alert, Gilbert; these monks are too content.'

Blackstone and those with him left the monastery before nightfall with a blanket roll and dried food. There was no sense sleeping when his instincts had alerted him. They trudged back up the hills towards the ruined houses. Each of them checked the markings on the doors. It appeared that the prior had spoken the truth: there were faded red crosses but they were only visible close to.

'Will, you and Meulon find one of the houses on the lower path. John and I will stay here and keep watch on the track across the ridge. We hunt tomorrow.'

'What are we looking for, Sir Thomas?' said Meulon.

Blackstone shook his head. 'I don't know but I don't like the idea that these monks have remained untouched by routiers. One of us sleeps; one stays awake.'

'Meulon's snoring will wake the valley,' said Will Longdon.

'And your farting will sound like rolling thunder,' answered the throat-cutter.

'Then clench your buttocks and tie up your jaw,' said Blackstone.

'And what about the dead?' said Longdon. 'Are their spirits clinging to these ruins? I've no wish to wake in the night and feel the chill of a spectre. A man would be hard pressed not to cry out.'

'The chill you feel will be the metal of my knife jabbing you to allay the stench, fool,' said Meulon, tucking his bedroll beneath his arm.

'Aye, treat this with irreverence, you Norman oaf, but it is known that those unshriven souls dragged from their bodies cling to the last thing they knew in this mortal world.'

'If they start to haunt us then I'll bend you over and point your arse in their direction. That will cleanse the place of any evil spirits better than a priest with a cross.'

'All right,' said Blackstone. 'Enough. We stay silent through the night unless something unusual occurs.'

Will Longdon grabbed his blanket and war bow. 'Like damned ghosts,' he muttered.

'Like damned ghosts,' said Blackstone. 'Or those who might wish us to join them.'

Killbere beckoned Alain de la Grave to him.

'You're familiar with a monastery?'

'My father took me on his travels when he patrolled his lands. We rested in a monastery.'

'Good. Go to the scriptorium, admire the monks' work. Be humble. The Benedictines like humility. After a while express interest in what it means to be a monk, tell them that being so young and not suited to a life of indulgence in a wealthy household you have often considered taking up the life. Tell them that you venerate such a place as this that has stood for hundreds of years and ask if you might see the chronicle of the monastery.'

'Why would I do that, Sir Gilbert?'

'Because you're an idiot and well suited to the life.' Killbere sighed. 'Because, boy, no monk, prior or abbot ever keeps a journal of their own lives when living in a place like this but a record is kept of events that affect the monastery. See what's been written. If there are those who are patrons, remember their names; if travellers are given accommodation see when they came and who they were. What we are after, lad, is anything that will tell us more about this place. Understand?'

'Yes, Sir Gilbert.'

'Off with you then, and if the bell rings for compline see if you can avoid being persuaded to go with them because night prayers drone on until a man has no choice but to fall asleep.'

The young Frenchman nodded and left. Killbere looked down the length of the dormitory. Some of the men had rolled into their blankets; others tended their wounds, helped by Jack Halfpenny and Perinne. Killbere tapped Perinne on the shoulder. 'Leave Jack to see to that for now.'

He turned; Perinne followed him to the door. 'Perinne, I want night guards posted. Nothing obvious. Find places where we can watch for anything suspicious.'

'Are you expecting trouble?'

'No, but Thomas wants an eye kept open. He's not happy about this place. More than that I don't know.'

'Then we should have men in the stables to protect the horses in case there's trouble.'

'Yes. And when Jack has finished tell him to seek out places where the archers might be effective. They need range and an open place to shoot. Don't put the men there, but have him determine where it should be. Just in case.'

Once his orders had been given Killbere found himself a deep sill and propped his back against the stone wall from where he could see the central courtyard and some of the cloisters where monks sat and contemplated whatever it was that monks contemplated when not on their knees or bending their backs. He had scavenged another piece of cheese and bread and watched as crow-shuffling monks hunched their way towards the church. The bell for vespers rang out and two or three monks started lighting the night lamps in the dormitory and latrines. He would forsake his bed tonight and watch from this vantage point because there was one thing he had learnt over the years: Thomas Blackstone's instincts needed to be listened to.

Killbere had nodded off but Perinne poked him. He awoke without a sound, hand already on the knife at his belt, but Perinne's fist closed over it. No sense risking being stabbed by a veteran whose reflexes had kept him alive longer than most fighting men. The dull glow from the cresset lamps cast their shadows over the monastery. He stared into the shadows where Perinne pointed. He saw nothing. Then a monk scuffed his way towards the church. Killbere looked at Perinne with a questioning look. Perinne shook his head and made a small gesture for him to be patient and stay looking at the shadows. Nothing moved. Then the dull clanging of the bell sounded again. Vigils. It was midnight. The monks made their way into the cloisters from their dormitory and after a few more chimes the bell fell silent. Perinne eased his arm forward to where a shadow was changing shape. Moments later two monks skirted the wall; they kept their profiles away from the light but their movement made the darkness shimmer. Killbere followed them until they reached the porter's gate. The gatekeeper stepped out quickly in a practised movement, eased the gate open just enough for the two men to pass through, and for the spluttering night light at the porter's lodging to show that both men carried bedrolls tied across their backs. The gate closed.

'Anything else?' Killbere whispered.

Perinne shook his head. 'They might be going on a pilgrimage. Need to set off early,' he said quietly.

Killbere grinned. Which was as likely as breakfast being served with the boiled haunch of a pig.

The high ground and forests muted the monastic bells. The pinprick of lights from the areas lit behind the monastery's walls flickered like distant stars. The path leading down towards the monastery was a black tongue leading to the gaping mouth of the valley. There was sufficient light in the night sky for Blackstone to see two bent figures begin their climb up the steep track. He pushed the toe of his boot into John Jacob, who lay curled with his back pressed against the wall of the house where they were keeping watch. His squire made no sound of complaint but got quickly to his feet and followed Blackstone's gaze. The monks made good progress, their life of physical labour and, no doubt, their journeys across the hills allowing them to make good time. As they drew closer Blackstone could hear their laboured breathing. They were not big men. No monk was ever as well muscled as a fighting man, but there was sufficient night light for him to determine by their progress that they were wiry and agile. As they drew level Blackstone and John Jacob stepped out. The shock of seeing them caused the two monks to cry out. They stumbled, but Blackstone had already brought his fist down on the side of one monk's head. John Jacob quickly assaulted the other, a hard blow to his stomach bringing the man down onto his knees. Two more dark shapes were quickly making their way up the track.

'These are the only two,' said Meulon as Will Longdon wheezed behind him in an attempt to keep up with the big man's strides.

'Bring them inside,' said Blackstone.

Meulon and John Jacob manhandled the two monks into the derelict house.

'Bind them, put them in that corner and between us we watch

them until morning. It will be first light soon.' With a final look out into the night, he found a piece of ground less strewn with rubble and threw down his blanket. The night chill caused no discomfort. He closed his eyes and was soon asleep.

CHAPTER THIRTY-SIX

It was close to mid-morning when Blackstone led the others back into the monastery. Meulon carried a small deer carcass across his shoulders, brought down soon after dawn by one of Will Longdon's arrows. Men greeted them from where they loitered seemingly relaxed, but Blackstone noted that they had been placed strategically either to kill any monk attempting to attack them or, should an enemy approach from outside the walls, to easily seize a vantage point.

Blackstone beckoned one of the monks. 'Take my man to the kitchen. He'll butcher the deer and give you the offal to cook. We will share the meat. Prior Albert has given his permission.'

Meulon followed the grinning monk. Cooked liver, kidney and heart were a welcome treat and if the big man was as skilled with a knife as their own cook then there might even be enough to go around. At the very least the deer's bones would be put into the soup.

Killbere followed Blackstone to the water trough where he washed his face and hands. 'Two men left at midnight,' said Killbere quietly.

'We have them,' said Blackstone, shaking the water from his hair. 'Tied and gagged. They can't raise the alarm.'

'No doubt they were willing to tell you what you needed to know.'

'Once Meulon raised his knife to their throat. It frightened them enough for them to piss themselves and tell me everything.'

'And?'

'Prior Albert had instructed them to go to Felice and tell them that

English brigands had sought shelter here and that we would soon be travelling north. It would have given them time to ambush us.'

'The bastard prior is in their pay.'

'No doubt.'

'It fits,' said Killbere. 'I had the monastery chronicle looked at. There's enough largesse from this Countess Catherine de Val. And before her, a year or more back, her husband. His death was recorded. Killed at the hands of skinners like he said, but butchered. He had a bad death.'

'Is there a good one to be had? Anything else?'

'Nothing of use to us. I sent the boy. He did well.'

'Well, now we must act normally. Another few days here will suit us. Bring the men together.'

While the monks were engaged in their duties Blackstone gathered his captains and Tait, with the sergeants and ventenars, and told them what had happened during the night. 'I'm going to send two men to take the monks' place. Once they deliver the message that we are riding north it will draw out troops from behind the town's walls. By the time they move to ambush us we will already be on the road and lying in wait for them. Tait, I want you to go into the Felice with one of Beyard's Gascons.' Two or three of the men gestured they would be willing to go with Tait. Blackstone pointed to one of the men, Othon. 'You go with him, you're about the right size for one of the monks' habit.'

'Sir Thomas,' said Alain, 'Master Tait might raise too much suspicion. They will recognize his accent. I should go.'

The men looked at the youth as if he had declared himself the next Pope. One of Tait's men called out, 'You think they would believe you to be a novice? You're a lord's son. You need to be a rough-tongued commoner like Tait here.' The men jeered their agreement and Tait grinned.

'Aye, boy, you'd need a few years of tavern life before you were ready to escape and come to a place like this.'

Killbere grabbed Alain's hands and turned them palm upwards. 'You've barely enough calluses to show you abuse yourself, let alone work the land.'

The men laughed as Alain blushed. He snatched free from Killbere's grip. 'I could say I worked in the Scriptorium,' he blustered.

'Not if you were a lay brother. You would have to be ordained and you would be tonsured,' said Perinne.

Alain stood his ground and faced the grinning men. 'My accent would not be questioned. If the wrong man is sent into Felice then it will be you lying dead in the mountains. You can shave my head if that will convince everyone.'

Blackstone placed a hand on the boy's shoulder. 'We do not doubt your courage. But you're too young to be ordained.' Blackstone hesitated for a moment. 'But you make a good point about Tait's accent.'

Killbere tugged at Blackstone's arm, pulling him a few paces out of earshot. 'Thomas, do not consider sending the boy into the town. It gives him the perfect chance to betray us. He's French. You humiliated him. And even if he does not then if Cade is there he might recognize the boy from when we were in Sainte-Bernice.'

'He barely caught sight of him. When we stepped into the courtyard there the lad was behind us. Cade and ap Madoc were looking at us.'

'You cannot risk the men's lives,' insisted Killbere.

'They are already at risk,' said Blackstone.

Killbere sighed. 'Thomas, Perinne was barely with us when Cade rode with the men. You had sent him off to follow the brigands' tracks. We need a man we know and can depend on.'

Blackstone thought on it for a moment and then beckoned Perinne to him. 'Perinne, I want you to go into Felice. Cade won't recognize you. Not wearing a habit and a cowl.'

'Of course,' said the stocky fighter.

'You'll need to shave your beard,' said Killbere.

The fighter grinned. 'Aye, well, that will give some relief from the lice.'

227

Blackstone still looked troubled about his decision.

'Cade rode with Meulon's men. He won't look twice at me. Who goes with me?'

'I'll send the boy.'

'Thomas,' Killbere sighed.

'His accent will help.'

Killbere knew there was no point in arguing. 'All right. Perinne, when you get to this Countess Catherine at Felice and you're questioned tell them you have been a lay brother here for only a few months, that way if there has been any contact between the monastery and the town recently they won't expect to recognize you.'

Blackstone turned back to face the expectant young Frenchman. 'Alain, you will be a new lay brother who has sought sanctuary here because the English killed your family.'

'Thank you, Sir Thomas.'

Blackstone turned to Tait. 'Did Chandos strike anywhere south of where we fought the Bretons?'

'We met resistance at Les Choux some months back but it was little more than a skirmish,' said Tait. 'The town surrendered quickly.'

'Do you know it?' he asked Alain.

'No.'

'Tait? Who were the burghers?'

The hobelar shook his head. 'I don't know, Sir Thomas. I was in the field searching out any ambush.'

'I went into the town with one of Sir John's captains,' volunteered one of Tait's men. 'All I know is the mayor's name was Riveaux. He was killed.'

'It's enough that English troops killed Frenchmen for you to have fled,' Blackstone told Alain, 'but if your father was the mayor then that adds strength to your story. You will have to maintain the lie if you are questioned, but there's no reason for them to do that if they believe the prior has sent you.'

The young man smiled, flush with enthusiasm. 'I will not fail you, Sir Thomas.'

Killbere grunted. 'Fail us and you will also die. Remember that.'

'I will, Sir Gilbert,' he answered, the brief moment of joy at being chosen evaporating.

'All right. Alain and Perinne will leave on foot today. I'll tell Prior Albert that I am posting sentries on the ridge. Meulon, Will, Renfred: choose two men per post, that way when we send men out the lad and Perinne can slip away. Will, you take them up to the ruins, see them dressed and make sure those monks stay securely tied.' Then he addressed his long-serving friend: 'Perinne, you and the boy will take the monks' habits and their bedrolls. Go due north to Château de Felice. It's two days on horseback, so three full days or more on foot.' He looked at Alain. 'It will be hard going. Perinne will not carry you. You stay the pace.'

'I will, Sir Thomas. And Master Perinne will have no cause to be slowed by me.'

'Good. Perinne, we will use the lad's accent to allay any suspicions so you will let him do the talking. Act slow-witted so that the questions go to him.'

'No difficulty there, my lord,' said Will Longdon. 'Perinne once went to the wrong woman's bedchamber and climbed in next to her husband.'

Ribald laughter was quickly quietened by a gesture from Killbere. 'Best watch your arse, boy,' he said to Alain, softening the threat with a grin.

Blackstone kept a cautious eye on any monks who might pass but so far there had been no sign of any of them being suspicious of the gathered men. 'By the third day we will find an ambush site on the route. This Countess or William Cade will know how long the journey is from here so they will send out their men to entrap us in good time. And we'll be waiting.'

CHAPTER THIRTY-SEVEN

Perinne set a steady pace and for the first day Alain struggled to keep up. His feet were soon blistered and that night after Perinne laid a fire the seasoned soldier examined the young man's feet – despite his initial objection.

'When you first start riding you get blisters on your arse, but at least you can keep moving. These blisters on your feet – they will soon bleed. Piss on them and let them dry and then see how far we can go tomorrow. Bleeding or not we have to get to Felice in the next couple of days.'

Alain knew he was in no position to argue with the grizzled fighter. 'The monk's sandals and habit chafe,' he said.

'Mine too, but you just ignore it.'

The young Frenchman felt out of his depth and knew that his ambition was getting the better of him. He felt the weight of insecurity press on him, remembering how, on the ridge when the Bretons attacked, his terror had overcome his desire to kill those who had inflicted such brutality on his family. Had it not been for John Jacob that day he knew he would have fallen beneath Breton swords. And when Blackstone took him through the routiers' camp and showed him how to kill sleeping men he had thought he had become more capable but the truth, he realized, was that he was unable to match the toughness and stamina of the men he rode with. And now this truth was borne out by a day's march across stony track. Even the monks seemed more resilient than he.

'I'll be all right,' he said.

The stocky fighter glanced at him as he rolled out his sleeping blanket. 'There's no choice in the matter, lad. Sir Thomas has given us a job to do. And when you piss on your feet do it over there away from me. I don't want the stench in my nostrils.'

'I will, Master Perinne.'

'Christ's sake, boy, stop calling me that. We're supposed to be monks and we can't risk Cade remembering my name. Call me Brother Othon or you'll get us both killed. All right, Brother Alain?'

The young man grinned and nodded, pleased the veteran was talking to him because the day's walk had been in silence. 'Should we not tell each other about ourselves? If we are monks serving the same prior would we not know where each came from?'

Perinne pulled his blanket over him and reached out to nudge another piece of wood into the fire. 'Lay brothers join a monastery for different reasons. I'm supposed to be so dull-witted I'm only good for clearing shit from the animal pens so you and I would have no cause to talk in the dormitory or when we eat. And the less we know about each other the better because then our lies will not become confused. I don't know you and you don't know me because we work in different places in the monastery. Understood?'

'Yes, I understand.'

'Then get some sleep because we leave at first light.'

Alain moved away from his companion to the furthest limit of the light cast by the fire. He looked down at his blistered feet and urinated over them, being careful not to soil the rough cloth of the chafing habit. In that moment he felt a wave of self-pity come over him. Only recently he had been the son of a respected knight to whom common men dipped their heads in greeting when he rode by. And now here he was pissing on his own feet, lower in status than even a common monk. Tears stung his eyes as sharply as did the urine his blistered feet.

In his mind's eye he saw his mother and the man he called father. Blackstone had stopped him from seeing their mutilated remains but he remembered the fouled sheet in which they had been carried to their grave. It took little imagination to picture their savage death. He snorted the phlegm from his tears and spat. His resolve stiffened. He must never allow self-pity or fear to grip him again. He turned and nestled his meagre bedding closer to the fire. Tomorrow he would keep up with his battle-hardened companion.

The château sat on a craggy escarpment and took its name from the town that surrounded it. Some stone-built houses buttressed the outside of the walls, adding strength to the walls' defences. Beyond these twenty or so dwellings the walls themselves remained Felice's main fortification, enhanced by the craggy rock face that dropped down below them. Attackers would be observed approaching across the bottom of the rocks and would then face a seemingly impossible climb in the face of resistance. Château de Felice seemed impregnable.

A shadow high in the sky caught Perinne's attention. It was a buzzard and its keening cry heralded death. And Thomas Blackstone was miles away so it had to be calling out for him and the boy. Perinne watched it soar high, imagining its eyes locked onto his. Would they both die inside those walls? Perinne glanced at the lad. Thomas Blackstone wanted him to survive but would it cost Perinne his own life? He spat. Fuck the damned bird. It could seize William Cade's soul when the time came.

Perinne gazed across the rugged hills to where the jagged bedrock supported the château as it rose above the low-pitched house roofs. 'Doubtful if God's lightning could destroy a place like that,' he muttered. 'No matter how many Sir Thomas might kill out here he's going to have to get the men inside those walls.'

'How?' asked Alain. 'I see no way.'

'Me neither, lad. Once we are inside we need to keep our eyes peeled so that we can see if there's any weakness anywhere. We make a tally of how many armed men there are because when they send some of them out to ambush Sir Thomas they'll leave enough to defend the town. Remember, we tell them there are less than twenty men at the monastery. With luck they will send twice that number to try and capture our comrades.' He glanced at the young Frenchman. 'All right, now you have to start thinking like a damned monk. You will lead the way to the gate and tell the guards who we are. I will be playing the role of the dullard behind you. Don't be too damned cocky just 'cause you can find words to spout that others might not. Simple words, boy, just deliver the message. You remember all that we spoke of today?' He pulled the leather coif tight onto his skull.

Alain de la Grave nodded. This final day's journey had been different from the first. Perinne had questioned him about his childhood to see if he had been baptized and knew the psalms; that he could offer a blessing if need be. They had spoken about the monastery, testing him where the buildings were situated, when they ate meat, when they did not. Where the latrines were situated and the name of the old porter who had spent most of his sixty years living in the monastery. Everyone would know Brother Gregory's name. Enough familiarity of the place if questioned, not enough to show they knew more than they should.

'All right, Brother Alain, lead the way. Grip that staff and find purpose to your stride. We deliver important news from Prior Albert for Countess Catherine. No one else. Just her. If we are separated because you're the one who bears the message then you will be facing her or the bastards she protects. Understood?'

'Aye, Brother Othon. I understand.'

Perinne crossed himself and took a deep breath. 'Then God bless us both.'

They walked along the muddy track that meandered through the scattered households of dirt-encrusted villagers who grew crops and raised livestock. Villeins stopped, heads bowed, expecting a blessing when the two monks passed. Alain muttered a few words in their direction and then they reached the bridge that led to the path up to Felice's iron-studded gates. A deep-running river swirled below. Perinne looked left and right. The causeway bridge seemed the only way into the town. The river flowed at an angle from the low hills and did not encircle the walls. Now that they were closer he could see more clearly that the ragged dry gully cut along the base of the rock face. Above this the houses that leaned against the town walls formed another defensive barrier. A walkway had been built from great timbers and then planked so that it gave the appearance of an extended balcony stretching across the front of the houses. It was to all intents and purposes a wooden street that allowed the householders to walk around the walls to the gate. The broken ground below the wooden props holding up the walkway made it difficult to clamber up, as did the sheerness of the walls. And this approach could be easily defended by the householders pouring boiling water or throwing missiles down onto any attacker. It was obvious to Perinne at that moment that no matter how many of the garrison troops or skinners Blackstone killed outside the walls, the town could not be taken. They were on a fool's errand.

Sentries on the wall called down to the soldiers at the gate and the two monks were admitted. A broad courtyard greeted them, as did the several corpses hanging from a gibbet. The bodies were torn and disfigured. The guard at the gate saw their stunned surprise. 'Routiers. They're starting to stink. The crows have had their fill of them. They'll be in the river in a few days, along with the others that were brought in.'

Perinne and Alain needed no prompting to cross themselves. The carcasses showed savage injury, and if Perinne and the Frenchman failed such would be their fate. The raptor's prescient cry had warned them. This was a place of death. Narrow streets cut away between houses that huddled wall-to-wall. It seemed at first glance that the alleyways were inhabited by tradesmen: blacksmiths and carpenters shared the start of one street on the left of the courtyard; cooks, bakers and butchers another on the opposite side. The stench of acrid smoke from the forge was overpowered by the mouth-watering odour of baked bread. Alain's stomach growled.

'We have a message from Prior Albert,' said Alain to the sergeant who stepped from the guardroom. Alain looked across to the other side of the gate into what looked like a small armoury. The soldiers who loitered in the area were relaxed, the boredom of their routine reflected in their lack of interest towards the two monks. The sergeant turned and called to one of the other men.

'Take them to the Countess,' he ordered.

The man so ordered pulled on a skullcap helmet and nodded for the two men to follow him. They skirted the rotting bodies on the gibbet and after a few hundred yards the dirt alley became paved. The passage was wide enough for a cart and horse and rose quickly, turning into a steep curving street that led to the château itself where it rose above the town. In some houses they heard infants crying, in others pots being clattered. As they trudged behind their escort a different breed of men appeared in doorways. Alain recognized their garb as similar to that of the routiers he had seen at his father's house at Sainte-Bernice. They were not his parents' killers but they were William Cade's mercenaries. And they were dangerous.

'Selling your arse, brother?' one of the men called as they walked past, lowering a beaker of drink from his lips. 'You're young enough.' He smiled a toothless grin. 'I've impaled monks before now,' he said and stepped out to harass them. 'Impaled them with my sword.' He laughed and dodged forward to rub the back of his hand against Alain's cheek. Alain sidestepped, eager to avoid confrontation. Perinne tried to crowd in on his shoulder to block the brutish routier. The man had clearly had too much to drink. The routier pushed Perinne aside. 'Don't get in my fucking way,' he said.

Perinne's muscled bulk barely moved from the shove, which surprised the belligerent man, but before he could make any more of it the escort turned.

'They are from Prior Albert. The Countess does not allow any harm to come to these monks. Leave them be,' he threatened.

'Or what?' snarled the man.

The garrison soldier was no match for the killer but he knew he had one weapon that would surely stop him. 'Or Master Cade will hear of it.'

The drunk snarled and then turned his back.

Perinne's heart beat faster. They were being taken to the Countess but perhaps William Cade was also waiting. He prayed that neither he nor the young Frenchman would be recognized.

CHAPTER THIRTY-EIGHT

The higher Perinne and Alain climbed towards the château entrance the more of Cade's mercenaries they saw. The two of them exchanged glances, wondering whether the Countess used these men as bodyguards or if it was they who kept her as prisoner. Their escort spoke to two of Cade's men at the entrance to the château's courtyard, and then turned back. The mercenaries then pointed them towards the main door where even more of Cade's men stood. They were getting ever closer to the centre of the web that might entrap them. What seemed obvious was that the mercenaries were a barrier between the Countess and the townspeople below and although there seemed to be more garrison troops than skinners it was here with these men the power and strength lay.

William Cade stepped out of the doorway. Alain and Perinne stopped.

'What brings you here?' said Cade.

'My lord,' said Alain, bowing his head, 'we have information from Prior Albert but he asks us to deliver it to the Countess Catherine.'

William Cade stepped closer and looked at the two men. It seemed that he was the final barrier to pass before being allowed inside. He studied the two men, eyes going from one to the other. He grabbed Perinne's wrist, who had the good sense not to resist as Cade examined his hands. 'What work do you do at the monastery?'

Perinne grinned like a village idiot. 'I keep the livestock pens clean, lord,' he said, lifting his chin proudly as if he were the prior himself.

The men at the door behind William Cade laughed. 'He cleans out the shit,' one cried.

'Aye, and he smells like it,' said Cade, turning his attention to the younger of the two men. He carried out the same examination on Alain's hands. 'You're no lay brother who works the fields.'

'No, my lord, I am a novice and have only been at the monastery for a few months.'

'Your hands sweat. What frightens you?'

'Perhaps it is the exertion of the hard journey and... I am unused to being in the company of fighting men.'

Cade grunted. 'Answer me.'

'Most of my time is taken with study and I am often given duties in the kitchen.'

Cade was taking nothing at face value. He stared at Alain, who did not turn away. 'Then you will know the fat bastard who prepares the food and tastes it more often than he should. Name him.'

Alain did not hesitate in his answer. 'Sir, I think you are mistaken, I do not know when last you were at our sanctuary but it is Brother Simon who prepares the food with the grace of God and he eats sparingly. Perhaps the brother you speak of served in the kitchens before I arrived.'

William Cade said nothing: it seemed his question had been a bluff, as much a bluff as Alain's answer. It was possible Cade had never visited the monastery in person.

The mercenary stepped back and looked at the two men. 'I need to see that you do not conceal any weapons. There are monks who think they carry out God's will by killing those who seek the pleasures of this world – and the Countess is no stranger to pleasure.' He gestured for them to raise their clothing above their waists.

Alain and Perinne lifted their habits, exposing their nakedness. One of the men behind Cade spoke out again. 'Don't let the Countess see the lad's weapon, William; she will be keen to see it raised in anger.' The men laughed. 'Monk or not, he bears more than a message from the prior. He carries his fortune between his legs. Perhaps it's a gift for her.'

'And I'll be the first to take it with a knife should he try and deliver it,' Cade snarled.

Alain lowered his eyes and his habit.

'He blushes!' the man taunted.

'He's a novice, for Christ's sake,' said another. 'Probably never even seen a woman, never mind knows what to do with one. Fodder for the monks.'

Cade pushed past them. 'All right. This way. Not you,' he said pointing at Perinne. 'No one who shovels shit need go any further.'

Alain glanced at his companion. There was the briefest of looks between them, a warning, a moment of alarm, but Perinne quickly took on the mantle of a dullard. 'God bless you, brother, but even a man who serves the animals needs food. A scrap perhaps? It has been a long journey. Is there a kitchen where a humble brother might be given a crust?'

Cade nodded to one of the men who loitered at the doorway. 'She'll want them rewarded for their journey. Take him to the kitchen yard. Feed him. This one will eat when he's delivered the message.'

'Bless you, bless you,' said Perinne, bowing repeatedly until one of the men grabbed his arm and turned him in another direction.

The chill of fear gripped Alain as he followed the murderer Cade into the château's gloom.

Two guards who wore the Countess's blazon stood at the carved door. They were older men, and looked to be retainers from the time the Count had lived, sworn men who protected the widow. Men, Alain thought, who would not be threatened by William Cade's reputation. They stepped forward and blocked the door.

'He has a message,' said Cade, nodding towards the monk at his side.

One of the men stepped into the room and a moment later reappeared and allowed Cade and Alain to enter the Countess's quarters. The room he was escorted into was in stark contrast to the unfurnished and unheated entrance hall. Light filled the room from windows that overlooked the town and the countryside beyond. Richly embroidered tapestries hung over the harsh stone walls and a massive fire blazed beneath a granite mantel. His sandalled feet were cushioned on woven rugs that lay over the rush-covered floor. Two large, ill-bred dogs lurched from the warmth of the fireplace and went as if to attack as he and William Cade entered the room. A woman's voice carried from the far side of the fireplace, her sharp retort bringing the dogs obediently to heel at the woman's side where she sat in a carved chair softened by silk cushions. Alain squinted at first because the light from the vast windows obscured his vision of her. Cade pushed him closer.

'Two monks have come from Saint-André's monastery,' he said and moved to her side. She held a small embroidery frame on her lap and did not look at him for a moment as she pulled a thread through the material.

'Who are you?' she asked without raising her eyes.

'I am Brother Alain, my lady.'

'And the one I saw from the window? Your companion?'

'He is a lay brother, his name is Othon.'

'Prior Albert usually sends Brothers Pibrac and Dizier. Why has he sent you?' She raised her eyes and looked at him.

Alain stood ten paces away but from the moment his gaze fell on her he felt his heart quicken. She was the most beautiful woman he had ever seen. Black hair framed her face with the sheen of a raven's wing. There was colour in her lips and her cheeks bore the blush of the fire. Her dark green eyes ate into him but he could not resist staring at the rise and fall of her breasts, which seemed to be barely contained in the rich fabric of her dress. The heat from the blazing logs seemed to penetrate the coarse cloth of his habit as he felt warmth creep into his groin. The taste of fear that had soured his mouth as he entered the château was now thick with the sweeter taste of lust.

She stared. A hint of a smile at the corner of her mouth. Perhaps, he realized, she knew the effect she had on him.

'Well?' she asked with a softness of tone that lulled him into a stammering reply.

'My... lady. I... I do not... know why. Perhaps... perhaps because one is in the infirmary and the other is doing penance for raising his voice in anger at another brother.'

William Cade studied him and did not wait for the Countess to make any further comment. 'Do I know you? Have we met before?'

'I think not, unless you once prayed in the church at Les Choux, which is my home,' Alain said quickly, desperate to answer without hesitation but at the same time frightened that Cade might know of the town.

Countess Catherine muttered a sound of delight. 'William. You have prayed in a church rather than pillage it?'

Cade grunted. 'I don't know the place. But I have seen you somewhere.'

Alain swallowed hard. 'I have a common enough face.'

'I think he has a beautiful face,' said the Countess, ignoring the quick glance of irritation from Cade at her remark, staring with delight at the young man before her. 'A novice,' she mused. 'Well, I wonder whether a monastic life will prove suitable for you, Brother Alain. Perhaps you should wait a few years.' She pressed the needle through the linen.

Alain's heart would not calm. A vein in his neck pulsed and he felt the embarrassment of an erection beginning.

'Very well,' she said, concentrating on her needlework. 'What message does Prior Albert send?'

Alain concentrated; this moment was the culmination of his journey and the trust placed in him by Blackstone. 'Seventeen men sought sanctuary which Prior Albert gave gladly. They paid him with gold.'

Cade's eyes registered at the mention of plunder.

'They are mostly English but there are others,' Alain continued. 'Some French and German, I think, but I never spoke to them. They were kept in the guesthouse.'

'And when will they leave the monastery?' asked the Countess, some of the warmth lost from her voice.

'Prior Albert has told them to come north, towards Felice.

241

He told them there is plunder to be had here. I am to tell you that they would leave the monastery two days after Brother Othon and I began our journey.'

Cade looked down at the Countess, who seemed more interested in her embroidery. 'I'll send forty men,' he said. 'Thirty of your garrison and ten of mine. That will be enough to overwhelm them.' A thought occurred to him. 'Do they have archers?' he asked Alain.

'No, my lord, only hobelars,' he lied.

'I'll get the men ready; they can ambush them easily enough,' said Cade.

'William, do not send so many of mine, they are not as skilled as yours. Ten of my men. No more. Make up the numbers with your own men – and do not forget that we want some prisoners,' she said, glancing up. 'They must be taught a lesson.'

Cade didn't like the idea of leaving so few of his men in the town. They were already outnumbered by the Countess's troops. If she should ever turn against him then their numbers alone would be sufficient to overwhelm his own. But there was an incentive to use his men rather than the garrison's. Cade's fighters had the experience to defeat a smaller force without killing them. Garrison troops would be less skilled in the field. Cade stood to make money from the encounter.

'As you wish. I have no desire to lose my bounty on those we deliver to you.' He looked at Alain. 'I'll take you to the kitchen, then you can be on your way.'

Countess Catherine eased a silk thread into her design. 'You would have us neglect our hospitality, William. Look at Brother Alain's feet. They are cut. They need attention before we send him back. Have food brought here. He should bathe and then his wounds can be attended to,' she said matter-of-factly. 'And then he can join me in prayer.'

Cade glowered. The bitch was grooming a novice monk to take to her bed. He resisted the urge to grab her throat, to show her that he would not be humiliated. Much good it would do him. If he killed her in a fit of rage, made her suffer for the power she held over him, it would be hard to escape with his life, no matter how tenacious his men were in a fight. The garrison troops would cut them down. And should she survive such an attack then he had no wish to suffer the pain she could inflict on a man. He swallowed his pride together with the words of condemnation. As he strode past the young monk he swore to himself that he would carry out his threat made against the novice. Once the bitch had taken her pleasure the youth would be of no concern to her and then he would geld him.

CHAPTER THIRTY-NINE

Blackstone and Killbere lingered on the road to Felice. They had allowed good time for Alain and Perinne to reach the town. Once the message had been delivered soldiers would be sent to ambush Blackstone that same day. If the two bogus monks had reached the château by early morning then Blackstone had planned to be a half-day's ride from the city walls. A chill wind persisted from the higher mountains but the men made little effort to warm themselves other than riding with their cloaks wrapped securely around them. They were on the alert for an attack and would be ready to discard them the moment their enemy appeared. Blackstone had picked fifteen men to ride in column behind him while the captains rode on his flank with their men out of sight. If Alain and Perinne had delivered their message and suspicion had not been aroused then a force outnumbering those on the road would soon appear. Blackstone had made the two captured monks ride with them on the pack horses until they were far enough away from the monastery on foot not to be able to raise any alarm. They were given food, drink and a blanket and sent back.

'I don't suppose William Cade will ride out against us himself. So that means after we kill those he sends that we will have to seek him inside the walls,' said Killbere.

'You think it is not worth our effort?' Blackstone said.

'I'm thinking it's going to be difficult to root them out. God knows how many men this Countess has under her command. Street fighting is a dirty business, Thomas, you know that. We will lose men and as yet we have no means to scale walls. If they are forewarned then they will be ready. What do you propose?

That we take on their clothing once we kill them and pass ourselves off? By the time we reached the town gates the sentries would know our real identity.'

'I don't have a plan, Gilbert. Not until we are there. We must see the lie of the land. But I want William Cade to pay the price for hanging young Peter Garland, and to find out where Gruffydd ap Madoc has gone. If Beyard brings more men to us we need to offer them some enticement other than allowing them to claim territory. And for that we need the gold that was seized from us. We'll find and kill William Cade, Gilbert. I made that promise. It needs to be done.'

'Well, it's better than having to stand outside a town's walls and hear those inside bleating like sheep that they do not wish to swear allegiance to Edward. At least now we do what we do best, but it might take months to track down the Welshman and who knows how many men he will have drawn to himself by then? Beyard had better not be languishing in an Avignon brothel.'

'Perhaps I should have asked you to go and raise troops with him and then you could have kept an eye on him.'

'Ah, now that would have been sensible. In fact, there is a very fine brothel in Avignon which I would recommend.'

'No nuns?'

'Thomas, do not tempt God's wrath. Nuns in brothels? That is near enough blasphemy and—' He stopped his playful chastisement as he saw movement ahead. 'Horsemen. Ready yourself.'

William Cade's men were over-confident. They sought a quick killing, sweeping down onto the few men they saw on the road. Their intention was to kill a dozen and capture the rest; that way Cade received his bounty.

Blackstone and Killbere raised their shields and spurred their horses. The men behind them quickly formed an arrowhead formation. They had chosen this place carefully: the road ahead widened to one side where rough mountain grass swept upwards into a forest. This expanse of rising ground forced their attackers to sweep out into the grassland. Cade's men were seasoned fighters and their attack did not falter. They quickly swept wide in an attempt to encircle Blackstone's horsemen but they had not anticipated the few men they thought to quickly defeat would meet them with such ferocity. A cry of alarm went up from one of Cade's routiers when he identified Blackstone's blazon. These were not the down-at-heel skinners they had been expecting.

Blackstone's bastard horse barged into the nearest mount. Blackstone felt its power surge through his legs as if the beast had deliberately gathered its strength and lunged with such force that the other horse was knocked off its stride. Its rider struggled to control it and his raised sword arm was unable to strike. Blackstone eased the reins, letting the antagonistic beast have its head, and rammed his sword point beneath the man's armpit as the bastard horse's momentum carried him past the fatally injured routier. Barely a few strides behind him Killbere and the other men thudded into the attackers. The thwack of horseflesh striking horseflesh and the clash of sword blade on metal mingled with cries of exertion and pain. The first assault took Blackstone's men clean through the attackers' ranks and they wheeled their horses in a tight turn ready to strike again. Unsaddled horses ran wild, their riders dead or dying on the ground. The garrison troops fared badly, unused to such violent close-quarter battle on horseback. Defending a town in a position of strength was different from this sudden onslaught. As Blackstone's men urged their horses back into the fray those they attacked broke and ran, scattering in a desperate attempt to escape. More were brought down as Blackstone and Killbere struck at them again but some slipped past, laying the flat of their sword blades against their mounts' rumps, urging the terrified beasts to gallop faster. Blackstone and Killbere reined in and let the routiers ride across the grassland. The edge of the forest shimmered as Will Longdon's archers stepped forward and quickly bent into their bows, shooting into the retreating men. The horsemen swerved this way and that, shields raised above their heads. Some of the yard-long arrows punched through shields into men's shoulders. Others struck exposed legs and horses' flanks. The animals whinnied and screamed and fell headlong, throwing some riders down, crushing others beneath their weight. But still there were those who evaded the arrow storm and raced for the road back to Felice and safety. As they spurred their mounts at the far edge of the grassland more riders suddenly appeared, Meulon and the other captains, sweeping around from the edge of the forest to cut off the few survivors block their path and hack the men down. The routiers were overwhelmed, but one man gambled and spurred his horse away from the track obstructed by these new horsemen. He lashed his horse up the rocky ground – perhaps he knew the landscape and where the animal tracks ran because he guided the horse expertly this way and that – but it seemed a desperate gamble for no escape route was visible.

Blackstone raised himself in the saddle and waved Wolf Sword above his head. 'Stop him!' he bellowed and then gestured with his sword towards the retreating figure.

Renfred was already in pursuit and another three quickly followed but their horses balked at the steep, uneven ground. Renfred's horse stumbled, almost throwing him. Meulon spurred his horse along the road to try and cut off the horseman but it soon became clear that he had escaped. The big Norman spearman and the others turned back to the grassland as Will Longdon led his men down to the dead and wounded. While Jack Halfpenny's men tugged free their bodkin-tipped arrows from the flesh of man and horse, Quenell's archers killed the badly wounded routiers and drove spikes into dying horses' skulls, putting them quickly out of their pain. The blood-slicked grassland upset some of Tait's horses, causing them to fight their reins. Some of the mounts tried to bolt, cursed at by their riders, until finally they settled and were brought back to where Blackstone gathered the men. Three of his own men were dead, as were two of the Gascons. William Cade's routiers were experienced and had fought hard. Thirty-seven men lay dead across the open ground, two more on the road.

'Is Cade among the dead?' Blackstone called to those going among the bodies.

'He's not here,' came Meulon's reply.

'We must push on, Thomas,' said Killbere, wiping his blade clean. 'That man will ride like the devil's chasing him and warn the town. I pray to God that the lad and Perinne have started their journey back because if they are still there when he returns then Cade will know he has been tricked.'

'You think I don't know that?'

'Thomas, no plan is ever foolproof,' said Killbere. 'The bastard was lucky and it looked as though he knew the ground.'

Blackstone gathered his reins and spurred the bastard horse towards the road. It was a race now to try and reach Felice before the escaping horseman raised the alarm. The two-faced god of war had been on Blackstone's side but could as soon turn away and give his blessing to a man's enemy. The lumbering horse settled into its uneven stride. More horses pounded behind him. The heavy thud of their hooves were as war drums beating out their urgency.

CHAPTER FORTY

Perinne had been fed and then ignored. A monk wandering through the lower rooms and passageways of the château was no cause for alarm. Perinne was already worried they had not been allowed to leave Felice. The message had been delivered and there was no reason for them to be kept in the town. If Blackstone launched an assault while they were still inside they would be the first to die. He glanced up at the sky but the buzzard was not in sight. He searched for a safe place to hide for himself and the boy and for any means of escape. As he had sat in the kitchen he'd eaten slowly, so that he could listen to any gossip. The fireplace was tall enough for a grown man to stand upright in; it burned logs three feet long and the meat that turned on the spit told him that the Countess did not believe in eating sparingly. A sawtoothed rack supported an iron kettle that simmered with hot water. His clothing made it impossible for him to secrete a weapon but he had identified where the knives and meat cleavers were kept. Moving around afterwards without challenge he observed where the garrison troops were in force and where Cade's men were billeted. He made his way to where he last saw Alain and William Cade disappearing into the château's main hall. When he asked where his brother monk was, the men smirked and sent him on his way. Their behaviour was enough to tell him that either the lad was inside with the Countess or William Cade was questioning him, suspicious, perhaps, that he recognized him. If violence was going to be inflicted then he reasoned that it would be this very day, should Alain be unmasked. Failing that Blackstone would be at the walls by that night.

* * *

Serving women had filled a wooden bathtub and then left Alain in a room that was heated by the rising steam and the seasoned logs burning with a deep glow in the stone fireplace. Food had been brought, and the Countess had watched him eat sitting self-consciously away from her at the small table. She remained silent as she continued her sewing but her eyes seldom left him. He ate delicately, small mouthfuls at a time, wiping his mouth with the napkin, barely able to stomach the food. Anxiety made his hands tremble. The woman's scent was as delicate as a spring flower and he found it almost impossible not to watch her – as she watched him. When she asked if the food was to his liking he kept his eyes down and muttered his gratitude. The urgency to leave and return to Blackstone was stifled by his desire to be near this woman. When he had finished eating she called for the serving women to show him where to bathe.

The deep, hot water lulled him. The exhaustion from the journey and the burden of fear soaked away. He suddenly snapped awake. How long had he slept? The water was only warm. The door opened and one of the serving women came in and asked if he needed more water. He declined and asked for his habit but she told him the washerwomen were boiling the dirt out of it. She lifted an embroidered robe. The Countess had sent this. Once the woman had left the overwhelming desire to escape seized him. He climbed out of the wooden tub and padded naked across the stone floor. The door was locked. He went to the window and stood on a footstool and saw that the sheer drop ended on the rocks far below. Panic began to crush him and the curse of self-pity gnawed at him once again. For a moment it seemed this weakness would drown him but, as before, he found his resolve. He must find Perinne. The veteran would know how to escape. He heard women's voices beyond the door, followed by the turning of a handle. What he had taken to be a garderobe covered with a heavy curtain proved to conceal a door. This opened and the Countess stepped into view. Her head was bare, dark hair loosened. The robe she wore was sheer and the darkness of her nipples pressed against the flimsy material.

'You must rest now, Brother Alain, and let me attend to you,' she said, her tone as natural as if he were a welcome guest. He had not yet raised his eyes from her breasts but as she extended her hand he walked, dreamlike, towards her, unaware that he still wore no clothing. She took his hand and led him into her bedchamber. The room flickered with dim light from beeswax candles and more scent. The sheets on the canopied bed had been turned back. And as he faltered, quivering with the promise being offered, she turned and cupped his face and gently, like a mother with a child, touched his lips with her own. His chest pressed against her silky arousal and then he was lost to a drunken state that made him nearly weep with desire. The only words he heard as they settled on the bed were her whispers. *Slowly, slowly.*

The alarm was raised hours later as church bells pealed. Perinne heard the clamour first and thought for a moment that it was a call to prayer and that the last thing he wanted was to be dragged into reciting psalms, prayers or blessings as a monk. He hoped his dullard character would excuse him. And then the cries overtook the bells, rising above their clanging. By the time they stopped he had made his way to where he had determined would be the safest place to hide. No matter how dark and narrow some of the streets were, if a hue and cry were raised then every man, woman and child would seek him out. A door led from the kitchens into the solar, the two great fireplaces back to back divided by the chimney's shared wall. The solar was unoccupied; the Countess's rooms were elsewhere and he suspected that was where Alain would be. As the cooks and servants ran outside he went quickly through the kitchen, lifted a carving knife and a cleaver and then closed the adjoining door between the two rooms behind him. The solar's grate was cold but there was warmth coming through from the kitchen fire on the other side of the wall. He stepped into the fireplace and then raised his hands until they touched what seemed to be a ledge which was the inner beam of the fireplace's hefty mantel. It was wide enough for him to lie on. He would stay concealed for as long as it took for the fighting to start and then he would lower himself and kill as many as he could before he was overwhelmed. The young Frenchman, Alain, was abandoned to his own fate.

William Cade's voice echoed in the chill passageway and at once Countess Catherine's guards banged on her chamber's door and told her that only a single survivor had returned from the sortie. The seductress called for her servants to dress her and looked at the boy who had given her pleasure. Alain de la Grave, as defenceless as a newborn child, was standing before her, still without any clothes.

'Stay here until I call for you. You'll be safe. No one will dare pass my guards. Understand?'

He nodded.

'I will have the laundress return your clothing.'

There was nothing he could do other than to get back into the bed and cover his nudity with the sheets that still bore her scent and the musk smell of sex. The raised voices cleared away any headiness from the indulgence of the previous hours. What was important now was not to panic and to brazen out his story. After the Countess left the room he opened and closed trunks searching for any men's clothing. Rather than wait for William Cade to convince the Countess that he, Alain, had misled them and caused the death of Cade's men, he would try and find Perinne, and if he couldn't do that then at least he would get out of this room that was his prison. His search for clothing proved fruitless. One of the bodyguards opened the door and threw his habit at him.

'Get dressed,' he commanded and waited, the door still open behind him; the second bodyguard was nowhere to be seen. Alain supposed the man had accompanied the Countess. Whatever else he felt, fear and anxiety aside, he knew he was not the same person he had been hours before. He pulled the habit over his head and tightened its rope around his waist. The sandal straps rubbed against the nicks and blisters but he ignored their bite.

'Follow me,' said the guard.

'The Countess told me to stay here.'

'She wants you outside.'

He hesitated. If Cade had convinced this man to seize him then he might soon be dead. His hesitation caused the guard to step forward and fling him from the room. 'Outside, you crow bastard.'

As he was pushed down the passageway he heard the clamour of raised voices and the sound of running feet. He stepped outside and saw people running for their houses, while others were being ushered from outside through the town's gates. He saw William Cade on the walls organizing men, and the Countess walking the parapet ahead of him, her cloak gathered around her, the second guard who had once stood at her door shadowing her. There was no sign of Perinne. Had he been killed or captured or gone into hiding?

'Up there,' said the guard and put a hand in his back to urge him towards the stone steps that rose to the parapet. As he reached the top of the walls Cade turned and saw him approaching. He took a couple of strides, grabbed a handful of his loose habit and slapped him hard. Alain went down on his knees, his ears ringing. He tasted blood.

'Enough!' the Countess called, but the look on her face told Alain that she no longer cared if more pain was inflicted on him.

Cade dragged him to his feet and hauled him to the Countess.

'Did you lie on purpose?' she asked. 'About the routiers at the monastery? Only one man returned. He said they were ambushed by hundreds of men.'

'I don't understand,' he said, realizing that Blackstone had inflicted a defeat on their men and that someone had survived. Bad news had brought the possibility of retribution against him.

'Thomas Blackstone swore revenge,' said Cade. 'How the fuck did he discover where I was? How has he brought hundreds here?'

253

Alain's confusion was genuine. How could there be an army at Blackstone's back? Then it dawned on him that the survivor had exaggerated, perhaps to stave off any punishment from being defeated by a small force.

'I did not lie. I saw less than twenty men. I did not know the man's name. Prior Albert gave me the message and I delivered it faithfully, my lady,' he said, bowing his head, knowing that what had gone on between him and the Countess had been nothing more than fleeting hours of intense sexual gratification with the most beautiful woman he had ever seen and who had captured his heart at first sight. How foolish that all felt now as she gazed at him with a look of regret.

'Perhaps,' she said. She looked at Cade. 'He's yours.'

'No,' he cried out. 'I beg you, Countess. Please!'

Cade snatched at him. 'I told you what would happen and now I will keep my promise. And before you die you'll tell me where I've seen you before.'

Alain twisted free, squirmed for freedom but Cade's fist clubbed him unconscious to the ground.

Cade looked at the Countess. 'We man the walls and bring every villager inside. No one sleeps. Light braziers and torches. I'll order the men to bring hot pitch and rocks. If he tries to scale the walls the crossbowmen will kill enough of them.' He grinned with anticipated success. 'Your husband chose well. Felice cannot be taken. Thomas Blackstone will die in his attempt. And when I take his head to the Dauphin I will have reward enough to buy you and this château.'

He kicked Alain's limp body down to the yard twenty feet below. It landed heavily. A leg twisted and broke. Cade called down to his men below: 'Take him to the cellar.'

The Countess looked out across the empty countryside that might soon be filled with an army ready to try and seize her home and inheritance. She turned to Cade.

'You had better make sure this Thomas Blackstone does not breach the walls, William. It is you he comes to kill.'

CHAPTER FORTY-ONE

Blackstone and his men approached the broken ground that lay several hundred yards away from the high walls. They had made good time and had sight of the château just as the sky eased into darkness. Using the rising ground to conceal themselves they peered across as the red glow from the burning torches and braziers illuminated the ramparts.

'Well, they're expecting us,' said Killbere. 'Not that they have too much to worry about. I doubt I've ever seen a more impregnable stronghold. You could spend a month building ladders and still not reach the top. Besides, we'd all be dead by the time we got halfway.'

Blackstone studied the defences. There was no apparent sign of vulnerability and to try and attack across the causeway bridge and burn down the iron-studded gates would probably kill every man who tried. 'Every place has its weakness, Gilbert,' he insisted.

'We don't know how many men serve the garrison or what numbers William Cade has,' said Will Longdon. 'I would need my archers on those walls to shoot down into them and then we would all have to fight our way up to that château.'

'The wind is at our back,' said Meulon, pointing a finger towards the wisps of smoke from the town's chimneys. 'They'll have stables close to the outer courtyard near their guards' quarters. We could use those braziers and torches to burn them out, then the smoke would smother the houses and streets. We've done that before. And horses running loose will add to the chaos. If we fight through in small groups, then we would have a chance to get up there because a killer like Cade will be in the safest place there is. In the château.

All we have to do is get inside.' As he spoke Meulon winced at his own suggestion. The assault still seemed impossible.

'Alain and Perinne are most likely dead by now,' said Renfred. 'If they aren't then they're either imprisoned or in hiding. If we find a way in then they might be able to get us into the château.'

The men fell silent. No one had a good enough idea of how to breach the high walls.

'William Cade could die of old age in there,' said Jack Halfpenny. 'I'll wager most of the people of Felice are already under their blankets and sleeping soundly, knowing we cannot reach them.'

Blackstone raised himself a little more and gazed into the darkness. 'Perhaps not. Look at the château. I can see candle- and firelight flickering in most of those rooms. But down here? Nothing. The village is deserted. They've taken everyone inside.'

'We could use those houses for cover,' said Renfred.

'That only gets us so close,' said Gilbert.

Blackstone pointed towards the houses that pressed against the walls. 'Every window in those houses is dark. We have rope and hooks to scale that timber walkway from the gully below. We create a diversion and once we are onto that wooden walkway and into one of those deserted houses we cut through the roof and then we're only feet away from the battlements.' The men murmured their approval. By taking everyone inside the walls the defenders had gifted them a means of gaining entry. 'Meulon, have Tait take a dozen men on the left flank of that gully in the opposite direction from the houses. Tell him to keep out of crossbow range. Single file, every man carrying a burning torch. They need to be seen – make it look as though they are searching for a way inside. Once we are over the walls they double back and follow us.'

'And the woman? This Countess? What do we do about her?' said Killbere. 'She's not done us any harm. From what we know she helps protect the villagers in the district from routiers. That she kills them is nothing less than what we've been doing, nothing less than the treaty would have us and the French do.'

'But she's with Cade,' said John Jacob. 'She's using routiers to trap routiers.'

'Or she's beholden to them in some way,' said Killbere. 'Perhaps she is even his hostage. We don't know. Going after Cade and rescuing Perinne and the lad is one thing; killing a countess and her men is another. Even King Edward would think twice about this and he's a harsh man when it comes to retribution against a defiant town.'

The role of the Countess had not been considered by any of them but now that Killbere had raised the issue it became part of the problem of assaulting the town of Felice.

'Women. They always complicate a man's life,' said Will Longdon.

'For all we know she's dead already,' said Meulon. 'Cade's men rode against us but there were few of hers who fought. We don't know how many men are in there, Sir Thomas, and who is to say that there are not patrols beyond the walls. If there are they could strike at our rear. The woman is less important than our horses.'

Meulon made good sense. And Blackstone knew that everyone was aware of the risk they took. He turned away from the manned battlements, pressing his back against the boulders. He looked to where the men waited; the horses had been moved further back into dead ground, hobbled and corralled by fallen branches. He would have to leave men behind to guard them. But to fight through the streets of a town and then try and find a way into a guarded château would demand every man he had. The danger was that if they were isolated in the narrow confines or if they finally secured the château enough of the enemy might escape and stumble across their horses. To lose their mounts would be a disaster.

'We saw no sign of any patrols. And they are expecting an assault. I'll wager they have every man armed and waiting. Inside, not out. Once Tait's men have shown themselves have them come back here and act as a rearguard for the horses and supplies.'

'We could do with them inside the walls,' said Killbere.

'I know, but we have taken towns with fewer men. We strike silently. Kill those who resist. The objective is the château,' said

Blackstone. 'And we cause no harm to the Countess or her house-hold.' He turned back to study the houses that buttressed the walls. 'Will, Killbere and I will go onto the walls through the middle house. You will take your archers left and right. Jack and Quenell will break through the roof on that furthest house. See it?'

Will Longdon looked to where Blackstone pointed. 'We need to kill the crossbowmen first. And then if we can drive the others from the walls then it's up to you to deal with them, Thomas. All we can do then is hold the battlements. We'll be hard pressed if they counter-attack from the town.'

Blackstone glanced at the veteran archer.

Longdon shrugged. 'It can be done,' he said and grinned.

'Hold the walls. Keep the archers there. Don't come into the streets. I will send men to you once we have taken the château.' Blackstone looked at his captains. 'Ready the men.'

Blackstone watched Ralph Tait lead a dozen of his men, blazing torches held aloft, as they skirted the gully that encircled the walls. There were shouts of alarm from those who manned the ramparts and Blackstone and his men waiting below the wooden walkway saw torchlight moving hurriedly along the top of the walls in Tait's direction. They heard the clatter of crossbow bolts striking rocks but they fell at least fifty paces short of where Tait led his men. As Blackstone's men ran quickly through the deserted village towards the houses against the wall the captains sent some of them inside the hovels to scavenge for tallow candles or oil lamps. To clamber inside those houses pressed against the walls meant that they would have to risk lighting their way into the rafters.

Blackstone's men huddled below the wooden walkway as grappling hooks quickly found purchase. The men climbed up hand over hand and then crouched in the darkness, checking that no sentries had heard the bite of steel into wood or seen men's shadows flit into the houses. No door was locked and no sound came from any abandoned dogs. The citizens of Felice had bundled up their chattels and fled into the town.

The dim glow from the spluttering candles was enough to show each group of men the open stairs that led upwards. A half-landing gave another turn to the stairs and then they saw that half the roof void had been boarded for storage. Meulon went down on one knee and Renfred clambered onto his shoulders; then he reached up onto the edge of the boarding and hauled himself up. He crouched as he pressed his palms upwards onto the slate roof. John Jacob followed and attached a rope beneath one of the rafters so that the others might clamber up once a hole had been made. Renfred pushed his fist firmly against the nailed slates, which were brittle with age. Two or three broke at the same time and he whispered quietly to his companion to take the broken pieces from him. The old roof gave way quickly in response to his efforts and there was soon a hole broad enough for the likes of Blackstone and Meulon to climb through. They, like the others who followed, bore their shields across their backs.

Renfred eased his head and shoulders into the night. The battlements were only feet away and as he looked in the distance he saw that most of those who guarded the walls were focusing on Tait's men. Will Longdon, Halfpenny and Quenell's lightly armed archers had moved even more quickly and made better progress. Darkened figures were already scrambling through the roofs left and right and spilling quickly onto the walls. Renfred bent down into the flickering shadows below and urged the men-at-arms to hurry. The men's heaving effort was punctuated with curses as they tried to stoop below the low rafters. There was room for only three men at a time to crouch and then get through the hole. Killbere was struggling to climb up the rope that led to the rafters. He swore, sweat in his eyes, his age and the weight of his mail and weapons halting his progress. Meulon reached down and grabbed his arms and hauled him unceremoniously onto the half-platform.

Blackstone was soon on the walls; then Meulon heaved himself over the ramparts, followed by a cursing Killbere. One of the men behind them put his foot through the roof slates and the break sounded as loud as a crack of thunder. Blackstone and Meulon leaned across the battlements and pulled men across in quick succession now that those below were moving quickly.

One of the archers hissed, 'For Christ's sake, hurry. They're starting to come back to their posts.'

Blackstone bent low and ran left along the parapet. In the distance Felice's men were turning back with their torches. Tait's men had done all they could do but the crossbowmen among those who guarded the wall could quickly bring down Blackstone's running men as they made their way to the steps that led down to the courtyard. Blackstone had John Jacob at his shoulder while Meulon had peeled away and taken his men to the right of the breached wall, racing for another set of steps. Will Longdon's men were crouched, backs against the battlements, barely visible in the lee of the walls. And then a cry went up from one of the approaching sentries. Blackstone was already taking the steps two at a time, running towards the fleeting shadows of the garrison men below, who ducked and weaved between the hanging corpses in their attempt to cut him off. If the attack was isolated on the walls before it got into the alleyways then Blackstone knew his assault would be contained. He felt the air whisper past his face and then heard the metallic strike of a crossbow bolt against the stonework. One of the men behind John Jacob grunted; there was the sound of a bolt piercing mail, flesh and bone. The man tumbled into space and fell.

Will Longdon and his archers stood close together, two abreast on the rampart, as many men as the width of the walkway would accommodate. The first two loosed into the approaching men, saw and heard their arrows strike, and then quickly pressed themselves back as another two shot into the crowded men at the far end of the parapet. In a rapidly moving sequence of shooting and manoeuvring Will Longdon's archers gained thirty paces more. As Longdon's bowmen drew and loosed so too did Halfpenny's men, buying time for Meulon's men-at-arms going in the opposite direction. Men cried out below. Commands echoed across the courtyard. Blackstone heard the hard breath of shadowy men at his shoulder, saw out of the corner of his eye Killbere strike out towards four men who ran at him. Renfred was at his back just as John Jacob was at Blackstone's, and then these shadowy men who loomed behind Blackstone fanned out and clashed into the defenders, who hesitated, uncertain whether to throw themselves at the attacking men or retreat into the gloom of the narrow streets and try to hold back these silent killers.

And then a chapel bell clanged out its desperate warning. Its incessant clamour echoed around the houses and walls, calling the town to arms.

CHAPTER FORTY-TWO

Perinne heard men shouting and women's fearful cries as the château's servants ran to wherever they thought might be a safer place. And then as the voices died away he heard the clanging bell. He quickly eased himself down from the soot-filled chimney and grasped the weapons he had taken from the kitchen. The attack had started and he needed to do what he could to aid its success. As he ran into the kitchen he saw two garrison soldiers preparing to throw water over the deep-seated kitchen fire, a fire that could be used against the defenders. They turned suddenly as the wild apparition of a soot-streaked monk attacked them wielding a meat cleaver and a knife. Startled, they dropped their buckets and fumbled for their swords, yelling in alarm. But Perinne's momentum carried him into them, sweeping the cleaver down across the nearest man's shoulder. It dug deep into bone; the man went down screaming. He writhed but the cleaver was embedded. Perinne grabbed the second man, who had turned to run, and plunged the knife down into the gap between throat and shoulder. Fatally wounded, the man went down. Perinne turned quickly and, placing his sandalled foot on the other man's chest, yanked free the embedded cleaver. The man's eyes rolled, his mouth opened, but his scream halted as the pointed knife plunged into his throat. Perinne needed as much surprise on his side as he could get and hoped that the men's death cries had not alerted others.

He stopped, listened for any sound of approaching guards and then quickly went to the stone larder where pig carcasses hung. He dragged three of the dead pigs to the outside of the kitchen. Looking down across the town he saw spurts of red from burning torches, flames that flickered as their bearers ran in and out of darkened streets. Muted cries of alarm and defence carried through the night. Somewhere in the distance a donkey brayed and dogs yelped and howled. He ran back into the solar and gathered an armful of the rush flooring. Back outside it took little time to build a small pyre: it would not cause damage but it would guide the attackers up towards him. Taking a shovelful of coals from the kitchen fire he quickly got the dry rushes burning. With a final visit to the solar he yanked aside a tapestry from the walls and dropped it onto the flames. Once the fire took hold the old threadbare tapestry flared and engulfed the pig carcasses whose fat fuelled the flames.

In a final effort to feed the flames he dragged kitchen stools and a bench to build the pyre higher. He went back into the kitchen and barricaded the door into the solar. If Blackstone's men saw the beacon in time then they would fight their way quickly up to the château and this door would give them a way into the main rooms. And somewhere inside was the Countess and, he hoped, the young Frenchman.

There was little sign of any townsmen. Most had barricaded themselves into their homes and the few militia who had ventured out into the streets retreated quickly when they saw the violence inflicted on the garrison troops and William Cade's routiers. The rumour that an army of mercenaries was at the gates fuelled the town's fear. As Blackstone and his captains moved rapidly through the narrow alleys Will Longdon and the archers secured the walls. The braziers had illuminated the archers' targets and as Longdon and his men advanced left and right along the parapet soldiers and crossbowmen retreated down into the town square. The town walls were three-sided with the château forming the fourth quadrant, whose rear walls were so sheer that they could never be assaulted.

The fight progressed through the streets upwards towards the flaming beacon. Pockets of resistance formed at street corners where barricades were quickly thrown down to impede Blackstone's advance. But, shields raised, he and the men at his shoulder battered their way forward into the makeshift barriers, his spearmen thrusting their weapons forward, jabbing into the lightly armed defenders, forcing them to reel back. Grunting and cursing with effort they strode on, hacking their way clear. Many of Cade's men retreated across the open space of another square towards the town church, whose bell had now fallen silent. Men, women and children – villagers who had sought sanctuary in the town – huddled along an outside wall of the church. There were more than a hundred of them cowering, terrified by the darkened figures who swarmed into the square. Children wept and their mothers screamed at the sight of men being cut down mercilessly.

Blackstone saw that the church door had been forced open by retreating soldiers. Killbere ran after them with half a dozen men and rammed sword and spear into the narrow gap, slashing at those soldiers who were trying to heave the doors closed from inside. Blackstone broke away and faced the terrified villeins.

'Stay here!' he bellowed at them. 'No harm will come to you if you do not run or resist.' The huge scar-faced man was enough to provoke even more fear in them. They clung to each other as Blackstone turned back to the church. Killbere's efforts had succeeded in forcing the heavy wooden door open and as Blackstone got there he saw the church was crammed full of townspeople and that the few soldiers who had forced their way inside had pushed their way in among the refugees, clutching slashed arms and hands from their efforts to resist the doors being shoved open. Blackstone knew there was no sense in trying to reach them; it would only cause slaughter among the huddled mass.

'Close the doors and guard them,' he said. 'If they surrender disarm them and let them live.'

The heavy doors slammed closed and Killbere ordered the men with him to stay and do as Blackstone had commanded. Then: 'Up there,' Killbere gasped and spat the phlegm of exhaustion. 'Someone's lit our way.'

Blackstone looked around the square and saw Meulon advance from one of the side streets having fought his way through to join up with Blackstone to make the final assault up the curved route to the château.

'I couldn't burn out the stables,' said Meulon. 'The villagers and their livestock were penned at the back – sixty or more peasants with their wives and children. But there's a beacon up there at the château.'

'We see it,' said Blackstone.

'Our backs?' asked Killbere. 'Any of these murdering bastards ready to strike at us?'

'I saw none,' said Meulon, still breathing heavily from his exertions. 'Some of Will's archers are coming down off the walls.'

'Send a man back, tell them to advance only to where they can use their bows. Let them secure the squares. I don't want to lose any archers in street fighting. Any sign of Cade?'

Meulon shook his head. 'He's either barricaded himself in a house or he's up there,' he said, tilting his head towards the château, shimmering in the light from the burning pyre which illuminated the way towards it.

Blackstone quickly assessed the surrounding houses in the square. The resistance had been lighter than he had expected and the town had been secured quickly but there was still no sign of the man he had come to kill or of the woman who ruled here. 'How many have we lost?'

'Four men dead as far as I know,' said Meulon. 'Some light wounds.'

'We cannot risk the townsmen rising up once we have pushed up to the château. Meulon, hold your men here. With Will Longdon's archers on the walls and those that come into the square they should be enough to protect our backs. Gilbert and I will take the rest of the men up to the château.'

Meulon immediately turned away and ran to organize his men.

'Do not race me to the top and start the killing without me,' said Killbere.

'Don't worry, my friend, Cade and his men will not surrender without a fight.' Blackstone's grin broke the darkness that played across his face. 'Shall I find one of those braying donkeys to carry you up there?'

'Thomas, I swear you have no respect for your elders.' Killbere snorted snot from each nostril. 'I'm pleased I taught you well.' With that he turned and strode briskly uphill.

CHAPTER FORTY-THREE

Perinne stood his ground in the kitchen as men on the other side shouldered the connecting door. They knew that this was a way in for their attackers. The château's main doors were locked and barred but this kitchen access into the solar was the weak point and someone had barricaded it from the kitchen side. And even if the defenders barricaded the door where they were, those entering the château through the kitchen could burn the door down. Whoever was in the kitchen needed to be stopped and the outer door closed. The defenders' choice was to open the main doors and flank whoever was in the kitchen from the outside, or to push through whatever was blocking this door. Going outside seemed a greater danger than trying to force their way through.

Perinne had dragged the heavy kitchen table used for preparing food across the door but the more the men on the other side pushed the more it gave. It would not be long before they breached his defence.

He wrapped a kitchen cloth around his hands and lifted a pot of hot water from its stand above the flames. The table shifted. Men swore and heaved and then three soldiers appeared, shoulders against the door. They pushed hard enough to force the heavy table aside. Big men, blood-flushed faces, beards flecked with spittle from their efforts. One was already clambering over the table to reach Perinne, who hurled the hot water at him. As the man's hands went up to his scalded face Perinne threw the pot at the others and picked up his cleaver and knife. He did not wait for them to clamber forward but lunged at them, throwing himself across the table and stabbing one of them in the face. The other brought down his sword and Perinne felt the blade cut through his habit. It seared his flesh. The pain spurred him: he rolled, felt the squelch of blood on his back and prayed his left arm would work as he raised the knife in an attempt to block the second strike. The blow was hard and forced his blade away but his effort deflected the slash that would have taken his arm. He swung his free arm and struck down with the cleaver. It cut through the skullcap helmet and embedded itself into the man's head. He fell without a sound, the force of his falling body yanking the cleaver from Perinne's blood-soaked hands. He winced in pain from the slash on his back but ignored it, dropped to the tabletop and began pushing it back against the door. The sudden sound of men at the kitchen door made him swirl, knife in hand.

Blackstone and John Jacob with two men crouched ready to attack: they saw the bloodied monk. 'Perinne!'

Perinne grinned and leaned back. Blackstone strode quickly to him as others stormed into the kitchen. 'You look like a monk from hell,' he said, looking at the soot and blood that covered the fighter. The cut on his back was deep enough to need attention. Perinne slumped. The fight had gone from him. Blackstone half supported him to a stool. 'All right, my friend. I have you,' he said. 'That wound needs attention.'

Perinne gave a dismissive gesture. 'Through there,' he said, pointing to the door. 'The solar and then the other rooms. I think there are more men in the château. I held here as long as I could but... you came just in time.'

John Jacob had already ordered men to guard the other side of the door they had breached.

'You lit the fire?' Blackstone said.

Perinne nodded as Killbere came into the kitchen; sweat streaked his face and he was breathless. 'A good defensive château should always be built on high ground,' he wheezed, 'but not when I have to attack it.' He moved across to where Blackstone stood with Perinne. He unceremoniously tugged Perinne's shoulder down so he could poke a finger into the wound. The stocky fighter winced.

'Get Will Longdon here to stitch it or – better – sear it with one of those irons in the fire,' he said. 'But do it quick.'

Perinne looked at the veteran knight, realizing that the urgency in his voice meant the wound was worse than he thought.

'Aye, get it done,' said Killbere in answer to the unspoken question. Perinne nodded.

'Find some wine,' Blackstone ordered a couple of men waiting at the door. Others were already crowding in ready to join the fight. 'Brandy if you can.'

Men quickly rummaged on the shelves.

'Where's the lad? Where's Alain?' said Blackstone.

'Don't know. He was taken inside to the Countess when we got here. That's the last I saw of him.'

One of the men stepped out of the larder, a clay flask in hand. 'Brandy, Sir Thomas.'

Blackstone gave it to Perinne, who drank thirstily, then coughed, and drank more. 'Merciful Mother of God, this is going to hurt like hell.'

'Hurts once and then it's done,' said Killbere and took the flask from him, swigged heartily and handed it back.

'You go on,' said Perinne to Blackstone and Killbere. 'I've no wish for you to hear me cry out. Cade and his men are inside somewhere.'

'Bellow like a calving cow,' said Killbere. 'I've brought the walls down about my ears before now when I've had a wound cauterized.' He rested a reassuring hand on Perinne's shoulder.

Blackstone sheathed Wolf Sword and laid aside his shield. He eased Perinne to his feet as Killbere picked up the piece of cloth that had been used to lift the pot of water. He twisted it and put it between Perinne's teeth; then Blackstone laid him face down on the table and ripped the habit open further to expose the cut. He nodded to Killbere and two others to hold Perinne's arms and legs as John Jacob pulled out a hot riddling poker from the coals. They wasted no more time. Blackstone seized a cloth, wiped away the blood, tipped brandy into the wound. Perinne's back muscles bunched as the liquid stung and then John Jacob laid the red-tipped poker across the wound. Flesh sizzled. Perinne bellowed and then passed out.

'Leave him on the table,' said Blackstone, arming himself again and pushing through the knot of men who had gathered in the solar. They peered into the gloomy interior. There was no sign of Cade's men or any garrison soldiers. The stood silently listening for any sound that might alert them.

'Man's stupid if he only holds upstairs,' said Killbere quietly. 'We could set fire to the place and let them roast in hell.'

'He didn't hold the town, he had no militia and how many of his men did you see? Not many.'

'No,' agreed Killbere. 'A few levies, and a handful of Cade's men. They were on the walls. It was mostly garrison men in the streets. We killed enough of Cade's men when they tried to ambush us. If he has more men then he would have pitted them against us. We've killed most of them.'

'So where is he? How many men can he muster?' Blackstone looked at the men who accompanied him. 'Then if he doesn't have enough men to fight he has something to bargain,' he said. 'Alain. He holds the lad.'

'Or this Countess is being held prisoner,' said John Jacob.

Blackstone nodded. 'All right. John, you take four men and search these rooms down here. Sir Gilbert and I will take the others to the upper rooms.'

The men raised their shields and followed Blackstone and Killbere up the stone stairway that turned onto a half-landing ahead. No cresset lamps flickered, plunging the stairs into deep shadow that verged on darkness. Blackstone stopped halfway and turned to the men behind him.

'When we turn up there our backs are exposed to anyone on the landing above and if they have crossbows then we die here. Be ready. Sir Gilbert and I will draw them out.'

Blackstone and Killbere trod carefully forward and then as they reached the half-landing that exposed them to those above and behind them they quickly turned raising their shields. They had no sooner exposed themselves than the sound of crossbow bolts being loosed cracked the silence. Blackstone and Killbere, backs pressed against the stairwell, crouched as two quarrels struck close by. No sooner had the men on the stairs heard the taut bowstrings loose than they charged past Blackstone and up onto the landing above. Experience had taught them that if crossbowmen laid an ambush then they would release their bolts all at once in their determination to kill their enemy. As they raced up the stairs they were quickly proved wrong. There must have been four archers on the landing because another two quarrels struck the first two men who fell back dead into those who followed. The attack faltered but Blackstone and Killbere were already pushing their way through the stumbling men.

'Forward! Keep going!' Blackstone yelled.

He and Killbere were quickly in the near darkness and saw shapes of men moving against them. Dim light caught sword blades and a sudden cry of 'Attack!' bellowed from whoever held the landing. Blackstone braced his shield, pushed his arm forward, felt the impact of an attacker's sword and thrust Wolf Sword instinctively, feeling its sharpened point bury itself into the nearest body. No sooner had he and Killbere pressed forward than the men behind them were quickly at their side and their shield wall forced the defenders onto the back foot as they closed. Once the cries of defiance were spent the thud of shield against shield and blade against flesh and mail became a muted, grunting effort to kill. Light spilled onto the landing as two of the grappling men fell against a door which gave way, exposing a fire in a grate and candlelight. Killbere and Blackstone saw there were no more than eight men defending the landing. Three others were already dead at their feet. He and Killbere punished them with a sustained attack. Soon there were only five men standing. They cried out for mercy. Blackstone raised his sword to halt the attack. Killbere commanded the cornered men to lower their shields and drop their weapons. They were Cade's men and had fought more stridently than garrison troops.

'We'll die here if we must with sword in hand but we'll not be butchered defenceless,' one of them declared.

'Throw down your weapons and you'll live,' said Blackstone as he stepped across men's corpses and levelled Wolf Sword at them. The routiers looked uncertainly at each other but when their leader threw down his sword and shield the others followed.

'William Cade. Where is he?' said Blackstone.

One of the routiers pointed up the continuing flight of stairs. 'He's with the Countess Catherine. Her rooms are up there. Sir Thomas, I beg you, let us live.'

'How many more men are with him?' snarled Killbere, pressing his face closer to the defeated men.

The man who spoke for the others shook his head. 'Sir Gilbert, I don't know. There are few of us left now but the Countess has men loyal to her.'

Killbere looked at Blackstone. He was ready to kill the men who had surrendered. Blackstone shook his head.

'There were two monks sent here. One younger than the other. Where is he?'

'I don't know and that's the truth,' answered the mercenary. 'When the alarm was raised we manned the walls and then fought through the streets. This was to be our last place of defence.'

John Jacob and his men pounded up the stairs. 'Nothing below, Sir Thomas.'

Blackstone gestured to one of his men who had fought on the landing. 'You and five others seize these men and take them to Meulon. Have them bound and held. If any one man tries to escape kill them all.'

Blackstone and Killbere turned for the upper storey. John Jacob was a stride behind them. 'Still no sign of the French lad.'

'We'll find him. He's here somewhere,' said Blackstone as they reached the top floor. Two double doors faced them. The men let their breath settle. 'John, break down the doors.'

John Jacob stepped forward with one of his men. They braced their shields and rammed the door. They flew open. Blackstone faltered at the doorway. Across the room, seated by the comfort of the fire, was a woman of rare beauty. She was dressed in fine silk clothes and wore precious gems that caught the light. She had the bearing of a queen ready to receive homage rather than a woman who might be facing imminent death. An armed guard stood either side of her. Big men who looked ready to die at her feet. Each held a sword in one hand and a snarling dog on a chain in the other. An older man stood respectfully just behind the seated woman.

'I am bailiff to this noble household and Countess Catherine de Val. Who is it that invades her home and kills our men?'

'I am Thomas Blackstone and you harbour a murderer and a thief and for all I know you aid and abet his killing.'

The bailiff took a half-pace forward but before he could speak the woman stood. There was a slight tremble in her voice.

'I am Countess de Val. Do not judge me until you know me better,' she said. The Countess made a slight gesture to the part of the room which was obscured by the doors.

Blackstone stepped forward.

'Is this the man you seek?' she said.

William Cade was on his knees, arms bound behind him and gagged like a captured thief, guarded by another two garrison soldiers.

CHAPTER FORTY-FOUR

Blackstone ignored the bailiff and the two men holding William Cade and with half a dozen quick strides put his boot into the kneeling man's chest and sent him sprawling. His guards were too startled to react quickly enough and they took faltering steps backwards away from the scar-faced Englishman. Blackstone turned and looked at the Countess. 'Stand your men down or have them and your dogs slain.'

'And you will do what with me?' said the Countess defiantly.

'I will question you and expect answers. And then I will decide your fate.'

'The Countess has the protection of the King of France,' the bailiff said.

'I've never liked him,' said Blackstone. 'I won't ask you again. Send your men out and tell them to surrender their weapons to my men. And keep those dogs chained and under control.'

One of the bodyguards stepped closer. 'We are the Count Henri de Val's sworn men and since his death we serve my Lady Catherine. We do not leave her alone with you.'

Blackstone gauged the two hefty men. They could be killed and overwhelmed but their fearless loyalty was something that could be respected.

'Very well, stay with her until she commands you to leave.' He looked towards the two men who stood with William Cade. 'Have these men surrender their weapons and take the dogs. What needs to be said should be done without their snarls interrupting us.'

The bodyguard looked at the Countess, who nodded her assent. Without hesitation the two men handed over the chained dogs and the two garrison men lay down their swords. Blackstone's men stood aside from the doorway as the muscular beasts were taken from the room. There was a moment of calm once their threat had been removed. Blackstone laid aside his shield and slipped Wolf Sword into its scabbard. There would be no assault from the two men who guarded the Countess unless she so ordered, but it was obvious to the men and to the Countess that they would die before they even reached Blackstone, with or without sword in hand.

'You align yourself with this scum,' he said, meaning William Cade.

'Am I to be questioned like a common prisoner, sir? I do not discuss my private affairs in front of unwashed, bloodstained soldiers.'

Her courage and defiance in face of the brutal-looking men who gathered in the doorway impressed him. 'John, have these men taken downstairs, secure the main doors to the château and send word to Meulon to give safe passage to those who sought sanctuary in the church and the square. Have the people return to their homes and take their livestock and chattels with them.' He faced the Countess. 'Does that give you some assurance, my lady?'

'I am grateful,' she said. There was warmth in her voice, enough to easily entice him to stay in the room with her.

'Do you have a physician who serves this household?'

'An apothecary in the street below the church,' she answered.

'Fetch him for Perinne,' Blackstone told John Jacob, who stood ready to pass on Blackstone's orders, 'and leave three men outside the door.' He nodded his dismissal.

As the men clattered down the stairs, Killbere closed the door behind them and pulled off his sweat-soaked helm. He walked across to a table that bore a flagon of wine and a tray full of glasses. He hesitated momentarily and looked at the Countess. 'With your permission?'

'You assault my town and kill my men and you ask if you may help yourself to my wine?'

'Killing your men is thirsty work, but there's no need for bad manners,' said Killbere, pouring the wine.

Blackstone pulled off his gauntlets and took the glass of wine Killbere offered and slaked his thirst. He laid his helmet on the table.

'We were sent into a trap by Prior Albert. But we learnt of his treachery and ambushed the men you sent to kill us. The prior is in your pay.'

'I seize routiers who terrorize my people. I capture and kill them in revenge for my husband, son and daughter who were murdered by them two years ago. I make no apology for using men like William Cade to entrap them. I take pleasure in my revenge. I inflict pain on them at every opportunity. I knew nothing of you or the men who ride with you. Prior Albert considered you mercenaries.'

'We are men on the English King's business,' said Blackstone. 'A treaty has been signed and agreed by your King and mine. I enforce that treaty.'

'And Château de Felice is not ceded to English rule. You have no right to do what you have done,' insisted the bailiff.

'I came on Felice by chance in my search for Cade,' said Blackstone.

'Be careful whom you kill and why you kill them. He also has protection. He serves the French Crown,' the Countess said.

Killbere snorted at the news. 'Thomas, this bastard was planted on us!'

Cade's muffled curses meant nothing. Killbere pulled off his gag.

'Listen to her. She's speaking the truth. You harm me and word will get back to Paris,' said Cade.

'We don't intend to harm you,' said Killbere. 'We're going to kill you. Traitors deserve a slow death. An Englishman serving our blood enemy should be made to suffer. And you must pay for killing a young archer who was promised safe conduct.'

Cade squirmed and tried to get off his knees. Killbere pushed him back again.

'Kill me and you lose your gold. Kill me and you won't find the Welshman.'

'You're wrong on both counts. You'll yield that information when I ask for it,' said Blackstone, with the implied threat of torture. 'How much did you pay him for delivering routiers to you?' he said, turning to the Countess.

She waved a hand at the bailiff who opened a linen chest and hauled out a small sack of coin. 'This is what he arrived with and I gave him more.'

'Bitch!' Cade hissed with disbelief.

'William, you're a fool. You are easily betrayed by your own kind. Once your men failed in their ambush and we were told that we might be attacked it wasn't difficult to discover its hiding place. I paid the man who betrayed you well.'

The bailiff dropped the sack at Blackstone's feet.

The Countess made a slight gesture towards the sack of gold and the bound prisoner. 'Take the gold, and take him. He means nothing to me—'

'Whore!' Cade yelled and earned a cuff across the head from Killbere.

'That's no way to address a noble lady,' said Killbere. He smiled at the Countess and dipped his head in respect.

Countess Catherine barely took a breath after being interrupted by Cade's insult. 'King John and the Dauphin will hear of what you do here. Be it on your own head.'

'This whore bitch—' Killbere struck him again. Cade spat blood but he shook the blow away as if it were nothing more than a wasp sting. 'She took me to her bed. She will take any man to her bed.'

'Not any man. Only those I choose,' she answered coolly and sat down, easing a crease from her dress.

Killbere smiled and bowed slightly. 'I am at your service, Countess. A decent bath and a clean linen shirt and I am no longer the ruffian you see before you.'

Cade laughed derisively. 'She's a bitch on heat who goes for your throat. Watch it doesn't get cut. She took your false monk to her bed. The young one. She fucked him into manhood.'

Countess Catherine de Val showed no expression other than to stare expressionless at Blackstone and Killbere.

'Where is he?' said Blackstone to Cade as Killbere grabbed a handful of his hair and yanked back his head.

Cade spat bloody phlegm at Blackstone, and laughed for a second before Killbere gave him more than a wasp sting blow. He fell back, barely conscious.

'When you attacked us, Cade had him taken to the cellars,' said the Countess.

Blackstone grabbed Cade, hauling him to his feet. 'You,' he said, pointing at the bailiff. 'You show the way.'

The bailiff received a nod of consent from the Countess and then quickly moved to open the doors.

'Sir Gilbert Killbere is a veteran knight who has long served Edward of England. He stays,' said Blackstone. 'Gilbert, if her guards make any move against you call for the men outside. And kill her.'

The doors closed behind Blackstone.

Killbere helped himself to more wine and this time took a glass for the seductive woman whose eyes smiled at him. 'Would you?' she asked.

'Regretfully, yes,' said Killbere.

She took the glass. 'You have killed many women?'

'Hundreds,' he said.

'You are a liar, Sir Gilbert,' she said, raising the glass to her lips.

'Only about some things,' he said. 'Not about the beauty of women. Never that. But, as insurance against such an event as your early death, I drink to your health. And beauty.'

'I accept,' she said. She raised a hand and with the slightest of gestures commanded the two sworn men to step away across the room. 'You have the temperament of a gentle man,' she said softly: an intimate compliment whose tone of voice she did not wish her keepers to witness.

'I am versed in love and war, madam.'

'Well versed?' she asked, glancing at him over the rim of her glass.

'Experience hard won,' he answered.

'And my wellbeing might be in your hands?'

'Should that occasion arise it is possible that I could persuade Thomas Blackstone not to cause any harm to befall you. He is a man of insolence and intemperate ways. A legend at war feared across the country. He even tried to kill the King of France once. Violence is not even second nature to him. It is his first.'

'Then I am at your mercy,' she said. 'Is that the truth?'

'It would appear so.'

'Truthfully?'

'I seldom lie, my lady. Better that a man be known by his words as well as his actions.' Killbere stood in front of the fire, warming his back. It was a good enough reason to step closer to her. She smelled of flower fragrance and he imagined breathing it deeper were his face resting on her naked flesh.

'Sir Gilbert, would a woman who fell under your charm allow you the freedom to wander, like a travelling minstrel?' she probed. 'Would such a man as yourself not have a family? Children perhaps?'

'No woman has yet caged my heart, Countess. And as for children, well, there are none that I know of.'

'Perhaps you do not possess the passion or the... ability to do what is necessary when holding a naked mistress in your arms,' she taunted him. 'Your beard is slight: perhaps the state of the hay suggests whether the pitchfork is any good. There seems little more than the fuzz that ladies have in certain places.'

'Given that we play the game of truth or dare, Countess, perhaps you have more hair between your legs than I have on my face.'

'I have none,' she said.

Killbere dared to lean forward and take her hand to his lips. 'As they say, my lady, grass does not grow on a well-beaten path.'

CHAPTER FORTY-FIVE

The bailiff scurried ahead of Blackstone as he forced Cade down the stairs. The bailiff led him past the kitchen where the apothecary was tending to Perinne's wound. Blackstone pushed Cade outside where survivors of the attack were being held in the courtyard by Blackstone's men. He beckoned John Jacob to accompany him.

'If your friend beds the whore tell him to make sure there is no knife close to hand,' said Cade. 'She held a blade at my throat because I accused her of sleeping with the King or his sour-faced son. She's probably been had by everyone at court.'

'Keep moving and spare me your thoughts on the Countess. She is of no interest to me.'

Cade grunted derisively. 'What kind of eunuch are you, Blackstone? Are you telling me you didn't feel the urge to rape her?'

Blackstone ignored the crude taunt as Cade led him down into the dank and musty cellars. 'Where's the Frenchman?'

Cade sniggered. 'Your attack saved him. I was going to geld him. He's there.'

Blackstone gripped Cade's collar and moved deeper into the darkness. He reached out and touched the metal frets of a cage. It might have been dog pens or the château's cage for holding prisoners; whatever its purpose it stank of soiled straw and fetid air. Water ran down the walls, further chilling the atmosphere.

'Alain,' Blackstone called, but there was no reply. 'Where is the key?' he asked Cade with a shake of his collar.

Cade looked up at a hook in the wall behind Blackstone. John Jacob took it, opened the cage door and stepped out of sight into the darkness at the far side of the cage.

'I have him,' said John Jacob. 'He's more dead than alive.' He grabbed the unconscious young Frenchman beneath his arms.

'Get him outside,' said Blackstone. And as Jacob pulled him free Blackstone pushed Cade into the cage and locked the door. 'You'll stay there until I decide when I'm going to kill you.'

Cade pushed himself against the bars. 'Blackstone, you are hunted. The French want you dead. You're a plague on the House of Valois. I was paid to ride with Chandos so that I might kill you but I decided to take your gold instead. If the Welshman hadn't arrived I would have found a way to cut your throat in the night. But I decided my chances were better served running with ap Madoc. I know where he is. And he has the rest of your money. Let me live and I will tell you where. Let me live and I will ride away. I don't care what you do with my men. There are always others, but I will stay well away. You have my word. What do you say, Blackstone? Come on, killing the Welshman will give you more pleasure than killing me.'

'Killing both of you would please me more,' said Blackstone and then followed John Jacob.

Once they had dragged Alain into the daylight they saw that he was badly hurt. His leg was twisted at an unnatural angle and pieces of broken bone pierced the skin. It was matted with dirt and excrement from the foul cage. His face was caked with blood and one eye was swollen and closed.

'He took a hard blow, Sir Thomas. I can't rouse him. And that leg...' John Jacob let the words hang.

Blackstone nodded. He knew as well as his squire how badly injured the leg was. He saw Perinne being helped from the kitchen. He was weak but would survive. He shrugged off the helping hands of the men who supported him, cursing at them and getting the usual rough response from his comrades, but the coarse exchange was all in good humour. Blackstone called up to them. 'Perinne? Don't tear open the wound. That's an order. You rest. There's enough brandy to give you sleep.'

'Aye, Sir Thomas, and the apothecary has given me a tincture for the pain and bandaged me. I'll sleep for a week.'

Blackstone beckoned Renfred over from where he stood with his men guarding the captives. The German captain ran to his sworn lord. 'How many of their men do we hold?'

'Near enough seventy.'

'Find a stretcher and have four of them carry this lad to the apothecary's house. I want it done gently, Renfred. We must give him every chance we can. Then use a dozen or more of the garrison men to get rid of those corpses that are hanging in the square. Keep the rest of the prisoners bound and guarded until I know what we're doing next. Where's Meulon?'

'At the town square.'

Renfred needed no further orders and ran back, shouting his own commands. The elderly apothecary stepped carefully down the steps to the courtyard.

'I am told you are Sir Thomas Blackstone,' said the old man. 'I have done all I can for the monk's wound.'

'He's no monk. And you will be paid for your skills.'

The old man could not hide his surprise. 'I am grateful, my lord. I thought it likely that I would be put to the knife once I had fulfilled my duties.'

'Not by me or by my men. Can you help this lad?' he said. The old healer was gazing down at the unconscious Alain.

'He's alive?'

'Barely.'

'Not for much longer.'

'Can you save him?'

'That leg is poisoned; those bones cannot be mended.' He extended his arm for Blackstone's support, which was given, and he knelt next to Alain. After a cursory examination, he took Blackstone's arm again and stood. 'I might help the head wound, and the swelling on the eye. But the leg. No. Impossible, Sir Thomas. You need a barber surgeon.'

Renfred appeared with a stretcher and four garrison prisoners.

'I don't have a barber surgeon. I have you,' said Blackstone.

The bailiff was dismissed to arrange food from the kitchens for Blackstone's men while the injured Frenchman was taken to the apothecary's house. There were no facilities for surgical operations so Blackstone swept aside the foodstuff and plates on the kitchen table and had the lad laid on it.

'Old man, you will save this boy. I made a promise to his father that I would cause him no harm and that means I offered him my protection. Attend to his wounds.'

The old man's watery eyes gazed at the broken body that lay unconscious in his kitchen. His hands trembled slightly. These hard-looking men who crowded the small room frightened him, and the towering figure of Thomas Blackstone, taller than the door frame and who looked to have the strength of a bull, could snap his neck in a moment's anger should he change his mind and decide that his healing skills were of little use.

'I will try,' he said. 'Cut free his clothing and fetch me hot water from the fire. Go into that room there' – he pointed without looking at the adjoining chamber – 'find me a linen sheet and tear it into strips this wide.' He spread the palm of his hand. Renfred went in search of the material. The old man looked up at Blackstone. 'You are a scarred man, Sir Thomas, and to my eyes you have been so for many years. Were you grievously wounded?'

'I was. After Crécy. I was a boy.'

'And the physician who cared for you, he was a man of great experience?'

'He was.'

'Then I beg you do not compare me to him. I am a humble apothecary. Send one of your men to the corpses that hang in the

283

town square and bring me maggots. They will be feasting on the dead flesh and I will use them to feast on this stench in his leg. Trust me in this matter.'

'I have used maggots before in wounds,' said Blackstone. 'John, go down to the square. Take one of those pots. Do as he asks.'

'And these men?' John Jacob asked, meaning the four prisoners.

'They stay here. We'll need them to hold the boy down.'

'We will help you, Sir Thomas,' said one of the men, grateful to have been spared.

Alain stirred. The air raised gooseflesh on his torso. He started to regain consciousness.

'Lift his head gently. Let him sip this,' said the apothecary, passing Blackstone a small dark glass bottle. 'Do it, my son. It will ease his pain and cast a shadow over his mind. If we are obliged to take his leg, let us spare him the pain and anguish of it.'

Blackstone moved to the awakening young man and gently lifted his head. 'Easy, boy.'

Alain de la Grave's uninjured eye opened and stared at the scar-faced knight who bent over him. 'Sir Thomas...'

'You're safe,' said Blackstone, dribbling the potion into the injured man's lips.

Alain gripped his wrist. 'Cade is here. He beat me.'

'I know. We have him. He'll pay.'

'And... Perinne?'

'Wounded but alive.'

Alain sighed as the potion began its work, and loosened his grip on Blackstone's arm.

'Forgive me, Sir Thomas... I... I failed you. I could... not escape in time... and warn you that Cade was here.'

'You played your part well,' said Blackstone. 'Your father would be proud of you.'

The young man smiled gratefully and Blackstone saw that he was drifting away under the effect of the drug. Blackstone made a silent promise that should the boy live he would tell him the truth about his father, who was the wellspring of his courage.

'Cade beat me... but... she... betrayed me to him... She... gave me... to him,' Alain said almost in a whisper, so gentle that Blackstone had to put his ear close to the boy's lips.

'Who?' asked Blackstone, already knowing the answer but wanting to hear it from the young man.

'My beautiful Countess...' said Alain, a tear easing down his cheek; and then he fell into his drug-induced sleep.

CHAPTER FORTY-SIX

Renfred stayed with the garrison soldiers at the apothecary's house awaiting John Jacob's return. As Blackstone strode across the courtyard Meulon came from the opposite direction.

'We are giving William Cade a chance to be fed and have any injury he has attended to. Go into the cellars and cut his hands free and have him secured to the cage bars. Give him a blanket, food and water. No brandy or wine. I want him rested and sober for the morning.'

'It would be less trouble if I just cut his throat,' said the big Norman.

'No, Meulon, I want him to fight for his life. I promised him a painful death and he shall have one but I won't kill a man who is without his strength. See to it.'

'Aye, Sir Thomas.'

'Have you checked the stables?'

'Warm and dry and plenty of fodder. Only Cade's men had mounts stabled here. These garrison troops had no need. '

'Good. Pick men to go and bring in our horses. I will have John Jacob fetch my horse. Is everything here secure?' said Blackstone, scanning the walls, rooftops and streets.

'We hold the town and the château. Will and Jack still have their archers on the walls. The gates have been opened long enough for the villagers to return to their homes. The last of the livestock is going out now and then the gates will be barred.'

'No man is to go anywhere alone. Two men together, no matter how mundane the task, Meulon. We are not welcome here; let's not gift them a lone target should anyone seek revenge.'

286

'What are we to do about the prisoners?'

'Once I have the Countess's word that they will not raise their weapons against us I'll release them, so keep them guarded until then. The bailiff will organize food from the kitchen but it will take too long to feed us all. Find women in their households to cook. Feed our men and then the prisoners. Pay the women for their effort and food. We don't want them pissing in it.'

Meulon gave him a quizzical look. 'There are seventy garrison solders, enough to cause trouble if they take it into their heads to try to take back the town. They'll know every street and alleyway so we would be hard pressed.'

'The Countess was using Cade to draw in mercenaries and then kill them. The French King has two armies searching out and killing routiers, Chandos clears towns of these skinners and our own King has promised they would not be used to hinder the treaty. What crime has she committed? She has a cruel heart and an appetite for men, but I cannot take this town from her – and even if I desired to we don't have enough men to stay here and command it. So we will let them go when I have secured her word,' said Blackstone, and then as an afterthought: 'For what it's worth.'

'Then I will arrange a double guard on the night watch and have the men stay vigilant. There is little sense in trusting a woman who entraps men and then inflicts a bad death on them.' He spat into the dirt. 'Even if they are skinners.'

Blackstone made his way up to the Countess's rooms. He heard laughter behind the closed doors. The three men who guarded the entrance had been joined by four more. They smiled as Blackstone approached. One of them was the hobelar Tait.

'What are you doing here, Tait?'

'I brought my men inside the walls once the gate was secured. Some of the villagers were already going back to their homes and when I searched for you I was told you were here but Sir Gilbert damned near kicked my arse when I interrupted him. So I thought

I would wait here until you returned. I relieved one of the men you had left here at this door.'

'You did well last night. You drew their attention and their crossbowmen. Your men are safe?'

'Aye, my lord. It was a simple enough task you gave us.'

'Stay here until food is arranged for the men. I have matters to attend to. Do not think that because we hold the town that we are safe. There might be some belligerent townsmen who think they can slip out into a darkened alley and plunge a knife into your neck. The sooner we are done with this place the better.'

'Yes, Sir Thomas, I understand. My lads are scavengers, they'll find themselves food and they wouldn't trust the Pope when walking down an alley so they'll be wide enough awake for any attack.'

'Good. You tell your men that the captains have orders to pay for anything we take. What's happening in there?' Blackstone asked as another peal of laughter was heard.

Tait shrugged. 'You would think the Countess might be more sorrowful. Her men are dead or captured, her town taken and she must still wonder whether she herself will come to any harm. Perhaps it is Sir Gilbert's charm that pleases her.'

'Then I should have brought one of the scribes from the monastery so that such an event might be recorded in the history books. Sir Gilbert's charm is best expressed in battle.'

'My lord?' said Tait, not understanding.

'He has none,' Blackstone explained and then pushed open the doors.

'Thomas, there you are,' said Killbere, who was sitting on a footstool between Countess Catherine and the fireplace. He had a glow to his face that was not only from sitting close to the warmth of the flames. He grinned foolishly. 'Come, my friend, join us. Our hostess has brandy that would grow hair where there is none!' He chortled, glancing at the Countess who, barely suppressing a smile, fixed her gaze more intently on Blackstone.

Blackstone's grim countenance showed he had no wish to be inveigled into the Countess's hospitality. 'Our hostess is our prisoner. She has no privileges until she proves herself willing to co-operate,' he said.

Killbere stepped to his friend's side and spoke quietly so that the Countess could not hear. 'Thomas, she is more than willing.' He grinned foolishly again.

'Has the wine and brandy on an empty stomach addled your brain?' said Blackstone quietly. 'Do you know how dangerous this woman might prove to be?'

'I think you should leave her to me. I have a certain finesse in these matters,' Killbere told him. Then, in little more than a whisper: 'You do what you have to do and I will do what needs to be done here.'

Countess Catherine stared boldly at Blackstone. It was almost like a challenge. It seemed likely that she would desire nothing better than to come between him and his friend. Then she would have won a victory of sorts over him.

Blackstone looked past Killbere. 'You gave a young man to your killer as a man would toss a dog a bone.'

'Alain?' She shrugged. 'I could do nothing else. I thought he had lied to us. Had I not done so then who knows what Cade might have done to me. I have men at my shoulder who would die for me but even they would not have stopped him. I value my life. I have seen what men like Cade are capable of.'

'You flit from seasoned killers to innocent young man between your sheets, and then you betray and abandon both.'

'I am a woman alone in a violent man's world. I have sworn soldiers at my command. I rule this territory. I am no chattel; I am permitted by law to sign legal documents, to buy and sell land and goods. I am a woman whose husband and family were cruelly slain and I will not take any lecture from a heathen mercenary like you. I am a countess in the realm of King John. I have authority. Do not dare, sir, to tell me whom I might or might not take to my bed.' She hurled the glass into the fire, where it flared briefly as the brandy spilled.

Killbere glanced with raised eyebrows at Blackstone and then slowly released the breath he had held as Blackstone had been berated. 'I'll stay,' he said quietly. 'And smooth things over.'

Blackstone ignored his friend. 'Countess, you are confined to these quarters. Once we are secure here you will command your men not to raise arms against mine. If you do this then your remaining soldiers will have their weapons returned when we leave. Sufficient men remain to protect you and to hold this town. But you will no longer have men like Cade to draw routiers here to their death. If you refuse to command your men then they will die.'

'And when I give this order, if I give this order, and your men have taken whatever you permit them to take—'

'They will take nothing more than food and drink and fodder for our horses which we will pay for,' interrupted Blackstone.

'Very well, and what happens then?' said the Countess.

'We leave Felice. After I kill William Cade.'

CHAPTER FORTY-SEVEN

Blackstone inspected his men's positions, taking Renfred with him. It was obvious that he had too few men to effectively hold the town for any length of time. Townspeople averted their eyes as the two men walked through the narrow streets. The air was still crisp and he knew they had been blessed with the dry weather for the attack on the town.

The two men made their way down into the open square where the corpses had been hanging but had now been removed. Meulon and his men were shepherding some of the garrison prisoners whose work party carried bundles of faggots and cut timber. The gates were open and guarded by Will Longdon's men on the walls.

'Sir Thomas, we have too few men to patrol the walls at night so Will Longdon and I are putting markers out to burn near those village houses,' said Meulon. 'There's a French army out there only a few days away. If for any reason they decide that they would rather hold this place than us then we don't want any surprises. The archers will have their distance marked.'

'Warn the villagers to stay in their homes after curfew. These small towns are not as strict and they have no police to enforce it,' said Blackstone. 'Are the horses stabled?'

'John Jacob and his men brought them in.'

'Take the braziers from the walls and place them in the square. Better that we see anyone within who might try and take us by surprise than for our men on the parapet to be seen by the fires. Cade made the mistake of showing us where his men were.'

Meulon nodded and turned away to carry out Blackstone's orders.

'Renfred, I want our men to take over the soldiers' billets. Make sure that the cooks know where they are. Have the garrison men locked in one of the buildings before dark once they have been fed. They may only be garrison troops but they fought well and there'll be veterans among them. No fighting man likes the taste of defeat and if they see a chance to strike back at us then they could seize it. They might have a hidden cache of weapons. Caution is the best defence we have now. Remember, no man walks the streets alone. When that is done then find me: there is more we need to do to protect ourselves.'

Renfred beckoned one of his men to him and they made their way towards the soldiers' quarters as Blackstone went up onto the walls. To one side he saw Jack Halfpenny and Quenell still holding their archers in place. Will Longdon and his men controlled the front wall over the town gate. He saw that Meulon's men were stacking firewood to be lit as beacons with the veteran archer directing their positioning.

'How far?' Will Longdon called to those below.

'Two hundred and forty-seven,' came the answer as Blackstone joined him.

'Mark!' cried Will Longdon. 'Thomas, we can do little more to secure the town. How long do you intend to stay here?'

'All being well we will leave in a day or so. I would like to find out where the Welshman has gone but even on pain of death Cade would lie so it would serve no purpose to torture him.'

'I would still take my knife to him if you'd permit it. The bastard's men nearly killed me and he hanged Peter Garland for the pleasure of it.'

'I know, Will, but I'll fight him tomorrow. He'll be dead by the time the church bell rings for midday prayers.' Blackstone let his eyes take in the defences. 'As you said, we have done all we can do to secure this place but something is wrong. I feel it. We are more vulnerable inside these walls than we are out.' He watched as Felice's carpenters repaired the roofs he and his men had used to clamber onto the walls. He turned his gaze across the town's buildings and the château that towered beyond them. 'There's a woman up there who commands loyalty from these people. She inflicts revenge on routiers and she still has sworn men who serve her. And to these townspeople we are nothing more than English mercenaries.'

'We didn't kill any of them in the attack and Meulon says that we pay for the food we take.'

'It means nothing to people who hate routiers and who served her husband and now her. She wields power. She's unafraid. And that makes her dangerous.'

Before darkness fell Blackstone and John Jacob made their way to the apothecary's house. Alain lay strapped to the old man's table, a blanket covering his chest and thighs. His wound had been packed with maggots. The young Frenchman trembled with fever, and sweat streaked his face and torso.

'I dare not administer any more opiate to him,' said the apothecary to Blackstone and John Jacob in the dim candlelit room.

'You have the skill to keep him alive, though.'

'Medicine is brought together by astrology, the use of herbs and the will of God. I have not studied the heavens and profess to have only a lifetime of skill with the plants and potions at my disposal. I have taken urine from him. His water was green after first being red. It tells me he is infected. I do not see how he can live.'

'The colour of a man's piss doesn't kill him,' said John Jacob.

The old man shrugged. 'I can only tell you what I know.'

'And the bones in his leg?' said Blackstone.

The old man sighed. 'You have seen wounds like this before?' he said, exposing the wound more clearly to the candlelight. 'Tell me what you see now.'

The stench was bad enough and even though the maggots had eaten away much of the dead flesh Blackstone knew the poison could soon kill the young man.

'The leg must go,' said Blackstone.

'And it is doubtful he would survive. I have never seen it done,' said the apothecary.

'I have,' said Blackstone. 'But he'll surely die if we do not cut off the leg.'

'I have no skill in this,' said the apothecary.

'Send for the town butcher and have your blacksmith prepare hot pitch. Once the leg is off what remains needs to be seared.'

The apothecary scuttled from the room and called a servant to do Blackstone's bidding.

Blackstone wrung out a cloth in a bowl of water and bathed Alain's face. He had tried and failed to keep the young man safe.

'I have never seen a man survive this,' said John Jacob. 'If it were me I would be happy for you to kill me now.'

The apothecary heard. 'You cannot murder a man so injured.'

'How many battlefields have you seen?' said Blackstone. 'We kill out of mercy as well as out of anger. This boy is one of us. His parents were cruelly slain and butchered by routiers. And I promised his father that no harm would come to him. He has courage. He deserves a chance.'

'What you propose is barely a chance,' said the apothecary. 'The pain that will be inflicted on him is enough to kill him. I do not have enough medicine to help him.'

'You have henbane?' said Blackstone.

The old man nodded. 'Of course.'

'Mix henbane and brandy. It will make him unconscious to anything done to him.'

For a moment the old man looked uncertain. 'How do you know this?'

'I saved a woman once who was thought to be a witch but she was a healer and if she were here now she would tell you to do the same thing. His heart is strong enough and if it isn't then he will die in his sleep.'

Alain shuddered as the fever gripped him. Blackstone looked helplessly at the maggot-infested leg of the young man who had only wanted to prove himself. The apothecary's door opened as the servant brought in the town butcher. The well-fed man sweated from the exertion of hurrying and while he wheezed, regaining his breath, he gazed at the man strapped to the table. He placed his belt of implements down on a table, licked his lips and swallowed hard.

'You are to take off this man's leg. Above the knee. What do you need?'

The butcher's eyes widened. The two fighting men frightened him. He stuttered with uncertainty. 'A... a block. Beneath his leg.'

'You've brought a bone-cutting saw and knife?' said Blackstone.

The hapless man tugged out a saw and a long curved-bladed knife. His hands shook uncontrollably as he also tugged free a cleaver from its pouch.

'Mother of God, Sir Thomas, he'll tear more flesh and cause more damage. This isn't a pig's hock.'

The sight of the crude instruments and the fear in the butcher's face made it plain that the man would be less than useless if the bone saw jammed and to hack off the leg with a cleaver was too brutal an act. Blackstone had seen men's legs taken off in less than a minute by barber surgeons on the battlefield. 'We packed Perinne's wound with honey and had it stitched closed. Perhaps we need to try that here before we take the leg.'

'And how do we get the bones back inside his leg?' said John Jacob.

Blackstone studied the two sharp pieces that pierced the wound. 'Butcher, go back to your house. We will call you again if you are needed,' he said. 'Be quick. It will soon be curfew.'

The butcher hurriedly gathered his tools and was ushered out.

'Rinse out the wound,' Blackstone told the apothecary's servant. 'Use brandy. Get every maggot out of that wound and do not touch those broken bones.' He looked up at the apothecary. 'You have honey here?'

'Some.'

'Enough to press into the wound?'

'Yes.'

'Get it. And mix the brandy with henbane.'

The old man and his servant did as Blackstone demanded.

'What do you plan to do?' said John Jacob.

'Whatever I can,' said Blackstone. 'Go and fetch Will. Tell him he's to stitch the lad's wound so he must bring his needle and cord.'

'You intend to push back the bones,' said the apothecary realizing the only course of action left beyond amputation. 'Very well.' He turned to his servant. 'I will clean the wound. Mix me eggs and flour.'

The servant disappeared into the back of the kitchen and through a door to a larder.

'I will mix a paste that sets and will help hold the leg in place. It is a treatment I have used once a broken leg has been straightened.'

It didn't take long for the wound to be flushed clean of the wriggling maggots and for the cup of sleeping draught to be eased between Alain's lips. Blackstone instructed the apothecary to tear strips of a linen sheet into bandages. By the time Will Longdon arrived Alain was asleep. The wound looked raw and the broken bones appeared to be more prominent now that much of the dead flesh had been reduced. The apothecary smeared honey into the wound.

'I can't stitch that,' said Longdon.

'You've got the cord?'

'Aye, silk from an arrow fletching.'

'Get it ready.'

Whatever Blackstone had planned Longdon knew better than to argue. He threaded the silk in a curved needle that resembled a sailmaker's awl and then dipped the silken cord into the brandy flask. Blackstone stood at the side of the table and placed his hands gently either side of the protruding bones. 'Will, stand opposite me. I will push the bones back together in his leg. I'll hold until you stitch each side. John, you and the old man will bind the leg with the bandage. Ready?'

The men nodded. Blackstone repositioned his hands slightly, gazed at the shattered bones and tried to imagine how they might fit together. It was not the same calculation as laying a dry stone wall, of finding how each piece of rock might fit neatly together for strength, but there was a part of him that instinctively saw how it should be done. And then he pressed down. They heard a crunch and a grinding sound and Blackstone was momentarily surprised how much resistance there was to pushing the bones back into the leg. The young man's leg muscles were as tight as a bow cord.

'John, take hold of his foot and pull on his leg.'

The bones chafed together and submerged into the open wound. 'Now,' said Blackstone. Will Longdon bent to the task and quickly made long looping stitches to close the wound and then doubled the silk cord back to tie the skin together in smaller stitches as Blackstone shifted the weight of his hands to accommodate him. When Longdon had finished and cut the cord, Blackstone kept his hands in place holding the leg straight with his weight.

The apothecary's servant placed a deep bowl on the table. The sticky mass it held was almost firm to the touch. The apothecary smeared the thick plaster mixture over the leg and, when satisfied, instructed what to do next.

'Bind the leg tightly, top to bottom,' he told John Jacob.

When the task was completed the men stood back and looked at the sleeping young Frenchman.

'My servant will sit with him throughout the night,' said the apothecary. 'If he is still alive in the morning then... well, then we will see. He is in God's hands now.'

Blackstone and his two companions stepped out into the last remnants of daylight. The church bell rang for vespers but the streets were deserted. The clear evening settled into near darkness. A dog barked somewhere, answered by another. The braziers were already lit in the town's main square. Blackstone knew his men were tired, he felt it himself, but they needed to be alert this night. He imagined himself to be one of the townsmen, or a survivor from the fight. If he were going to strike an enemy who had taken his town he would wait until the attackers' exhaustion claimed them. Blackstone's men had ridden from the monastery, fought Cade's men and then assaulted the town the previous day and night. They all needed sleep.

'Will, John and I will walk you back to your post, and then we will find a place to keep watch ourselves.'

As they turned into the main square the bell stopped ringing and an eerie silence settled over the town of Felice. What was it that made Blackstone's skin crawl? He was no stranger to sensing the spirits of the dead. There had been much cruelty in the town, and its very name had spawned a woman heedless of the suffering she caused, a woman who took delight in seeing men die slowly at her command. Shadows from the braziers might easily be ghosts haunting the dark alleyways, beckoning the living to join them.

'If they come they will come tonight,' he said quietly. But he was uncertain if he meant the living or the dead.

CHAPTER FORTY-EIGHT

Killbere had eaten well from the food supplied from the kitchen for him and the Countess. They had teased and tempted one another with innuendo and at times outright suggestive talk. This woman, who enjoyed the pleasures of men at any time of her choosing, kept Killbere's lust simmering. They had both drunk too much by the time the bell rang for night prayers, three hours after vespers.

The candles flickered in pools of wax; only the fire that Killbere had fed from the faggots and logs during the day gave the room sufficient light for him to see the Countess's features. He risked her anger by lifting the sleeve on her dress and exposing her arms. It was a flagrant breach of etiquette that might have earned him a cuff around the head, but she had pressed herself back into her chair and luxuriated in his touch. He stroked her bare skin with the back of his hand, keeping the roughness of his palm and fingers away from her silken limb.

Her eyes half closed. 'It is late,' she said sleepily. 'It is time... for bed.'

He kissed the palm of her hand and gently bit the raised part at the base of her thumb, the Mount of Venus.

She pulled away. 'I did not give you permission,' she said without any malice.

'I did not need it, my Lady Catherine.' Killbere stood and offered his hand. She took it and raised herself so that she stood close to him. Killbere made no move towards her.

She raised her eyebrows. 'You do not desire me?'

He smiled. 'To go further I need permission.'

'And to bathe.' She stepped away towards her bedchamber's door and then turned back. 'Though I do not find your smell disagreeable.'

'It is honest sweat, my lady,' said Killbere.

She murmured a soft mewling sound and shrugged. 'Permission is given.' She walked past the two stoic bodyguards who had waited against the far wall. Neither man glanced at her or looked at Killbere as he picked up his sword belt wrapped around its scabbard.

'Don't be alarmed if you hear her cry out,' he said as he passed them and then closed the bedroom door behind him.

The sweet scent of beeswax candles mingled with her own fragrance; the room was heavy with desire as they faced each other and undressed in a slow dance of sensuality as each piece of clothing dropped to the floor. When she was naked she lay half propped on her bed and watched as he sluiced the dirt and sweat from his body with water from the bowl on her nightstand. By the time he had dried himself he was aroused and as he approached the bed he nipped the candle wicks until only two remained, bathing her body in a gossamer of shadow and light.

As the hours passed there was nothing gentle about their coupling and she fought him with a passion that matched his own. When they were spent they fell back into the softness of the feather mattress and rested, and then began again until finally the wine and exertion claimed them both. Killbere was barely awake and close to succumbing to his own exhaustion. As his eyes grew heavy he laughed aloud. The beautiful and sensuous woman beside him curled her body in slumber and snored like a grunting soldier.

Darkness cloaked the room, the faintest glimmer from the night sky barely showed their shapes in the bed.

The dull ringing of the church bell for night prayers echoed across the rooftops.

It was midnight.

And the killing began.

* * *

Silent men, their boots bound with rags to dull the sound of their footsteps, scurried like rats through the darkened streets. They were townsmen who would march as militia in support of the garrison troops when called to war. They were sullen, belligerent men who hated the English and their victory over King John. The traitor William Cade served a purpose for the Countess and whatever sins he had committed as a routier were forgiven when he delivered mercenaries into her hands. Forty men had answered the call of the Countess's bailiff, men who kept their weapons hidden under floorboards in their homes, men who were urged by their women to kill the invaders who had spilled blood on the streets. It made no difference to them that they had been spared rape and death by a benevolent Englishman; years of bitterness fuelled the hatred coursing through them.

They had used their knowledge of the labyrinthine vaults that lay beneath the château and released William Cade from his cell. Cade forgot any thoughts of escape now that the citizens of Felice had risen up. There was still a handful of Cade's men imprisoned and they were released by the blacksmith who opened the lock that secured their prison. They were soon armed and took command of the townsmen. They would overwhelm Sir Thomas Blackstone's men.

William Cade knew exactly how to defeat Blackstone's outnumbered troop. Whispered commands passed from man to man as they approached the town square, an attack of two columns, each down a side street left and right, who would storm the walls and kill the archers first. Once their threat had been removed, half of the force who had remained in the courtyard near the château would kill Blackstone's men who were billeted nearby. Then those of Blackstone's men who remained would be caught between those who attacked from the town square and others who would act like beaters on a day's hunt and drive Blackstone's men onto the attackers' swords. Cade would once again take his place in the whore's bed.

301

He cursed. The damned bell kept clanging. It would wake the dead. The tolling of the hour was also an arranged call to arms but the idiot on the end of the rope needed to stop before its insistence awoke Blackstone's men sooner than was needed. He turned to one of the townsmen who ran at his side.

'The church! Tell them to stop.'

The man grunted an answer and turned away. Despite the darkness he knew exactly which side street led to the church. Hadn't he been born and raised in Felice and never left except to help kill those who threatened the valley? He'd known the old Count, had carted wood up to the château – still did – since he was a boy of seven with his father. The long-handled axe he carried would be cutting down more than trees this night. He slowed, placed a rough palm on the stone wall that he knew would guide him into the square and the church where the slow-witted Marcel would be heaving on the rope. He was soon across the open ground and pushing into the ancient church. A candle burned near the figure who heaved on the rope. A bundle of clothing lay on the stone floor near the bell ringer. It meant nothing.

'Marcel! Cade says to stop. Damn you.'

The man let go of the rope but by the time he turned the axeman had realized that they were not rags that littered the dark floor. He swung back his axe. The bell ringer seemed to move so quickly that by the time the axeman was ready to strike the man was an arm's length from him and the sudden pain in his heart pierced the darkness of the church as a lightning bolt seared through his brain.

Renfred stepped over the dead woodsman.

Everything that Blackstone had predicted was already taking place.

William Cade led the mixed force of garrison troops and militia into the town square past the gallows, as a garrison sergeant-at-arms, with his men who had been released, pounded into the far side from the other street. A wind had picked up, funnelled along the valley and striking the village and walled town. It smelled of rain: a gathering storm that would soon hurl itself against those who fought in the narrow confines of Felice. Men would falter once the rain chilled their muscles, but if luck was on their side they would beat the storm before it reached them. Cinders and sparks flew from the braziers in the square as the wind whipped their flames. Cade gestured left and right for the men to scale the steps that led up to the walkway. The crenellations obscured any archer's silhouette against the night sky but as his men ran along the walls there was no sound of assault. No body fell, no man cried out.

Cade stopped beneath the gallows. Men broke the silence and shouted that the walls had been abandoned. It made no sense to the mercenary. Would Blackstone have stood down his prized archers from guarding the walls? Were they sleeping? Did he think that walls did not need defending? Before he could satisfy himself with an answer he heard the sudden clash of a fight near the château. Men's voices were raised in fear and anger. What had happened? If the other half of his force had trapped Blackstone's men between them then his plan had worked. No matter that the archers were not at their posts; perhaps they already lay dead in their beds, betrayed by the cooks like the rest of Blackstone's men. In his mind's eye he saw that those of Blackstone's troop who had survived being knifed in their beds were now trapped beneath the château's walls. 'Turn back!' he bellowed. 'The courtyard. We have them!'

It was time to kill the scar-faced knight and claim the glory and the reward of the French King and the gratitude of the Countess, who by now would have killed Sir Gilbert Killbere.

CHAPTER FORTY-NINE

Countess Catherine had allowed herself to sleep after the vigorous lovemaking with the veteran knight. He had shown no lack of stamina and she concluded that the gratification that she had received had been worth the time she had spent drawing in this man who was clearly senior to Blackstone and who would have taken control of her town. Keeping Killbere in her quarters had left the younger Englishman to organize his men. And from what the veteran told her over the hours that he had sat at her feet by the fireside, Blackstone was doing only what Killbere had instructed. Blackstone was a man who yearned for command but whom Killbere kept in check. When the veteran knight had left the room to relieve himself in the garderobe she had instructed her bailiff and the two bodyguards when to strike.

As the night bell rang she opened her eyes and then nudged her back against the weight of the man lying next to her. He did not awake. She counted the first ten chimes so that her mind was clear and then, easing her dagger from beneath the mattress, rolled quickly, plunging its blade into where Killbere's head would rest on the pillow next to her. The moment the knife struck home she cried out. No gristle or bone met the blade. Only a pillow. His body had been replaced with the heavy bolster. Kneeling up, breasts free from the entwining sheet, her mouth gaped as the doors burst open. The outer room's fire glow threw the heavy shadows of the two armed bodyguards over her as a naked figure stepped behind the first man and plunged a sword between his shoulder blades; when he fell the second man turned, but the quick-moving Killbere had a dagger in his other hand that swept upwards, catching the

304

man in the throat. He went down, hands clutching his gurgling wound. The shock of the attack and her failure to kill Killbere momentarily stunned her.

Killbere, ignoring the dead men, stepped quickly towards her and she recovered. She spat at him and screamed a curse, jabbing with the knife. He easily stepped aside and swung his blood-smeared hand across the side of her head. She fell heavily. Killbere threw her knife far enough away and strode through to the other room where Tait and his men were trying to force the door that had been barricaded by the bodyguards. He tossed aside the heavy chair and pulled away the table that had been pushed beneath the door handles. He opened the doors. Tait and his men gawped at the naked figure of Sir Gilbert Killbere in the firelight, blood-stained sword in hand.

'Don't just stand there looking like a damned virgin who's seen her first cock. Get down to the fight,' he barked.

At the top of the town Blackstone stood with John Jacob, Meulon and Renfred and their men, backs against the high walls at the base of the château. In front of them lay twenty or more dead or dying militia and garrison troops. Earlier, during curfew, Blackstone's men had moved away from their billet. They had waited silently, unmoving in the blackness, watching the militia gathering their force, releasing the garrison troops and hurriedly and quietly organizing their strike into the town. While Blackstone and his men knelt behind their shields, merging their dark forms into the depth of the archways that spanned the base of the walls, the town force had split into two, and the garrison men had gone quickly into the billet to kill. They had swiftly emerged again, uncertain and disorganized, after finding the room empty, and been instantly attacked by Meulon and his men from one angle and Blackstone head on. They had raised no battle cry. It was the garrison men who bellowed in fear. They fought where they stood. And died.

There looked to be more than a hundred garrison soldiers and town militia who tried to fight their way clear. Four of Meulon's men fell: a slight cost because of the efficiency of their killing.

After the sudden impact of his surprise attack Blackstone had retreated with the men back to the wall where they braced themselves for the counter-attack that would soon come once the survivors had gathered themselves. Blackstone had chosen his ground and put all of his men in one killing area. The smaller courtyard beneath the château's walls favoured his outnumbered men. It obliged the greater force to funnel into a tight arena where they could be contained and slain. Men would jostle each other trying to reach Blackstone's men; their ability to fight effectively would be diminished. Will Longdon, Halfpenny and Quenell stood unseen above the men in the yard, having earlier run from the walls onto the road that curved high up to the château, which eventually became the vast terrace that looked down across the town; from there the archers had watched that first conflict below as Blackstone and his men seemed to appear from nowhere to kill the unsuspecting Felice troops.

William Cade pushed his way into the disordered men as they jostled at the mouth of the courtyard.

'Move forward! Forward!' he yelled. He addressed two of his men close by who had fought in the confined space. 'What's happened? Where's Blackstone?'

The men turned contorted faces on him. 'We should get out while we can,' one of them said, trying to push past Cade, who snatched at him. Cade's grip and ferocious snarl were sufficient to stop the panicked routier.

'What's happened here? I ask again: Where is Blackstone?'

'His men are back against the wall. We can't see them. There aren't that many but...'

'We outnumber them!' Cade spat.

'Aye, but we have garrison troops and militia at our backs,' the man bleated.

'With me,' Cade insisted as he shouldered his way through the gaggle of men into the courtyard. Too frightened to disobey, the man and his companion turned back with Cade.

Cade edged closer to the perimeter of the courtyard. It was so dark he could only make out that the dark lumps on the ground were men's bodies.

'If their men have their backs against the wall then they have no escape. We have blocked the streets down into the town. They are caught like rats in a trap.'

'Aye, but not one man here wants to go forward into the dark.'

'Then fetch torches,' said Cade. He shouted to the gaggle of men that choked the entrances to the streets: 'Fetch torches!'

Men pushed their way into houses and soon re-emerged carrying lanterns and flaming reed bundles. Cade snatched one of the torches and stepped forward. He took a few more tentative steps, the flames held high allowing him to see the dead. Beyond them, backs pressed against the arched wall, Blackstone's men's dismembered faces glared at him like gargoyles from above their shields.

Cade turned back to the ranks of men who waited ready to attack. 'See how few they are! They have no escape. Take back your town. Kill these men and hang their bodies for the crows!'

Encouraged by how few men faced them the militia and garrison troops raised their voices and their weapons. Their ragged line surged forward, jumping and stumbling over their dead in the flickering torchlight. Blackstone's men did not move. A savage cry rose up from the attackers. They would slaughter Blackstone's men where they stood. As they reached halfway across the courtyard a different sound came from the darkness above: a rippling of the air whose significance could not be determined by those who heard it above the cacophony. A sudden and terrifying force struck them down. A mighty hand had hurled a death storm of bodkin-tipped arrows into them, tearing flesh and muscle, felling a score of men who writhed among the abandoned torches that sparked and spluttered as men's bodies rolled across them in their death throes.

Screams rent the night air as another flight of arrows whispered and hit with a sickening thud. Cade had crouched, then fallen as arrows found their mark in men next to him. An arrow struck the ground close by, its impact making the yard-long shaft quiver. Cade scrambled to his knees as Blackstone's men suddenly ran forward into the disarray.

Cade's mind raced through his fear. Every man that Blackstone had under his command was either in this courtyard or on the terrace above them. If the townsmen retreated they would be pursued but there were still enough of them to slow Blackstone's men. And that would give him time to escape.

Two of his own men had survived. Wide-eyed with fear they too crouched, using the dead as shields.

'The stables!' Cade shouted to them.

Killbere had bound the unconscious Countess with torn sheets and locked her bedchamber door, then hurriedly dressed and run down to where Tait and his men stood at the main door where Perinne held his post. The injured man wore only breeches and shirt, its linen cloth stained from his unhealed back wound. There seemed little chance that the townsmen would attack up the snaking roadway now that the archers had slain so many.

Killbere glanced at Perinne. 'Where's Sir Thomas?'

'Below in the yard.'

'Perinne, stay here. Guard the stairs. There'll be no assault on the château with Will's men here but if you see the bailiff you hold him. He's not to go up to the Countess. Tait, you and your men with me.'

Tait and his handful of men ran behind Killbere down the curved roadway that led back into the town. Below him he saw the militia and garrison troops who had survived the blizzard of arrows turning in retreat and jamming the narrow streets. Their force was spent and they would either return to their homes and lick their wounds or try and escape into the nearby village knowing the town walls were bereft of bowmen.

'Sir Gilbert? Do we burn these bastards out?' shouted Tait.

'In good time. First we make sure they never strike at us again. We'll see if anyone holds the town square and gates.'

The roadway's slope pulled at Killbere's leg muscles, he was tired – with good reason, he told himself – but the first stinging drops of rain against his face freshened him. He and the few men with him had the advantage that no retreating militia had yet reached any of the side alleys that would bring them onto the roadway. Those men in full retreat were now fighting for their lives as Blackstone's men hacked at their backs. It didn't take long for Killbere to reach the town square. The gates were closed and the walls were still unmanned. He suddenly realized that if enough retreating men flooded the area where the gibbets stood then he and Tait's men would soon be overwhelmed. It would be better to kill those they could and let the others escape into the night.

'Open the gates,' he ordered. The hard rain stung their eyes as they lifted the crossbeam free from the gates. They dragged open the heavy studded doors, which soon became a maw into the blackness of the countryside and the muted shapes of the village obscured by darkness and rain. They heard the cries of approaching men funnelling down through the streets. It felt as if the Almighty had finally thrown His displeasure against the murderous town as thunder rolled across the mountains and the clap shook the ground they stood on. Killbere and Tait and his men formed a line and as the first desperate survivors spilled into the yard they struck at them and caused more chaos.

The survivors, blinded by the rain, saw these men and in their panic they could not know they were the only ones who faced them. The rain finally drenched the braziers and those who could ran for the open gate. Thirty men ran past Meulon's swordsmen, who struck from the side streets, and soon fell dead in the mud.

Meulon and Renfred appeared from one side street as John Jacob and others came from another. Men still ran from them and Killbere was content to let them disappear into the storm beyond the walls. Exhaustion was already claiming Blackstone's fighters as the lack of sleep and the action in the past two days drained them. When Meulon came into the yard by the gates Killbere sheathed his sword.

'It's done,' he said. 'Close the gates.'

Meulon grinned, raised his sword arm and let out a roar. The victorious men with him bellowed into the slashing rain.

'Is Sir Thomas not with you?' asked the Norman fighter.

Killbere squinted into the rain and looked around at the soaked men. Only a couple of the braziers still flickered, protected from the wind by the town walls, but he could see that Blackstone was not among them. 'John?' he asked Blackstone's squire.

'He followed Meulon.'

'I didn't see him,' said the throat-cutter.

'Is he wounded? Did he fall?' asked Killbere anxiously. A fleeting memory stung him. When he and Perinne had stood watch that night at the monastery Perinne had told him of his fears for Blackstone. Of the raptor's keening, of it first rising into the sky above Blackstone. How it had dogged their journey. Killbere had spat and scoffed at Perinne's superstition. Theirs was a life ruled by the cruel bitch Fate.

But the confined spaces of the narrow streets and the mêlée of the fighting meant it would be easy not to have noticed a man go down. It had been suffocatingly close during the hard-pressed killing.

Killbere shrugged the tiredness from his aching body. 'We must find him,' he said and led the way back into the town's streets.

CHAPTER FIFTY

As Blackstone had fought in the courtyard he had seen three men break away once the archers had done their killing. They had squirmed their way through the crowd at a crouch but Blackstone had recognized William Cade. Blackstone skirted the edge of the butcher's yard, using his shield and Wolf Sword to cleave past three or four desperate and fear-fuelled men who tried to stop him. He could see Meulon pressing home the attack yard by yard and John Jacob forcing his way along the opposite flank. Blackstone suddenly found himself in an alley where the rank smell of sweat mingled with that of blood and excrement. Eviscerated men rolled in agony in the dark as their comrades trampled their spilled intestines.

Here and there windows were opened in the houses as women prepared to tip boiling water onto their enemy, stopping only when they saw that it was their own menfolk who fled in panic, screaming from their wounds. Light spilling from the shutters in a brief respite from the darkness allowed Blackstone to see where Cade was running. It looked as though he was heading towards the stables, but was it to hamstring Blackstone's horses or an attempt to escape?

One of the garrison troops blocked Blackstone's way. The man had strength enough to force him back a pace and he fell over a dead body behind him. He smothered himself with his shield as the man hacked down. In the quickness of a breath Blackstone dropped his guard and lowered the shield, looking at the dark shape that was trying to kill him. His deliberate attempt to draw the man in succeeded: his assailant boldly stepped forward, ready to strike the fatal blow. It allowed Blackstone to hook his boot behind the man's leg and tumble him backwards. Blackstone quickly recovered and lunged Wolf Sword down into the man's chest.

Women were screaming from the open windows, which still gave sufficient light as he searched desperately ahead, but there was now no sign of Cade. Blood trickled down his face from an earlier blow and it began to blur his vision in one eye. He lifted his face to the stinging rain and let it wash the blood away. He had turned his back on the street cluttered with bodies and panic and shouldered his way down a passage. He tried to remember the streets' layout from when he had walked them checking his men's defences but the darkness of the running battle had disorientated him. And then, more by chance than anything else, he caught the pungent smell of the stables on the wind.

As he edged around the building he could hear the unsettled horses shifting in their stalls. A flicker of an oil lamp passed across a half-open door. Blackstone bent down and groped in the dirt for mud at the base of the building. It was malleable in his fingers, not yet soaked by the rain. He pressed it into the cut on his forehead to stem the blood and then crept closer to the opening.

Three men were saddling horses in the dim light. One horse shied as Cade tightened the girth strap. He cursed and punched the horse, then kneed it in the belly and wrenched the cinch another two notches tighter. Blackstone caught snatches of conversation above the driving rain. The men would ride into the square and then Cade's men would open the gates. As Blackstone got closer he sensed there was dissent from the men but Cade raised his voice and Blackstone heard the words *King* and *reward*. As rolling thunder broke across the town roofs one of the horses reared. Blackstone took the half-dozen strides into the stable and killed its rider, whose arms were raised sawing at the horse's reins. Blackstone stepped quickly between the panicked beast, which slammed itself against the stall, and the second man who desperately tried to draw his sword as his horse turned and pushed him almost into Blackstone's arms. Blackstone headbutted him. His nose split, head whipping back before he could utter a cry. As the man went down beneath the horse's hooves Blackstone sensed the rapid shadow that came between him and the oil lamp on the wall. He ducked, avoiding the knife strike from Cade, and rolled beneath the panicked horse, using his shield to protect him from the thrashing iron-shod hooves. The headbutted man grappled with him, spitting curses through his bloodied nose. For a moment it seemed that Blackstone could not break free, trapped as he was beneath his shield and the man alongside, and then one of the hooves caught the man's head. Blackstone heard the bones in his face crack. He pushed himself clear of the horse as Cade tried to get around the agitated beast. The horse was now between Cade and Blackstone, who threw his weight against the horse's rump in an attempt to reach the killer. In the confines between wall and stall and with the wild-eyed horse dangerously shifting its weight Blackstone's shield became a hindrance. He slipped it from his arm and threw his weight against the horse again, forcing it aside. He flung his shield at Cade, who fell back but recovered quickly as one of the remaining horses whinnied and bolted into the storm. Cade slashed a high guard strike down onto Blackstone's blade. Blackstone parried it, half turning, ready to let the momentum of his body cut across Cade's exposed chest. But no sooner had one horse made its bid for freedom than the others followed, knocking Blackstone off his feet. His head smashed into the stall's wall. Instinctively he rolled clear as wood splintered from Cade's sword thrust where a moment before his head had been. Cade's strike had all his strength behind it and his blade sank into the soft old timbers. He tried to yank it free but was forced to abandon it.

Blackstone was on his feet as Cade ran for the door. Cade snatched a baling fork, turned and jabbed the double tines at Blackstone. One of the narrow points pierced his mail and drew blood high on his arm next to his shoulder. Had he kept his shield the iron tip would have jammed into it but now the strike made him half turn his shoulder away from the next thrust. The rain thundered down on the slate roof; horses whinnied, crushing their weight against the walls of their stalls. The flickering oil lamp's dull orange glow threw a muted veil of light across the two men who crouched facing each like ancient gladiators, one with a long-handled spiked fork, the other batting away its jabs with his sword. If Cade caught Blackstone's sword blade between the two tines he could twist it away and gain the advantage. As Blackstone jabbed again he deliberately threw his free arm forward, ramming it between the two tines. His strength forced the haft to twist in Cade's hands. Cade snarled as Blackstone wrenched the baling fork out of his hands, but he had the agility to avoid Blackstone's strike, which would have taken him across the shoulder and cleaved him to his hip. As Blackstone regained his balance and shook his arm free from the pronged fork Cade snatched a sword from one of the fallen men and then backed away further towards the door. Neither man spoke, cursed or threatened. Each had his eyes locked on the other. Cade knew he had a chance to kill Blackstone. The bigger man was quick on his feet but the half-light and confines of the stable gave the lighter man the advantage. He could duck and weave and if he could deliver a maiming blow the legend that was Thomas Blackstone could be ended.

Cade's eyes widened with confidence. Blackstone's left shoulder had dropped. The stab wound must have gone deeper into his packed muscle than Cade had at first thought. But Blackstone showed no sign of pain and he strode forward again as Cade pulled a length of chain from a wall hook and swung it. Blackstone winced as the links struck his wounded shoulder. He faltered. Cade grinned. He swirled the chain again and this time entangled Blackstone's sword arm, snaring the crossguard. Blackstone was defenceless. His left arm drooped; his right was snagged. With a cry of triumph and a darting stride forward Cade lunged. He was on his toes, limited in his movement by the taut chain on Blackstone's sword arm. And then the chain tightened further and pulled him off balance. He stumbled forward, his sword point dipping off target, and before his leg muscles could correct his fall Blackstone's left arm swung forward and gripped his throat. Blackstone had fooled him. Stiff with shock, he choked. Blackstone held him in a crushing grip. Then, as his sword dropped, his hands grasped Blackstone's wrist in a vain attempt to relieve the pressure, and he saw Blackstone easily shake free the chain. His efforts to disable Blackstone had been useless. He was the one who had been duped and drawn in. Eyes bulging, spittle running from his lips, he gurgled as his breath was closed off from his lungs. His legs fought and kicked but made no impression on the tall man holding him. Blackstone brought the suffocating man's face closer to his own.

'I promised you a slow death,' said Blackstone, and threw him to the ground. Gasping with relief and barely conscious, Cade fought for his breath. Through bloodshot, watering eyes he saw Blackstone stand over him. A trickle of blood ran down the Englishman's scarred face and for a moment in the flickering glow of light he appeared to Cade's fear-struck mind as the Devil's disciple.

'Where is the Welshman?' said Blackstone.

Through the depth of his pain and knowledge of certain death Cade knew he could have one last victory over the English knight. He shook his head and rasped, 'You'll never know.' His breath wheezed in a pitiful laugh.

Blackstone swung the chain across a roof beam. He secured it and tested its strength. 'You will take a long time to die, William Cade, and then I'll put your head on a pole outside the gates. Tell me where he went.'

Cade had no fight left in him. 'When I die, you whoreson, the Dauphin will know of it and... he will... know where *you* are.' Cade wheezed again. 'It's over... you... bastard. Even you cannot... fight an army.'

So, the French had always intended to try and kill him, Blackstone realized. And the army that searched for routiers also searched for him. By now Chandos would have been at court and the King and his son would know where Blackstone had been seizing the towns for Edward. It would not take long for messengers to reach the army and for them to hunt him down. Chandos would not be able to help him now that Blackstone and his men operated alone.

Blackstone dragged a bale of straw beneath the chain. He reached down and hauled Cade to his feet. Cade made a feeble attempt to struggle but Blackstone easily had the measure of him and banged his head with a short sharp knock against the stall wall. It was enough to make the man cease. Blackstone twisted the chain around his neck and lifted him onto the teetering, uneven bale. Cade had no choice but to reach up and grab the chain above his head but when Blackstone's sword tip sliced through the binding string the bale collapsed. Cade kicked and wriggled but he was unable to support his body weight with his hands on the slippery chain.

Blackstone stood back and wiped away the blood from his eye. 'You hanged young Peter Garland,' said Blackstone. 'Now Satan and his imps wait for you in the darkness.' He sat tiredly on another bale, leaning against the wall. He pulled off his helm and eased back the coif beneath it. Sweat and blood caked his beard but he did not mind the discomfort from the stinging wound. He had known far worse.

He tilted his head slightly so that the blood did not obscure the sight of Cade slowly choking to death.

CHAPTER FIFTY-ONE

Blackstone and his men soon came together. He gathered the captains in the drenching rain. Some of the men, like Blackstone himself, had minor wounds that could soon be attended to.

'How many men did we lose?' he asked.

'Seven dead,' said Meulon.

Blackstone nodded wearily. 'All right. The gates are barred and the town dead clutter the streets. It's time the men got some sleep. Take everyone into the château. Use the lower rooms and light the fires. See what you can find in the kitchen and dry out the men's clothing. There will be no more fighting here. The storm will see to that, and tomorrow the townspeople can clear away their dead.'

The captains gathered their exhausted men and made their way back to the château where they barred the doors. Once the fires were lit men quickly fell asleep, even ignoring the prospect of scavenging for food. Blackstone and Killbere trudged upstairs to the Countess's rooms with John Jacob.

'You didn't kill her,' said Blackstone.

'I struck her hard enough to stop her gelding me with a dagger.'

'She will never stop hating us or men like us. I can understand that,' Blackstone said.

'She kills and tortures for pleasure, Thomas. A she-wolf if ever there was one.'

Their footsteps scuffed and echoed up the stone stairs. 'I've known a woman take up arms in revenge for the death of her family. Blanche de Harcourt raised a mercenary army when I failed to save her husband back in '56. She was a formidable woman,

Gilbert. I can see some of her strength in this Countess Catherine. She holds her dead husband's fiefdom and survives as best she can.'

'Aye, well, feel sympathy if you must, Thomas, but you did not come whisker close to having a knife plunged through your head after a night's passion.'

'Perhaps she was left with no choice when you didn't succumb in her arms,' said Blackstone, ignoring Killbere's scowl as they walked through the Countess's room to her bedchamber.

The Countess was conscious but remained tied up as Killbere had left her, still naked and shivering as the fire in the room had died down to embers. Her hair was in disarray and the bruise from Killbere's blow discoloured her cheekbone. Killbere stepped forward and hauled her to her feet. After the fighting he and Blackstone looked even more threatening than when they first arrived at Felice and she made a slight protest of resistance, but he held her firmly and then draped a robe around her. He chastised her quietly as if she were a child.

'Did you think I spent those hours with you only to offer myself up as a sacrifice?' He tenderly eased a strand of hair from her face and kissed her forehead. 'Your hatred has poisoned your heart. We would have left you in peace but now your soldiers and militia are dead. So too is William Cade.'

'And now your men will rape and plunder,' she said sullenly. 'You have already lain with me so whose turn is it next?'

'None of that will happen,' said Blackstone. 'The weather has turned against us so we will stay a few more days. The citizens of Felice can bury their dead and you will stay here in your rooms. Your bailiff and ladies can attend you.' He turned to John Jacob. 'Build up the fire, John. Then we'll drag these bodies onto the landing outside the rooms.' Blackstone stepped closer to Killbere and the Countess. 'Your servants can be summoned to wash away the blood from the floor. Shall I fetch the apothecary to treat the bruising on your face?'

'I want to address my people and for them to see that even I could not escape your brutality.'

'And have you claim I raped you?' said Killbere. 'No, my lady, you will stay here in these rooms until we leave Felice.'

The fire crackled in the hearth and the flames quickly flared. Killbere stayed with Countess Catherine as John Jacob and Blackstone bent to the task of dragging the first of the guards' bodies through the rooms and onto the landing, leaving a track of blood soiling the floor.

'I will send your servants at first light and have them bring hot water for you to bathe and fresh reeds for the floor,' said Killbere as the second body was heaved away. He undid the bindings on her wrists and ankles. 'You see, Countess, you tried to kill the wrong man. Thomas Blackstone is in command here, I simply misled you into thinking I was.'

'So that I might take you to my bed believing you were the one who would protect me.'

'Believing I was the man you were going to kill,' said Killbere. 'We both played our parts.'

She turned her face away.

Killbere picked up her undershift from the floor and handed it to her. 'Clothe yourself, my lady. You will cause no harm tonight.'

Blackstone and John Jacob stood in the doorway as the Countess clutched the gown about her. As they left her chambers Killbere followed them to the bedroom door. He lowered his voice. 'Your passion does your beauty justice. I have never loved a woman as I have you.'

For a moment it seemed she was going to answer him for a smile played on her lips, but then she spat vigorously at him.

He grinned. 'Though I have been with whores who could spit further. And should we have a child what shall we call him?'

'Get out!' she screamed.

Killbere closed the door and turned to face Blackstone and John Jacob. He shrugged. 'You never know, my offspring might one day rule Felice.'

* * *

The men were back on the walls by dawn the next morning. The respite of even a few hours' sleep had strengthened them. The rain had stopped but a bitter wind barrelled down the valley. As daylight broke and the townspeople ventured out the wailing sound of grief rose up. Blackstone's fighters had released the town priest from where he had been locked up by the militia before they started their attack the previous night, and Blackstone had ordered him and the bailiff to round up townsmen to begin clearing the bodies from the muddy streets. Handcarts were needed so Blackstone allowed men to be brought in from the village outside the walls to help. There was little point in Blackstone addressing the townspeople to tell them that they had brought the carnage upon themselves and he suspected that word was already making its way to Paris that Thomas Blackstone had invaded and slaughtered the innocents of Felice.

'We'll stay here until this storm eases,' Blackstone told the captains. 'It will get colder; there'll be snow again on the mountains. Keep the fires burning so that men can stay warm when they come off duty.'

Perinne limped into the square with Ralph Tait and three of his men. Perinne raised Cade's severed head. 'Where do you want this?'

'On a pole at the far end of the causeway so that those who enter the town will see it. Have a notice made that it is William Cade: a routier lackey of King John.'

Tait turned and told his men to set the pole where Blackstone wanted it. 'Do we feed Cade's body to the pigs?'

'Throw it in the river. Why poison good pork?'

The men grinned as the dead man's opaque eyes gazed up at the man who killed him.

Blackstone made his way to the old apothecary's house, doubtful that the young Frenchman would have survived the night. He was admitted by a tired-looking servant who had been charged to keep watch over the injured man. The servant huddled by the kitchen fire as the apothecary greeted Blackstone. Alain's head was propped up by a small cushion, his body covered with a blanket.

'Does he live?' asked Blackstone.

'The fever broke,' the apothecary said and bathed Alain's face with a damp cloth.

'His leg?'

'Another day or more until we know,' he said as the young man's eyes opened.

'Until you know what?' said Alain sleepily.

Blackstone grinned and placed a hand on the boy's arm. 'Until we can see whether you're able to ride or not,' he lied.

'Sir Thomas...' he said weakly, 'where am I?'

'We took the town, remember?'

'Oh... yes.' He tried to raise himself. 'My leg?'

Blackstone put an arm beneath his shoulder and lifted him gently. 'It is set and bound. We did all we could do. And the apothecary gave you enough potion to fell an ox. But here you are, stronger than my bastard horse.'

He grinned. 'Then I shall soon be able to rejoin you.'

'Soon,' Blackstone assured him. 'While you slept we fought William Cade and the townsmen. There's much to tell you and there's no hurry.'

'And Cade?'

'Dead.'

'By your hand?'

'Yes.'

Alain sighed. 'I wish I could have seen it.'

'You'll see his head on a pole. Now, I and the men need some rest. I'll have you moved to a room in the château where this good man can attend to you when needed.'

The answer satisfied the young man and he lay back down and closed his eyes. The apothecary gave Blackstone a look that told him the young Frenchman was not yet out of danger. As Blackstone stood at the door he pressed a gold *mouton* into the old man's hands. His eyes widened and he shook his head.

'I cannot accept this much,' he quietly protested. 'You must realize that the boy might still die and at the very least that he is most likely to lose the leg.'

'Keep it. You kept the pain from him and you will have to buy more medicines. I am grateful for your efforts. I'll send men to have him taken to the château.'

The apothecary bowed his head in gratitude. 'Then I will also prepare ointments for your wounded men. That dried dirt in your hair shows a scalp wound. It should be stitched.'

'I'll have my centenar attend to it. I'm sure he'll take pleasure in pushing a needle through my scalp.'

The door closed behind him. John Jacob had placed men there once dawn had bled into the night sky. By whatever means these things happened the townspeople would likely know that the young Frenchman was not a monk sent by Prior Albert but that he was of the men who had slaughtered so many of their kin. Until the lad could be moved to a safer place then two men would guard the apothecary's house.

Blackstone was obliged to step over and around some of the crumpled bodies that littered the narrow street. Women sobbed as they identified their husbands or sons. The town had paid a high price and the hatred behind their stares as he walked past them stabbed at him like a dagger point. John Jacob dogged his lord's footsteps, walking three paces behind, hand on his sword hilt, watching that the hatred did not boil over into an attack. Blackstone regretted their grief. He too knew what it meant to lose loved ones. Also, these villeins' lives were hard and the lack of a man meant additional poverty and hardship. He raised his face to the wind and thought he sensed snow in the air. He hoped not. He wanted to escape from Felice in good time and meet up with the Gascon captain, Beyard, who he hoped had gathered more men to ride with them. The fighting here was over but he had no doubt that a greater conflict awaited them if William Cade had not lied. If it was true the Dauphin and perhaps the French King had decided to order their army to kill Blackstone should he cross their path, then he would be obliged to try and defend himself. The fact that he had already fought Marshal of the French Army d'Audrehem's men-at-arms in a skirmish meant that King Edward might also abandon him. It would be seen that Blackstone had broken the treaty.

His thoughts were interrupted as a woman cried out when she turned over a body. Dirt half covered the face of a boy, probably no older than Blackstone's own son, he realized. The woman cleaved the child to her, pressing him to her chest. The lad's arm had been hacked off and he would have died from the shock, loss of blood and the previous night's bitter temperature. Yet it made no difference what finally killed the lad: the woman's son was dead. She bared her teeth at Blackstone, cursed him with such fury as only a grieving mother could and then began throwing mud at him. John Jacob stepped forward to stop her but Blackstone held out a restraining hand and let the mud splatter him until the woman's venom abated.

'Remember, John, I know what it means to lose a child to violence.' He wiped the mud from his face and walked on, bringing the silver-wheeled goddess Arianrhod to his lips. He would go to the church and light a candle to honour the memory of his murdered wife and daughter and to give thanks that his son was safe in Florence.

PART THREE

BROTHERHOOD
OF THE SWORD

February 1362

CHAPTER FIFTY-TWO

The Florentine bankers, the Bardi, had wealth, which gave them influence and favour in the court of the English King, but their priest, no matter how hard he prayed, Torellini, could not influence the Almighty. The Marquis de Montferrat, allied with the Pope, friend of Thomas Blackstone and trusted by Florence, had entertained Torellini and his charge long enough for the snowstorms to blow clear of the mountain passes. The rain that swept the valleys on the far side of the mountains coated the crevices and routes in a blanket of snow. Although these routes were kept open throughout the year, those that travelled from Italy into France, or those who took the pilgrim's way on the journey to Rome, depended on the knowledge of the mountain village guides and their strength and skill in traversing the treacherous passes. Father Torellini had separated the pilgrim party that had set out from Florence, sending the genuine pilgrims and their Knights of the Tau escort further north towards the Brenner Pass, which would take them across the trade route to Lyons, a pilgrimage that would be noticed by the Visconti. And if the Milanese lords had planned Henry Blackstone's assassination they might already know that the attack in Florence had failed. If that were the case then this group of pilgrims escorted by their protectors would draw their attention. The Marquis de Montferrat had been waiting north of Genoa to take them through the lower passes to Avignon. But even here where the snow was not as deep as on the higher passes the weather demanded they stay with Montferrat in one of his castles until a safe route could be determined. Once Montferrat had been made welcome by the fortress's commander and Torellini had been ushered into the great hall to share wine, a blazing fire and the promise of safety, Henry had slipped away from his escort and climbed the steps to the walls.

Braziers with half-cupped iron guards on one side of their baskets shielded the flames from the wind, but the buffeting snow had passed and a blue sky streaked across the mountain peaks and scattered its diamond-bright light across the meadow that lay below the castle.

'Boy? You know this place?' said Fra Foresti when he traced Henry's whereabouts. He had seen the look on the lad's face when they arrived. For once he did not reprimand his young charge for absconding from his care, realizing that ghosts from the past might haunt the high plateau and that Blackstone's son might have seen them.

Henry Blackstone knew it only too well. Knew it and dreaded it the moment they had arrived. His body trembled as he steadied himself and dared to step closer to the parapet in a test of his own courage. His eyes squeezed shut and then he opened them and gazed down to the ground far below. He knew exactly where the skeletal remains of the killer would be. The air stung tears into his eyes. He wiped them away in case the Tau knight mistakenly thought him weak. He had not realized that the young guardian hospitaller had moved quietly to his side, had not heard the crunch of his boots on the snow or the rustle of his cloak.

'Henry?' said Fra Foresti quietly.

Henry's gaze stayed fixed on the treeline that edged the snow-covered meadow. 'Before snow comes there are Alpine flowers here. They cover the meadow like coloured snowdrops. There's a lake behind us. Its water is cold enough to snap a man's bones but men once forded it to rescue my mother, my sister and me.' He dared a step closer to the edge. 'The man who imprisoned us held Agnes and me over the edge. He asked my father which of us should die.'

'Your father was here?'

'Down there. He fought three men and then... You remember John Jacob and Will Longdon?' he asked, turning to his guardian, who nodded in assent. 'They swam the lake and climbed up the wall with their men and attacked. And saved us. Yes, I know this place. There was a great battle here. The flowers were watered with men's blood. My father's young squire was butchered near here and the man who killed him was slain by my father in single combat. His body was spreadeagled and left as a warning. There,' he said, turning his gaze towards the plateau's edge. 'Somewhere. I can't see it. But it's there.' He looked up at the Tau knight. 'And here,' he said, touching his temple. 'I see it all. I always do.'

'The Savage Priest,' said Fra Foresti, suddenly realizing where they were. 'La Battaglia nella Valle dei Fiori.'

Henry nodded. 'Why would I come to this place again? Why would I be brought here?'

'It is coincidence. Or God's will. You must decide.'

Henry remained silent. The memory of the place held him. To revisit it was to be assailed with the fear he had known back then. The thoughts of his dead mother and sister were as haunting as the eerie sound of the wind across the rock face. His hand touched the sword pommel at his belt. It had been his father's squire's sword, given to Henry by his father when its brave young owner was butchered. It had been given to honour Henry's courage.

'Memory can trespass on a man's heart,' said Fra Foresti. 'But it can also serve to strengthen his resolve. You have walked a stony path over the years but I see in you a strength that is unique for a boy your age. Those mountains are hidden by the snow just as you are clothed by a generous spirit. Both disguise an unyielding stubbornness not to be conquered.'

Henry shivered and then did as his father had always taught him and calmed the urge in his body.

'Let us eat and find some fireside warmth,' said Foresti. 'And then we can pray in the chapel. Will you join me?'

The wind hurried the clouds away exposing Alpine peaks that soared into the blue. Henry nodded. He had passed this way once before and now he would turn his back on the grim fortress that held his memories captive. The guardian mountains beckoned.

The moon glowed across the vast snowfields peppered here and there with the distant glimmer of small mountain villages. The untrammelled crystal carpet glistened as far as the eye could see, its sweeping curve of downhill contours would lead Niccolò Torellini down into Provence and then the papal state of Avignon.

Henry Blackstone slept wrapped in his blanket, back turned towards the burning logs in his room's fireplace while below in the great hall the reality of what lay ahead was discussed by the three men who were responsible for his safety.

'Provence has been swept with routiers these past months,' said the fortress commander. 'This castle guards the way for those who go and fight in Italy. But it is impossible to say what you will find down there. No routier has ever respected a pilgrim.' He gestured away the servant who had poured wine for his lord and his guests. The boy bowed and left them to the warmth of the fireplace.

'And they will not change their murderous ways now,' agreed Torellini. 'We must pray for good weather so that we may reach Avignon as quickly as we can.'

Niccolò Torellini knew it was because of him that they had only made slow progress along the Via Francigena and then into the mountains. He was getting old and his back ached from the horse's gait and the mountain's dampness caused his bones to grumble. But he made the declaration in such a manner that no one would question his ability to keep up at a faster pace.

'I can go no further,' said the Marquis de Montferrat. 'Provence belongs to the Queen of Naples and she would not welcome my presence. And Savoy is on their northern border. If that peacock Count Amadeus hears of my incursion then I and my men would be trapped on the wrong side of the Alps. You will have to go unaccompanied from here.'

Torellini nodded. 'I knew as much and did not expect your protection any further, my dear Marquis. I am grateful you shielded us from any attempt by the Visconti to cause us harm.'

The grizzled Piedmont lord poured another beaker of wine. 'You cannot be certain they are responsible for the attempt on the boy's life. If they were I believe we would have had a fight on our hands no matter how carefully we travelled.'

Fra Foresti considered their ongoing journey. 'Count Amadeus of Savoy allowed Blackstone and his son to travel through his territory when they took the French Princess to Milan. Perhaps he could be called upon to offer us protection once we reach the lower plains?'

'Who's to say he is as benevolent now? A lot can happen in two years and he is still aligned with the Visconti,' said Montferrat.

'But he serves the Pope, which goes against their wishes,' said Foresti.

'No, no,' Torellini said, raising his hand to halt any further discussion of who might help them. 'We travel on alone. We are only days away from safety in Avignon. We must look to ourselves. The boy is of value to someone and we must just pray that his presence is not discovered going into France. He is cursed with his father's name.'

'But he is blessed with his parents' courage,' said Fra Foresti. 'He sleeps in a place that held his family captive years ago when he was a boy. His father killed the Savage Priest here.'

At the mention of the murderous killer's name, Torellini crossed himself. 'I had forgotten. Of course. I had not given this place any thought.' He tugged the fur collar of his cloak tighter around his neck. It was a draughty castle despite the fire. The thought flitted through his mind that it might be more than the invasive wind, and there might still be malevolent spirits who clung to the place of death.

A shaft of moonlight beamed down from a high window. Montferrat glanced up at the clear sky. 'A raw night. The wind will hold and the snow will fall further north. You should take your chances tomorrow.'

They left the high citadel as the sun struck its walls. Fra Foresti led the way, his horse going forward uncertainly into the knee-deep snow as they followed the mountain guide. The sharp crunch of the broken surface hung in the still air. Henry followed, and behind him the man who had held his father's near-dead body before the boy was born and who was determined to see the son safely delivered to his father's side. They stopped at the frozen skeletal remains that still hung, tied with wire, the shield's blazon weather-beaten. The alpine wind and glacial temperature had turned what was left of the man's skin into blackened leather. Henry jumped down from his horse and wiped a gloved hand across the stone slab that rested below the gibbet. The words of warning as to who had killed this vicious murderer and the promise that all men like him would die had been chiselled by his father and would remain long after the Savage Priest's blackened flesh finally flaked from his bones.

'I saw him die,' said Henry as he climbed back into the saddle. 'And I was glad of it.'

He smiled at Fra Foresti. He had laid the ghost to rest.

CHAPTER FIFTY-THREE

Beyard, the Gascon captain had travelled as far south as the bridge at Pont-Saint-Esprit, the walled town twenty miles north of Avignon. He had gathered men from disparate groups of routiers with promises of serving a legend of war who would grant them control of conquered towns and districts. That meant profit from *patis*, protection money, from the towns and villages, enough to keep a band of men in food and comfort year in year out. The men were mostly Gascons, troops who had served and were still loyal to the Captal de Buch, and once these men knew that their lord's captain rode with Blackstone it made easier their desertion from the coalition of brigand forces that controlled the lower Rhône Valley. Thousands of brigands in bands of varying sizes, some less than a hundred, others several hundred strong, were scattered across Provence and Bas-Languedoc, a shifting mass that nudged the Mediterranean coast and sought refuge in the mountains. If they ever came together they would amass an army of five or six thousand. Many of these routiers had tried to fight in Spain but once the truce had been called between its warring princes they had drifted back and were already edging their way up the Rhône Valley, wary of being trapped between two French armies that hunted them.

Beyard's proposal was not welcomed by all the mercenaries. Many were footsoldiers, unemployed now that war had been abandoned between France and England, their ranks swelled by archers and criminals, penurious knights and minor lords who had lost their lands. Their view was that Blackstone did the English King's work hounding routiers out of towns that had been ceded, which meant he was an enemy of the brigands. Beyard skirted trouble – all he needed was a few hundred men he considered trustworthy enough to fight at Blackstone's side. There were many more who came forward to offer their services but were rejected, their crimes too great for Blackstone to have accepted them. It was already a negotiated part of the agreement with those Beyard had recruited that they would be granted a pardon by Pope Innocent for their part in the destruction and killing that had gone on throughout the south of France. Other mercenaries who drifted from band to band sought leaders who would give free rein to their lust for plunder and rape; such fighters drifted into the mountains where men of ill repute gathered like-minded followers; the Bretons were recruiting further north after their recent defeat, as were routier commanders like John Amory and John Cresswell, Englishmen who already held garrisons in more than a dozen towns. Others had drifted even further north and found refuge with the Welshman, Gruffydd ap Madoc.

Beyard left his men on the far side of the River Rhône and requested entry through the gates of Avignon. The walls had been reinforced and there were more soldiers on the battlements, men who had heeded the call from Pope Innocent to help protect the papal city. He would have been denied entry were it not for his service with the Captal de Buch and the warrant given to Thomas Blackstone by Sir John Chandos. The document was scrutinized by various guard commanders as he was conducted deeper into the city sanctum, past the luxurious palaces belonging to the cardinals and the bustling streets that thronged with courtiers and tradesmen. Soldiers jostled shoulder to shoulder with bankers and court messengers. The wealth in Avignon consumed vast supplies of luxury goods. Food was in abundance, court officials sported fine clothes of silk and velvet, their cost easily explained as courtiers vied with petitioners in bribing the officials to be heard. Beyard began to yearn for the more simple dishonesty of fighting men rather than those in this money-grubbing city. He was given a cot and a mattress in a guard commander's quarters while he waited to be summoned for his petition for clemency and forgiveness to be heard for those men who would join Thomas Blackstone. He would never be granted an audience with Pope Innocent himself but he hoped that the liberal use of Thomas Blackstone's name and the knight's association with King Edward of England would help speed through the suffocating bureaucracy of Avignon.

After three days he had heard nothing and drifted into a brothel for distraction and pleasure. On the fourth day, as he made his way back to the bleak, dismal rooms that were his quarters, he saw a man approaching through the crowd and despite the distance between them he sensed the cloaked figure was making his way towards him. The man had glanced once or twice in his direction and caught his gaze, then turned away, easing his shoulder through the herd of people. Beyard's hand went to the pommel of his sword but the crowd pressed him, which would make it difficult to draw the blade. He shifted his hand to the knife at his belt. The cloaked figure had ignored him and gone past him, nudging people aside. Beyard scoured the crowd ahead in case the cloaked figure was a decoy to draw his attention away from an assassin or a thief. It was likely there would be men here who harboured ill will towards Thomas Blackstone and those who sided with him, and of course he had mentioned freely that he served the scar-faced Englishman. His attention was held by a rough-looking villein who carried stacked baskets on his back, a rope that bound them together across his forehead. His curt, gruff voice called out for the crowd to make way as he forged through the press, opening up a passage ahead of him. A perfect ploy to suddenly ram a blade between a victim's ribs. The distraction was Beyard's downfall as a man's iron grip clutched his knife arm and a whispered warning from the cloaked figure behind him told him to do as he commanded or the blade that he felt pressing in his lower back would leave him dead on the ground. The knife point nudged him quickly away from the busy street and Beyard knew the chances of twisting free from it were too slim to risk making the attempt.

The man's pace quickened as they went this way and that.

335

Beyard stayed silent, looking for any opportunity to turn and fight, but found none, so determined was his assailant's determined stride along alleys whose narrow walls seemed to have been chosen to make it impossible to resist. Finally Beyard was pushed into a wider corridor of marble floor and religious frescoes that colour washed the walls high into ornate ceilings. A courtyard beckoned through soaring arches as the cloaked figure guided him through a gilded door and into a scented garden where a rill trickled water from a gently spurting fountain. For a moment the contrast between where he had been quartered these past few days and this luxury distracted him. Then, with a firm push in his back, he was shoved further into the sunlight that streamed into the enclosed garden. He turned, ready to fight, but the cloaked figure pulled back the hood of his cloak and stood ready sword in hand. Beyard would be dead before his blade left its scabbard.

'You use Sir Thomas Blackstone's name with abandon,' said the figure.

Another voice came from the far side of the garden. 'And that means you are either a charlatan or are trusted.'

Beyard turned. Despite the winter sun's rays that reached into the garden the old man was dressed in a pale cassock beneath a fur-edged cloak for warmth.

'I am the Gascon Beyard. I serve the Captal de Buch, but I fight with Thomas Blackstone. If there is disagreement between you then I will stand in Sir Thomas's stead and defend his name. But if you wish to murder me then be done with it.'

The cloaked figure sheathed his sword and stepped in front of Beyard as the old man beckoned Beyard forward.

'You seek a pardon for fighting men. I can arrange that. This is the house of the Florentine banker, Bardi. I am his servant. And God has looked kindly on me because I cannot go much further. You are the man we are looking for,' said Niccolò Torellini.

CHAPTER FIFTY-FOUR

After several days the town of Felice was still mourning the death of those who had served in the militia and the married men of the garrison troops. The town was occupied by foreign fighters led by the Englishman, Thomas Blackstone. The curfew was strictly enforced but church services were permitted. Resentment festered but no one had dared raise more than their voice against Blackstone's men who patrolled the walls and streets. The outlying villagers had been brought in with their handcarts to help take the dead to the graveyard. The ground was still hard but Blackstone allowed the town priest to take as many of the townsmen as he needed to dig graves. Felice's carpenter fashioned eighty-three crosses but after the attack Blackstone refused to pay for them and instead instructed the Countess's bailiff to recompense the carpenter. Countess Catherine de Val, still confined to her quarters, was allowed a servant to attend her.

'How much longer are we staying?' said Killbere as they gazed across the landscape beyond the village roofs. 'The weather comes and goes but we should take advantage of these clear spells.'

'I want to be rid of this place. It reeks of treachery and death. But Alain is not yet ready to travel,' said Blackstone.

'There are still a half-dozen towns that need to swear allegiance. That will take us into summer and by then we should decide where to go. We cannot linger because of the lad's wound. We have to leave word for Beyard so let's take him back to the monastery. We can make a litter for him and leave him in the care of the monks in their infirmary. They won't cause him harm. Not now.

And we can meet up with Beyard as he makes his way towards us. We could do with his reinforcements.'

Blackstone nodded. 'I also thought we should do that. If we stay much longer who knows who will come over those hills? Word will have reached the French King by now and unless Chandos can be convincing enough then the French will want us dead. The Countess and William Cade were in their pay.'

'It will make no difference,' Killbere said, looking down at Cade's head on its spike outside the main gates. 'The French don't need an excuse to come after you but doing Edward's bidding has shielded us so far, and I'll wager Chandos won't defend us unless he is put into a corner.'

'We gave him victory over the Bretons. He won't abandon us. Even so, the French won't need to excuse themselves to him or Edward should we be killed.'

'And this place can be defended, but we would be starved out if they laid siege. And if they bring enough men, then, well... they might throw themselves at us like plague dogs. We've been here too long.'

Blackstone knew Killbere was correct but he had been holding on hoping that the young Frenchman would recover from his injury. 'Talk to the men, Gilbert. We will leave tomorrow; there's no point in waiting any longer. We will give the Countess back her town.'

'You've spoken to her today?'

'No. I avoid her.' He glanced at Killbere. 'You've not tried to bed her again, have you?'

Killbere snorted. 'Mother of God, Thomas, I performed heroically that night. I was the old stallion in the herd. I rose magnificently to the occasion. I will be honest and say that I have not known a woman before with such appetite and vigour for the act of coupling. Her knife attack aside, she damned near killed me.' He grinned.

'Good to know you raised the flag for England,' said Blackstone, smiling back.

'It was a battle standard!' said Killbere.

'Then best you stay clear of her. If she finds you that irresistible we can't have her following us across France.'

As Blackstone went down the steps from the parapet, his shadow John Jacob fell in beside him. As they walked up towards the apothecary's house windows and doors slammed closed. Since they had buried their dead the townspeople avoided any contact with the man they held responsible. Once they had collected the apothecary John Jacob took the old man's satchel of medicines and they slowed their pace to suit him as they walked up to the château. Perinne sat in the warmth of the winter sun on the terrace. He got to his feet as Blackstone approached. It was obvious the man's wound was still painful and he wore his jupon open over the loose linen shirt.

'We need to take a look at your back,' said Blackstone. 'I don't want anyone unable to ride because of their wounds.'

'I'm healing well,' said the sturdy man. 'No need to fuss over me as if I were a feeble woman.'

'All well and good,' said John Jacob. 'But there's at least one woman in this château who would inflict another wound on you for saying it.'

Blackstone gestured. 'Let us see it now.'

Perinne sighed and tugged free his coat and shirt, then bent his back muscles so that the ugly welt could be examined. The searing-hot iron had blistered the skin and when his muscles were flexed the gash looked ready to split. The apothecary ran his fingers down each edge of the wound. He nodded to himself and then bent to open his satchel.

'Keep the wound dressed.' He handed Perinne a small hessian sack of herbs. 'Can you make a poultice?'

Perinne dropped his shirt and nodded.

'This is comfrey,' said the apothecary. 'Let the poultice cool and then cover the wound. Bind it with fresh linen every day for as long as the herbs last.' He turned to Blackstone. 'He must not be put to physical work or raise a sword in anger until the time comes. If the wound splits...' He shrugged. Who knew what might happen.

Perinne looked from the old healer to Blackstone. 'Do as he says,' said Blackstone and placed a hand on the apothecary's shoulder. 'Now the youngster.'

They went past Tait and his hobelars, who guarded the kitchen and main door into the château, and on into the lower rooms. In one with a south-facing window, which allowed the sunlight to stream in, Alain lay covered with a fur-lined cloak with two blankets on top. The boy shivered despite the warmth from the fire. Tait sat with him, keeping a moist flannel on the boy's forehead.

'Has he slept and eaten today?' said Blackstone.

'I got some broth down him a few hours back. But he is neither awake nor asleep. The fever came on him a few hours ago,' said the nursemaid hobelar. 'Master Apothecary gave me ground fennel liquid for his fever. I dribbled some into him but the fever has not reduced, my lord.'

Blackstone acknowledged Tait, who then shuffled past the three men to wait outside. John Jacob pulled back the bedclothes and he and Blackstone wrinkled their nose at the smell. The apothecary lifted the long linen shirt to above the young Frenchman's knee. The leg was swollen. Pus and crusted skin gathered along the stitched wound. Angry red fingers clawed up Alain's leg into his thigh. The wound had festered. The apothecary lifted the lad's shirt higher. Blotches, some as big as the palm of a man's hand, had formed and peeled on the skin of his stomach and thigh. Pustules clung to the bare flesh.

John Jacob crossed himself.

'I thought we had held back the poison, Sir Thomas, but it's gone from his wound into his blood. For these past days I have bled him but I have no cure for this.'

'If we take off his leg? Will that stop the poison spreading?' said Blackstone.

'Now there is no choice, Sir Thomas. It is his only chance.'

'John. Fetch the butcher.'

* * *

Perinne watched the shadow circle high in the sky. The buzzard was mocked by high-flying crows but the raptor ignored their determined attempts to chase it away. It lingered, soaring higher. Gazing down. Waiting for the next man to die.

They carried the young Frenchman into the brightness and warmth of the winter sun. Blackstone summoned Ralph Tait to fetch Will Longdon, whose wound-stitching skills would be needed, and then had his men who guarded the château's door carry the heavy kitchen table outside. Some of the townspeople gathered in the courtyard below where only nights earlier other blood had been spilled. As three or four people at a time stopped to observe what was about to happen, John Jacob hurried the butcher before him. He wore a belt of pockets that held his cutting and paring knives and clasped a saw and a cleaver in his fist. This was the second time he had been summoned to the ailing Frenchman and once again he was sweating more from fear than the rush through the streets.

Meulon strode alongside them carrying a small pail and an earthenware jar. 'This is better than hot pitch. Clay and turpentine will seal the stump. I took these from the carpenter and the potter,' he said, placing his cargo to hand near the supine body.

'And this seals the wound and stops the poison?' asked the apothecary.

'We don't know. We have seen barber surgeons on the battle-field use it. They soak the wound with turpentine to keep the flesh from rotting and then pack it with clay.'

'Very well,' said the old man. 'I am no surgeon, all I can offer is to try and subdue his pain.'

'Few men can stand this agony,' said Blackstone. 'Whatever you administer make it a draught that will keep him asleep throughout.'

The apothecary hesitated. 'There is only one mixture of herbs I can give him now. I have a preparation of three parts black henbane, one of ground poppy seeds and one of hemlock. If he

341

survives he will remain unconscious for three days, perhaps more. The potion itself is dangerous.'

'Get it,' said Blackstone. 'He'll die anyway.'

Will Longdon boiled his silk thread over the kitchen stove and Meulon stood ready to use his strength to hold the young man down should the apothecary's mixture not take hold soon enough.

'You have brought a curse on this town!' one of those in the growing crowd called. 'And pain and death will be inflicted in return.'

Blackstone and the others looked to see who had cried out but the shuffling crowd hemmed in whoever had cursed them.

'Get back to your homes,' Renfred ordered.

'How many of us will you kill before we obey?' a woman snarled.

'How many will die before you run?' said Killbere. 'Get back to your rat holes, you vermin, or I will come among you.'

Renfred signalled for some of his men to move in on the crowd, who quickly dispersed before any violence could be inflicted on them.

Blackstone pulled the butcher to him. He took the meat cleaver and the saw from him and placed the bone saw on the table. 'It needs a clean cut. If you hack the bone it will splinter.'

The man nodded dumbly as he looked down at the young man who sweated and shivered on the table. Will Longdon raised the infected leg and placed a block of wood beneath it. He tied cord above and below the wound.

Blackstone pulled free the butcher's knives and examined them. The paring knife had the keenest blade. 'When you pare a pig's haunch you cut through skin and muscle and pull the skin back?'

The butcher nodded.

'Then, when you remove the bone there is enough skin remaining so that a cook can pack herbs and spices before threading with string and cooking.'

'Yes, my lord,' said the butcher feebly.

'Then that is what you will do here. Leave enough flesh to stitch over the cut bone,' said Blackstone. 'Keep your hand steady, saw cleanly.'

The men gathered around the stricken Frenchman. Each had a

role to play. The apothecary lifted Alain's head and poured wine mixed with the opiate liquid between his lips. 'I am uncertain how much to administer,' he said. 'Too much and I kill him before you begin to cut, too little and the pain will not be sufficiently blocked.' He stepped back and nodded at Blackstone. 'I dare not give him more.'

Alain de la Grave's breathing and tremors eased. Blackstone nodded to Meulon, who leant his strength against the lad's shoulders. Blackstone stood opposite the butcher and held the broken, infected leg. The butcher licked his lips nervously. A moment of calm settled as everyone waited for the cutting to start. A sudden flurry of crows fluttered from the château's roof, their cawing alarm startling everyone. A bad sign.

'Do it,' said Blackstone to the frightened butcher. 'Put your mind to it. And cut.'

'Where?'

Blackstone touched a hand's breadth above the swollen, pus-filled wound and poisoned tendrils, and a finger's width below where Longdon had tightened the cord.

The butcher hesitated, took a deep breath and bent to the task. Alain's unconscious body bucked slightly as the curved blade found nerves. The man cut with the expertise a butcher learns over the years. A bucket on the floor at the end of the table caught the blood that quickly swamped his hands. The butcher looked startled for a moment, being more used to butchering dead animals.

Blackstone saw the look of alarm as he raised his eyes. 'Quickly now. The bone,' said Blackstone.

The butcher wiped his bloody hand on his apron and picked up the bone saw. Blackstone reached across and tugged back the flap of skin, exposing the bone, giving the butcher a clear view of what had to be done. The saw moved back and forth. The pain must have reached deep into the young man's unconsciousness because despite the opiate he suddenly bucked and tried to rear up. Meulon and Blackstone held him down but a low cry of agony reached out to them all. And then he fell back.

'Finish it,' Blackstone commanded the butcher as the apothecary placed a hand on the lad's chest and then placed his face close to his mouth.

'He still lives.'

The leg came free. Killbere reached for it and dropped it into an empty wood basket. Will Longdon shouldered the butcher aside; the man was dazed from his experience. The veteran archer swabbed the gaping wound with turpentine and then, as Blackstone raised the stump to ease the bleeding, quickly stitched the flaps of skin over the cut. The apothecary's servant stepped forward with the pot of malleable clay. Blackstone dipped his hand into the pot and spread the contents thickly and evenly over the wound. The apothecary then placed a piece of clean linen over the clay and bandaged the leg. If they had been at prayer in the church and watched the marked candle burn down they would have known that it had taken less than two minutes from the moment the first cut had been made.

The men stood back from their efforts.

A lone crow dropped silently from the roof and settled near the basket, its crippled gait taking it closer to the severed leg. Killbere moved so quickly that the bird had no time to escape. His sword slashed down and the bird fell dead.

'We'll have no bad omens hovering near the lad,' said Killbere. 'Have the leg taken to the blacksmith and burnt,' he instructed Tait, who in turn ordered one of his men forward.

'Meulon, take him back to his cot. Master Apothecary, you and your servant stay with him a while,' said Blackstone. 'Butcher, you will be paid for your work here today.'

The butcher bowed his head and gathered his knives and saw. As Meulon lifted the unconscious Frenchman from the table, one of the men sluiced it with a bucket of water.

Killbere spat out the foul taste that the stench from the poisoned leg had left in his throat. 'I'll go and kick the priest's arse and have him light a candle and offer up prayers.'

The men filtered away as Blackstone turned his face to a freshening breeze that blew across the lingering smell of blood and disease. The sooner they could leave this place the better. He felt a tinge of regret. He had failed to tell Alain that his true father still lived and it was from him that he gained his courage. Was it going to be too late? It seemed unlikely the lad would live. And if he did? What use could he be? There could be no employment as a soldier. What was left? A life of poverty begging on a vermin-infested street in some town? Regret struck him. Why had he not let the boy die? He knew why. Because it had been his intent to avenge another youngster that had brought them to this murderous place. If a life could be spared from the slaughter that had occurred here, then it should be saved.

Blackstone kicked the crow's bloodied remains into the court-yard below. Let it rot there on the blood-soaked ground.

CHAPTER FIFTY-FIVE

Blackstone went into the château and the room he shared with Killbere. He was covered with gore from when Alain's heartbeat had pumped blood across him as the leg was taken. He stripped off his jupon and shirt and used the washbowl to sluice the blood from his hands, face and body, and rinsed water through his hair. As he turned to take a bolt of cloth to dry himself he saw Countess Catherine in the doorway. Her dark hair had been curled and plaited and the bruise on her face was covered with pale make-up, but she was dressed more simply than when he had first seen her. Still, her plain attire could do nothing to hide her beauty. She was barefoot and wore no rings on her hands or bracelets on her wrist. For someone like the Countess it appeared to be an act of penance. She had approached so silently that he had not heard her and he wondered whether she had a hidden knife. But the tightness of her gown would have made such concealment impossible.

'You're confined to your quarters. I had your doors locked,' he said.

She stepped into the room but did not approach him. 'There is more than one key,' she answered. 'And more than one door.'

'What is it you want?' he said without any warmth in his voice. He would not accord this woman any clemency that might still linger in his heart.

'Does the boy live?'

'Why should you care?'

'I took him to my bed. I enjoyed his youth. I did not wish to see such a beautiful body broken.'

Blackstone pulled on his shirt. He had no wish to linger in the same room as this temptress – because that was surely what she was. And he could not deny the same urge he felt towards her as he had done in the beginning.

'He's likely to die. The broken bones poisoned his blood and we were forced to cut off his leg.'

She showed no sign of remorse. 'It is your actions that have resulted in his misfortune and brought death to my people,' she said matter-of-factly. 'We are both to blame, Sir Thomas. I for wishing to avenge my own family by luring routiers here and killing them, and you for seeking the same vengeance on William Cade. I am no pious woman, as you know, but these circumstances were surely governed by God's hand.'

'God favours no one in a battle. We all cry out His name to bless us and to keep us safe. He is deaf to our entreaties. It was not God who brought us together; there are other spirits of misfortune that punish us. I wanted only William Cade. I was going to leave this place without harm but you have a lust for killing that is even more than your lust for sex.'

'And you condemn me for it.'

She had taken another step closer, like an animal approaching a trap. Cautious but daring to test the danger of what lay ahead. Blackstone did not move, sensing creature instincts were at play. Was she laying poisoned bait for him?

'You know you will be hunted now. Those who escaped from Felice will have carried word of what you have done here.'

'Being hunted is nothing new to me or my men.'

'Your enemies increase every year you roam like a dispossessed ghost. You should stop and find a place that grants you safety and a way to feed and clothe your men and to make money with ease. There would be no need for you or your men to die when the French King or another routier leader finally traps you.'

Blackstone gazed at her. He could not take his eyes from the hollow of her throat where a rhythmic pulse beat. It had increased in its intensity and a warm glow had seeped into her neck and face. He realized she was offering herself to him.

347

'You wish me to stay here?' he said.

She stepped yet closer. 'I am a widow who must defend this town and this fiefdom. You have killed my garrison and many of my militia so I cannot offer my people safety any longer. I need a man no one would dare challenge and if that man had his own soldiers then it would prove an agreeable arrangement.'

'And you would wish me in your bed,' he said gently, lowering his voice to match her inducement.

'I would welcome it,' she said. 'And you would become Lord of Felice.'

He could smell her scent as she came within arm's reach. She was offering him lust and power and yet she stood before him like an innocent. A virgin bride demure before her husband.

'And I would have money?' he said, already tasting his desire for her.

'I have enough gold and silver coin and more will come in *patis* once you offer your protection here and beyond,' she said, her voice almost like a whisper from a lover.

'I would have to leave while I looked for the Welshman I hunt. I don't know how long that would take.'

He could feel her breath on his face. It smelled of sweet-scented herbs. He bent his lips to hers and touched them lightly. Like a huntress she had drawn him in and slowly she tightened the noose on her prey.

'Not long... not long... Thomas. He's in the mountains south of here. He camps at La Roche. Cade told me. Kill him and come back to me.'

Without haste her tongue sought his and for a moment he embraced her. So slow was the kiss, so delicate her tongue, it took little imagination to know how sweet the lovemaking would be.

He held her a heartbeat longer, she raised her head and looked up into his smiling face, and then Blackstone tipped the jug of water over her.

Drenched, she shrieked and shuffled back. Shock etched her face. She snarled and hurled herself at him but he easily wrapped her arms around her and her thrashing kicks had no effect on him.

'Be quiet or you will be hurt,' he warned her.

Her cries brought Meulon and two of his men to the door.

'Do as I say,' he insisted, 'or I give you to my men.'

Her head sank as her struggles eased. He pushed the bedraggled woman away from him. She fought the men who grabbed her arms but she was easily held. She spat at Blackstone as he pulled on his jupon. 'You are a bastard, scar-faced Englishman. You are a plague on France and I wish to God that I could have hung your body in my courtyard.'

Blackstone nodded. 'And had you succeeded your King and his son would have rewarded you with anything you had asked for,' he said evenly. 'I admire a woman who will fight for justice. I've known women like that. I respect their courage. But you are not one of those women. At first I thought you were. You are twisted in heart and soul and surely it will be that same God you proclaim who will condemn you. I do not. I despise you.'

She screamed a torrent of abuse at him. Meulon clamped his broad hand across her face until she gagged and quietened.

'Don't smother her. Let her breathe.'

No sooner had Meulon's hand released her than she drew breath and cursed Blackstone again. The throat-cutter went to strike her but Blackstone stayed his hand.

'She's a creature who won't be silenced until the devil takes her back to his fold. It's time we left this place of misery.'

How many more nights would they have to spend here before Alain was able to travel? He had once thought Felice to be the name of a woman but in reality it was a place of torture and death ruled by a voracious she-wolf. Cade was dead and Gruffydd ap Madoc would soon be found. He nodded at Meulon. 'Keep men at her door, search her servants each time they enter. She has keys of her own. And there's another door. Look in her bedchamber. Block it. She is to be kept inside.'

'I will curse you, Thomas Blackstone, every day you live,' she said.

'And your voice will join the multitude of others.'

'I swear I will be there when you are caught and your limbs are severed from your body and your ugly, scarred head is on a spike at the gates of Paris,' she hissed through bared teeth.

'Be sure that my eyes gaze on you, Countess. I would want to see the withered hag that you become. Old, bent and crippled, your wanton life will wither you, your shrivelled skin and toothless gums will give flight to what beauty you have today.' He smiled. 'I have no such journey to make. My face will never be my fortune.'

CHAPTER FIFTY-SIX

Dank mist clung to the countryside around Vincennes. The Seine seemed to suck the grey air down to its surface as if reluctant to relinquish its smothering blanket. The Dauphin sat hunched in an ermine-lined robe, his feet pushed towards the blazing fire. No matter how warmly he dressed the chill would not leave his bones. He ached and his nose dripped. His watery eyes gazed at the blurred flames and he craved the warmth that summer would bring, knowing he would be happy to endure the suffocating heat. But this was only the middle of February and the trees stubbornly refused to leaf and herald the approaching spring. The French army had made progress, sweeping aside some of the routier bands; the army's ranks had swelled to four thousand after extra taxation had been imposed by the King. Men from the eastern provinces had been united under Jean de Tancarville's command and they had begun their march south while those under Arnoul d'Audrehem's command scoured the Rhône Valley, digging the mercenaries out of their rat holes and destroying them. The routiers would soon be crushed between the two armies.

Simon Bucy entered the room and bowed. He was breathless.

'You wheeze like an old crone, Simon. This weather will put us all in an early grave.'

'Sire,' he said as if agreeing; and then: 'The King—'

Before Bucy could complete the sentence the Dauphin arched upright in expectation. 'He is ill?'

Was that a note of hope in the Dauphin's voice? wondered the King's counsellor. 'No, sire, the King is well.' He hesitated, expecting at least a sign of relief from the frail son. There was none.

Charles remained passive and, if anything, appeared to be irritated by the intrusion for anything less than his father's imminent collapse. The King had gone to claim Burgundy and he had stayed in Dijon.

'No, highness, but I am instructed to advise you of news that he has received.'

'From Florence?' the Dauphin asked, again hopefully.

'No, sire. Nothing has been heard from there. Messengers have reached us about an attack on Château de Felice.'

The Dauphin looked nonplussed. 'Where?'

'Countess Catherine de Val. Count Henri's widow.'

'What concern are they to us?'

'Count Henri was a loyal nobleman, highness. He was slain by routiers two years or more ago. You allowed the Countess relief from taxation because she entrapped routiers and for using—'

'William Cade.'

'Exactly, highness. Now Cade is dead.'

'She killed him? Even though he lured routiers behind her walls?'

Simon Bucy suppressed the sigh of exasperation. His face remained passive. 'Sire, Château de Felice was taken by Thomas Blackstone. His men burned and raped. Blackstone killed William Cade.'

The Dauphin's face sagged. 'If Cade was tortured he would have told Blackstone who sent him.' He gave it a moment's thought and shrugged. 'That is of no consequence. What of the Countess?'

'One of the garrison men who escaped said that she was alive when he left. But Blackstone's men had pillaged and killed with abandon. It is not known whether she has survived.'

'It grieves us to think that a loyal widow who waged her own war against these vermin might succumb to the likes of Blackstone.' The Dauphin stood and tugged the cloak around him. He smiled. 'Our father must take action against him. He has legitimate cause now.'

'There is more information that the King has not yet been made aware of. Nothing is yet clear and we do not know whether the reports are first hand but, because the King desires to travel to Avignon, I thought you should be the first to hear what we have discovered,' said Bucy, clearly enjoying the privilege of bearing important information.

The Dauphin waited. 'Are we to die of exhaustion awaiting your news?'

'Sire, our envoys travelled down the Rhône to ensure that the army had secured his route. Our people in Avignon report that Pope Innocent is ill and in his weakened state we were fearful that he might grant an amnesty to the routiers who press close to the city walls. I was concerned for the King's ongoing comfort and safety. The Pope has excommunicated the mercenaries who demanded payment in return for raiding elsewhere, but we have heard that he has pardoned one group of brigands. The circumstances are not clear and we do not know why but there was word that they were Thomas Blackstone's men.'

Bucy was gratified to see that the news focused the Dauphin's attention.

'He is in Avignon now?' said the Dauphin, shocked.

'We are uncertain, but his name was heard many times. We assume it to be true.'

'The Pope has pardoned him and his men?'

'It would appear so.'

'Why would he go to Avignon?' The Dauphin considered the possibilities. 'Unless... unless he is leaving France to go to Italy. You say we have heard nothing about his son in Florence but is it possible that Blackstone has? Is he retreating to Italy to be with his son?'

'It is doubtful, sire. Our sources say his men are riding north from Avignon.'

'Here? Or... do they intend to invade Burgundy? It is a prize the English failed to secure in the past. We do not understand. Our northern army is between the King and them.'

'Other routiers gnaw at the edge of Burgundy, highness. If he is joining these others then they might be arriving in force.'

The Dauphin fell silent; thoughts of Blackstone demanded concentration. 'If our father places a bounty on Blackstone now and the Pope has granted a pardon does that not cause a conflict between the Holy Father and ourselves?'

Bucy hesitated. Let the young Dauphin see that he, the wise counsellor, thought deeply on the matter before answering. As always it added weight. 'Not if Pope Innocent was pressured to do so,' he said as if he had considered the ramifications. In fact he knew already that no such conflict would exist should the King of France bring the weight of his authority to bear against Blackstone. 'If the Pope lies sick and there are brigands at the gates of Avignon then what value can there be in granting such a pardon? It does not absolve Blackstone from rape and murder and further atrocities. There is also rumour that before Château de Felice and after he destroyed Saint-Aubin, he and a marauding band struck at Sainte-Bernice-de-la-Grave. There was a great slaughter and mutilation of the worst kind. And it appears the young son, Alain de la Grave, was taken hostage. Nothing is known of his welfare.'

The Dauphin's parchment skin creased into a smile. 'I laid traps for Blackstone, and my plan in Florence to kill his son and blame the Visconti might still bear success, but now Blackstone places his head in a noose of his own choosing. He will find no favour now with Edward. He can no longer serve the English King and secure the towns ceded under the treaty. Here is proof that he has taken matters into his own hands and benefits as much as any common mercenary.'

Bucy watched the agitated Dauphin stand and pace back and forth, fists clenched. 'Sire, hardly proof. May I beg to remind you that all of this is only rumour. That the messenger from Château de Felice might be exaggerating events there. Yes, of course we know Blackstone sacked Saint-Aubin, but as to the rest of it...?'

The Dauphin glared at Bucy. 'Rumour serves our purpose. Told convincingly enough it becomes truth.'

'And dare we deceive King Edward? If he discovers that—'

'Edward has forced a foul treaty on our father!' the Dauphin interrupted. 'We fought that treaty with you at our side. We denied Edward even more territory. We will take France back one day but if there is an opportunity to impugn Blackstone in the eyes of his King then we will not hesitate.'

The Dauphin had found a new energy and strode from the room with a subservient but worried Simon Bucy in his wake. Merciful Christ, Bucy prayed quietly, grant those who labour to restrain an impetuous king-in-waiting the ability to control his actions. The Dauphin sought satisfaction against Thomas Blackstone with an unquenchable thirst. But if the allegations against the scar-faced knight were proved to be nothing more than exaggerated tales and the all-powerful English King learnt of it, then Edward would find a way to inflict further punishment and humiliation on the French Crown. He would decide that the French were undermining the treaty. Bucy followed the man to whom he had committed his loyalty to a room where a dozen courtiers and advisers waited and clerks had quill and parchment ready.

'We desire that word be taken to our father bearing news of Thomas Blackstone.'

The clerks started writing as the Dauphin settled himself by the fireplace and a servant poured him wine.

'There is now sufficient evidence that King Edward employs a mercenary knight who hides behind the official duties imposed by his own King,' said the Dauphin. He glanced at the gathered courtiers. 'It would not be the first time that Thomas Blackstone has defied his monarch.' He saw the clerks scratching away. 'No, no. Do not write that.' He gestured at the clerks to wait and then signalled he was ready to dictate again. 'We entreat our beloved father to summon Sir John Chandos and deliver a formal writ of complaint. We implore him to send word to the English King that the atrocities committed by Thomas Blackstone will be a cause of concern to him and that we will pursue such criminal and foul activities in defence of our treaty.' He raised a hand to stop the scribes writing. 'Edward has vowed to rid us of these brigands. He cannot in good conscience employ this mercenary in his service.' The Dauphin glanced at Bucy. 'We will bring Edward's force against Blackstone as well as our own.'

Bucy felt a grudging respect for the ailing Dauphin. He had thrown a wide net to entrap Thomas Blackstone and even if each attempt failed he now reached into the very heart of England and was in effect blackmailing Edward. The English King could not object to the French hunting down his own chosen captain, and if Edward feared his will had been thwarted by a rogue knight who placed the treaty in jeopardy then he would have his chosen commander Chandos stop Blackstone. The physically weak Dauphin might spend his days in his library rather than enjoying the hunt at the King's side, but his mind was agile and as cunning as a rodent finding its way into the grain store. Perhaps, Bucy dared to think, when the Dauphin Charles came to the throne he would be known as the Rat King.

CHAPTER FIFTY-SEVEN

The Gascon captain Beyard had led Fra Foresti and Henry Blackstone out of Avignon as Niccolò Torellini remained to recuperate from the arduous journey across the Alps. That a loyal captain serving Blackstone had arrived in the same place as Torellini's foothold in southern France could only be an act of God. And that Beyard had been sent by Blackstone to recruit more men gave the old priest even more comfort. But the sooner Beyard departed from Avignon, where whispers travelled more quickly than the wind, the better. If Blackstone and his small band of men were less than ten days away then his son could be delivered safely and with more protection than Torellini could have hoped for. Once he had secured the Pope's pardon for the Gascons under Beyard's command he embraced the son of the man whom God and Fate had brought into his life.

'Tell your father that I send him my heartfelt wishes and that I beg his forgiveness for allowing you to be placed in danger while in my care,' he told Henry.

'Father Torellini, my father would never bear you any ill will. It is I who must beg your forgiveness because my presence in Florence caused an attack to be made on me and that you have been obliged to journey so far from the comfort of your home.'

'A gracious answer, my boy. You have been educated by the finest minds and you have learnt good manners and the importance of respect. But you have also been close to death before and forced to defend yourself and I know you do not take killing lightly. But your journey is not yet over and you may once again be required to take your sword in hand. It is then, as happened in that street

357

in Florence, that you must set aside the laws of reason and the language and emotion of the schoolroom and defend yourself.'

'I am in good hands, Father Torellini,' said Henry, acknowledging the two men who were now his guardians for his onward journey to his father.

Beyard gathered the men he had recruited but made no mention who it was that travelled with them. It was enough for them to know that the Tau knight had promised to escort the young man in his charge to Canterbury on pilgrimage. As they rode cautiously towards the agreed meeting place with Blackstone they saw increasing signs of French troops on the banks of the Rhône. More men were gathering than they had seen before and if the French army was marching from the north to entrap the mercenary bands then their ranks would soon be swelled by these thousands of men moving up from the south.

'Do we make ourselves known to the French?' asked Henry.

'No, we have had skirmishes with them. We did not know whether their attack was deliberate or whether they mistook Sir Thomas and thought us a band of routiers.'

'If my father serves the King and there's a treaty then why would they now wish to deliberately attack him? The French would bring King Edward's scorn and anger upon them.'

Beyard looked with uncertainty at the Tau knight. How best to answer the boy?

'He has a point,' said Fra Foresti. 'If you and these men cannot appeal to the French for further protection then that means you are fearful of them. But it seems impossible that we will be able to avoid them on this journey.'

'Avoid them we must, Brother Foresti, and Master Blackstone is correct. We might be mistaken about their intent but it is my opinion we would be safer in routier hands than with the French. The war was won but a treaty can be tested. Who knows what Edward might sacrifice to see his ceded lands brought under his control? A king would not lose sleep over the loss of one of his captains if it meant keeping hold of peace.'

'Then we are thankful that good fortune has brought you to us,' said Fra Foresti.

Beyard wasn't listening. His attention had been caught by his outriders, who urged their horses from the high ground ahead. He spurred his own horse away from the Tau knight and Henry but the Gascon's sense of urgency was infectious and the column of men quickly followed.

Beyard heard only a few words of his outriders' report and then, wheeling his horse, followed them at the canter. They crested the ridge and looked across the valley below. On the far side, a thousand yards distant, he saw fluttering banners and a mass of men. They were moving across a battlefield. His eyes swept the expanse beneath them. Hundreds of corpses littered the field. The killing must have ended only hours before. Loose horses stood and grazed, ignoring the twisted dead. Others had fallen alongside their riders. It looked to have been a sudden confrontation.

'French army,' said Beyard as the other men caught up. He pointed to the indistinct huddle of men in the distance.

'Routiers,' said one of his outriders. 'Caught like rats.'

'They came down that plain between the hills and the river and had nowhere to run,' said another man-at-arms.

'Beyard!' called one of the Gascons from down the line of men who were gazing at the slaughter. 'Look sharp!'

The Tau knight and Beyard looked to where the man pointed. Horsemen, several hundred yards away, were riding hard towards them.

'Rearguard ready to kill stragglers,' Beyard shouted. 'Too many. We must outrun them!'

He yanked his horse around and spurred it towards the higher ground that lay two or three miles away. If they could make the rocky, forested heights their pursuers might have second thoughts about attacking them uphill. Beyard realized that if they survived they would need to find sanctuary behind the walls of a town because the countryside was crawling with determined French troops. And if Blackstone was travelling towards their rendezvous then he too was riding into an overwhelming force. But there was no way he could be warned. He looked across to where the Tau knight and Henry Blackstone whipped their horses. At least the boy could ride. The test would come if the outnumbered men were obliged to fight. Beyard did not wish to be the man who told Thomas Blackstone that his son lay dead in a sodden field of blood.

CHAPTER FIFTY-EIGHT

Blackstone had suppressed his impatience and desire to be free of the Countess and Felice. The apothecary had pleaded with him to delay his departure so that Alain had a chance to survive the butchery on his leg. So Blackstone had delayed. Waited and kept the men sharp, once their wounds were healed, for Gruffydd ap Madoc's camp in the mountains would likely be a stronghold that would take its toll on Blackstone's men in an attack. Patrols went out every day but there was no sign of French troops making their way towards the château. Finally, at the end of the month with bad weather looming, they took their leave.

Blackstone's horsemen rode slowly through the gates of Château de Felice. The town's walls had no sentries. Felice was left to defend itself and its predatory Countess Catherine de Val as best it could, a depleted citadel that now had only its sheer walls to repel any invader. The blood-clogged mouth of William Cade gaped in a silent curse. His blind eyes, already taken by the crows, denied his departed soul the sight of the victor leading his men away to seek further retribution against Gruffydd ap Madoc. Cade's skull would rot, or the townspeople would cast it into the river; either way the time of the routiers at Felice had ended.

Countess Catherine stood at her window, the fire in the grate cold, her gown loose, her skin puckered from the wind that swept down the valley. She wore no make-up; her hair was unkempt, her mind desperate. Every ambition to avenge her dead husband and children had been crushed by the Englishman. Her town was defenceless, her people fearful and she had nothing to comfort their grief. She watched as the line of horsemen faded into the distance. She had given Blackstone the Welshman's location. That Blackstone and his men would be outnumbered and surely killed when the Englishman found the man he hunted brought her no satisfaction. She had gambled and lost. How long would it be before the people in the town turned on her and sought out the gold that still remained? She was a defenceless woman utterly alone. How could she carry on?

She gazed down the sheer walls to the jagged rocks far below. It would take only a few terrified breaths before her body smashed into the gully. Then the barren life that beckoned and the impending assault from her own people would be averted and she would, at last, find some kind of peace by joining her husband and children. She raised her face to the wind and let it chastise her body a moment longer, then called to her servants to bathe her and prepare her finest clothes. She stepped away from the window and its temptation.

A better day would come.

Other men could be bought and power regained.

Alain de la Grave lay tied onto a litter. Blackstone had kept the pace slow during the first day and stopped frequently to attend to the young Frenchman, but he knew he could not pursue the Welshman or fend off any attack with the injured boy slowing them down. Given that they were carrying an invalid, Blackstone had decided to avoid taking the ceded town that he intended to secure for Edward, knowing that Beyard would by now be making his way northward with any men he had recruited. As they edged towards the monastery he knew he had to risk the boy's life again. He would leave him in the care of Prior Albert, the man who had betrayed them. 'Unless we meet Beyard coming north we will have to leave word at the monastery,' said Blackstone.

'These scab-arsed monks might smother the lad or let him rot,' said Killbere.

'I'll give them cause not to do that,' said Blackstone as they eased their mounts into the forest for the night.

Killbere and Blackstone dismounted and pushed through the low ferns to where fallen trees and a rocky outcrop created a natural encampment. Killbere ran his hand across the velvet coat of the moss-covered deadwood.

'Damned forests are always wet, Thomas. My bones ache from it. I have been denied the comfort of a feather mattress with a woman whose teats would please a wet-nurse and any suckling babe. I thought myself well suited to the life of lord of the manor at Felice. My cock ached for her, and in time my heart would have come around as well; now all I have are aching bones. A poor exchange.'

Blackstone tethered the bastard horse and pulled free the saddle. He tore a handful of ferns and rubbed its sweat-slicked back. Muscles quivered as it turned its oversize head, fixed its glare on him and then shifted its weight. Blackstone moved carefully out of reach of the iron-shod hooves. 'Too many old wounds, Gilbert. All of us – including him,' he said, meaning the horse. 'She would have gelded you one day. That or cut your throat – as she tried to do. She had an appetite for men. You would not have lasted long in her embrace.'

'I was prepared to risk it. I'm the same age as the King and unlike him I do not have many opportunities to wallow in comfort. She would have been a demanding woman, I know that, but I am up to such demands. And, I have to confess, that as far as my heart is concerned, she was more radiant than even my nun.'

'The nun who fornicated with every monk in sight.'

'I forgave her once I broke their heads. You don't understand women, Thomas. They have needs like us. Imagine being cooped up in a convent or a château. Dear Christ, the boredom. I pitied the Countess. What was there beyond embroidery and torturing routiers? Eh? Sexual gratification tempers the soul and banishes boredom.'

Blackstone finished hobbling the bastard horse. It snapped at his head as he bent to tie its front legs. He deftly avoided the yellow teeth and despite its belligerence ran an affectionate hand over its cheek. 'I was thinking we should go south after we've finished the

King's business and dealt with the Welshman. Find an abandoned garrison, somewhere near a monastery, maybe find you another of your nuns. A place where the sun ripens the vines and the monks make good wine. Or perhaps even go back to Elfred and the men outside Florence. Or bring them to us. Elfred is even older than you. He would settle for a quieter life now, I'll wager. '

'We should do it soon, Thomas. The King will continue to find us work more fit for tax collectors than fighting men.' He followed Blackstone's example and rubbed grass and fern over his horse's back. 'But the likes of you and me cannot stay idle for long. We were born to fight. What would life be without something to stir the blood? We should think about the Moors in Spain. The Spanish will pay us well. There are sea breezes and food enough for an army. And the winters down there are warm. None of this dank misery with thousands of skinners on one side of the river and thousands more Frenchmen on the other. Let them fight among themselves. The Moors have built palaces rich with gold. A couple of good years of plunder and I could buy my own castle.'

'And do what with it? Stand on its tower and survey your land? Farm it? Plant crops or vines?'

'Servants, Thomas. They do all the work. We sit back and enjoy the rewards of our efforts. Merciful God, we could have done this a dozen times already. Imagine. Slave girls from the east, nuns from local monasteries, women from anywhere. I'm not fussy like you, Thomas. It's not my heart I offer them. And it's not for ever. Just long enough to rest and see which way the wind blows us to our next conflict.'

Blackstone carried his saddle and blanket beneath the tumbling boulders. He found a patch of deep fern and crushed the plants beneath the blanket, then settled his saddle as a pillow. He undid his sword belt and wrapped it around Wolf Sword's scabbard. 'I would ride away quietly, Gilbert, but there are too many enemies who await their chance to kill me. I'll rest when I'm dead.'

'You need a woman,' said Killbere, settling his own blanket down. And then, remembering the women Blackstone had known since his wife died: 'Perhaps not. You and women upset the order of the planets.' He sighed. 'I need a piss. Think about what I said, though. Spain is warmer than Italy, the women are hairy but they have no inhibitions. Not like some of these damned Frenchwomen who think their cunny is a vault full of silver. No, a Spanish woman's skin is fragrant, her hair is black like silk, glistening with sweet oils. We could do worse if only for a couple of years. Three perhaps. But, I agree, no longer. Then, by God, we would be like armoured stallions ready to fight the devil himself.'

Killbere glanced down at Blackstone. The hard, seasoned knight, the boy he had dragged to war all those years past, lay curled in on himself, his breathing deep and regular as he slept. The veteran knight looked around as the men organized themselves. Years of campaigning meant they were sharp, every one of them, as keen as a honed blade. They knew what to do and when. Blackstone could lead an army of men like these and every one of them was worth shedding blood for. In truth, he told himself, despite all his talk of castles and rich women, there was nowhere else he would rather be than among them.

CHAPTER FIFTY-NINE

On the slow journey back to the monastery Blackstone had kept the injured Alain close by his own campfire and through the nights made sure the young man had warmth and food. The amputated leg showed no sign of turning foul but he had followed the apothecary's instructions and had the dressing changed each day. Now Blackstone and his men waited outside the monastery Saint-André-de-Babineaux as John Jacob hammered his fist on the gate and rang the bell.

'Open it, you lovers of the Lord, or be prepared to meet him,' he shouted.

Killbere shifted in his saddle. 'Thomas, were it not for the lad and his need for care, would we have burnt this place to the ground for their treachery and sent these pious, lying bastards into the forest and hills so that the wolves and bears might fill their bellies?'

Blackstone grinned. 'I would have sent the prior on a pilgrimage to Canterbury on his knees and helped him on his way with a sack of pig fat on his back to help attract them.'

The leather-faced porter's head appeared in the viewing hatch. Blackstone and Killbere could hear the trembling voice from where they waited.

'He's afraid to give us entry,' John Jacob called.

'Tell him he has no choice. We have an injured man. We claim sanctuary for him,' Blackstone answered.

Killbere sighed. 'We need to make better time, Thomas. Who knows if the Welshman is still at La Roche? He'll outnumber us so we'll need to ride with caution once we're close.'

'We are still refused,' called John Jacob.

'Mother of God,' groaned Killbere. He stood in his stirrups

and bellowed. 'Open the gates, you Judas whores, or we'll send our men over the walls.'

John Jacob trudged back, shaking his head, to where his horse was held. 'The old gatekeeper has strict instructions from the prior.'

'This is hardly the time to start a siege, Thomas. Let us scale these puny walls and teach them a lesson.'

'Let's try the front gate first,' said Blackstone and nudged the bastard horse forward. As he reached the double wooden doors he tugged the rein to bring the great war horse's rump against them. Then he eased his weight in the saddle and the horse obliged, pushing itself back, gathering strength, pressing its front legs into the dirt until its weight splintered any holding bar on the other side of the gates. Blackstone quickly turned the beast and forced his way through. The monks were gathered, huddled together for strength and confidence, but they soon broke and scattered as Blackstone urged the horse forward. Killbere, John Jacob and Meulon followed, leaving the rest of the men at the open entrance. Blackstone dismounted and pushed his shoulder against the locked door that led to Prior Albert. It quickly gave and once inside he strode down the passage and saw the prior running into his rooms. Blackstone heard a lock turn. He kicked at the handle, throwing open the door. The prior, shaking with fear, was on his knees before a simple crucifix on the wall. Blackstone grabbed him by the collar and threw him onto his cot. The weight of the man's body splintered the cot's legs and Prior Albert slithered to the floor, his habit up around his waist.

'Get to your feet and cover yourself,' said Blackstone.

As the prior scrabbled to adjust his habit Killbere came into the room. 'I've sent Perinne into the kitchens.' He pointed at the quivering prior. 'You and your fleabitten brothers are close to death. Do you wish to pray before we take our blades to you? Your Countess won't be coming to help you this time. We killed all her men and the routier scum she sent to ambush us. Did you think we wouldn't come back, brother betrayer? We offered you peace and goodwill. Now you'll pay with your lives.'

Blackstone stepped forward and placed a restraining hand on

Killbere's shoulder. 'Now, Sir Gilbert, we caused Prior Albert's monks no harm but he was likely frightened that we might have been skinners not men on our King's business,' he said, looking down on the kneeling prior.

'Yes. Yes, I was convinced you were men like... like...'

'William Cade,' said Blackstone.

'Exactly,' said the prior, seizing on the excuse.

'There, you see, he was fearful of his own doubts,' Blackstone said to Killbere. 'Like a man who doubts his own faith.' He looked at the prior. 'Do you doubt your own faith?'

'I do not.'

'Then you believe that the Almighty will protect you.'

'I do.'

'And yet you lost your faith when we were first here, otherwise why would you have betrayed us?'

The prior's mouth opened and closed as his thoughts raced for an answer.

'He is a false believer. Kill him now and burn the place to the ground,' Killbere growled, taking a stride forward.

Blackstone restrained him again and turned to the prior. 'I am certain that if we grant these monks our mercy they will offer their prayers for us and care for our wounded comrade. Is that not so, Prior Albert?'

'With all my heart I swear that to be so.'

Blackstone's body blocked the prior's view so that he could not see Killbere grin. Their little game of threat and the promise had worked. Killbere stormed out of the room and turned with a final pointed gesture. 'If he's lying God himself will strike him and scorch this place from the face of the earth.' He turned away.

'Now,' Blackstone said to the prior, hauling him to his feet. 'You will prepare the infirmary and instruct monks who are skilled in treating wounds. And then your kitchener will feed my men. Understood?'

'I will do everything you ask and will pray for you.'

'Pray for yourself, brother prior. You still need forgiveness for your betrayal.'

* * *

The monks attended Alain de la Grave with gentleness. Clean sheets covered with woollen blankets and a fire in the infirmary ensured his comfort. Herbs and ointments were prepared and a wicker cage was placed over his amputated limb to keep the weight of the blankets from his wound. While Killbere and the captains went about billeting the men and stabling the horses Blackstone watched the monks go about their business. The young Frenchman was still gravely ill but he was conscious.

'The monks will prepare a potion for your pain,' he said.

'I am cast out of the world, Sir Thomas. I cannot serve you and I can no longer serve myself. Better that I should have died,' Alain said weakly.

'No, your courage demanded that we tried to save you.'

'Like this?' he said bitterly, barely able to suppress his tears.

'You are not a child, Alain. You will bear this like any fighting man. Your life has changed but you have a life,' Blackstone said sternly. 'I have seen sturdier men than you die from amputation. You have fierce blood in your veins.'

Alain tried to raise himself in the bed but his strength had not yet returned. Blackstone resisted the urge to step forward and help him. Sweat blistered the young man's face. A monk preparing fresh linen dressings across the room moved to help him.

'No!' Alain said. 'Leave me.' The monk glanced at Blackstone who gave a gentle shake of his head. The brother turned away and returned to his duties while his young charge persevered and finally propped himself up.

'And what would you have me do with this half-life you've condemned me to?' he demanded.

'What you did at Felice took courage. It will not desert you. Once that wound is healed you'll use a crutch and you will move as quickly as many men on two legs. I've seen men tie their half-leg by straps to a saddle. You'll be able to ride. You will do what you can and make the best of it.'

'I won't be able to fight,' he insisted.

'No, likely not, but you're an educated man. There are towns and villages who need teachers. You might have only one leg but you have a brain which is more than a lot of fighting men have.'

They fell silent. Blackstone went to him and touched his arm. 'We are riding south tomorrow to seize and kill Gruffydd ap Madoc. I could not leave you at Felice so here is where you will stay until you are healed. No matter how long it takes. No harm will come to you here. And when my business is done I will look for you again.'

Alain nodded but Blackstone could see his words offered no comfort.

'You are stricken, Alain, but that does not make you any less a man.'

'How are you so certain?' he answered. 'How can you know?'

'Before we arrived at Sainte-Bernice and found you I spoke to a man cursed with leprosy. He guided us through the forest near your town. He had served King John and years ago fought us at Poitiers but the leprosy brought him to his knees. His family was taken from him; the son he loved was raised by another man. He understood that despite the pain of that loss he had no choice but to accept it. He was one of the bravest men I have met and he lives his life with fortitude and courage.'

As Blackstone quietly told the story he thought he saw in Alain's eyes a glimmer of some lost childhood memory.

'His name was Robert de Rabastens. He was your father.'

Disbelief gripped the young Frenchman. Finally he stared at Blackstone, his voice strained. 'My father was Mouton de la Grave. Lord of Sainte-Bernice.'

'He honoured Robert de Rabastens and took you to his heart. Now you must honour both these brave men.'

A tear spilled from Alain's eyes. He quickly wiped it away and regained his composure.

'Honour is all we have left to us,' said Blackstone. 'Find where yours lies, hold it close and let it serve you.'

CHAPTER SIXTY

The men and horses were rested and fed and after the prior had prayed for them they left. Behind them the prime bell for morning prayers rang out across the rocky hillsides.

Blackstone did not look back. What lay behind a man was past. It was Killbere who turned and glanced at the monastery as the column of men meandered across the valley track. 'I hope the lad survives. It feels unusual not having him with us.'

'I thought you found him a burden,' said Blackstone.

'God's tears, Thomas, I found you a damned burden when you were a clumsy oaf that I first took to war, but I persevered.'

Blackstone smiled. 'He'll survive. He has youth on his side and he has the urge to live. I told him about his father. He thought him dead.'

'Aye, well, a leper is the living dead.' Killbere crossed himself. 'I will die with a sword in my hand or with a woman in my bed, God willing.' He shrugged. 'But it seems likely that the way ahead will not offer me the choice. If the French have heard about Felice, then they will have an excuse to hunt us.'

'They don't need an excuse,' said Blackstone. 'It will soon be a time of reckoning, Gilbert. One way or the other we will not be able to avoid the French army.'

Killbere snorted and spat. 'Then just as well I ploughed a furrow with the Countess.'

It took three days of steady riding for Blackstone's men to reach the Loire and another to find a ford. Blackstone and his men had skirted the broad swirling river with its treacherous currents and sinking mud until coming across a broad shallow expanse of the waterway. They sat in their saddles two hundred yards from the bank in cover behind a village of huddled, reed-thatched houses, waiting to see if the crossing was safe. There had been no sign of riders on the far bank but the bulrushes that grew in the shallows' mud and the trees beyond could easily hide an enemy.

'This is the best we will get, Thomas,' said Killbere. 'But who's to say local troops don't use it to go back and forth?'

Blackstone studied the muddied banks and approach to the ford as the air from the river was swept onto them by the northerly wind. 'Cow shit,' he said. 'Smell it?'

Killbere wrinkled his nose. 'I thought that was Will Longdon and his archers.'

'Aye, Sir Gilbert,' said Will Longdon from further along the line of horsemen. 'But when archers fart men die. And you are still in the saddle.'

'And I've a mind to have your scab-arsed archers swim across further upstream to see if your foundering draws any attention from an enemy on the far side.'

Blackstone pointed beyond the village to the ford. 'It's shallow enough for local villagers to herd the cattle across, so there must be grassland on the other side. There's nothing but forest here.'

The wind carried no sound of voices, only the flitting smoke from the hovels' roofs and the gentle baying of cattle. Then herdsmen appeared from beyond the houses and began to whip a dozen cows across the ford. Blackstone and Killbere watched as the men waded knee-deep, their cries urging the cattle forward easily audible, but no soldiers appeared on the far bank to establish who it was that called out. Blackstone led his men forward to follow the cattle herders. The villeins were alarmed at seeing armed horsemen suddenly splash into the shallows behind them yet they had no choice but to hasten the cattle and let them scramble ashore wherever they may. Blackstone's men rode among them, using the cows' splashing hooves and ululating panic to smother their own heavy hoofbeats. Anyone hidden beyond the riverbank would have their guard lowered by the usual sound of the villagers bringing across their livestock. The men spurred their horses on, swords drawn against any troops who might be guarding the crossing unseen. Once up the bank the men saw a stretch of open meadow that led to wooded rising ground. But the pasture was trampled as if a column of horsemen had cut across it and merged into the forest.

'Thomas! Our flank!' Killbere called.

There was a surge of activity in the treeline and men stumbled into the open. They were footsoldiers and no more than thirty of them. They were French regular troops, a contingent of infantry who would have been part of a larger group of scouts or raiders. It was unlikely that they were alone without mounted men-at-arms in support.

Blackstone wheeled the bastard horse away, hesitating to strike at such hardened men, even though they had been taken by surprise. His men veered and quickly re-formed forty yards from the footsoldiers, who crouched, clearly frightened, shields high, ready for these horsemen to attack. They edged back slowly towards the trees.

'Hold!' Blackstone called, to keep back his own men as well as to stop the Frenchmen. 'We serve the English King and enforce the truce. We take the allegiance of the ceded towns. I am Sir Thomas Blackstone.'

At the mention of his name the French soldiers spoke hurriedly among themselves and retreated faster.

'Sir Thomas?' Meulon called, asking whether the men should attack.

'No!' Blackstone ordered. The French were now well into the trees where they formed a line, shields high. They were not running, they were waiting.

'Sir Thomas, they see us as their enemy. They're too few to attack us but there'll be horsemen somewhere,' said John Jacob. Blackstone's men restrained their horses, who had picked up their riders' uncertainty. And then the bastard horse yanked its head so hard that the reins were nearly pulled through Blackstone's grip. It turned away from the trees and faced the empty stretch of meadow. Several hundred yard-long paces away the breeze ruffled the treetops. The grass wavered. The bastard horse snorted, muscles quivering; it raised its ugly misshapen head and with ears erect pawed the ground.

'Be ready,' Blackstone called. There was no sign of any movement, no sound of hoofbeats, but Blackstone trusted the horse's instincts even more than his own. 'Meulon, watch those men in the trees.'

And then they felt the tremor rumbling through the ground.

'Will, get your archers back.' There would be no time for the lightly armed archers to defend themselves if they were caught between an approaching attack and the men in the forest. Will Longdon's men spurred their horses away. The veteran archer glanced over his shoulder as the horizon blurred and a smudged line of colour rose like a winter sunrise. Surcoats of blue, gold and red. Crimson and black banners and fish-tailed pennons. Heavy horses thundering towards Blackstone; men with shields raised and sword and mace ready to strike. It was impossible to gauge how many charged across the meadow but it was a great many more than the few Blackstone commanded. Longdon covered three hundred yards and then leapt from his horse. His archers did the same, abandoning their mounts to run free. He watched as Meulon wheeled left into the treeline with a dozen or more men and Blackstone led the charge into the approaching horsemen with Killbere and the others. Once the men clashed, horses would surge through the English ranks.

Longdon's bow was already clear of its waxed linen bag, the heart of yew bent, its cord strung on its horn tips. All was done with rapid, practised ease as his eyes stayed on the approaching horsemen and now he saw that they outnumbered Blackstone three to one. At least. There was a gentle hump in the meadow behind Blackstone as his men galloped forward. The ground had been pushed up – perhaps a long disappeared tree stump had been there. It made no difference whether it was an unmarked grave, rotted tree or creatures from the underworld clawing their way from hell. It was a marker.

'A hundred and eighty paces!' he cried as the bowman lined up each side of him. 'Rising ground! Seen?'

The archers quickly found it and called their acknowledgement. They pushed a handful of arrows into the ground at their feet, nocked the first and waited.

The French men-at-arms had been returning to the footsoldiers' position when they saw the armed horsemen who looked no different than the routiers they were hunting. Given the distance between them they spurred their horses into a canter and then a gallop whose impact would smash the lightly armoured men. What the French could not see through their visors as they advanced, sweat already stinging their eyes, breath sucked in through the heat of their helms, were the archers who had retreated behind the line of approaching horsemen. Men who rode tightly together, urging their horses into a canter and then suddenly splitting to veer left and right, leaving a half-dozen men in the centre. The urge to kill surged through the Frenchmen. These routiers had no discipline and if some had already peeled away to escape then they would be hunted down at leisure.

The bastard horse's lumbering gait barged between two horses, forcing them to swerve. The man-at-arms to Blackstone's right could not swing his sword from that angle but the one on Blackstone's shield arm twisted in the saddle and struck. Blackstone took the blow on his shield as he rammed Wolf Sword into the other man's unprotected side. No sooner had they clashed than the Frenchmen's speed carried them through. Killbere and John Jacob, who were half a length behind Blackstone, thundered into the enemy. Blackstone heard screams and the thud of bodies hitting the ground. Horses were whinnying and cries of alarm rose up from the Frenchmen who had lost control of their galloping mounts. Blackstone's men had ridden and struck at the canter, and their slower pace made it easier to wheel their horses around to see their attackers in disarray. The Frenchmen who managed to steady their mounts – leaning back in their saddles, yanking their horses' bits, tearing at their mouths – were once again bearing down on the Englishmen. But the English who the French thought had broken and run had now turned onto the Frenchmen's flanks, effectively encircling them. Other French men-at-arms had galloped on towards the line of men who stood, backs arched, faces skyward. The Frenchmen's laboured breathing and curses trapped inside their helms stopped them from hearing what sounded like the wind ravaging the forest, creaking the trees' boughs and releasing a sudden whispering gust. They were twenty horse strides from the underworld's creatures' attempt to claw them down into their lair and by the time they reached the archers' marker the arrows had stung man and beast.

Meulon had barged into the trees with his men, their mounts trampling the footsoldiers, but the confines of the forest made manoeuvring the horses too difficult. His men quickly dismounted and fought those who had not turned and run. The Norman used his shield like a battering ram and Renfred's and Tait's men hacked and cut their way into the crumbling French line. It was grunting, sweating work despite the cold. But the men's blood was up and the horses had already done damage to many of the footsoldiers. Meulon's men, working in twos and threes, chased the scattered French, overpowering equally those who stayed to fight, alone or in pairs, and those who ran and foundered in the undergrowth and whose fear tormented their last moments of life. Those who turned and begged for mercy were also killed.

The archers could not loose more arrows because of the proximity of Blackstone's men so they dropped their bows and ran to despatch the wounded French with knife and sword. No mercy was granted, except for a quick death. Four of Blackstone's men lay dead on the grass but the French were routed. One knight had seen the futility of their attempt to break through these vicious fighters and signalled a retreat. He and a handful of survivors galloped to escape and Blackstone watched as, once clear, he reined in his horse and turned to look at Blackstone's men. He must have called out to his three companions as they too forced their horses to slow and then turn. The knight wore good armour and his distinctive yellow shield bore the image of a stag's head. He waited mid-field. His horse's lungs heaved, but its rider sat upright, sword at his side, facing Blackstone. The three knights who accompanied him drew alongside. Blackstone saw the knight raise his visor and say something to the others, who then held back their horses as he urged his own forward. He stopped eighty yards from Blackstone and waited again, sword lowered.

'Hold your ground,' Blackstone called, raising Wolf Sword and signalling his men to halt any further attack. He pushed the bastard horse into a trot and drew up ten paces from the stag's head knight.

'I am Sir Godfrey d'Albinet. You have committed a slaughter here today on great and good men who serve their King.'

'It's not the first time I have thinned out your King's ranks,' said Blackstone.

The knight frowned. And then he looked more intently at the worn and battle-scarred shield on Blackstone's arm. The blazon showed a mailed fist grasping a sword blade like a cross. The words *Défiant à la Mort* were etched in black lettering.

'Blackstone,' Sir Godfrey muttered.

'Sir Godfrey, I did not wish this conflict. You brought it on yourself. I serve the English King who takes only what is rightfully his.'

The French knight became agitated. 'You are a brigand and wanted for atrocities on women and children. You have raped and murdered. You are no different than the routiers we seek to destroy.' He looked around at the corpses of his men strewn across the field. Archers were going among the dead stripping what wealth could be found as they tugged free their arrows. 'Had I seen your archers...' He let the words trail off in regret.

'What? You wouldn't have attacked?'

'I would have returned with more men and taken you on your flanks.'

'The result would have been the same. And you are wrong about me and my men. You have been lied to.'

'Our King does not lie. He has issued a warrant.'

'Your King wants me dead; so too the Dauphin.'

'For your crimes.'

'For my success. Rumour and lies serve their desire to have me dead and for noble men like you to die trying to kill me. Surrender and you will live. I will accept your word that you will not fight and I will release you on parole.'

Sir Godfrey spat a globule of phlegm onto the ground towards Blackstone. 'Surrender? To a murderer?'

'To an English knight,' said Blackstone. 'You and your three companions. I will not ask you to remain silent about where you saw me, but I will hold you to your word and accept your parole.'

For a moment it seemed the Frenchman might agree. A look of acceptance crossed his face but then he shook his head as if listening to his own voice of reason. 'I cannot,' he said. 'There is no honour surrendering to you.'

'Is there more honour being killed by me?'

'You would have your archers slay us?'

'I would kill you myself. Don't die needlessly, Sir Godfrey.'

'You are confident that you can defeat me, but if it is I who defeat you, you will either be dead or my prisoner. What chance would I have against your men?'

'You would be free to go. My word is my honour.'

Sir Godfrey glanced over his shoulder. 'My companions will fight with me. Choose your men.' And with that final abrupt demand he wheeled his horse around and returned to his companions.

Blackstone rode back to Killbere and told him of the French knight's decision.

'I wish these bastards would know when they are beaten. Their arrogance chafes,' said Killbere as he drank wine thirstily from a flask. 'All right, who fights with us?'

'John Jacob and Renfred.'

'Aye, they'll finish these noblemen off in good time and they'll have belts of silver and daggers encrusted with precious stones. Decent plunder. I found only a few rings on those I killed but I gave them to Will Longdon's lads. They took good care of those horsemen.' He sighed, corked the flask and gathered the reins. 'But the archers are going to need more arrows if we ride into any more of these French. We could steal a few barrels of arrows from Chandos and Felton if we could find them but I dare say they are warming their arses somewhere in a nobleman's great hall and bedding his servant girls. Right, let's get on with it. I'll need food in my belly before it gets dark. Fighting always gives me an appetite.'

Blackstone called to Renfred, who had fought with Meulon in the trees. The German caught his horse, which had wandered a few feet from the killing, and led it to where Blackstone, Killbere and John Jacob waited.

'Sir Gilbert and I will take the centre. John, you and Renfred draw the other two away. I suspect they will want me dead quickly so they'll strike at me first. If you attack the man on the right flank his sword arm will be hampered by his position until he breaks and turns. This isn't a tourney. The two of you go at him, kill him and then attack the fourth man.'

'Wait,' said Killbere, and pointed across the field. The knight's three companions had suddenly spurred their horses in an attempt to escape through the far group of Blackstone's men who had encircled them. They rode tightly together, knee to knee, which made it impossible for Blackstone's men to stop all of them. One at least would be sacrificed, perhaps two, but it was certain that one would escape. Perhaps Sir Godfrey had not taken Blackstone's word and thought the archers would kill him? Whatever his reasoning, it seemed he was prepared to fight alone in an attempt to allow others to get away and warn the French about Blackstone.

They watched as the French men-at-arms broke free and hit Blackstone's stationary line of horsemen. The impact carried two of them through as the third was hemmed in and killed. Half a dozen of Blackstone's men gave chase. The French knight, too, watched his men's bold attempt and then turned his horse to face Blackstone.

'I'll take him,' said Killbere and was about to spur his horse but Blackstone blocked him.

'No, he made his choice. It's me he wants.'

Sir Godfrey dropped his visor, raised his shield and then dug heels into his horse's flanks. The war horse's hooves tore up the ground, sending up clods of turf. It was obvious the French knight was an experienced fighter. Blackstone just managed to hold back the bastard horse, who fought the bit and then lowered his great head, until his rider eased the reins slightly and the muscled beast unleashed its strength. Blackstone cursed as its uneven gait unbalanced him. His open-faced helm made him more vulnerable should the French knight find a way to jab at his eyes or slash his face. He tucked his chin onto his chest, raised the shield to just below his eyes and steered the pounding horse with his knees and heels. Sir Godfrey was swirling a spiked flail, the length of its chain meaning he would be able to strike before Blackstone could deliver a sword blow.

Dammit, stay straight... Straight, for Christ's sake. He swore silently as the wayward beast beneath him took it upon itself to suddenly veer. It was an uncontrolled movement that saved Blackstone's life. The Frenchman had altered his strike. No longer was the flail swirling around his arm in a sweeping arc; the knight's skill had allowed him to bring it down, rather than across Blackstone's body. It would have torn the shield and half his face away had the bastard horse not changed direction moments before the two men collided. The length of chain wrapped around Blackstone's sword arm and the spiked ball bit into his mail. The speed of the two horses meant that the Frenchman galloped past Blackstone and his strength pulled Blackstone from the saddle. Blackstone tumbled in the air and landed face down. The effort tore the flail from Sir Godfrey's grip and he heaved on his horse's reins and drew his sword as Blackstone thumped into the ground.

The impact had torn Blackstone's helm away and as he groggily raised his head, spitting dirt and grass, he saw Killbere in the distance place a restraining arm on John Jacob. This was Blackstone's fight. He clambered to his feet and shook free the shield from his arm. With Wolf Sword in his right hand and the retrieved flail in his left he braced himself as the Frenchman charged him down. The knight bent down from the saddle, bringing back his sword arm in a sweeping blow that would be hard to deflect. As the wide-eyed horse was almost upon him, so close that he saw its blood-flecked nostrils and smelt its breath, Blackstone sidestepped, swung the spiked chain and caught the horse's leading leg. He did not have the strength to haul the horse to the ground but as he bent his back and dug in his heels the horse's leg was snagged for a vital stride, and that made the beast falter. The flail's handle slipped through his hands but the stumbling horse had thrown the unbalanced Frenchman.

As the horse danced away, kicking free the entangled chain, Blackstone strode towards the man who had determined to kill him and gain favour from his King. He got to his feet, dazed, and pushed up his visor, turning on his heel, looking for the Englishman. As he spun he saw Blackstone. Eyes wide with surprise he raised his sword. Too late. Wolf Sword's honed steel blade rammed into his face, through his skull up into his brain.

He fell back, arms wide; his body shuddered and was then still.

Blackstone reached down and pulled free the inlaid silver sword belt and scabbard from the fallen nobleman. Dead men's plunder was his bounty.

Blackstone and the French were once again at war.

CHAPTER SIXTY-ONE

La Roche was not a town but an area made up of craggy rocks and, in places, dense woodland. The hillsides rose and fell, their boulder-strewn forests making travel arduous. Blackstone and his men travelled for days through the remote hamlets; many were little more than a handful of wattle and mud hovels next to a muddy track, rutted deeply from handcarts. Where the ground had become impassable the locals had laid cut ferns and branches to accommodate their donkeys' passage. Most had no livestock other than a pig or a milk-giving goat. Blackstone questioned these forest dwellers, who knew the woodland as well as any wild creature, but none had seen or heard of brigands led by a grey-bearded man who wore silver armbands and silver and gold rings on his fingers.

Ancient foresters' tracks were often overgrown but Blackstone's scouts found a route wide enough to support oxen dragging felled timbers to some charcoal makers in their crude woodland hamlet. These people had no wealth for routiers to plunder so their safety was guaranteed. A nearby monastic cell supported a few monks who had struck out years before to bring God's grace to these peasants. The monks themselves were as filthy and unkempt as those they tried to help and they had learnt the bitter lesson that trying to survive by growing crops in the unyielding ground kept them in a state of near starvation and dependency on those to whom they had come to offer spiritual succour. The woodcutters and charcoal burners trapped and shared what little food they had with the monks. It seemed a small price to pay for salvation.

'It's time we stopped,' said Killbere. 'We've been chasing the bastard for too long. This ground will exhaust the horses. We'll suffer injury at this rate, Thomas.'

Blackstone nodded. The small clearing they had entered offered new-growth saplings and overgrown ferns and bramble. There was no sign of boar or other animal tracks and the last woodcutters' hamlet was less than a mile behind them. It was unlikely that wolves would venture this close to a settlement. He turned to his squire. 'John, we encircle the clearing. Separate the horses, no more than ten hobbled at a time. If we are attacked we will only lose some of them. Have Will and Jack hunt us some fresh meat. Sir Gilbert and I will camp below those boulders.' He glanced up at the rustling branches and gauged the wind direction. 'Latrines to be dug down there beyond those rocks.'

John Jacob needed no further instruction and turned his horse to relay Blackstone's commands to the captains.

Will Longdon and Jack Halfpenny brought down four deer, one of which, when gutted and skinned, Blackstone sent back to the nearby woodcutters. They could only snare small game for their pots so to have an English bowman bring down big game was cause for celebration. Their fires burned brightly and even though Blackstone's men were deep in the forest the rising ground where they camped showed them the village's flickering light in the distance. Blackstone's generosity was repaid next morning when a scurvy-looking wretch made his way into the camp.

'Sir Thomas?' said Meulon as he led the peasant woodcutter up the path to where Blackstone and Killbere were washing in the stream that tumbled down the rocks. Blackstone pulled his head from the water and dragged his fingers through his hair. The tall Norman pointed behind himself, past the woodcutter. A monk, his tonsure unshaven for days, his face stubbled with ingrained dirt, smoke smudges encrusted on his wrinkled skin, was panting towards him. John Jacob had stopped him twenty yards downhill, waiting for Blackstone's command to allow the monk closer.

'Said he had to speak to you and you alone. I searched him. He has no weapon,' Jacob called.

'My lord,' said the woodcutter as he knelt respectfully in the dirt. 'This monk bade me bring him to you. I am blessed by him if you will see him.'

'Get up,' said Blackstone. 'No need to kneel before me.'

The woodcutter rose as Blackstone beckoned the monk forward. Sweat streaked the man's face despite the chill air. 'My lord,' said the monk, bowing slightly.

'You promised this man a blessing,' said Blackstone.

The monk looked nonplussed.

Killbere wiped a cloth across his chest to dry off the stream water. 'A blessing. A promise of heavenly gratitude. A touch of your grubby hand on his lice-infested head.'

'I have a message for Sir Thomas Blackstone,' said the monk, paying no attention to Killbere's chiding.

'Monk, you had better not ignore this knight,' said Blackstone. 'Or he will baptize you again in this icy stream.'

The monk, surprised, glanced at the half-naked Killbere, who did not appear to be anything more than a pock-faced hobelar. Then he clasped his hands together, bowed his head and muttered an abject apology.

'Give the man his blessing, then,' said Killbere.

The peasant woodcutter, rank with stale sweat and woodsmoke, grasped the monk's equally grubby hand and kissed it. The monk winced, even though his own stench was no different to that of the man whose spittle wet the back of his hand. He fought the urge to step away but the two half-naked men in front of him scowled with annoyance. He made the sign of the cross, muttered a benediction, and when the peasant pulled off his cap, the monk placed his hand on the matted hair and finished his blessing. The toothless woodcutter's gums grinned at Blackstone.

'My lord, me and mine are here to serve you.' He bowed again and then returned the way he had come.

'What do you want?' Blackstone asked the monk.

384

'I have a message for Sir Thomas Blackstone,' repeated the monk, looking uncertainly from Blackstone to Killbere, who raised a hand and pointed at Blackstone.

The monk began his message again. 'I have—'

'Merciful God in heaven. No wonder you have been cast into this wilderness,' said Killbere. 'You must have bored your abbot to death. Give us the damned message.'

The monk fumbled in the small leather purse on the rope around his waist and teased out a leather cord bearing a small silver medallion. He reached forward, offering it to Blackstone. It was the same silver-wheeled goddess that he wore around his neck.

'He says he will meet you at the Roman aqueduct but that you are to come alone.'

CHAPTER SIXTY-TWO

The ancient aqueduct spanned a narrow valley. On Blackstone's side of the vale five of the arches soared up above the treeline. He looked across the open ground, which gave him a clear view of the level ground behind him and the similar view of the landscape opposite. If there were an ambush it would be from archers concealed on the lower slopes in the treeline. Killbere had cursed and threatened to send Will Longdon and a dozen archers to protect him but Blackstone had insisted he honour ap Madoc's demand and forbade anyone from following him. The monk had made his way beneath one of the arches and called out that Thomas Blackstone had arrived. His voice echoed along the curved stonework, then carried across the expanse of the valley. Blackstone watched the trees on the opposite side for any movement. There were no archers riding with Gruffydd ap Madoc when last he saw him but it was not impossible that he had gathered English bowmen to him in the time that had passed. The movement, when he saw it, did not come from the opposite side but from further down the open ground beyond the arches on Blackstone's side. A lone horseman, a man who seemed too big for his own sturdy mount, eased into view and halted.

The startled monk turned quickly. 'Sir Thomas, that's him.'

'I know who it is. Get back to your work and prayers, brother monk.'

The unkempt cleric needed no further urging and strode away quickly and as he disappeared back into the forest beyond the clearing Gruffydd ap Madoc rode forward at a leisurely pace. Blackstone watched him. There was no sign of the Welshman glancing left or right, no sense of him being wary or of readying himself to give a signal to any hidden men. As he reached the arched pillars ap Madoc dismounted and tethered his horse. He stood waiting. Blackstone looked around again. There was still no sign of men in hiding. The forest was as it should be. The birds flew; the breeze ruffled the treetops. He dismounted, walked the bastard horse closer and then tied his rein off on a secure tree. The Welshman watched him approach and then sat on a boulder and pulled off his helmet.

'Thomas, I bear you no ill will. Whereas you wish to see me dead.'

'You hanged one of my archers and tried to kill my centenar, who nearly died trying to save him.'

'Ah, Thomas, you know in your heart it wasn't me. What purpose would I have to do such a thing? I had your gold coin; I had two hostages. All I did was make sure you didn't come after me in a hurry. It was William Cade and his men who strung up the lad and attacked your archer.'

'You didn't stop him.'

'I knew nothing of it until it was too late. And now you hound me, running me down like a beast of prey. You know I'll not allow it. We'll fight and one of us will die. And it won't be me. I don't want to kill you, Thomas. I swear it.'

Blackstone tossed the Celtic charm to him. 'She won't save you.'

Ap Madoc caught it, kissed the figure of Arianrhod and put the cord around his neck. 'Knew that would tell you who sent it,' he said. He drank from a flask and then offered it.

Blackstone made no response.

'It's good brandy. We took it from... I forget. Someone we butchered along the way.' He swallowed again and then corked the flask. 'We could fight it out here and now, Thomas, but your gold is with my men, so you would die a poor man. And this place here' – he waved a hand at their surroundings – 'is no battle-field, no place of glory. Not the place for a legend to die. Face down in a muddy stream, beneath some relic of a monument from another time.'

'Perhaps I care less about the gold and more about avenging a boy archer.'

'Oh, for God's sake, man. The lad died at the end of a rope at the hand of others. Leave it be. No beardless boy is worth us drawing blood even if I had done it. I told you—'

'William Cade is dead. I killed him,' Blackstone interrupted. 'He was in the pay of the French King and his scheming son. They have failed to kill me again.'

The Welshman seemed momentarily surprised that Cade had been tracked down. 'Ah, well, then, your blood-lust should be satisfied with that. I hope the wretch died badly.'

'We fought together in the past, Gruffydd. You, me and Gilbert. We served our King and now a tide of killing has swept across France and forced us apart. We each went our own way, no longer brothers in arms. We cannot have regret for what could have been.'

'I am sincere in my wish not to see us fight, Thomas. I swear that.' He kissed the silver-wheeled goddess again. 'She protects us both, but if we go at each other like crazed dogs all it proves is that you want your money back. Did you take Cade's share?'

'Let's finish this now,' said Blackstone. 'Once you're dead I'll follow your men and get back the gold.'

Gruffydd ap Madoc sighed and stood. He pulled on his helmet. 'Thomas, I will trade you.'

'For what? The money?'

'No. Your life or mine. Perhaps you will kill me, perhaps I you. I think it better if we both live.'

'Beyond the gold there's nothing I want from you except to close the account of a young archer's death. You gave your word and he died without priest or mercy.'

The Welshman walked slowly towards Blackstone. He stopped at arm's length. Too close for either man to draw a weapon. 'Have you heard from Lord de Grailly's man? The Gascon captain, Beyard?'

Blackstone's heart skipped a beat.

'No, I thought not.' Ap Madoc stepped away. 'Thomas, I was down near Avignon when your Gascon went among the routiers.

He has a persuasive tongue. He convinced enough of them that your promises were as good as... gold.' He grinned. 'Me, I believed him as well. Though I can't see you granting me the seneschalship of anywhere other than hell.'

'If you have harmed him, Gruffydd, then my revenge will be doubled.'

The Welshman rolled his eyes and trembled his hands. 'See, it's terrified I am.' He guffawed. 'I never met him. Christ, Thomas, it's not for me to kill a Gascon like him. Look to the French for that.'

'He's dead?'

'Soon will be.'

'He's prisoner?'

Ap Madoc snorted and spat. 'Is his life worth trading for mine?'

'You talk too much.'

'I'm a Welshman. We love to talk. And fight.' He grinned once more. 'Thomas, it is our language that is the bedrock of your mother tongue. We savour it like a good wine.' He paused, but when he spoke again his words still tumbled lightly. 'He's not my prisoner, no. But he is imprisoned, for want of a better word. Now, would you trade him for my life?'

'I would not.'

'I thought not,' said ap Madoc. 'No, indeed. I thought you would not. So, I asked myself: What *would* Thomas Blackstone trade to let the matter between us rest? And I thought: I know, something more precious than a sack of gold, greater than a loyal man-at-arms. Now, what do you think that might be, eh? Shall I give you a clue? A scholar, brave as a boar facing a hunter, and as sharp and bright as that Wolf Sword that you'd love to use on me.' He stopped, eyebrows raised, watching Blackstone's reaction.

Blackstone's mind raced to the obvious conclusion.

'Ah, you've got it then. Aye, Thomas, your lad was being escorted from Florence. I don't know why. A priest and a knight of the Tau with him. They sought sanctuary at Avignon. They heard of your Gascon and made themselves known to him. I don't know the details but perhaps he offered to bring them on to you.'

'Where are they?'

Gruffydd ap Madoc pulled his fingers down his beard, studying the renowned knight he had momentarily reduced to a concerned father.

'Say it is over between us, Thomas, and I will tell you where they are, and I will even fight at your side to help release him. I have more men with me now than I had before. I know where the brigands ride and I know their captains. Routiers are being hunted by the French, who are everywhere. Together, with you leading them, you could finish off these bastard Frenchmen once and for all.'

Blackstone took a pace back. Wolf Sword was suddenly in his hand. Gruffydd ap Madoc smiled and extended his hands away from his own weapons.

'What good would that do?' he said. He spun around following Blackstone's gaze and realized that Blackstone had drawn his sword because of the horsemen who had appeared in the distance, beyond the aqueduct behind him. Routiers or Frenchmen? It made no difference. The two men stood no chance. They ran for their mounts. The Welshman spurred his horse, yanked the reins and held the panicked beast as he called out to Blackstone.

'Brignais! It's held by mercenaries. They are trapped behind the town's walls by a French army! You are in my debt, Thomas. Do not forget it!' And then he galloped across the valley.

Blackstone turned the bastard horse to where his men were encamped. He would lose the approaching horsemen in the depths of the forest, but knew he could not afford to lose time in reaching his son. The remaining corner of his heart capable of love was besieged with fear.

CHAPTER SIXTY-THREE

The woodcutter repaid his debt to Blackstone. Despite his skinny frame he ran tirelessly through the vast forest, outpacing the horses that followed him. Before the midday sun rose above the treetops on the second day, he slowed and gestured to Blackstone, indicating the moss-covered boulders that tumbled into a wood-strewn gully. At first Blackstone could not see what the wiry man was pointing at. His toothless grin seemed to imply he had a secret and he scrambled surefooted down the awkward slope, pushing himself through waist-high ferns.

'God's tears, Thomas, I hope he doesn't expect us to ride down there. I thought he was going to show us a way out of this forest and avoid the French,' said Killbere as he watched the woodcutter reach the bottom of the gully.

'He will,' said Blackstone. 'There's something down there he wants to show us.'

The woodcutter began to pull aside undergrowth and then called for Blackstone to go down to him. Blackstone handed his reins to John Jacob and clambered after the man. It was treacherous going but he persevered, for as he pushed through the ferns he saw debris from a broken wagon wheel and what looked to be scattered remnants of planking that would have served as part of a cart's baseboard. When he reached the woodcutter he saw what he had exposed. There were four barrels, some cracked open but mostly intact. The man grinned and nodded his head excitedly. 'For you, my lord, for you.' The man took a small chopping axe from his belt and hacked away one of the barrel lids. Blackstone bent down and reached inside and felt the familiar soft touch of goose feather in the palm of his hand. He closed his grip and pulled out a handful of arrows.

'Soldiers came this way months ago and their wagon fell, my lord. We hid these barrels because we were afraid and did not know who to trust. We wanted no trouble. We buried the wagoners' bodies.'

Blackstone grinned and placed a hand on the man's shoulder in gratitude. He looked up to where the mounted men stared down at him and he raised his fist, clutching the yard-long arrows. 'Will, Jack, Quenell, down here.'

Will Longdon and his archers would rather starve than have their arrow bags empty and – now that they had bundles bound and tied to a pack horse – like hungry men at a feast their spirits lifted. Every man would have at least four sheaves and from what Blackstone had told them about the French army attacking the town where his son had sought sanctuary, they would need them. When the arrows were secured the woodcutter ran on like a tireless dog ahead of the horsemen until on the fourth day of travel from the mountains and forests of La Roche they reached a clearing close to where the sky stretched beyond the confines of the trees. The clearing exposed tracks etched across the rolling countryside. Smoke rose from distant hamlets and sunlight caught a slithering narrow river that twisted towards dark smudges in the distance that could be more woodland or perhaps further villages. Once Blackstone's eyes adjusted to the distances the multitude of bare feathered sticks that clung to hillsides were revealed as stakes holding rows of vines like silent, stationary soldiers.

The forest dweller spat phlegm and let his eyes gaze across the vast expanse that was denied him in his day-to-day existence. Then he clambered on top of a boulder and pointed to one side. 'Five leagues,' said the woodcutter. He turned and looked at Blackstone but there was no smile on his face this time. 'Brignais, my lord.'

Blackstone eased his horse alongside their guide. Beyond the landmarks the ground flattened into a plain and Blackstone saw a speckled mass of movement that his eyes soon told him was a barely moving mass of encamped men. It was the French army under Jean de Tancarville's command. And they numbered in their thousands.

From his vantage point Blackstone spied out the best route to take them behind the French army. To reach his son behind the walls of Brignais seemed an impossible task. The town was built on high ground and the French would need time to defeat its defenders. He saw a low stone bridge across a narrow river that would funnel the troops and knew, if it could be blocked or enough of the enemy killed on it, that might slow the French attack sufficiently for him to find a way inside.

'There could be danger behind us, Thomas,' said Killbere as they slowed their horses, approaching within a thousand yards of the rear of the French, using irrigation channels as cover from any sentries patrolling the perimeter. The water course was shallow, the ground yielding to mud beneath the horses' hooves.

Blackstone looked back. Killbere was correct. If French reinforcements arrived across the undulating land behind them Blackstone and his few men would be trapped between the two forces.

'Don't worry, Gilbert, by the time any more French arrive, we'll most likely be dead.'

'Ah, always pleased to hear that you have a plan,' said Killbere. He grinned but there was a look of resignation at the impossible task that lay ahead. 'When the time comes, Thomas, we must retreat up there. Those of us alive.' Killbere pointed to where one of the fields on their flank rose up; the spring vines were still bare but they would offer good defence once the men were obliged to retreat. They could hold a first wave of attack from there but it would not take long for the heavy horse to trample them and the vines into the ground. Desperation would make them sell their lives dearly, and it seemed to Blackstone that their only hope would be to join Henry and the Tau knight behind the walls.

A roar rose up from the French army. Blackstone dismounted

and crawled to the top of the water channel's lip. The French had thrown another attack against the walls. It would soon be dark and Blackstone could barely make out the assault but the narrow bridge did indeed slow the French as they swarmed forward. The defenders were hurling rocks and stones down on those below their walls. Scaling ladders were being pushed away and the French were dying. Yet sooner or later the overwhelming numbers of attackers would prevail: the defenders would not be able to kill enough French, and those left would clamber over their own dead to reach those inside.

Killbere, Meulon and John Jacob joined Blackstone on the wet ground and peered across the ditch's wall, each of them gauging the strengths and weaknesses of the attacking force. Meulon glanced at his comrades in puzzlement and then gazed back at the French ranks. 'Look hard. Do you see what I see?'

The men kept looking. What had Meulon spotted and they had not?

'There's another drainage ditch a few hundred yards behind them, which would get us closer if we could reach it unseen,' said John Jacob.

'He's right,' said Killbere. 'Over there on the left you can see where this ditch leads into it. We could get close enough to count the hairs on the back of their necks, but there are so few of us against so many of them. Still, it's close to that bridge and the town gate. Perhaps we could move through them at night?'

Blackstone glanced across at Meulon, who smiled.

'There's more than that,' said Blackstone. 'What have you seen?'

Meulon raised his eyes across the parapet again and waggled his finger back and forth. 'They have no rear pickets. There are no sentries, no rear defences; everything they do is focused on the town.'

For a brief, incredulous moment the other three men looked again.

'Arrogant bastards think they're too many to worry about a rear attack,' said John Jacob.

'And we are too few to take them on. But if we had Felton

and Louis de Harcourt with us we could make them bleed,' said Killbere.

Blackstone remained silent, his mind racing to find a way through the blind spots and reach the gates. There were thousands of infantry and crossbowmen, and at least a third of the force would be knights and men-at-arms on horseback. Even if they got halfway under cover of darkness – a troop of men riding at the walk, unhurried, as if they belonged with the French – could such a daring plan be successful? One challenge and they would be overwhelmed.

'What banners do we see?' said Blackstone.

'Men of Lorraine, and there's Jacques de Bourbon's...' said John Jacob. He winced; de Bourbon was a renowned fighter.

'Lyonnais, Bourbonnais, the Count of Forez... Christ, there's as many noblemen here as we killed at Poitiers,' said Killbere. Turning his back on the host he pulled free his helm, scrubbing his palm over his sweat-streaked hair. He grinned. 'Kill a few more of their high and mighty and King John will have a seizure. We'd save Edward a lot of trouble.'

'There are men from Savoy out there as well,' said Meulon.

The men slumped down the ditch wall. 'We can get Will and his lads closer tonight, Thomas,' said Killbere. 'We need to see if there's a gap in the French ranks tomorrow or whether there's another route we haven't seen.'

Blackstone nodded in agreement. The water channel was wide enough for a dozen men to gather across. He summoned his men.

'There are too few of us to cause these thousands any harm, but they have no defence in their rear. Tonight we will walk the horses through these ditches – we cannot be seen – and then we will wait until dawn to see what can be done. If Will and his archers take up position on the rear of the ditch then any attack can be repulsed. French horses will die here and their riders with them, but once arrows are loosed it's only a matter of time before footsoldiers come swarming. Then Will and Sir Gilbert will form a defensive line beyond those vines.' He looked at the grim faces that stared back at him. 'I will not ask you to strike through their ranks with me. Too many of us will die. If the diversion is enough and we cause chaos among them, then I will get through and reach my son.'

'And I,' said John Jacob.

'Me too,' said Meulon. 'I know young Henry and wish to see him safe.'

'And Beyard owes me money,' said Renfred, 'so best I come with you, Sir Thomas.'

'And I have no wish to sit here with my arse in freezing water,' said Perinne. 'The more of us at your side the better.'

A murmur of agreement rippled through the men.

'We'll have no damned disagreement here,' growled Killbere. 'If Will and Jack and Quenell and their lads do their killing and then ride free of their infantry when they turn on them... then we all go. Beyard will need help in there and I'll wager there's fewer than two hundred manning those walls.' He looked at Blackstone. 'We are in agreement, Thomas. We have fought too hard together over the years.' He looked at the grinning faces. 'None here will see you strike out alone.' He stepped to his horse and took its reins. 'Besides, you and that bastard horse of yours would probably get lost without us and you would end up in a cage and carted off to Paris. Then where would your lad be? And there I was thinking we could all end up in Italy with good wine and plump women.' He sighed. 'We will have to forsake those pleasures for another time. You see how obvious it is, dammit. You need us.'

CHAPTER SIXTY-FOUR

Beyard was bloodied. He had grappled with a determined French-man, one of the hundreds who had clambered onto the walls, and taken a blow to the head. Blood trickled into his eyes until the scalp wound caked dry. His men fought hand to hand, beating skulls with rocks, slashing and stabbing with any weapon to hand. And once again they had pushed away the scaling ladders. The few defenders of the castle at Brignais had fought on every wall and their numbers were dwindling. As darkness began to seep across the landscape he and his men counted their losses. Fra Foresti had joined the routiers on one of the walls after extracting a promise from Henry Blackstone that he would stay clear of the fighting and help servants carry water buckets to those who fought. Water had soon given way to gathering and carrying rocks to hurl down. Henry had helped break down a low stone wall and like a beast of burden carried a yoke across his shoulders bearing rubble. Young men and children scurried here and there responding to cries from the men on the walls. Exhaustion was claiming them all and they knew it was only a matter of time before the sheer weight of French numbers swarmed over the walls. And then a final stand would be made in the small castle.

As the daylight faded so too did the last attack of the day. When they had arrived at Brignais it had turned out that Beyard outranked everyone in the garrison and its defence had fallen to him. He had reached the hilltop town with little time to spare. His 150 Gascons, along with Henry Blackstone and Fra Foresti, were too small a force to challenge the hordes of French who swept down the Rhône Valley to destroy the routiers riding north intending to invade the Duchy of Burgundy. Beyard's party had been caught in the middle. When they had retreated into the mountain foothills they had joined forces with a small band of routiers who told him of a mercenary stronghold held by a few men at Brignais. It could not have been a more unfortunate place of refuge. The French army already pressing south of Lyons had descended, seeking a routier by the name of Hélie Meschin, another Gascon who had once served the French, and had become a brigand when released from their service. He was nothing more than a gangster who occupied towns and villages and the routiers quickly learnt that the French had decided to trap and kill him. That he had slipped their net and taken to the hills was ignored, if it was ever known, because the rumour was that Blackstone himself was behind the walls.

Beyard shouted his orders. 'We need lances cut down and sharpened. Three men on every lance.'

Weary men nodded their understanding and began to gather their weapons ready for another assault whenever it might come.

'Fra Foresti,' Beyard called to the Tau knight, who was helping to carry a wounded man down from the walls. The hospitaller handed responsibility to another and joined the Gascon captain in the yard.

'They will breach us tomorrow,' said Beyard. 'We cannot hold the walls. What shall we do about Henry? We cannot escape through the French lines. If I and my men stay do you think the French would honour a Knight of the Tau and a pilgrim in his charge?'

'Possibly, but it's a great risk.'

'No greater than staying here,' said Beyard. 'You can tell them that you were captured and held by us.'

Fra Foresti fell silent. Beyard put a reassuring hand on his shoulder. 'We have to get Henry out. Once the French break through they'll kill every soul here. Man and boy. We could not even disguise him as a servant. This place will be burnt to the ground and all of us with it.'

'Have you thought why they have committed their army to

destroy this insignificant place? It's held by so few. What threat does Brignais offer?'

Beyard shook his head. 'We don't need to know why. They are scraping the land clear of routiers. We are in the wrong place and I am sorry for bringing us here.'

'You know there was an attempt on the boy's life. He is worth more than gold to those who seek to hurt his father.'

'You think all of this is because of him?' said Beyard. 'Thousands of men to seize a boy?' He stared at the injured being carried away and the dead being laid out in the dirt of the yard. 'No. That cannot be.'

'Someone tried to kill him, Beyard. Perhaps their intention is not to seize him.'

Beyard sighed. 'Merciful Christ, if they killed him then Sir Thomas would set this world on fire and he would be hunted down by every prince and nobleman. Every beggar and assassin would have just cause to kill him.'

Fra Foresti looked to where Henry was helping to tend the wounded. 'We are not to know what reason lies behind this. All we can do is stand our ground. In his last breath the boy must declare who he is and then his name will either save or condemn him. Capture or death. That is all that remains.'

Blackstone and his men led their horses along the deep channel. At its end it turned into another drainage course. The evening breeze was in their faces so the smell of men and animals reached their nostrils. Being downwind gave Blackstone's men the advantage and as they peered over the top of the high ditch wall they heard voices of the French troops settled about their thousand fires.

'They're damned fools. Look at them. We could walk among them and cut their throats. No sentries. Not one,' said Killbere quietly. 'Damn, they're so close now I could spit on them.'

The rear ranks of the French army lay 150 yard-long strides from where the men hid.

'The French commanders have no need to fear anyone,' said Meulon. 'Not with so many. Who is there to strike at them? No one in any strength.'

Blackstone studied the scattered troops. 'We'll place Will and his lads behind this ditch. They'll kill enough to get their attention and then we ride through. The French have a well-trodden path towards the walls. They funnel themselves across the field. We'll ride in on that. I wish we could have got you closer, Will. Killing them on the bridge would have slowed their advance. But we will have you strike them once you see us attacked. Until that moment I and the others will ride hard and fast. It might get us close.'

Will Longdon lay flat on his belly like the other men at his side. 'Come the morning I'll have Jack and Quenell take their men back fifty paces behind us. They can shoot first: the range will be good to kill the French at the back and when Jack brings his lads forward mine will already be shooting deeper into the French ranks. We'll kill them in waves. Just like the old days,' he said, grinning.

'As we try to reach that bridge they'll turn on you, Will. We'll have a fight on our hands but you won't have time to get the horses free from here and that vineyard is three hundred and fifty yards,' said Blackstone. 'You'll be running for your life.'

'Thomas, when any of them come at us they'll be stumbling over their own dead. Then they have to get across this ditch with us on the other side and the horses below them. We can buy enough time for you and the others to gallop through. And with a few thousand Frenchmen chasing us, we'll get to that vineyard quicker than an arrow falls from the sky.'

Blackstone turned and looked along the huddled men and horses who waited silently in the darkness. Once again he had given every man the opportunity to leave and once again they had ignored his pleas that many of them would die while trying to reach the gates. His son would have every chance to live but so many of Blackstone's men would die in the attempt.

The odds were too large. For a moment he considered abandoning his son because trying to reach him would see the death of so many of the men he held dear. The sacrifice was too great.

Killbere was the closest man to him and despite the darkness he must've seen the doubt crease Blackstone's features.

The veteran knight whispered, 'It's all right, Thomas. They'll die for you tomorrow as they would any other day.'

CHAPTER SIXTY-FIVE

The men slept as best they could, each tying their mount's rein to leg or arm. Horses relieved themselves, shifted their weight and half slept, like their riders who lay in their animals' filth, curled in on themselves on the wet ground, giving no thought to the following day or their fetid conditions. A man's stench meant nothing when he was soon to be covered in gore. As the pre-dawn light crept across the sky they roused themselves. Stiff from the wet ground, they rubbed warmth back into their muscles. Some scooped shallow water from the bottom of the ditch and freshened their faces. Blackstone gripped Will Longdon's arm and embraced the man who, like Killbere, had been at his side since the first day he had gone to war. No words were needed as the veteran archer clambered up the rear of the ditch wall, keeping his men low against the skyline as they crawled into position.

The French army slowly awoke, their fires wafting the tantalizing smell of cooking over Blackstone's men. But it would not be the first time he and his men had gone into battle hungry. They fussed their horses, pressing their palms against their soft noses, giving them their familiar scent. Girth straps were tightened. Some knelt briefly in prayer. Others spat the night's foulness from their throats. Most relieved their bladders. They had all been told what was expected the moment Thomas Blackstone mounted that bastard horse of his. God willing the beast would trample its way through the French ranks, some muttered quietly among themselves.

The barely lit day showed their grinning faces. Best to be at the French while they scratched their balls and yawned themselves into wakefulness.

Blackstone would lead his men to the end of the ditch where its grassy walls were low enough to spur their horses up and into the unsuspecting French. Then it was a race to the gates, shields high so that their enemies and their friends could see who it was who rode towards Brignais.

Perinne saw the shadow high in the sky.

'She's hunting early for men's souls,' said Will Longdon resignedly, and then placed a hand on his friend's shoulder. 'We must watch out for Thomas. Once they see him they will want him dead.'

Killbere undid one of his saddlebags and stepped towards Blackstone. He carried a folded banner. Catching Meulon's eye he beckoned the Norman captain to him.

'Your spear,' he said quietly.

Meulon looked at what he was holding and understood what was expected of him. He lowered his favoured weapon as Killbere took his time to secure the banner. Meulon shook it free and lofted it high enough for the men in the ditch to see it. Blackstone's war banner, the mailed fist grasping the sword blade in cruciform. Killbere held the bottom of the flag so that the words *Défiant à la Mort* were clearly visible.

'They'll know who it is who rides among them and kills them,' said Renfred.

'And those behind the walls,' said Killbere. 'We'll need them to open those gates damned quickly.'

Blackstone watched as Killbere did something he had never done before. He lifted the flag's hem and pressed his lips against it.

And then John Jacob did the same. And Renfred. Quickly followed by all the rest, the men shuffling forward to kiss the material.

Blackstone's heart beat hard. How many of these courageous men would remain alive in the coming hour?

And now they honoured him.

Silently the men followed Blackstone's example and climbed into their saddles. Blackstone was waiting for the dawn to break across the hills before urging his horse slowly forward because then the rising sun would blind the French and give his men another chance to survive longer than expected. Meulon held the flag-draped spear low. As soon as they threw themselves into their enemy he would hold it aloft. Renfred and Perinne would ride either side of him to protect Blackstone's blazon.

The bastard horse turned its head, nearly dragging the reins from Blackstone's hands. He yanked the belligerent beast's head back, but it repeated the movement. Its ears were up. Its nostrils flared. And it stubbornly resisted his heaving on the rein. Will Longdon suddenly appeared over the edge of the ditch wall, belly down.

'Thomas!' he hissed. 'Look! For Christ's sake, look!' he insisted, beckoning Blackstone who quickly dismounted and clambered up the bank.

He squinted into the dull light that still clung to the foothills and forests in the distance. A vast horde of men were descending towards them. Thousands of horsemen in a great extended line.

'Are they French? Their southern army?' said Longdon, a note of fear in his voice.

Blackstone concentrated on the fast-approaching men. Near another mile and they would be on them. He waited, uncertainty clouding his thoughts. If it were the French he and every one of his men would be dead before they even clambered out of the ditch.

Will Longdon's archers had resisted the urge to raise themselves from where they lay out of sight of the French but they turned and watched the approaching host with the same trepidation. They would be the first to die. They would have time to clamber back into the ditch but then they would be overwhelmed.

Blackstone's archer's eye picked out a solitary figure who rode yards ahead of the others. 'Not French,' said Blackstone. He grinned. 'Ready your archers, Will. They're routiers and they intend to attack.'

Blackstone quickly slithered back down the bank and mounted the bastard horse who yet again had warned him. 'Ready,' he called. He nodded to Meulon, who raised the banner. 'Thousands of routiers are at our backs,' he called. 'The Welshman redeems himself.'

He spurred the horse along the ditch and then turned, urging it up and over. Every man followed and in an extended line they hurled themselves over the parapet. The rear ranks of the French turned away from the cooking pots to look quizzically at the horsemen who galloped towards them, but within heartbeats their confusion changed to wholesale panic. As if from nowhere a storm of arrows fell into them. Men screamed; some tumbled across the cooking fires; others ran for their weapons, bellowing commands and shouting a belated warning.

Blackstone's horsemen had still not reached them by the time another hail of arrows fell. Will Longdon had moved his archers forward in two ranks, each ahead of the other, creeping their lethal assault further into the French until finally he held his archers in one extended line as the creaking bend of yew bows and the thwack of bow cords being released rippled through the still dawn air. And then heavy horse tore among the French, who ran in disarray. Trumpets blared as pennons and flags were raised and commanders, panic-stricken at the unexpected attack, tried to organize the men in defence. A thudding heartbeat thumped out from kettle drums, urging the French to form up and fight.

No sooner had Blackstone's men's horses trampled over the dead and the dying than another swarm of death followed as routiers plunged into the French flanks. Will Longdon ran his men hard towards the left flank of the encamped men in a move that would close the trap on those who thought of escape. The ground shook from the thousands of hooves as terror-laden voices hurled their agony into the morning sky. The surprise attack had caught hundreds of men unaware but as Blackstone forged his way forward others were forming a defence, determined to stop this advance guard of horsemen whose banner proclaimed it was Sir Thomas Blackstone and his men who hurled themselves into their midst.

Brave and desperate footsoldiers threw themselves at the riders, trying to stab and wound, to pull them down to the ground.

Most died or were trampled underfoot as the weight of the horses barged them aside. In the background a cavalry unit fought their way through their own ranks to try and cut off Blackstone's advance. These noblemen cared little for their own soldiers, forcing them aside with their mounts and causing them injury. The turmoil became panic. Blackstone's men were getting closer to the bridge. Routiers had charged into the far-flung ranks. Last-ditch battles were being fought. Small pockets of desperate men were organizing a defence. Howls of pain and roars of defiance rose up, sweeping over the battlefield with an urgency that struck hearts with despair and fear.

The flag carried by the horsemen was that of Jacques de Bourbon, one of the most able French commanders. Their horses were cloaked in caparisons, bright colourful trappings proclaiming their rider's wealth and status. The French were throwing their finest against these marauding horsemen. A footsoldier stabbed his spear at Blackstone; he felt its impact on his shield as another attacked him with a sword thrust, striking his armour-protected thigh. Blackstone heeled the bastard horse, letting its weight sweep them aside. Others reached for his reins but the speed and weight of the beast cast them off.

Meulon's horse was brought down. Frenchmen rammed halberds and spears into its chest and flanks. It fell bellowing in agony. Meulon tumbled down, narrowly avoiding its thrashing hooves. Some of the French who had struck at the horse had their ribs and skulls shattered by its flailing iron-shod legs. Meulon clambered to his feet as John Jacob and Renfred reined in their horses and protected him. Meulon hefted Blackstone's banner and thrust it into the German's outstretched hand. Riderless horses ran free. Meulon slashed and battered his way towards one. A sword thrust caught his shoulder, its point piercing his mail. Ignoring the pain he struck the man with the edge of his shield and, despite the roar of battle, heard the man's neck snap as its rim rammed beneath his chin. The horse panicked, wide-eyed with terror as men swarmed around it, but Meulon's strength took him onto its back and spurred it to follow Blackstone, who was closing on the French knights.

Perinne and Killbere stayed as close as they could to Blackstone, whose great beast of a horse was ploughing a furrow through the hapless infantry. With John Jacob they swung their horses to be a half-length behind his shoulder. Blackstone's men followed like a skein of geese behind their leader. The broadhead formation devastated the French footsoldiers but Blackstone was wounded. A crossbow bolt loosed at close quarters had punched through his shield and mail and plunged into his side. For a moment it looked as though he was about to tumble from the saddle but he quickly righted himself and spurred the lumbering horse towards the bridge. All of Perinne's fears surged. The great raptor had circled again. Thomas Blackstone was going to die.

One of the French commanders had rallied his men and blocked the bridge. Spears held low, shields locked, four ranks of men one behind the other stood ready to repel the attackers, determined that Brignais would still be theirs when this routier attack was eventually beaten. The French had reorganized. Killbere took a second to look left and right. Across the swarming men he saw the Welshman's routier force had pushed the French ranks further back. On the other flank Will Longdon's archers still loosed their arrows into the terrified footsoldiers. Fires burned out of control. Tents blazed. Smoke wafted across the confused field. And still Blackstone rode towards the town gates and the French cavalry that now came between him and the bridge.

Killbere raised himself in the stirrups and slashed down at a gaggle of men who struck at him. Desperate hands grabbed at his reins. An axe struck his shield, splitting it in two. He threw the useless shield from his arm and grabbed his chained flail, swinging its spiked weight at the axeman whose grimacing face was torn from his skull. On and on Blackstone's men charged. Every man seemed to bear a wound. Some lay dead. Horses ran wild. Jacques de Bourbon's knights bore down on Blackstone's lightly armed men, halting their momentum.

High in the sky a lone buzzard's piercing shriek carried across the cacophony below. Perinne heard the cry like a beckoning angel's call. For months the spectre of death had been waiting. It had passed him by with only a light touch and he had brushed it away. In that moment the battlefield fell silent. No sound existed. Figures blurred before him, men's gaping mouths silently hurling abuse and crying out in pain. Men weeping in fear, bodies contorted from their wounds. Everything slowed. Blackstone was being overwhelmed by two knights wearing armour and great helms. They swung axe and sword as they isolated him, desperate to slay the legend. Killbere and the others could not reach him as they fought their own battle. Renfred fell. The banner with him. John Jacob grabbed it. Meulon had driven his horse into the armoured knights and used his strength to shield Blackstone's squire. The men were outnumbered. How much longer could they fight through? It seemed they had all gone as far as they could. They were too lightly armed to fight these heavy cavalrymen.

One nobleman came at Blackstone on his blind side. Count Jacques de Bourbon desired nothing more than to cleave Blackstone's head from his body. Sunlight speared the low hills. It cast its crimson glow onto the bloodstained men who raised their hands to shield their eyes from its glare. Perhaps that parting of the heavens was a miracle. Perinne's horse surged forward through a gap that appeared and with a desperation born of his fealty to Thomas Blackstone blocked de Bourbon's war horse. The Count's head turned, his vision obscured by the narrow slit of his great helm. The silver-braided reins slipped through his gauntlet-clad hands as this routier dared to assault him. The roar of battle thundered back into Perinne's ears and the loudest cry was his own. Ignoring the sharp tug of his back wound he attacked de Bourbon with a ferocity that took the renowned knight by surprise. Blackstone half wheeled his horse, seeing Perinne trading blows. Perinne's attack bought him vital moments, and he turned and struck down the two knights clamouring to kill him.

Thomas Blackstone's men were gaining ground yard by bloody

yard and now the French were dying in greater numbers than Blackstone's own. Perinne's assault had forced the Constable of France to stand and fight, but Jacques de Bourbon had battled his way clear and now Perinne was assailed by de Bourbon's bodyguard. Perinne jammed his heel into his horse's flank, spurred it and yanked the rein, once again blocking de Bourbon's retinue from riding Blackstone down. Perinne's savagery nearly unseated an armour-clad nobleman and as the man struggled to control his war horse Perinne stabbed into the knight's ribs between the armour. Again and again, short rapid strikes that gave the knight no means to defend himself. He slumped. The wounded man's horse veered, causing more chaos.

Jacques de Bourbon's great war horse was forging a path towards the legendary Englishman as its rider spurred its flanks to barge Blackstone's mount. Glory awaited de Bourbon when the legend died here this day. The horses struck but it was the bastard horse that veered first; gathering strength in its haunches it wrenched the reins from Blackstone's grip as it swung its great head against that of de Bourbon's mount. The force of the horse's blow made the other beast toss its head; de Bourbon momentarily lost control just as Blackstone raised himself and struck his blade down against the man's neck – to no avail. Wolf Sword's blade skidded off the plate armour.

De Bourbon recovered quickly, and struck repeatedly at Blackstone, who reeled, feinted, and then leant forward with his shield to block the jabbing attack. Ignoring the wrenching tear in his side, he forced the bastard horse so that both men were knee to knee. They traded blows and then Blackstone urged his horse to step backwards, one, two, three strides and de Bourbon was suddenly stretching forward, unbalanced. Blackstone pressed his right leg into the bastard horse's side, kicked with his left and the weight of the horse turned sharply. De Bourbon recovered his seat and yanked the reins, trying to stop Blackstone's mount from thrusting its weight against his own. The Frenchman was forced onto his blind side and the impact of Blackstone's blows made him reel, his back arched, his arm raised to try and balance himself in the saddle. Blackstone dropped his own guard and lunged, ramming the blade hard and fast. Blood poured from beneath de Bourbon's armpit. His sword arm was now useless and as he rocked back Blackstone found that soft muscle beneath the knight's thigh and rammed in his blade. The renowned knight and commander tumbled forward over his horse's neck, mortally wounded by the scourge of the House of Valois. As Blackstone kicked his horse to try and fight his way through to the embattled Perinne, de Bourbon's squire reached his lord and tugged his master's horse aside, steering it from the fray.

Blackstone gulped air. His mouth was dry. His lungs heaved and the wound in his side gnawed at him. Sweat stung his eyes as he tried to reach Perinne but there were too many between Blackstone and his friend. Now others clamoured at Blackstone and Wolf Sword arced and swung into flesh and bone.

Two of de Bourbon's knights pressed Perinne. His shield arm covered the blows from one as he fought off the other. His blade cut across the knight's neck; the man's gorget saved him but the strength of the blow made him reel in the saddle, his arm sweeping back and catching Perinne's, throwing him off balance. Perinne felt sudden blinding pain as the other knight's blade found the space below his breastplate. The sword drove up into Perinne's chest. His head was thrown back. Blood flooded his mouth. He saw the shadow in the sky. And remembered the years at Blackstone's side.

The circling buzzard's broken cry called once again. *Per-inne, Per-inne.* All this time, he realized, it had been calling for him.

Blackstone saw his friend die.

The loyal fighter's strength and courage had been a constant companion since Blackstone had been a boy and now he had given his own life to save that of Blackstone. The loss gave added vigour to Blackstone's sword arm. He broke through the armoured knights; Killbere was at his side, face bloodied and with a leg wound that seeped blood into his saddle. The man's injuries made him no less lethal. John Jacob raised himself in his stirrups and lifted the banner higher. Blackstone's men, those who survived, wheeled their horses and drove them forward to reach the standard. All that lay ahead now were a few mounted men-at-arms and scattered groups of footsoldiers, and once through them they would need to assault the bridge – and a horse would not survive those spearmen.

As Blackstone and Killbere re-formed their men, the gates of the town opened. Beyard, and what looked to be a hundred men, charged out carrying lances cut down and sharpened to five-feet lengths. One in three men carried a lance; two others ran at his side armed with sword and shield. They bellowed their defiance and those who guarded the bridge had no choice but to face the counter-attack. But the bridge defenders were suddenly in disarray for as they tried to turn they found they could not bring their spears to bear. Blackstone charged forward into the mêlée and onto the bridge. Beyard's men planted their lances between the bridge and the gates and the desperate French, fleeing the approaching English horsemen, were forced onto them. Those not impaled were hacked down by the Gascon captain's swordsmen. By the time Blackstone had forced his way across the bridge Beyard's men had taken the brunt of the attack.

Blackstone's wound bled down his side and onto his leg but the embedded crossbow bolt staunched most of the flow. The bastard horse had suffered a dozen gashes. Killbere's shoulders slumped, his sword dangling from its blood knot. Beyard watched as Blackstone's exhausted men gathered. Meulon looked as though he had fought the French army alone. Blood caked his beard, a blade had cut through his mail and a raw, bloodied gash scarred his massive arm muscle. Renfred ran alongside John Jacob's horse, grasping a saddle strap for support while Blackstone's squire still carried the blazon. Everywhere across the battlefield French troops were surrendering.

Beyard gazed up at the wounded men. Fighting off his own fatigue he smiled and pulled free his helm. He nodded. No words were needed, not yet. He stepped aside, indicating that Blackstone should ride through his gathered men, who parted as the blood-spattered horse bore its rider to the gates of Brignais. As they entered Blackstone saw the dead and wounded laid out in the yard. A black-cloaked figure stood guard over the wounded men, sword and shield ready, and at his side stood Henry Blackstone, similarly armed, older and stronger than when Blackstone had last seen him, standing ready to fight with the sword given to him years before when he was a boy.

No longer.

His son was the reflection of Blackstone's own youth when he first went to war.

CHAPTER SIXTY-SIX

Killbere refused all help to ease him down from his horse despite his wounds. Blackstone concealed the crossbow bolt in his side, covering himself with his shield as he ordered his fighters to man the walls in case of a counter-attack. He had said little to Fra Foresti or his son; explanations would come later. It was more important to secure Brignais once again.

Beyard brought his men inside the walls and saw Killbere dunk his head in a water trough in an attempt to clear his head just as Henry Blackstone approached.

'With your permission, Sir Gilbert, I have a bandage to bind your wounded leg.'

'Aye, young Henry, let me sit. Bind it tight. I will have need of this leg for a while longer,' said Killbere in a rare moment of gratitude. 'It's good to see you again, lad. We journeyed some way to get here. It seems the French are determined to purge your father's name from their memory. They'll need better men than they've sent so far.'

The Tau knight gathered levies to take water to the fighting men who had made it inside the walls, and had others go among the wounded to follow Henry Blackstone's example in staunching their injuries with whatever bandages could be found. Blackstone winced as one of his men stumbled against his shield arm as they made their way onto the parapet. Meulon was close enough to see, and realized his sworn lord had been injured.

'Let me look,' he said, gently easing aside Blackstone's shield. 'They used a long-shafted quarrel. Best to snap most of that,' he said, looking at the crossbow bolt that protruded from Blackstone's side. 'We'll get the rest of it out later.'

Blackstone nodded and let the big man grasp the bolt shaft. The Norman captain glanced in anticipation at Blackstone who said, 'Do it.'

Meulon's strength snapped it easily but the pain from his effort stabbed Blackstone.

Meulon grinned. 'Just as well it didn't go in your arse.'

'Just as well,' Blackstone agreed and nodded his thanks to the big man.

They gazed out across the bloodied battlefield. Noblemen's banners and knights' pennons were being seized by routiers as some French survivors ran for their lives while others surrendered in their hundreds. Will Longdon brought his mounted archers towards the gates and John Jacob called down to the sentries to open them. Within minutes Blackstone's centenar led his men into the courtyard. They had all survived. They quickly dismounted, their horses mingling with the others. Longdon and his archers undid the last sheaves of arrows bundled on their saddles and ran up to where Blackstone and his captains waited.

'You killed more than we could have hoped for,' said Blackstone. 'Well done, lads.'

'Like the old days,' said Will Longdon.

'They couldn't get to us once you rode into them, Sir Thomas,' said Jack Halfpenny.

'And then the Welshman and his hordes took to the field,' added Longdon. 'My God, Thomas, the French were taken completely by surprise.'

'Damned fools,' said John Jacob. 'The arrogant bastards never thought to cover their rear.'

'It's a rout,' said Meulon. 'King John and his brat will lose sleep once they hear of it.'

'I saw Perinne go down,' said Blackstone. 'He saved my life. I want his body brought here as soon as the day is won.'

'I'll find him,' said John Jacob.

'And I will help,' said Meulon. 'We grow fewer in number.'

'And our grief increases,' said Blackstone.

Killbere had limped his way up the steps and joined them while below in the courtyard Henry Blackstone was organizing the levies to corral the horses, ensuring that only he handled the bastard horse. Foresti had the wounded and the dead moved into one of the nearby buildings.

'They'll see to it that our injured lads are kept safe,' said Killbere. 'Henry and his Italian guardian don't need to be told what to do. If the French were trying to reach your boy I'd say we got here just in time.'

'It comes at a cost, though,' said Blackstone, unable to disguise the pain in his voice.

Killbere looked the worse for wear, but he glared at the bloodied and saddened men around him. 'Mother of God. You men look like dung trampled by a herd of cows,' he said. 'How you let a ragged-arsed bunch of Frenchmen cause you such misery makes me wonder if you're past your best years.'

The men looked at the gore-splattered veteran and his own wounds. And then they laughed. His insult had taken their thoughts away from their fallen comrades for a few precious moments.

'And you look to be ready to enter a King's tourney,' said Blackstone.

'I would not waste my skill on such buffoonery. Jackanapes dressed as prancing lovebirds thrusting their cocks like blunt-ended lances, trying to impress a lady for a token. God's tears, *this* is what fighting men do. Tourneys. Entertainment!' He spat with contempt. '*This* is what we do.' He pointed across the ruptured field of death. Bodies curled, creatures devoid of life entangled in grotesque attitudes of death. 'But I am ready to lay my sword across his throat,' he said, pointing to the lone rider whose horse clattered across the bridge.

'Not yet, Gilbert, it was ap Madoc who told me Henry was here,' said Blackstone. He turned away and made his way down to the courtyard. The gates swung open at his approach and he stepped through to face the Welshman.

Gruffydd ap Madoc had been in the thick of the fighting and

it showed. He pressed a finger to each nostril and snorted snot; then he dragged a sleeve across his face and blood-matted beard.

'Thomas! A hard-fought day.'

'I did not expect to see you again,' said Blackstone.

The Welshman stared, looking his adversary over. 'Aye, well, you'd best get that wound seen to or you might not ever see me again. There are barber surgeons among us. I'll send them to you.' He guffawed. 'You lead a damned charmed life for a man who was once a bastard archer. Men like you sprout like great oaks from the bloodied ground.'

'What do you want, Gruffydd?'

'There's gratitude for you. Your lad lives?'

'He does and you have my thanks. Where did you find all those men?' Blackstone asked, giving a nod in the general direction of the battlefield and the routiers who were going among the dead and dying, stripping plunder and killing those who squirmed from mortal wounds.

'I sent word to every damned captain who had skinners under their command that Thomas Blackstone was about to take on the French army with a handful of men. They came for you, you dumb Englishman. More than four thousand of them. They heard your name and they rode hard. You and that damned reputation of yours.'

'And so that they could destroy a French army that hunted them.'

Ap Madoc shrugged. 'That was a bonus. We have Tancarville and a thousand prisoners and their ransoms.' He tossed down a sack. 'So I won't need your gold.' The meaning was clear. Gruffydd ap Madoc desired peace between himself and Blackstone.

Blackstone made no move towards the sack. Somehow the gold meant less than it did before. The two men held each other's gaze. 'Then spend your ransoms wisely, Welshman.'

Gruffydd ap Madoc's beard split into a broad grin. 'I will whore and drink my way to the next fight, Thomas. We came here to share a victory. Whether you like it or not we are a brotherhood of the sword.' He gathered the reins. 'Goodbye, Thomas.'

Ap Madoc turned his sturdy horse and spurred it away. Blackstone watched him ride into the battlefield where, in the distance, routiers were leading prisoners away. He went forward to pick up the sack but as he bent forward fire streaked through his side. He abandoned the attempt as fatigue and pain swept over him. It was time to retrieve Perinne's body and to have his wounded men and horses attended to. He would send Henry to pick up the gold. Right now he was too damned tired.

CHAPTER SIXTY-SEVEN

Killbere had cursed and spat as the barber surgeon sutured and bound his leg wound.

'You're stitching my damned leg, not embroidering like a woman. Get on with it!' he bellowed, swigging back brandy. 'Mother of Christ, Will Longdon and his fumbling fingers could stitch fletchings neater than that!' he complained as they looped the wound with broad stitches.

Before Blackstone allowed one of the barber surgeons to attend to his own wound he insisted they stitch the cuts and gashes on his horse. They hobbled the bastard horse and secured its great neck with ropes in a stall. It was Henry who placed one hand on its muzzle and soothed its cheek with the other. It fought the ropes but the barber surgeon was safe from the hobbled legs striking him. Only when plantain had been ground down in pestle and mortar and herbs boiled and mixed into it and then applied to his horse's injuries did Blackstone allow the surgeons to assess his own wound. There was some argument between the barber surgeons who hovered nervously over the pierced flesh. It had been suggested that like his horse Blackstone should be securely tied. One blow from those big hands because of the pain and bones would be broken – and they would not be the injured knight's.

'Let the wound fester,' suggested one of the two barber surgeons. 'When the wound is full of pus then it's easier to pull the quarrel free.'

'Cut the flesh and use the prongs,' the other argued. 'Or we could cut an exit wound and push it through.'

'If we open the wound and push strips of linen soaked in honey then that will soften the flesh,' said the first.

'There is no damned honey,' said Blackstone. 'Get it out now.'

The quarrel's head was no different than a bodkin-tipped arrow. Its flanged head had sliced into Blackstone's side. The hope was it had not broken his rib because then marrow would seep into his bloodstream and he would die. Its fifteen-inch length had been snapped earlier by Meulon but now the surgeons asked the big Norman to help hold Blackstone's shoulders when they probed and widened the wound and then inserted the prongs that would grip the quarrel head to ensure it did not detach when the shaft was extracted.

Meulon raised a questioning eyebrow at Blackstone, who shook his head. 'Bring Henry,' he said. Better that his son witness his father's courage than squirm and fight against Meulon's strength. Henry was ushered forward as Will Longdon and the others stood witness to the barber surgeon's attempt. 'You will help these men,' said Blackstone as the boy stood next to him. 'When they tell you to pour wine into the wound you will do it and then press the wound apart so that they can perform their butchery.'

'Yes, my lord,' said Henry obediently.

Sweat pricked Blackstone's skin as the surgeons probed. He kept his eyes on his son, who gave his full attention to the duty he had been assigned. The surgeons pressed the forceps into the wound and then, struggling because of the knitted strength of Blackstone's muscles, pushed in a finger and pulled the gash further apart, telling Henry to press against the muscle to help keep the wound open. The surgeons cursed, their own sweat dripping into the bloodied mess on Blackstone's side. And then one of them grinned. They had the crossbow bolt's bevelled head in their grip. It was intact and was not embedded in Blackstone's rib. They did not wrench it free but caused their patient more suffering as they eased it out through the torn flesh. Like two men who had been handed a gold coin they held the bloodied shaft aloft to proclaim their success.

Blackstone spat the leather-bound wood from between his teeth. 'This is no damned fairground. Finish it. Irrigate it with wine, let it bleed a while to flush the wound and then pack it with the same herbs you gave my horse. And hurry.'

As Will Longdon took the broken and bloodied quarrel and examined it with the interest of a man whose own arrow shafts caused death and injury, the surgeons did as they were instructed. Henry poured the wine and swabbed the wound with fresh linen; as the blood flow eased one of the barber surgeons pressed the herb balm into the lesion while the other dipped silk cord through wine and made ready to stitch closed the wound.

By the time they had finished Blackstone's shirt was soaked with sweat and blood. Meulon bent down and offered his sound arm to Blackstone and hauled him to his feet. Blackstone looked around at the gathered men. All had an injury of some kind. He put an arm on his son's shoulder. 'These men fought and died for you, Henry. You will always remember their sacrifice and honour them.'

Henry Blackstone looked at the gathered men and bowed his head towards them in acknowledgement. 'I will always do so,' said Henry. He turned and looked up at his father. 'But, my lord, it was you they followed.'

CHAPTER SIXTY-EIGHT

It took three days for news of the battle at Brignais to reach Dijon and the French King. and another six punishing days of hard riding for the messenger to reach Vincennes.

'Tancarville was defeated?' said the Dauphin in what was barely a whisper, unable to disguise his shock that more than four thousand men of the northern army could be defeated by a group of disparate mercenaries.

'A thousand prisoners were taken by them,' confirmed Simon Bucy, watching the Dauphin steady himself, fearful that the news might cause the frail man to collapse. 'Some escaped,' he said in mitigation.

'How many?'

'A… a few hundred.'

'Out of so many?'

'Sire,' said Bucy, dipping his head to express his shared sorrow. 'And Jacques de Bourbon died of his wounds.'

The Dauphin looked as though he had been clubbed with a mailed fist. Pain and disbelief in equal measure crossed his features. 'And our father?'

'He has departed for Avignon. It seems he seeks the solace of the Pope's blessing.'

The colour that had drained from the Dauphin's face was quickly replaced with an angry flush. 'Solace? Our father abandons Dijon, our people. France! For solace!' he bellowed. Spittle flecked his thin beard. He steadied his breathing. 'And what of Thomas Blackstone? Were the walls breached? Did they at least kill him?'

'The matter is… unclear, highness. There is some confusion.'

'Confusion as to whether he is dead or alive?'

'Information is unreliable at the best of times, your grace, but reports are that he led the routier attack against Tancarville's men. It appears that... well, that he was outside the walls and led a force of thousands.'

'We do not understand, Simon. We were told he was in Brignais.'

'It seems we were misinformed. But there is one thing that is absolutely certain, highness.' Bucy barely managed to keep the pained expression from his face. The Dauphin turned at the trusted counsellor's hesitation.

'Thomas Blackstone is in Brignais now,' said Bucy.

As the Dauphin fumed and his father rode towards Avignon, a second delegation from the French monarch, despatched by the Dauphin, reached King Edward at Windsor Castle ten days later. Their demand that Edward use his resources in France to hunt down and stop Blackstone's raiding were made with all the diplomatic skill the situation demanded but, none the less, with a forcefulness that could not be ignored for a second time. News of the French defeat added to the King's uncertainty about what to do with the rogue knight Thomas Blackstone, who had previously been blamed for destroying French towns, mutilation, rape and murder. It was essential that Edward gain the territory and the ceded towns guaranteed by his victory two years before; any further delay might fracture the already delicate peace treaty.

When the first of the French delegations had arrived it had been necessary to bring Sir John Chandos back to England to be questioned about Blackstone's supposed acts of brutality, which conflicted with the terms of the peace treaty. Chandos had defended Blackstone, refuting as best he could the allegations made by the French. He reminded the King that the French still allied themselves with the Bretons and they in turn still caused havoc. The English King made suitably comforting sounds of support to the French delegation and promised he would take action. He sent his royal cousin, King

John, blessings of peace for the future of France. But now he knew that he needed to decide what to do about the defiant Blackstone.

In Brignais the warm May weather helped ease the stiffness brought on by the men's wounds. The weeks that had passed since the battle had returned their strength but had not lessened their sadness at the loss of their men, especially that of Perinne. His story was told by Meulon, who recounted the years that had passed since Blackstone had met him and they had first fought together. Killbere related instances that brought smiles to the haggard men's faces. Fra Foresti spoke quietly in prayer at Perinne's graveside. And weeks later still, when he had returned to Florence, he explained to Torellini what had occurred and how the victory came about because Blackstone's name had been a clarion call.

The French who had fallen in the battle had been stripped of any wealth but, as most of the footsoldiers were arrayed for service by their local lords, there was little to be scavenged, other than clothing, by the villeins from nearby villages. It had taken only a few days for the bloated, naked dead to begin to stink. Scavengers pecked and tore soft flesh and took sightless eyes. Blackstone had Beyard's men ride among the villagers and order them to dig a long trench as a mass grave. By the time the thousands had been put beneath the ground it was the end of May and Blackstone prepared to lead his men, and his son, out of Brignais, northwards so that they might continue relieving towns of their French allegiance.

'Father, am I to stay with you now?' Henry had asked when alone with Blackstone.

'From what Father Torellini told you and the instructions he gave the Tau knight, it seems you are safer at my side than on your own. God knows how we continue your education. Your mother will not rest in heaven if I do not attend to it.'

'I brought books from Florence, and I will study for as long as I remain at your side. Perhaps my future will change when it is discovered who was behind the attack in Florence.'

'If anyone can find that out it will be the Bardi's priest. And if it was those vipers in Milan then we will take death to their door.'

'Father Torellini might never find out. It might not have been the Visconti.'

'Then we will take each day as it comes and be on our guard. I'll have the captains help train you and I will watch your progress. But until such time as I am content that you are proficient in both your studies and the use of a sword you will help with stabling and the baggage and return to being John Jacob's page.'

'Am I not too old to be a page?' he asked plaintively.

'You will receive no special favour here, son. Over the years you have earned the men's respect, now it's time to keep it.'

'I understand, Father.' Henry tried to keep the disappointment from his voice. Returning to his father had brought him no more status than he had before. He had made progress in his life away from the fighting men. Florence was the capital of culture and learning and now that too had been snatched away.

'And we will ride back to a monastery where I want you to meet a young Frenchman, not much older than you, who fought for us. He learnt to keep his hot blood under control. He sacrificed himself for us,' said Blackstone.

'He died?'

'He lost his leg. But he's courageous and a man can learn from those who have to find a different way to live. Your life has changed now, Henry, and there are lessons to be learnt beyond those in your books.'

Blackstone gestured for his son to pass the belted sword. The boy wrapped his palms around its breadth. The pommel held two halves of a silver penny that Blackstone had once split; he had given half to Henry's mother, keeping the other for himself. Then, when his wife was murdered, he had brought the two pieces together. His father had been only a year older than Henry was now when he fought at Crécy with some of these men. When he had lost his deaf-mute brother and slain the Bohemian knight who once owned the hardened steel blade etched with the Passau swordmaker's mark of the running wolf.

'Hold it,' said Blackstone, noticing his son's fascination. 'Go on,' he urged as the boy hesitated.

Henry gripped the hilt and withdrew the famed sword. Its fine balance was immediately noticeable.

'You think you're ready,' said Blackstone, sensing the boy's frustration at being given such menial responsibilities.

Henry's spine straightened, his chin lifted. His father had just taunted him. 'You know I've used a sword before. I can look after myself.'

'Oh,' said Blackstone. 'A man who thinks he's better than he is, is soon dead.' He studied the boy. 'All right, strike at me.'

Henry hesitated, doubt creasing his brow.

'If you can lay that blade on me I will give you whatever you desire. Horse, armour, weapons. Freedom. You can go wherever you wish. I want you with me, Henry, but you are of an age where you would prefer not to listen to your father. You're a man. Behave like one.'

The words stung. Henry sidestepped quickly, trying to touch his father's mail. The movement was deft but Blackstone batted the sword blade away with his arm. Henry tried again but now blood was pulsing through a vein in his temple. Once again Blackstone turned on his toes, balanced on his heel, half twisted and let Henry's strike take the boy past him. Blackstone cuffed him. Henry held his temper in check and danced quickly left and right, swinging the sword from high guard, slashing down, forgetting in that moment that now the blade could cause injury. Blackstone ducked and weaved easily and then quickly grabbed Henry's wrist. Suddenly Blackstone's knife was in his hand and he held it close to the boy's sweating face.

'And now you are dead.' He lowered the knife. 'I saw your rage, Henry. I know what that is. But you let it take you over. You are not ready. Trust me. I would not give you false acclaim. It takes time. Learn from men who are willing to teach you and swallow your pride. Killing a boy in the back streets of Florence is not killing a man in battle.'

Henry handed back the sword. 'Thank you, Father,' Henry muttered.

Blackstone resisted the urge to reach out and ruffle the boy's hair. He was too old for that now. And the years when he had yearned to embrace the boy had slipped through his fingers.

Henry watched enviously as Blackstone strapped on Wolf Sword. He knew he stood in his father's shadow. He was caged by his name and yearned for the freedom he had experienced in Florence. Thoughts tormented him. In the past he had used sword and knife, had stood and faced an enemy and fought with courage. And now he was to be relegated to fetching and carrying again. He would obey his father... until such time as he would defy him and strike off alone to seek his own place in the world.

Defiance. That was something else he had inherited.

CHAPTER SIXTY-NINE

'Riders, Sir Thomas,' called Quenell, whose turn it was to stand guard with his archers on the walls. Meulon and Renfred ran quickly up the steps. Blackstone followed while Killbere and the men were leading their horses from the stables.

'French or routiers?' Killbere called.

'Can't see yet,' Blackstone answered.

Killbere groaned. 'God's tears. We were ready to ride. What now? Henry! Take my reins.'

Henry ran forward and held Killbere's reins as the veteran limped up the steps to join the others. He peered across the open ground. The morning light cast low shadows, making the distant horsemen indistinct.

'If it's the French come to take back Brignais let's just give it to them. It's worth nothing to us now,' said Killbere.

'They can have it,' said Blackstone. 'But they may want payment in blood.'

Jack Halfpenny clambered higher and his archer's keen eyesight recognized the approaching column of men and their colours. 'It's Sir William Felton,' he called.

'Felton?' said Killbere. 'What the hell is he doing so far south? Perhaps he's come to reward us for kicking French arses.'

'We'll soon find out,' Blackstone answered. 'Open the gates,' he called to the men below.

Felton had two hundred or more men behind him who drew up on the far side of the narrow bridge as he rode across and halted a good distance from the walls.

'Something's not right here,' said Meulon.

'Thomas, this looks like trouble,' added Killbere.

Blackstone strode beyond the walls with Killbere and Meulon at his side. 'Sir William?' Blackstone called. 'The gates are open.'

'Sir Thomas, I am pleased to see you and Gilbert are unharmed,' said Felton.

'Unharmed now,' said Killbere. 'But we spilled our blood out there on the field. You hesitate.'

'I cannot bring my men inside the walls of Brignais, Gilbert, in case even more blood is spilled.'

Blackstone followed the Seneschal's gaze and turned to look at the archers who now stood along the wall's parapet. He turned back to face Felton.

'My men have a natural instinct for survival and you appear to pose a threat to us, Sir William. I fail to see why.'

'I have orders from the King.'

'Of France?' said Killbere.

'Sarcasm does not suit you, Gilbert. You know full well I speak of Edward.'

'Well, if you come here looking for trouble then it is natural that we think you serve King John and his snivelling offspring,' answered Killbere.

'Charges have been laid against Sir Thomas for actions in the field,' said Felton.

Killbere turned to Blackstone and lowered his voice. 'You hear that, Thomas? Felton's enjoying this but his arse is pinching arrowheads in fear.'

'And you would have us kill him and the King's men?' said Blackstone quietly. 'We are in a shit pit and we must see if we can climb out of it.'

Killbere looked towards the uneasy Felton and placed a finger on each nostril and blew free the snot. It was a gesture of contempt, but not one that could be proved.

'Killing murdering bastard routiers, and slaying a French army, who by all accounts sought to seize his son here in Brignais and who had already attacked us before we fought the Bretons, cannot be considered a crime,' Killbere said.

'Sir John Chandos and the governor Henry le Scrope await us at Calais. I am not here to argue the rights and wrongs, I have been tasked with escorting Sir Thomas and his men there.'

'God's tears, Thomas,' said Killbere under his breath. 'Le Scrope? He's an old war dog. He's been fighting since '33, a tough bastard and a good fighter. I knew him at Morlaix. He's a hard man. Now he holds jurisdiction in all criminal cases. Are we to be tried?'

Blackstone took a step towards Felton. 'Calais. The prison? And you bring so many men to protect us? Or do you arrest us?' he said.

'I have no warrant for your arrest but this escort was ordered by Sir John. You are to travel under the protection of my flag. The French have petitioned the King to strike against you.'

'Not with their northern army they won't,' said Killbere.

There was a murmur of laughter from the men on the walls.

'I've no liking for you or your men, Sir Thomas,' said Felton. 'I serve my King and he has ordered you be taken to the citadel at Calais. I have no interest in your fate but I will take you and if you resist we will answer with force.' He looked to where Beyard and a group of his men stood in the courtyard inside the gate, ready to repel any sudden attack should such foolishness prevail. Enough men would die before they even reached the gates now that the archers manned the walls. 'I'm told you have Gascons with you.'

'I recruited them,' said Blackstone.

'They will stay here or disperse. I care not. But they will not travel to Calais. Only you and your men are to be escorted.'

'Do you intend to have us disarmed?' said Blackstone.

'No, you are to ride as free men but you are under my command until I hand you over to Sir John.'

Blackstone looked from Killbere to Meulon. With Beyard's Gascons they had near enough two hundred men to match Felton's, and each of theirs was worth two of the Seneschal's, but to raise a hand in anger would cast them all into the wilderness.

'It's a pity they serve King Edward,' said Meulon quietly. 'Sir William has every right to be fearful of us. We would have little trouble killing them if they chose to fight.'

'If *we* chose to fight,' Blackstone corrected him.

'Goddammit, Thomas,' Killbere said, his voice hushed so that no word could carry to Felton. 'We could end our days in Italy. Would that be such a bad thing? The prison at Calais is a miserable end that I do not wish to endure.'

'It's not you they want, Gilbert,' said Blackstone.

'Well?' Felton called. 'Is there to be disagreement between us? Are you to submit to the King's command?'

Blackstone smiled ruefully at the men who had been for so long at his side. 'Let's see what Chandos has to say. Perhaps we can talk our way out of this.'

Killbere grunted. 'Aye, well, the trouble with that, Thomas, is that your tongue is not as eloquent as your sword.'

Beyard and his Gascons agreed with Blackstone that they would ride south to Aquitaine, secure in the knowledge that the domain fell under King Edward's control. They would wait until word came from Blackstone. He paid the men with gold that had been returned by Gruffydd ap Madoc and, to the annoyance of Sir William Felton, the Gascon captain and his men renewed their pledge of allegiance to Blackstone.

Blackstone and his men rode steadily northwards. There were few words spoken between Blackstone and the man sent to escort him. Sir William was clearly concerned that the French might be tempted to strike at them should they camp in the open country-side. Blackstone and Killbere admitted to themselves that the gruff Northumbrian knight was organized. He had arranged for them to rest most nights in towns held by the English King or in those ceded to him by the treaty. A treaty broken, the French insisted, by Thomas Blackstone.

In the mid-afternoon on the fifteenth day after leaving Brignais,

Sir William Felton crested the low hills and led his escort down through the salt marshes, land that flooded when the tides rose around Calais. Blackstone felt a tinge of regret as he remembered Gaillard, his murdered friend and captain who had guided him through these treacherous places years before when they went to fight the French at Calais. Little had changed except those who commanded the castle and the town. From the heights they could see that the streets were neatly laid out within the rectangular walled town and the curtain walls that surrounded the citadel and its keep sat snugly in the north-west corner. Perhaps, Blackstone mused, that would soon be his home when he was imprisoned. Killbere had asked what would happen if the English King was forced to make an example of Blackstone in order to appease the French and keep the peace. What if Edward executed Blackstone? He wouldn't be the first man to be sacrificed for the sake of a sealed bargain or an agreement made between royal cousins. Those whom God chose to rule did not have to show loyalty to those who served them. It was a question that could not be answered until Blackstone faced the charges brought against him.

'Well, if that is the judgment,' Killbere had concluded, 'they will have your men scaling the walls by night. You will not die alone, Thomas, of that I am certain.'

CHAPTER SEVENTY

Calais's outer defensive wall was surrounded by a moat and the southern gate accessed by a drawbridge, beyond which was a portcullis. The outer wall was buffered by a second curtain wall behind it. The space between the two was a gap wide enough for twenty men to stand abreast.

'A dozen years back we stood shoulder to shoulder there, Sir Thomas. Trapped the French and slaughtered them,' said Meulon as they waited beyond the great walled city.

Killbere drank from a wineskin and passed it to Blackstone. 'Aye, it was a hell of a fight.'

'We had our comrades still with us,' said Blackstone, watching as Felton made his approach towards the guarded drawbridge to gain entry. 'Matthew Hampton, Talpin, Gaillard, Perinne...' His voice trailed off. Ghosts of the men they had lost always rode among them.

One of Felton's captains approached them. 'Will? John?' Blackstone called. The archer and John Jacob nudged their horses closer. 'Killbere and I will be going in alone. John: you, Will and Meulon take care of Henry. He's a wild streak in him and he needs a watchful eye.'

'He won't run while you're in there,' said Will Longdon.

'And we will wait until you return,' said Meulon. 'We know this place. If matters turn for the worse then we can defend ourselves out here.'

'Sir Thomas, I should be at your side. I'm your squire,' said John Jacob.

'The fewer men who ride in there the better. It's me they want, and Sir Gilbert would have to be bound and gagged to stop him accompanying me and none of us would be prepared to try that,' said Blackstone with a grin. 'No, John, you were with Henry when it mattered all those years ago.' He looked at his three trusted companions. 'Keep him close.'

Felton's captain reined in his horse. 'Sir Thomas, Sir Gilbert, we are ready to enter Calais.'

'All right,' said Blackstone. 'Give me a moment longer.'

'Gladly, my lord.' The man hesitated as if considering what he was about to say so that his words would not sound disloyal. 'Sir Thomas, I serve Sir William and obey his commands but every man I know is aggrieved that you have been brought here. Many of us fought on the same battlefield and know your strength and honour. You and your men would have defeated us had you turned against us at Brignais. I thank God you did not.' The captain looked for a moment as if he had said too much. 'When you are ready, my lord.' He turned his horse and waited some distance away.

'You have more friends than we know,' said Killbere. 'Much good it will do us now.'

Blackstone grinned as he tightened the reins and turned to where Henry waited. 'You won't be coming with me, Henry.'

'But who will care for him?' said Henry, meaning the belligerent horse. 'No stable-hand will know what to do; he will kick them to death. He knows me. I should be with you.'

'I will give them instructions on how to deal with him. They will have to take their chances as you did in the beginning. Let us not argue, son: you cannot go with me. It is what it is. But you will have the company of good men around you. Listen to them and learn. There is always more beyond your books, but what you know they do not. So share your knowledge with them.'

'I will, Father,' said Henry obediently. 'Are we to wait here until your return?'

'Yes. John Jacob is your guardian while I am absent.' Blackstone knew that Henry still remembered when he was little more than a child and John Jacob had cut the throat of the man who had raped

Henry's mother. That bond would be hard to break. 'And let Will Longdon and Meulon tell you tales. There were adventures we shared that grow in the telling. But it gives them pleasure. Allow them that.'

'I'm lucky to have them care for me, I know that.'

The men were watching and Blackstone knew that Henry would be embarrassed if he reached out and held him close. He fought the desire to hold his son.

'I embrace you, Henry,' Blackstone said.

'And I you, Father.'

Calais thrived on trade, thanks to King Edward, and as Blackstone and Killbere rode escorted through the cobbled streets its merchants and citizens turned to watch the tall Englishman and his companion clattering along towards the north-west corner and the walled citadel and its keep. Many recognized the blazon on Blackstone's shield and jupon and rumours started as soon as Sir William Felton arrived. Whispers threaded through the streets, dancing ahead of the mounted men, rumours that were embellished as they jumped from tongue to ear. Betrayal, disloyalty, murder. Words that caused shock and started arguments among those who defended his name and those who were scandalized by it. If a knight with Thomas Blackstone's reputation was being taken to the citadel and the governor, then was the legendary knight about to be tried? Sir Henry le Scrope was known for meting out harsh justice. What had Thomas Blackstone done to deserve it?

The captain's voice carried to the sentries who manned the citadel's gates, which swung open as the horsemen approached, and as they thudded closed behind them Killbere turned in the saddle and looked at the defensive wall and the men who manned it.

'The Almighty himself would have trouble escaping from this place,' he said, 'and just as much trouble trying to breach it through those outer walls. Thomas, I fear we are soon to be without the creature comforts of this world. Do you think that

434

Countess Catherine made a complaint against me? I satisfied her lust with vigour. Perhaps she was aggrieved I left her. That would be cause enough for complaint.'

'Complaint perhaps that you were a wily old fox who denied her plunging a knife through your thick skull.'

Sir William halted before a set of doors. A court official came out and greeted him. Felton dismounted.

'Captain, I would urge no man or boy to try and stable my horse,' said Blackstone as he dismounted and tied the bastard horse to the hitching ring. 'And keep other horses a good distance from him.'

'I will do as you ask, Sir Thomas,' said the captain and shouted his orders to his men.

Killbere grunted. 'Should have let the beast loose, Thomas. We might need a distraction if we need to run.'

'With that leg of yours? I'd end up carrying you.'

'The day that happens I would go back to my nun and let her rub olive oil into my old muscles and offer prayers that I live long enough to pleasure her.'

They were beckoned forward by Felton. 'Follow me.'

Felton followed the court official through a bleak entrance hall, its heavy stone walls free from tapestry or decoration. King Edward's coat of arms was the only adornment. They turned into a passageway lit with cresset lamps, their dull flames throwing the men's shadows towards iron-studded doors. The court official pulled them open, revealing two armed guards who stood inside. Light shafted down from a high window and freshly cut rushes were spread across the floor. Blackstone and Killbere knew they were getting closer to the seat of power in Calais by the increasing comfort on display. A fire burned in the grate, upholstered benches and chairs were arranged near to it. Servants stood back in the shadows. A tall silver-haired man leant over a table bearing documents. He raised his eyes when Felton entered and let the document he was examining curl back into a roll.

'Sir William.'

'My lord governor,' said Felton to the severe-looking figure

435

whose clothing and demeanour were enough to proclaim his importance even without the chain of office around his neck.

Sir Henry le Scrope was fifty years old, man and boy a soldier, and for the past year his skills as an administrator rewarded with the authority to govern his King's jewels in France: Guînes and Calais. He studied the tall knight who stood before him and who did not avert his eyes. The two men facing him looked little more than unkempt brigands. 'Sir Thomas Blackstone and Sir Gilbert Killbere, you stink of the road and your clothing is still stained with the blood of the French.'

'My lord, we have not yet had the opportunity to bathe,' said Blackstone, 'and I remember seeing you splattered with French blood when we fought at Rheims. A man bears the marks of the duty he performs just as you bear your seal of office.'

'Your impertinence does not surprise me,' said the governor. 'Wait here.'

Sir Henry walked to another door beyond the fireplace and knocked.

'Christ, Thomas, do not antagonize the man who holds our fate in his hands,' Killbere sighed. 'Like facing a wild boar with nothing more than a stick.'

'Gilbert, they have not disarmed us; we are not yet prisoners. And when we are we can use that stick to poke the boar in the eye. Let us not yield too easily in this matter.'

The door was opened by someone unseen. The governor stood in the doorway and raised the rolled document. 'I have it ready.' He stepped inside when a muted voice summoned him. The door closed behind him.

'Where's Chandos?' whispered Killbere to Blackstone. 'He might defend us.'

'It looks as though the governor has already prepared our warrant,' said Blackstone. 'We are in the belly of the beast, Gilbert.'

Before Killbere could answer the door opened again and the governor faced them. 'Sir William, you are excused. Our thanks. Blackstone, Killbere, in here.'

Sir William Felton bowed his head and turned on his heel. No look of triumph crossed his features but his eyes expressed a satisfaction that the rogue knight had been brought to heel.

Blackstone and Killbere did the governor's bidding and stepped into a vast room. The warmth from a big fire reached them as soon as they entered. Candles were positioned around the chamber, but there was sufficient light from another large window to show woven rugs strewn over rush floors and tapestries hanging to help keep out the chill from stone walls. An iron chandelier bearing forty candles hung like a huge wagon wheel above their heads. Servants lurked in the shadows; an array of twenty or more court officials stood here and there. Sir John Chandos stepped forward, nodded at the two men and then stepped aside. It was a room furnished for comfort. Fit for a king.

Blackstone and Killbere caught their breath as King Edward turned from where he warmed his hands against the flames. His long flaxen beard and hair were shot through with slivers of grey. A second man rose from the embroidered chair that had been concealed by Chandos. It was the Prince of Wales.

Blackstone and Killbere went down on one knee. Killbere grimaced slightly at the pain from his wounded leg.

'We hear you were injured, Gilbert,' said the King.

'Sire, it was nothing. A scratch.'

'Get to your feet. Sir John, help him,' said the King.

No sooner had Chandos taken a step forward than Killbere pushed himself upright despite the discomfort. 'No need, my lord. With your pardon, I'm not yet ready to be nursed.'

The King of England stepped forward, away from his officials, closer to the two men. 'You did not know that your King and his son were here.'

'No, sire, we did not. We were not told.'

'Because, Thomas, no one knew other than Sir John and Sir Henry. What needs to be attended to here is a matter of grave importance. A matter that required us to travel here by night across the sea. The very treaty we have signed might be at risk.'

'Sire, whatever charges are to be brought should only be brought against me, no one else. Sir Gilbert is here as a loyal friend.'

'You were not given permission to speak,' said Sir John Chandos. Blackstone dipped his head, acknowledging his fault.

'We have received two delegations from the French King and the Dauphin,' said the King. 'They sought permission to hunt you down and asked that we lend our support with the troops we have in France. The charges against a knight under the command of our trusted Chandos were of such a serious nature that we were left with little choice but to give this matter our sincere efforts and best consideration. Over the weeks since the delegation reached us in England we were caused much vexation. Speak, Sir Thomas, explain to us how these charges came about.'

'Sire, my men and I have done everything to serve your good name. I cannot know the exact nature of these charges and would hope that, once I am told, your grace will give me the opportunity to explain.'

The King's face had not lost its stern look of displeasure. 'We doubt that will be necessary.' He returned to the fire and a liveried servant quickly pushed a second chair in place so that the King could sit and face the accused men. The Prince of Wales remained standing, gazing at Blackstone.

'Saint-Aubin-la-Fère,' said the King. 'A town ceded to us by the treaty. You burned it down after killing the lord who held it.'

'They betrayed you, sire. The agreement was broken. They tried to kill Sir Gilbert. I lost good men behind those walls. I reported the loss to Sir John.'

Somewhere in the half-light towards the back of the room was the sound of a quill scratching across parchment. Blackstone glanced towards it and saw three scribes seated at a long table copying down what was being said. *So, a trial it is and the evidence is being recorded against me. Questioned by the King himself.* He dared a glance at Killbere. Blackstone's young life had almost ended in a sheriff's court where only his own wit and help from Killbere had saved him. But this was no Court of Common Pleas.

The King gestured for the official to hand him the document. Edward stood and approached Blackstone. He held out the document that had now been folded square and sealed with wax and pressed once again with the royal seal. Blackstone looked at what was written on the front of the document. The three words hurled his mind back to his village in England and the day it started, all those years before, when Fate and its travelling companions Bad Luck and Misery had visited him, and he had begun his own boyhood journey that had brought him to this place.

'Sir Thomas Blackstone, you are to accompany our son, the Prince of Wales and Aquitaine, and to serve the English Crown as Master of War.'

HISTORICAL NOTES

In 1360 the Plantagenet King Edward III agreed to a peace treaty with the House of Valois after twenty-three years of fighting. He and his son the Prince of Wales had achieved magnificent victories on the battlefield. King John II of France, held as a prisoner in England after being captured in 1356 – though more like a pampered guest in the luxurious surroundings of the Savoy Palace in London – returned to a devastated realm. While King John had been in England it had been his son the Dauphin Charles who had effectively stymied Edward's invasion in late 1359–60 by steadfastly refusing to commit to a major battle. Charles was a shrewd and calculating Prince Regent who had vowed to reclaim as much of France as he could and who had rejected the original treaty agreed by his father the King. Once the new treaty had been signed there then began the process of handing over cities, towns and territory into English hands and their occupants swearing allegiance to the English. This was no straightforward task. A civil war raged for control of Brittany, which further complicated matters. The French claimed Brittany through their support of Charles de Blois, while the English claimed it through Edward's young ward, John de Montfort. It was a proxy war that continued even while the peace treaty was signed. The Breton mercenaries had no cause to acknowledge the English King's peace treaty.

King Edward sent the renowned Knight of the Garter Sir John Chandos to lead the negotiations with King John for the ceded towns to be handed over to the English Crown. He succeeded in gathering a thousand men to fight the Bretons in the Limousin where de Blois held territory. The Seneschal of Poitou, Sir William Felton, succeeded in defeating the Breton mercenaries in early 1362. In addition to this ongoing conflict the country was still plagued with mercenaries who swarmed throughout the regions, especially down the Rhône Valley. At times these bands of brigands came together and were sufficiently organized to number between ten and twelve thousand. The English brigands were obliged by Edward to renounce claim to the towns they held, but in reality the fact that they still raided and caused distress to the French Crown suited King Edward. The French, in an attempt to regain their own territory, often made payments to the brigands to encourage them to abandon the towns they occupied. Eventually, by increasing taxation and gaining financial support from major French cities, the French monarch managed to raise an army of the north under the command of Count Jean de Tancarville, the French Royal Chamberlain, with the renowned commander Jacques de Bourbon, Count de la Marche, Constable of France. Another army in the south was led by Arnoul d'Audrehem, Lieutenant of Languedoc. The expedition was a desperate attempt by the French to clear the mercenaries from the Rhône Valley and from any towns they held. In the small fortified town of Brignais in 1362 they thought to trap one of the mercenary leaders, Hélie (Petit) Meschin. The French army numbered nearly five thousand men, more than enough to destroy the defenders, but the French left their rear unguarded and Meschin organized a disparate group of mercenaries that outnumbered the French and defeated them.

It was after this defeat that King John II put into effect his desire to travel to Avignon and make the proposal to Pope Innocent VI that he, John, marry Joanna, Countess of Provence, Queen of Naples. (Since 1343 Provence had belonged to Joanna of Anjou, Charles of Anjou's great-great-granddaughter, a dangerous woman, at this date twice widowed, whose first husband had been strangled, it is said, on her orders. There is a touch of this violent and dissolute woman in my character Catherine, Countess de Val.)

443

It must have felt to the French officials that King John had abandoned France and it was rumoured that he yearned to return to the luxurious life he had enjoyed as Edward's prisoner in England rather than to try and rebuild a devastated and bankrupt nation. The shrewd Dauphin Charles waited in the wings. There were still unresolved issues in the peace process concerning the boundaries of territory which Edward claimed as his and which the French refused to cede. And so Edward now refused to renounce his claim to the French throne.

Many of King Edward's great knights and fighters, loyal friends who had been at his side since he seized back the crown from his mother and her lover Mortimer in October 1330, were now dead. The Earl of Northampton, Sir Thomas Holland, Henry, Duke of Lancaster, Sir Reginald Cobham, Sir John Mowbray, Sir William Fitzwarin. Death after death visited Edward. It was time to hand over the command of his territories to his sons, a strategy to give them authority and responsibility, ably assisted by trusted officials at their side.

The Prince of Wales was also made Prince of Aquitaine, that vast and resource-rich area in the south of France, with Sir John Chandos as constable and Sir William Felton as administrator.

It seemed a timely moment to honour and promote Sir Thomas Blackstone.

ACKNOWLEDGEMENTS

My thanks to all my readers who have made the *Master of War* series and Thomas Blackstone's adventures successful. On occasion I turn to some of these loyal fans when I need help with my research. When it came to finding a Welsh translation for the insult delivered by Gruffydd ap Madoc I asked fellow author and ex-broadcaster Nick Evans for his help. He, in turn, spoke to a Welsh speaker and between them they advised me how best to write the derogative term. What I discovered from their advice was that the Welsh language seems not to have such pointed unkindness as I had written and usually employs low-key, non-aggressive verbal insults. More like banter than harsh insult. The translation, then, is as pointed as I can make it. It might not be the exact interpretation but I hope Welsh speakers are generous enough to grant me some leeway.

My ongoing appreciation for the painstaking editorial skills and patience of my editor, Richenda Todd. My usual thanks to the enthusiastic team at my publishers, Head of Zeus, who have now come up with a brand-new set of covers that give the *Master of War* series a fresh look on the bookshelves. Nic Cheetham, my publisher, has made good inroads for Blackstone into the American market and Blackstone's legion of friends increases. Thanks to the efforts of the staff at Blake Friedmann Literary Agency and my agent, Isobel Dixon, other countries have also embraced Sir Thomas, Killbere and their men. More recently my German publishers, Rowohlt, have done a fantastic job of presenting the series to their readers. The books go from strength to strength, with audio editions read by Daniel Philpott and Colin Mace bringing another dimension to the series.

David Gilman
Devonshire
2017

davidgilman.com
facebook.com/davidgilman.author
twitter.com/davidgilmanuk